ALSO BY
MILORAD PAVIĆ

Dictionary of the Khazars

Landscape Painted with Tea

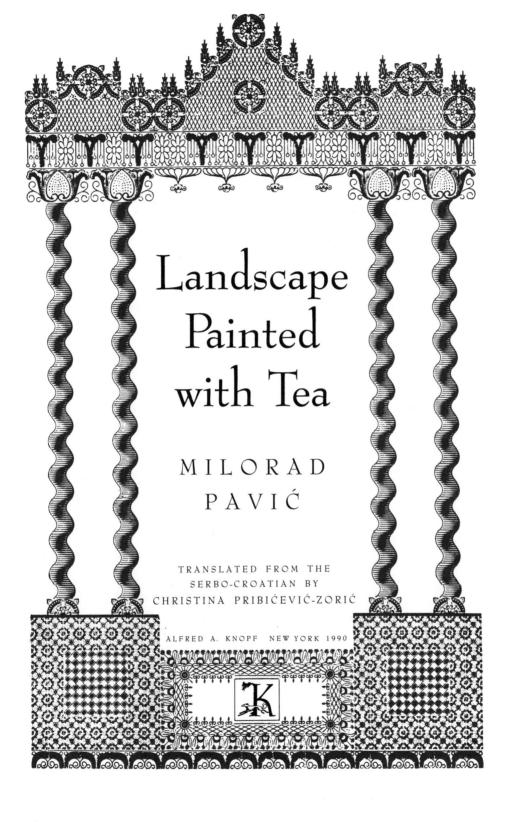

Landscape Painted with Tea

MILORAD PAVIĆ

TRANSLATED FROM THE
SERBO-CROATIAN BY
CHRISTINA PRIBIĆEVIĆ-ZORIĆ

ALFRED A. KNOPF   NEW YORK 1990

THIS IS A BORZOI BOOK
PUBLISHED BY ALFRED A. KNOPF, INC.

Library of Congress Cataloging-in-Publication Data
Pavić, Milorad.
[Predeo slikan čajem. English]
Landscape painted with tea / Milorad Pavić; translated from the Serbo-Croatian by Christina Pribićević-Zorić.—1st American ed.
p. cm.
"Originally published in Yugoslavia as Predeo slikan čajem *by Prosveta, Belgrade"—T.p. verso.*
ISBN 0-394-58217-9
I. Title.
PG1419.26.A78P713   1990
891.8'235–dc20   89-43379   CIP

Manufactured in the United States of America
FIRST AMERICAN EDITION

Contents

Landscape Painted with Tea

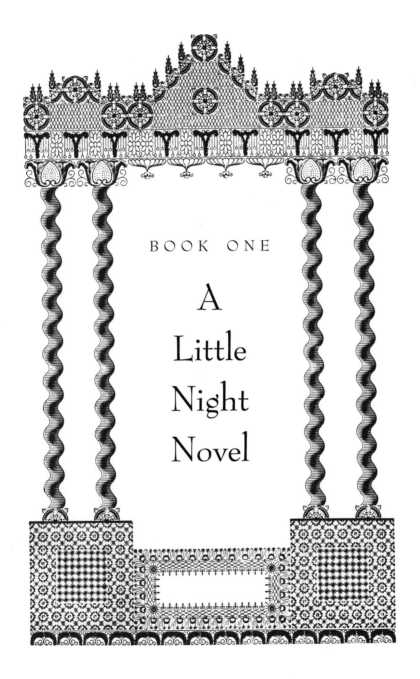

BOOK ONE

A
Little
Night
Novel

1

They wore the tips of their mustaches braided like whips. For generations they had not smiled, and wrinkles recorded the years in the upper areas of their faces. They aged from their thoughts, not their joys. They knew the Jews called them Edomites; they called themselves salt. It takes a long time for a man to use up a handful of salt, they thought, and were patient. They bore two signs: the sign of the lamb and the sign of the fish. To the lamb they gave cakes made with tears, and to the fish, a ring made of dough, because the fish is the bride of the soul. A long time elapsed, four to five generations, before one of them said:

"I like the talking tree best; it alone bears a double fruit, and on it one can distinguish between quiet and silence. For a man with a heart full of silence and a man with a heart full of quiet cannot be alike. . . ."

The one who had spoken came from Antioch, and he died without having clenched his teeth into the snarl of a beast, without fear or hatred, together with his fellow tribesman Ignatius, in Rome in the year 107 A.D. Just as in a grain of wheat one cannot see everything that is inscribed there, and inscribed are the kinds of spikes it will have, the size of the stubbles, and the number of new grains it will bring, so from his sentence one could not read anything in advance, but it was all already inscribed there.

When a little sleep came upon them, it was a veritable salvation from the horror in which they were compelled to live. But even in their dreams they were assailed by terrors, by beasts with freckled lips and navels instead of eyes, and they, like a drowning man on dry land, struggled to reach wakefulness, although the waves of the dreams kept spinning them in a circle. Thus, tossed back and forth between two seas, driven from wakefulness to sleep and from sleep to wakefulness, their bodies were the only link between these two kinds of horror. They were the mail. And they did not know that both the dreams and the edicts of Septimius Severus, Maximus of Thrace, and Valerius were forcing them to seek shelter under the very same tree mentioned in that sentence. So as not to be nailed to a cross or a windmill, so as not to be thrown to wild beasts or have their heads smashed against the closing heavy dungeon doors, so as not to be compelled to feed the morays in the fountains with their own fingers, ears, and eyes, they fled to the desert.

They dispersed across the wilds of Syria, Mesopotamia, and Egypt, hid in graves, in pyramids, and in the ruins of onetime fortresses, wearing their long hair wrapped under their arms and tied across their chests to keep them warm at night. They went into the mountains of Upper Thebes, between the Nile and the Red Sea, where bird-eating dipnoan fish live; they spoke Coptic, Hebrew, Greek, Latin, Georgian, and Syrian, or kept silent in one of these languages, unceasingly and unconsciously moving toward the tree from that sentence, like the grain of wheat that begins to germinate. And then they came to Sinai. And they finally understood the meaning of the words:

"A man with a heart full of silence and a man with a heart full of quiet cannot be alike. . . ."

As soon as that happened, as soon as the first hermit sat down in his own shadow and drank in the first dew, the fish and the lamb separated. Irrevocably and for all time at their disposal, they began to divide into two castes. Into those linked to the sun and those linked to water, into those with the lamb and those with the fish, into those with quiet and those with silence in their hearts. . . .

There, in Sinai, the former joined in brotherhood and began to live a communal life, and they were called cenobites, solidaries, *from the Greek*

koinos bios *(communal life). The latter (those under the sign of the fish),
were called* idiorrhythmics, solitaries, *because each had his own roof, his
own way and rhythm of life, and, isolated from others, spent the days in
total solitude, shallow but impenetrable solitude. These two castes, the
solidaries and the solitaries, cast their shadows far into space and time.
Because there is no clear borderline between the past, which grows and
feeds on the present, and the future, which, it would seem, is neither
inexhaustible nor incessant, so that in some places it is reduced or comes in
spurts.*

*When they traveled, the solitaries always carried their own plates under
their caps, a foreign tongue in their mouths, and sickles under their belts,
because they set out on their journeys individually. The solidaries, on the
other hand, always went in groups, carrying a kettle in turns, a common
tongue between their teeth, and a knife under their belt. At first, however,
they traveled through time more than through space. On that journey
through time, those of the solitary life took with them the stone of silence,
while those in the brotherhoods of communal life took the stone of quiet.
These two stones were carried separately, and the quiet of the one was not
heard in the silence of the others.*

*For idiorrhythmics each keep their own silence, whereas cenobites foster
a common quiet. The solitaries work silence like a field of wheat; they
plow it, give it space, extend the furrow, water it so that it may flourish, so
that it may grow tall, because with silence you can reach God, with your
voice you cannot, no matter how hard you shout.... The solidaries, in
cultivating their quiet, do not direct it toward God but, rather, extend it
like a dam toward the part of the world that does not belong to them and
that has yet to be conquered; they surround and enclose themselves with
quiet, and protect themselves with it or send it to catch their game like a
hunting dog. And they know that there are good hunting dogs and bad....*

"It's all a great misfortune in which we feel like fish in water," thought the architect manqué, Atanas Svilar, sliding into his fortieth year as though into somebody else's sweat.

He had studied at the School of Architecture in Belgrade from 1950 to 1956, which is when he learned that his upper lip was responsible for one thing and his lower lip for another: the upper was for hot, the lower for sour; he studied mathematics under Professor Radivoye Kashanin and wore a knitted cap with a whistle on top, attended Professor Marinkovich's lectures on prestressed concrete, and at the same time learned to recognize women who preferred mustaches for dinner. He remained famous for his unusual final senior exam, which created an uproar and left the School divided into two camps. While still a student, he noticed that one of the striking virtues of great writers was their silence on certain important matters. And he applied this to his own profession: here the unused space, equivalent to the unsaid word in a work of literature, had its form, the emptiness had its shape and meaning, just as strikingly and effectively as space filled with buildings. The beauty of the emptiness gave him the inspiration for the beauty of the built part of the structure, and this was evident and reflected in his designs. Preoccupied with the theory of sets, fluid mechanics, and especially the acoustics of closed spaces, he became and remained, in the opinion of those competent to judge, a brilliant expert. He was not a man to fool around with, and it was known that Svilar would carry fire in his mouth across the water, if necessary. His designs for the city's river belt, based on the premise that a river is always an older settlement than the town on its banks, attracted attention. The windows on his buildings always opened like loopholes, straight from the target to the eye rather than from the building to whatever was there outside, as is usually the case. He believed that humor in architecture was a bit like salt on bread, that there should be a door for every season of the year, a floor for the day and a floor for the night, because at night sound descends faster than it rises; he believed that when building the roof one should not only consider the sun, but also the moonlight, because the only good roof is one under which the egg does not rot. His hair was like straw, his sleep so swift and heavy it could shatter a glass. His left eye was aging faster than his right, and he had to don glasses to finish his project for a singles hotel and his draft of an art gallery, which was proclaimed the least costly design at a regional contest, but was never built. Svilar's projects simply did not sell. Rolled up in the closets of Svilar's apartment, or stuffed between double doors, they collected cobwebs for years.

"Buildings without shadows," Svilar's son called them.

"He measures and calculates here, and houses spring up over there, in the next world!" his peers would say, the hollows in their cheeks filling with darkness.

"If I had as many words as there are sheep in a pen, I'd understand it if nobody wanted me," Svilar joked, "but this way, I don't understand a thing!"

However, the devil had the last laugh. Despite his expertise, which was never disputed, despite his enormous working energy, which ruined his clothes and his hair, Atanas Svilar was simply unable to find a job in his field. And the drop of time cannot be wiped off the face with a sleeve, like a drop of rain. It stays there forever.

But nobody has tears in just one eye.

There was another noticeable thing about Svilar. Early on, as soon as he had developed a rough, broad, masculine mouth with which he could catch his own tear, he caught hay fever. From then on it attacked him every spring.

Besieged by hay fever every May, Svilar forgot the fragrance of flowers, but at night his sweat exuded such powerful smells of plants and flowers that they roused the house.

Married a long time, he had also spent two mature decades of his life without managing to earn a living from architecture. He did teach at a vocational school for building-constructors, but that was like talking about lunch instead of lunching. He continued to devote all his spare time to his drawings; indifferent to food and shy by day, at night he became so ravenous, eloquent, and hardworking that the back of his belt turned moldy. When his glasses got dirty, he would simply lick them and continue working. The years passed, he felt his saliva changing taste, he knew he was savoring some wines for the last time, he worked as though his ears were not planted on holes, but still he remained outside his profession and felt he was growing old in strokes, like a clock. Twice, at the ages of twenty-four and forty-two, he undertook ambitious projects, entire housing settlements, which were never transposed from paper to reality.

In the long summer nights, while pondering over his past life as he added wine to his water (because the reverse is a sin), Svilar usually asked himself two questions: how come he had hay fever for life, so that tea smelled to him like sweat, and how come he was unable to lay his hands on a real job as an architect, the work for which he was made. It was as though the right hand were more sinful than the left, after all.

One spring, when February was borrowing days from March, he finally decided to look up his old school friend Obren Opsenitsa.

"Maybe every person in this town has another person as the answer to his question," Svilar thought. Might that person-answer not be, in his case, Obren Opsenitsa? He found him in one of the bureaus that grant funds for urban construction. Opsenitsa was wearing a double-knotted tie, had white hair that curled at the ends like a hook and a smile that closed his eyes, and Svilar remembered how at school Opsenitsa used to turn his back on the person he was talking to and then suddenly swing around, letting loose with a terrific punch. He was a man who ate with a knife, omitting the fork, and was said to be so deft that he could replace the pits in cherries with the tongue in his mouth. Unlike other people, who basically knew what they wanted, he always had in mind what he did not want. And this proved to be exceptionally effective, catapulting him to the highest echelons of the city administration. And what he did not want, above all else, was people of his own generation. Just as some people are endowed with strength, others with speed or with a musical ear, so Opsenitsa was endowed with the unusual ability to develop and nurture fierce hostility, totally devoid of any hatred. This hostility was primarily directed against his own generation, most of whom had more schooling and ability than he had in the same field. Opsenitsa never made a public display of these hostilities (which, they say, were the cause of his cough), although he poured the better part of his energy and working hours into them, only to suspend them the instant they were discovered. That made him conceal the hostility all the more assiduously and adroitly, and put it, thus concealed, to maximum use. The person who was the target of these constant and ferocious clandestine attacks was like someone exposed to a constant infection whose source he could not pinpoint in order to take steps to protect himself.

"If you want to know whose enemy Opsenitsa is, look for someone who's having a bad time. That's him!"

That is what they said in professional circles. It was with such a former schoolmate that Svilar met that morning, while the wind devoured the rain. Svilar sneezed and shook hands with Opsenitsa, and they sat down at the glass-topped table. He gave him his latest drawings and asked him to take them into consideration at the next competition. Opsenitsa licked his fingernails, carefully looked through Svilar's portfolio, and had it entered in the books, and Svilar never heard another word about either Opsenitsa or his own drawings again. The two of them, one a top expert in his field, which nobody disputed, not even Opsenitsa, but without the financial power to ply his art, and the other without a professional reputation, but with financial influence in that very same field, were preordained to join together and work miracles. Yet the reverse happened. And then Svilar came to a conclusion. Opsenitsa's famous enmities were indeed his, but not the hatred in those enmities. That hatred came from somebody else. Like poison in a bottle, it merely traveled in Opsenitsa to its target, to Svilar and the others Opsenitsa thwarted.

That morning at breakfast, as he was thinking these thoughts, the milk curdled in Svilar's mouth and he felt that his vocation, his work as an architect, done outside of working hours and on paper, relegated to his spare time and unpaid, had become a vice. And he began to be ashamed of his drawing instruments and rulers and stopped touching bread with his hand forever. He ate it with a fork and knife off a plate. . . . He began to forget names and did not like their being mentioned too often in his presence. He was afraid of getting lost among so many names, as in a forest. He was also afraid of forgetting his own name one day, of having to stop for a moment when writing his signature, to remember it. . . .

He recalled with horror how once, when he was a child, he had gone with his father to the vineyard and had asked why they didn't cool the watermelon in the well.

"The well is blocked up," replied his father, "and wells, like living things, have their life span, and water, like man, can age and die. This one is dead, and now a new well has to be dug. . . ."

Svilar thought often now about that water. He was haunted by the feeling that he would never manage to get a building off the ground, to transpose its weight from numbers to a solid foundation and have its acoustics soar. It was exactly as though he were building on water. He had the impression that his street dawned on a different intersection every day, and he slept with his hand touching the floor, as though he were dropping an anchor from his bed. And after every waking, like a ship steered off course by a storm in the night, he had to reorient his bed, looking for the side of the world where he could get up. Afraid of these nights, which carried him at will, he began to renounce sleep, something he did not find difficult to do. His face transparent and sallow, carrying moles in that sallowness the way amber carries bugs, he roamed town night after night. And at this late age, when it was clear that the question was no longer how to succeed but why he had not succeeded in pursuing his profession, he turned completely from day to night, from his house to the city in which it stood.

At first, his nocturnal walks had no particular objective. He merely noticed that in walking he obeyed the traffic signs for motor vehicles. As though driving a car, he observed the No Turning signs and skirted streets closed to traffic. Sometimes he dreamed about these walks, woke up carrying from his dreams into wakefulness a tongue puckered with teethmarks, and realized that all the Belgrade streets in his dreams were one-way. It was then, to console himself, that he embarked on an almost unseemly enterprise, and his walks acquired an objective.

Several times, in the nights that guided him by their rumbling roar more than by the streets, he had come upon the forgotten places of his trysts as a young man. He noticed that he could not anticipate these places or recall them in advance, but that they announced themselves whenever he chanced upon one of them.

The entrance to a lit staircase leading to the darkness suspended high above. A bench chained to a tree. A fence with the unexpected shutter of a window. He was quick to recognize the places, but found it harder to remember the women he had taken there. Svilar started searching for these "sweet places" of his youth. He roamed the old houses of Belgrade that are flooded by the Danube when the water rises, knocking the barrels against the cellar door and tearing at the locks and hinges as though somebody were locked inside. Sometimes he spotted "dog windows" on the houses, those facing east, which only a few people could recognize nowadays, and fewer still put on their buildings. Dogs are fed through these "dog windows" on holidays, and birds are let in to get warm on St. Ilya's Day. He recognized the corners where the windows cross, spotted the streets where vertical winds blew in the spring and were crossed by horizontal winds in winter, and sweet memories once again opened before him like those shells that open only in the dark.

Memory gained upon memory, and on a map of Belgrade he began marking the places he had recognized during his nocturnal explorations, inscribing the names of the women he had had in these places. Their words and actions came back to him from the depths of his memories, and they seemed to mean more now than then.

"One sees into the past better by night than by day," whispered Atanas Svilar, and decided:

"All sexual acts in the universe are in some way connected, in some way they interact," and he hoped he would be able to find, in the messages of the women he had had, something like the equation of his own personality, something like an answer to the basic question that plagued him like hay fever: why had his life been barren and futile, despite the enormous effort invested?

And, strangely enough, bit by bit, something like a letter or a number, something like an answer emerged on the city map on which he had traced his own map of love. It was as though the common denominator of all his salient traits could be extracted from the secret messages left by his seed on the floor plan of the city. And one evening he sat down with the city map and read that message.

They usually went in the evening twilight to a half-demolished house in Vrachar from which the rain always flows into two rivers: the Danube and the Sava. They carried a bottle of wine and two glasses in their pockets, and the tip of her braid was always wet, because she liked to suck her hair. They wanted to catch that moment of pure sky, when all the birds have already descended and not a single bat has yet taken wing. They would enter a small glass elevator with its plush folding bench, small purple stool, mirrored doors, and light in the form of a crystal glass. It smelled of eau de cologne, of glue for paste-on beauty spots, and they sat down, put the bottle on the floor, the elevator in motion, and drank wine, their eyes traveling up and down the deserted hallways, while they kissed through her hair. It was as though they were journeying in a velvet-lined carriage. American bombs dropped all around them, Svetosavska Street was in flames, and when the air raid was over, they would go out to see what the "new town" looked like. The view opened up more and more each time, as entire buildings disappeared, and once, among the ruins, high up on the third floor, they recognized from the sole remaining picture and bookshelf the room where they had been served apple tea on a visit. A tap was peeing from that floor, and the bookshelf was swaying. One by one the books slowly slid off and, fluttering in the wind like birds on the wing, fell into the ashes of the ruins.

"Can you read which book is falling?" she asked him.

That day only one book was still left on the shelf. They waited for it to fall, but it only teetered. Then he took a stone and, in lieu of an answer, knocked the last book off the shelf, the way one picks a sparrow off the roof with a snowball.

"You don't like to read!" she observed.

"Books are painted intelligence!" he replied, and was surprised to hear her conclude:

"You like to talk, not read. And you know how to be silent. But you don't know how to sing."

In St. Nicholas Street, near the cemetery, in a small tavern that changed names more often than customers, so that everybody called it by its old name, The Sign, he acquired his first mustache. Every autumn the tavern-keeper plied the customers with wine that had caught a chill and inaugurated the tombola as soon as the stove, with its summer collection of cigarette butts, was lit. One evening, just when he had decided to take a card and try his luck for the first time, in came a woman with jet-black eyebrows perched above her nose like a comb—they looked as though they had been cleaved. She fired two eyes at him, as if he were some kind of rare game, then showed him the back of her head with its matted sweaty hair, and sat down. He filled in the card and listened to the melting of the strange silence that had briefly stilled the room when the girl entered. He watched how she dropped off to sleep and how, dozing on the chair, she slowly became younger than she really was, how from somewhere deep down, where the years were meted out, surfaced a smile that was only into its seventeenth autumn. That instant, as he gazed at the damp back of her head, he heard that he had won at the tombola and realized what he would win. He realized he would win that girl who was sitting with her legs crossed, smiling in her sleep over a chewed cigarette. It was too late to do anything. His number had been called and he had won his first woman at the tombola. He led her out, drowsy as she was, straight into the dirty, foul wind. When they parted in that same wind, it was already dawn. She gazed upon him for the first time in daylight and said:

"I know your type. You don't like wine and you mistreat water. You are afraid of daybreak. You are one of those people who think that the future emerges from the night, not from the day. Shall I tell you what you're going to do now, as soon as we part? You'll go straight to the fish market, to Djeram, to buy pickled peppers filled with cheese, and fish from rivers that flow from south to north, because they are tastier. At home you keep your cutlery separate, and you wash your own dishes, you fry and eat alone, because your family doesn't like the same food you do. You use both hands to serve yourself, you are a good cook and use a hot knife like the most experienced masters of the trade. You soak live sturgeon in wine, so that it reeks like a drunkard even after it's fried; you make soup of celery, which is heavier than other soups, and the plate under it can barely move.... And let me tell you something else: in cafés you and your kind have neither your own table nor your own waiter; you sit at the table alone and eat over six legs; you don't know how to be cheerful; if you clap, you clap with your nails, as though you were crushing lice. You are not one of those who spike eggs. And barbers and waiters ignore you."

They studied Sanskrit like mad, irregular French verbs before school in the morning, as if their lives depended upon it, from the Claude Auget books bought in the Henri Soubre French bookshop, which held the Hachette franchise at number 19, Knez Mihailova Street, before the war, English spelling in darkened rooms in the evening from the red Berlitz textbooks, German declensions at school from the yellow Schmaus editions, and at night, secretly, Russian words from the old prewar émigré press, received by Russian refugees in Belgrade. During the war, these lessons were dangerous and cheap, because under the German occupation it was prohibited to teach or study English or Russian. He and his friends studied them, keeping the fact from one another, often with the same teacher. So it was that for years they uttered not a single word in these languages, they pretended not to understand them, and it was only after the war that they shame-facedly realized that actually everybody of their generation spoke English, Russian, and French. And when they soon began forgetting these languages, they forgot them publicly, nostalgically remembering the times when they had learned them clandestinely. They had studied them under fat Swiss women, "Serbian widows," who would wish them a Happy New Year with a print of their rouged lips slipped into an envelope. For their Russian lessons they went secretly to former White Guard officers, émigrés from the Ukraine, who had beautiful wives and dogs and rigid mustaches, and who on their walls had hanging, like bats, enormous cavalry capes with a frame over the shoulders to leave free the hand that held the saber, and the hand that no longer held the saber. These teachers would sometimes sing to the strains of the balalaika, tossing down vodka between two words of the song so quickly that the song did not suffer. But he and his friends were not interested in the music—it hindered them from understanding the words—and they quickly returned to studying language, and that in itself fascinated them.

"Words grow on you like hair," his Russian teacher often told him, "and your words and your hair are black or brown, maybe secretly red, but sooner or later they will turn white, as we have all turned white. You can make what you want out of them, but they can also make anything out of you. . . ."

The wife of the Russian who had said that kept in a silk stocking all the hair she had cut off since leaving Russia. After every haircut, she would tie a knot in the stocking, and that is how she measured time. She no longer looked at the calendar, and she never knew the date or the day of the week.

Once, when he came for a lesson, he found her at home alone. She spoke no Serbian. She looked at him with her beautiful eyes, sucked at a button on her dress, and whistled softly into it.

"It's strange how you and others of your age study so many languages!" she said to him in Russian. "What do you want with all those thorns in your mouth? As though you were condemned to count every mouthful. I suppose it's because all of you are alone too much, and your memories are aging. Memory is not a circle; in the best of cases it is a very depleted circle. The memories inside us are not all the same age. You hope that languages will connect you with the world. But it is not languages that connect; you will learn them twice and twice in vain forget them, like Adam. What connects is whoredom. . . ."

And then she suggested that she give him a Russian lesson.

"Now I know whose dog answers to my name," he thought. She nuzzled up to him, gazed with her beautiful green eyes into his, and without a word wrapped her tresses around his neck. Then she tied them at the back of his neck and tightened the knot until their lips met. Moving her lips on his, she taught him how to say the same Russian word. The silent-contact method for learning foreign languages. Then she pushed him onto the bed, mounted the bed and him in it, and he learned for the first time how it was done in Russian. It was incomprehensible, but wonderful. Outside, it was snowing as though the sky were showering the earth with silent white words, and it all happened as though she were descending on him along with the snow, from infinite heights and in one direction, never pulling back for even a second, just as the snow or a word cannot return to the sky, to purity.

"You see," she said to him then, inhaling the air through her hair, "you don't need language to communicate. Whoredom suffices. But take care. You live best from whoredom on the first day, and then worse and worse with each passing day, until you fall low and rejoin the rest of the honest world. . . ."

She had a very shallow smile, and whenever she smiled one was bound to run aground on her nose. When she kissed him, he thought: "This is the kind of kiss duelists bestow upon one another before unsheathing their swords." He put down the oars for a moment and let the water turn them in the wind. They turned, and the wind slowly wrapped her hair around her neck. They had a dog and a newspaper in the boat. She read out her dog's horoscope in the paper and then took a drag from his pipe.

"Pay attention!" she told him. "Whenever there is a bitter taste in your mouth, you'll see something red on the lefthand side!" As she spoke, a strand of her hair fell into the pipe, and the golden wisp sizzled on the ember. They lay down in the boat, and the boat slowly pushed him deeper and deeper into her.

"She is lazy," he thought, "lazy even in making love." And this, he figured, was how she did it. But then she suddenly said:

"You want the water to father our child, not you. . . ."

That autumn another seven of his years ended; it had again been a weekly year in which he had done almost nothing. Tired and disappointed, far removed from his vocation, he barely comprehended that years, too, have their cycle, their holidays, their floral menstruation, and that this seven-year cycle persisted in him as well, and that seven years ago, just as now, he had been doing nothing. The number of days in which the world was created continued to reveal neuralgic spots. These weekly years were like navels on the body of time. Places where one time is separated from another by a knot, places where a knot interrupts the feeding of subsequent with previous time. That autumn he calculated that for three years now he had been groundlessly faithful to his wife, who had not slept with him for almost as long. He was spending time sitting idly at home, catching the rain on his navel and carrying his heart in his hand, when a Swiss German architecture magazine published several reports on his designs for medical buildings that had never been built. After dinner, he left the beans to soak under his tongue overnight, rubbed his chin with his shoulder, and read *Fachblatt für Architektur DBZ*, which had published his paper on the connection between ancient Byzantine urban architecture and modern building construction. Like the devil in church, he was at pains to recognize his own text. It was then that he first developed that pungent masculine hairy sweat in which mosquitoes drowned, which left towels moldy and gave cats a mute meow. And he felt that his professional knowledge was disappearing, that it was healing like a wound and vanishing like a disease after recovery.

He thought how there were already as many years in him as sentences in a story and he became alarmed. He began shortening his lovemaking, to where the beginning and the end touch.

She took his hand, opened it and gazed at it as though reading his palm:

"Slavia Circle is at the base of your hand, the place you should press if what is in me now gives you pain. The Sava River corresponds with the space between the index and the little fingers, and this is where neck pains start. Your index finger covers Knez Mihailova Street and designates head colds and nerves. The middle finger reaches Jovanova Street up to Neboisha Tower, and pressure on it eases sinus pains and the sense of smell. The stomach, somewhere around Teraziye Square, measures time at the base of the index finger, where the vein throbs. Finally, the ring finger reaches to the Danube bridge, designating the sense of hearing, and the little finger runs down Takovska Street carrying shoulder and appendix pains. Your life line goes over the Sava bridge, and there on the bridge it either breaks off or leads farther to the north. Remember all this, because, if your ear hurts, cross the Danube bridge and you'll feel better; if your shoulder hurts, go down Takovska Street and it'll cure you. . . . But illness is not the only reason why one should know these things. The city streets, like ships, have their course; they navigate following their own constellation, some to the south, under the sign of Cancer, others to the east, under the sign of Aquarius, and others yet follow Gemini. . . . Thanks to this connection between the streets, your body, and the stars, your paths, and your navigation routes, can be seen in your palm. And yet the town is not in your hand, you are in the hand of the town. You are tied to it like a cat to the house, and you see nothing else from it. You've never put even two seasons together out of town. Nor have you ever gotten the dirt of the earth on you properly. You've stayed under this town like women who stay under the same man all their lives, never wondering whether that man desires or wants them. . . ."

· · ·

He sat at his plate, looked at the spoon through the steam of the dilled milk soup, and wondered whose son his really was: that of Vitacha Milut or that of his lawfully wedded wife, Stepanida Djurashevich, Svilar by marriage. This is what happened the night he fathered his son:

He was fast at the time, and about him they said: "If nothing else, you can plant a tree in the handful of earth he can hold." He shaved his ears and had strong legs, which did not care how much the head had to carry, but his smile healed quickly, like a wound on the water. He ate with both hands at once, but his pockets were already full of chewed-off nails and mustache tips. In those days he and his young wife, Stepanida, often went to the Kalemegdan Terrace for dinner, to eat cheese pie with walnuts. One evening there they met Mrksha Pohvalich, a man whose face was so narrow he could touch both ears with one hand. He introduced them to his fiancée, Vitacha Milut.

"Why don't we switch to first names?" Atanas Svilar suggested to his new acquaintance, and immediately received an answer:

"All right, if your place is not too far away. . . ."

He threw a long look at Vitacha Milut, she blew him and his wife a kiss from the palm of her lip-embroidered glove, and then they started going out in couples: Mrksha Pohvalich and Vitacha, he and his wife, Stepanida, and a third couple, who were mutual friends.

The night he fathered his son, Nikola, the moonlight in Little Kalemegdan was the kind you enter from the dark, like a room. Under the Despot Stefan archway, somebody said:

"The stars are dancing, it's going to be cold!"

His wife, Stepanida Djurashevich, Svilar by marriage, was back a bit with the other woman, and for a moment he found himself alone with Vitacha Milut, whose fiancé was several steps ahead of them, talking to the third man of their group. In the darkness of the deep passageway, on one side of which you could hear the waters of the Sava and on the other the waters of the Danube, he suddenly kissed Vitacha Milut.

"A kiss is always cheaper than a tear," he thought, but he was wrong. Vitacha had saved "a mouthful" of wine from dinner and when they embraced, they mixed the drink in their kiss.

"I watched what you were eating," she whispered to him under her tongue, "and I ate the exact opposite: people who want a child should not eat the same food. . . ."

He felt that Vitacha was counting his teeth with her tongue, that she did not mind if the others discovered them, and that she was ready, right there in the park, to leave her fiancé. Her upper lip was salty with fear, her lower lip was slightly bitter, and her heart pounded as though it had been stolen. He felt her eyelashes graze his cheek, and Vitacha's hip on his stomach. He came out of the Despot Stefan archway consumed with desire, and as soon as the group dispersed in couples, right there, in Little Kalemegdan, in the park, still full of Vitacha Milut's saliva and with the penis she had made erect, he impregnated his wife, Stepanida Svilar, née Djurashevich, so frenziedly that to this day he was not quite sure to which of the two women his son belonged.

And the morning after, when he realized that he would never forget Vitacha Milut, it was already too late. He sought and found her in somebody else's bed. That night she had moved and for the first time had stayed overnight at her fiancé's apartment.

And so he stayed with his wife. And his son, Nikola Svilar, now sat before the father, under a head of hair resembling white feathers, in his sixteenth year, growing as though he were ladling days and nights from his plate, not soup. And for the umpteenth time, he tried to find some sign in the boy's features that would confirm his double origin. "If children were to take their mothers' surnames," he pondered, "whose surname should my son carry—that of Stepanida Svilar, née Djurashevich, or that of the 'first' mother, Vitacha Milut?" But, for the time being, there was nothing on Nikola to connect him with Vitacha Milut and her name.

He continued to meet periodically with Vitacha Milut and her husband, he watched how she drank as though biting the glass, and never again did he discover a single sign of her affection. But once, when they were left alone for a moment, she, with her own saliva, smoothed the eyebrows of his (at the time) still very young son, Nikola, and said:

"There are women who love only sons, and there are others who love only husbands. The problem is that a woman immediately senses a man to whom a woman's mouth is a mustache-binder. All women always go for the same men and always avoid the same men. Like those places on earth where dogs will never bark. And so some men are loved three times—first as sons, then as husbands, and finally as fathers—while others, those who were never loved by their mothers, will never be loved by their wives or their daughters either. Such men excrete and eat at the same time, like turtledoves. For centuries now, a good part of male America has been losing its virginity with black women, and a good part of Europe (its southeast) with gypsy women. Blessed be the ones and the others, because there is no greater mercy than to bestow upon such an unfed and unloved boy a piece of female bread. That is how you, who are not and will not be loved, lose your virginity. You will be faithful to women whom you don't love and who will not like sleeping with you. . . . That is why you will always search for a virgin. . . ."

After Atanas Svilar had made his notes on the city map of Belgrade and obtained a diagram of the sweet places of his youth, he suddenly thought he saw something like a message emerging in answer to his doubts. Had he been given just a little more time, just a day or two perhaps, he would have probably caught its meaning, maybe he would have quite accidentally turned over his architectural drawings and seen that his plans said the same thing as women. He would have discovered that the key words of that diagram drawn on the city map were: *silence, night, language, self-nourishment, water, town,* and *virgin.* . . . And that these words provided the much-sought-after equation of his fate. But this did not happen.

At that moment, outside, a catkin wafted by from a plane tree, wild wheat formed ears somewhere far off on the Danube, the sharp seeds of the onion weed scattered, the "bear ears" started to reek, and Svilar felt nauseous. He was already brown from the sun, but underneath that golden veneer lay a paleness, deep and constant like the moonlight.

The doctor was called in; he diagnosed another attack of hay fever, common at this time of spring, and recommended, as in previous years, a trip to the seaside.

The architect manqué Atanas Svilar and his son, Nikola, hurriedly packed their things, put salt in their pockets, and set out on their journey.

Their road, as all roads, did the thinking for them even while it was still empty.

2

For the first few centuries, they lived in the deserts of the Sinai. Then, one morning, a nail fell off a wall in Constantinople, and with it all the nails throughout the Byzantine Empire started falling off the walls. That nail, which had moved all the other nails, also moved the monks from Sinai and drove them to a new place. Their migration went like this.

When the Roman Prince Peter removed his helmet once and for all and had drunk from it his fill of wine, he decided to live an ascetic life. He looked for a place where nobody would be able to find him, a place where nobody knew his name. Such a place, everybody told him, did not exist in the empire. And then in his dream a woman appeared, shod in her own hair, with gloves knitted from that same unshorn hair, and she said to him:

"You will be protected by one of your fingers if you change your name." *The military commander had only three fingers, and for a long time he racked his brains trying to figure out how to interpret the dream. Finally, he decided that he should change his name, Peter (which denotes rock), to something that means the opposite of rock. And so he decided on water and boarded a ship, letting his new name, wanton water, carry him at will. His boat passed the island of Thasos and smashed against the underwater reef,*

and the water cast him onto a deserted piece of land. Having no idea where he was, he began to live in the kind of total solitude that makes nails peel and eyebrows turn gray. He divided the voices in his mouth into masculine and feminine, on Marian holidays he uttered only the vowels of his prayers, and on other holidays only the consonants. He probably never discovered that he was living and would die on one of the three fingers of the Chalcidice peninsula, on the cape facing the open sea, which in ancient times was called Akté. Word of his ascetic life reached Greece. They say he was betrayed by the birds he had taught to speak. One by one, they flew into Constantinople, alit on the masts of the ships, the females cawing the vowels, and the males the consonants of the prayers. Every Sunday, from the fleet in port, the birds on the masts could be heard spelling out "Our Father" and "Hail Mary."

Astonished and afraid, seafarers followed the birds and called the Akté peninsula, where Peter lived as a recluse, the Holy Mountain. But other monks would not have followed in his footsteps had they not been impelled to do so by a great misfortune, the kind that makes one forget the bread in one's mouth, and turns a new strand of hair white with every blink.

In the capital, icons appeared in the churches one morning, raised a mast higher than they had been the night before. It was whispered that the order had come from the basileus himself, so that the rabble of worshippers would not soil the holy cheeks with their kisses. But misfortune, too, walks step by step, and after the left foot it puts forward the right. A shipload of monks banished from Sinai arrived in the port of Constantinople. They were all icon-painters and all from the order of solitaries. By imperial decree, the ship of painters was watered only with colors and fed with the wood of the icons; it was stripped of its sails and left to the wanton water. The imperial stewards saw them off, taunting:

"He who sees the greenest of all green colors will be able to bring the ship back to port and save the passengers. . . ."

But not one of the painters ever found the greenest of all greens, although it brings luck, just as only a few died from having found the yellowest of all yellows, which brings death. And so the ship set out to sea, following the underwater winds, and smashed against the reefs of the Holy Mountain *where some of the painters drowned and others swam to dry land carrying their beards in their teeth.*

And then throughout the empire began the terrible persecution of icon-worshippers. First the soldiers took down the icon from the entrance into town, from Vlaherna, and then from the Church of Churches, and finally from the other temples of Constantinople and the vast empire, right down to the very last icon, depicting Satan. The nails rolled down the streets, and it was impossible to walk by without hurting one's feet. The imperial court began seizing the property of monasteries and individuals who continued to offer resistance by secretly keeping icons, even if they were turned to face the wall. These were chiefly monasteries of idiorrhythmics, dedicated to the Virgin Mary, and recluse monks, for they, in their solitude, most often paint, and it is no accident that the first icon-painter, Saint Luke, first painted the Virgin. Contrarily, the other monasteries, organized on the basis of communal life, did not take the persecution of icons and icon-painters too much to heart. They watched as the refugees and prisoners, their idiorrhythmic brothers from Sinai, from Cappadocia, from Constantinople and other places, were put on galleys without rudders or sails, and, like the former, were shoved out into the open sea and left to the elements. The currents carried them always on the same route, northward (this route is still called in some places the "painters' route") through the Aegean Sea, until the whirlpools spewed them out on the Holy Mountain, Mount Athos, and there smashed them against the underwater rocks, just as they had once cast Xerxes's armada onto the same sharp cape of the last peninsula in Chalcidice. And so it was that a large monastic settlement was founded at this site by the recluse monks who had survived the shipwreck. The center of monastic life thus moved from Sinai to Mount Athos.

But even here the imperial hand hung over them, the eye of the whip kept watch. The recluse settlers exiled to Mount Athos and other places were not permitted to renew their idiorrhythmic order; they were only allowed to enter cenobitic monasteries, and when they founded new ones, the new ones, too, had to be devoted to the Holy Trinity and based on communal life. Because the cenobitic monks were more immune to iconoclasm than the sol..... ver been particularly tied to icons or the matter of pa..... e masculine candles devoted to the

Holy Trinity of the Christian church were already burning, they lit a fourth, feminine candle for the Virgin Mary, and the iconoclasts in power turned a blind eye. When it came to slapping, the cenobites received only one of every three slaps. But this lasted only about one hundred years. Long enough for the soul to hide behind the brow.

It was the kind of day when they say: "Strike a thorn with a cane and up springs a flower!" It was on such a day that Atanas Svilar and his son, Nikola, found themselves at Matarushka Spa on the first night of their journey. Over the door of Svilar's small parental home hung a wreath, through which the cow was milked. They ate piping-hot dilled milk soup, and peering out of it were lamb's eyes. From these eyes Svilar saw that outside, where the streets had become warmer than the houses, the bracken promised another hard, dry spring with storms of pollen. His winter voice sounded strange in this new season. To have a quarter of the time against you every year is too much. . . .

Svilar's mother now lived in the house alone. Beautiful, tall, with transparent hands and nails painted pink by rushes of blood. For years, Svilar had recognized those hands and some of the gestures they made in his own hands and in the gestures that his acquaintances, and especially his wife, hated most.

When Svilar's father, Major Kosta Svilar, failed to return from the war in 1941, when it was heard that he had been killed and that a peasant had been seen one night crossing the Ibar bridge with a ram decked out in the major's fur jacket, Svilar's mother sat down on the edge of her bed and for weeks, as though waiting to go on a trip, she sat there, ready to follow her husband somewhere herself. When this did not happen, and when even in her dreams she began to realize that he was no more, she opened up her house to the black mourners, those merciless women who deal with the dead the way doctors deal with the living, passing on their art from one generation to the next. These women always came from the same nearby graveless village, where everybody either died in prison or was carried by troubled waters far away from any graves. They spoke and were silent through the coins in their mouths, they whispered that children should not be conceived in a year when the walnuts are hollow, they knew how to "drain the terror" from nightmares, and they rolled up navels by burning wool in a glass placed on the stomach. They never allowed questions about the age of the deceased ("Is it age we are burying?" they would say), and at the funeral feast they always sat at the second table, where, custom has it, one can reprimand the guests.

"Death is hard work; like plowing," they added, "it strains every bit of you as never before. And the weary worker should be looked after, all his needs tended to on time and in due order." They immediately took things into their own hands. The boiled wheat was to be prepared not by the deceased's family, but by a neighbor who afterward would boil the wheat every year on All Souls' Day, and if she fell ill would pass on this duty to another, younger woman. People came from the neighboring houses to slaughter what was needed, and each brought a candle. Then they carried into the house a cross the size of the man, dressed it, and prepared an empty grave for Major Kosta Svilar, in which they buried his suit, saber, and picture. Next the food was brought out for the soul. Volant meat went to the children, natant meat to the women, and ambulant meat to the men. For all forty days, a tray stood in the deceased's attic and on it a comb, a glass of water with sugar, and a slice of bread with salt. If, even after this period, the bread had not eaten the salt, or the water drunk the sugar, it was believed that something was denying the deceased access to the house. Finally, on Pentecost, a candle was affixed to the trumpet of a musician, and he played for the major's soul to rest in peace, until the candle burned all the way down. Then architect Atanas Svilar passed around the buttons off his shirt to the guests.

"He was redheaded, one of those who're baptized, but who knows whether a requiem will be sung for him. This way, at least we sang to his picture. . . ." And with those words the women departed and left them alone.

Time passed, Svilar's mother's hair turned gray, and her part grew fat. She roamed her sticky floors and rugs, which stuck to the soles of her feet at night as though they had been smeared with honey, and she often dreamed that her bed was full of cracked walnuts and was set like a table for three. Sitting at her table now were indeed three people, as in bygone times, only now they were her son and grandson instead of her son and husband. Atanas Svilar was now older than Major Kosta Svilar had been when they buried him in absentia, and now he increasingly thought of his father. Even this trip with his son was aimed in a particular direction, but he did not mention his objective to his mother. And that objective was connected precisely to the strange disappearance of Major Kosta Svilar. Atanas Svilar had decided to finally try and discover, after so many years, what had happened to his father who had disappeared in World War II. Since the doctor had recommended the seaside, he planned to set out with his son along the route taken by the major's former unit.

In 1941 it had been stationed on the border with Albania, and at the beginning of the war, in keeping with Plan "R 41," the major had nipped across the border and entered deep into enemy territory. While the other Yugoslav fronts were on the retreat, he bit the frost and charged. Nothing is more costly than a small success in a great defeat. Success in the midst of defeat carried Kosta Svilar away forever. According to one report, received just before the liberation in 1944, the last trace of Kosta Svilar after the capitulation of the Royal Yugoslav Army was somewhere in Greece. And so Major Kosta Svilar's son and grandson set out in that direction.

"All births are similar, and every death is different," Atanas Svilar thought, and took his illness along on the trip while his son, Nikola, took the major's guitar, stuffed with prewar money. That evening, before leaving Matarushka Spa, they sat at a wooden table still hot from the just-eaten soup and, keeping the purpose of their trip from Svilar's mother, they talked about entirely different matters. Svilar gazed at his son, thought how he was growing out of childhood, and tried to understand him. Childhood resembles no other time of life. It has something of the mystery and inaccessibility of the future. Once we leave it, childhood becomes as remote, opaque, and fateful as the future. It covers one end of our journey, just as the future covers the other. . . .

"Should I join the Party?" his son asked him just then.

"I don't know," replied Atanas Svilar, confused. "I don't know; maybe that's not something one should give advice on. I cannot save you from Tuesday and from Saturday."

"You were in the Party for thirty years, and now you don't know? How come? Just so we understand one another," the son went on, "I don't need an answer, but do you want me to tell you why you can't give me one? Today, when so many intellectuals all over the world are becoming reds, you're tired of the Party. Do people have to leave the CP for you to go back to it? Doesn't that seem like elitism to you?"

"And doesn't it seem to you that the Party is a mother to some and a stepmother to others?"

"Sure, when some treat it like their own home, and others like a hotel . . . You sneeze and you no longer know where you are, that's what you and your generation are like. If it's day for everyone else, it's night for you. But don't think you're the only ones. There are people like you everywhere, even in villages, where they make bread and on the bread put a navel, but they've never reached the city, just as you've never reached the country. You're the ones who are convinced that there's always somebody somewhere to take care of all the problems and that your time is still in the oven, when in fact your tomorrow has already been stolen by the magpie. Relying on yourselves and on the grit of your teeth, you wound up with a storm in your mouth. It was too late by the time you got to wear the pants, you say? That's true, but if I had been fourteen in the war, I would have picked up a rifle without waiting for the pants. And one more thing. As with rifles, so with women. One chooses a wife, not a mother. But you people didn't marry the women you loved and you didn't father us with them, like those who suck the change before letting it out of their hand. I don't know whether your luck has grown or not, but I do know that there is a gorgeous woman, Vitacha Milut, whom you once deserted for lack of courage. I don't know whether being faithful to a wife you don't love is a virtue, but I do know that you and your kind have never looked around you to see whose shadows you were treading on. You still don't know, even today, which of your hands is sinful, and which the one to slap with. The only thing your generation created, apart from bread that has already been eaten, it created in painting; only the painters among you were made of stronger stuff. Dada Djurich, Velichkovich and Lyuba Popovich, who went to France, the Mediala group led by Sheika, who asked for a passport but didn't get one, and the others who stayed, they opened a new age on canvas; they could say: Our daughter is as old as our house....

"That, of course, doesn't interest me at all; it's not my thing, all that stuff with paints and brushes, but what I can't understand is that it didn't interest you. You never realized that all those painters and their paintings belong to your generation. You couldn't have cared less about them. Yet they were able to imagine the future in space, not time; they resisted abstract painting, returned to the icon on the wall, reverted to the brush made of the human beard and the paints of the earth, turned back to their own image as the icon, and on it they found you, who had never seen them. They painted the presence of the absent, dogs running on human paths marked by dappled light, piglets replacing Rembrandt's corpse on the anatomy table. And that was the only instance of your generation's resisting someone or something, speaking out, swimming against the current, and they paid for their clairvoyance with the deafness that surrounded them. The rest of you remained high-school teachers, each of you sporting solitude like a cap. Have you ever wondered why your life has remained futile, as though you had been spending your time thrashing at snakes, as unfulfilled as dreams before Friday? Why the town in which you were born and grew up always thinks of you as a rose pepper, why you could never build a single building in that town, why they all re-mained on paper like fly honey? How it happened that that same father of yours, my grandfather Kosta Svilar, who was no civil engineer like you, just a plain old officer who could pee from a galloping horse, how it happened that he could build two houses, one in Belgrade, and the other here, and you not a single one anywhere, not even for yourself, so that you don't die in somebody else's? . . ."

"On days like this even snakes that have venom only on Fridays become poisonous," Atanas Svilar thought, listening to his son, to the boy who still adored grapes hot from the sun and ripe apricots in which you could almost feel the jam simmering on the branch in the heat. Atanas Svilar sat there and looked in amazement at his son, and then at his own hands on either side of the plate, and he could not recognize them. Two scalded goose heads peered out from his sleeves and tried in vain to swallow the knife and fork. . . .

He drank a glass of water and went to bed. The water seemed empty and full of holes, and in the morning, instead of his son, in the room with the porch where Nikola Svilar slept he found a note with the message:

> Bring me back an army shirt from Greece. They're in style now. If I need Grandfather, I'll find him myself. *Good luck.*
>
> *Nikola*

Assuming that Major Kosta Svilar had gotten out of Albania and into Greece by sea, Atanas Svilar set out for the Adriatic coast. In Bar he put himself and his car on a broad black ship bound for Corfu, filling his trouser legs with a cold wind, and his nostrils with saffron-smelling salt. When they set out from Ithaca for the Ionian islands, he placed a glass of wine on the railing of the ship and held the stem down with his finger so that it would not overturn. The red wine in the glass, out of solidarity with the briny sea, faithfully transmitted every move of the water. In the glass he now had a copy of the waves. "That's how it is with me," he thought. "I, too, am part of some kind of current that I'm transmitting without even knowing it. . . ."

Svilar was listless, he had transported his illness and hunger from land to the Ionian Sea and became increasingly sick and gluttonous, he felt like somebody who at a wedding feast had eaten the muzzle along with the sow's snout in the cabbage, and he hardly gave a thought to the objective of his trip. Hay fever held sway over him once more. He felt that the stars were thorny again and that that was what made his eyes blink. Admittedly, when they stopped off in the ports of Cephalonia and Zakynthos he did inquire about a Yugoslav unit that had retreated this way thirty years before and had linked up with British marines, who were still in the Peloponnese in April 1941. It was no use, not only because the people in the streets were young and did not remember such things but also because every eye on his journey had a different depth, like water, and Svilar was unable to communicate with people who ate yogurt with a knife and combed their eyebrows with a fork. Each word in their language had, like birds, its own guiding star, but the sky of these stars was invisible from where Svilar stood. As soon as he landed in the Peloponnese, entering a hot wind as though he were entering a furnace, two ship skeletons appeared on the shore like two gnawed fish bones, which were now slowly acquiring wooden meat through a shipbuilding technique that was the opposite of eating fish. In the ribbed shadow of these wooden bones, Svilar dipped his feet in the sea, on which the dust from his journey settled, and washed his inflamed eyes, breathing in the sea foam and iodine vapor like a fish. He lay down on the shore and fell asleep, taking into his dreams the intention of continuing his inquiry in Filiatra and in Sparta, but half-asleep he felt that the job was futile, that rain does not bread make. The water protected him from the land, the grass of the sea from the grass of the shore.

He was awakened by the screeching of car tires on the road. He opened his eyes and saw a red Mercedes slamming on the brakes. The car stopped, a dark object flew out of the window and rolled on the ground, and then the passengers jumped out, dragging a tall swarthy man behind them. They hauled him up against an olive tree, pinning down his arms, and the girl who had stepped out of the car with them unbuttoned his trousers and pulled out his prick. Then the driver, who had gotten out of the car with her, peed on the wretched man's sex organ. . . .

Taken aback, Svilar whistled through his fingers; the passengers piled back into the car and took off, leaving the man on the road. In their haste they closed the door on the girl's long blond hair, and as the door swung shut her hair flew in all directions, refusing to submit and enter the car, although they collected it by opening and closing the door of the moving car.

"Did they hurt you?" Svilar asked the stranger in German.

"Where there's treasure there's trouble," the man replied in Serbian. "They pee on your prick, then you can't sleep with a woman for the next seven days. But I won't need it where I'm going."

"And where are you going?"

In lieu of an answer, the stranger pointed his leg toward the north. He was a man of Svilar's age, about ten handfuls of salt, as they say. He was good-looking, but his looks were not the kind of feminine good looks one sometimes encounters in men, they were the kind of masculine good looks women sometimes inherit from their fathers. Around his neck he wore a wreath of peppers as hot as burning embers, and they made everything on him, from his mustache to his buttons and nails, so peppery that just to touch his things would make a man feel as though he had caught a disease, it was that burning sensation that makes the corners of one's eyes foam. Svilar immediately found that out for himself.

He bent down to pick up the stranger's things that had been tossed out of the car, and in the grass he saw a—gusle. He picked up the black instrument, actually a large wooden spoon sheathed in leather, looked at it, offered it to the stranger, and immediately felt his fingers prickle from pepperiness. He remembered that on the ship he had noticed a man with a gusle in a group of German tourists, and he offered to give the stranger a lift.

"Do you know Father Luke?" the stranger asked him as soon as they had gotten into Svilar's car and driven off.

"No, I don't," replied Svilar in surprise, but the gusle-man persisted.

"Never mind," he added, "he's bound to know you...."

"It's always Friday to him," Svilar thought, and focused his mind on the road ahead of him. At that moment his passenger in the back seat crossed his legs and started shouting at the top of his lungs to the accompaniment of the gusle. The song was monotone, the words in series of ten syllables, and it was immediately obvious that the singer had no ear and that he didn't need one anyway. There was only one string on his instrument, and with it he accompanied a kind of lament or disconnected speech, using only four of the seven intervals of the scale. It was obviously one of those songs that are not to be found in books but, rather, are learned from other singers and transmitted orally, like the pox. All in all, it really did seem like some kind of sickness of the language, an infection, carried from sentence to sentence, spoiling and constricting it to make it resemble the preceding one, even though it said something quite different. Svilar could not remember the song as he had heard it, but as he remembered it its title could be:

KARAMUSTAFA'S SONS

Back in the days when ways of lying were taught in schools in Greece, Mount Athos was administered by one Karamustafa-bey, a tyrant and an oppressor who used to say that one day in the week was God's and the other six were his. He had a horse that was rumored to pray in front of church on Sundays, and in the furnace a constantly burning fire which he called "Sophia," and with it he menaced and burned whenever he chose and whatever he chose to call to mind. From time to time, he would send a message to Mount Athos saying that he was going to set fire to Chilandar, one of the biggest monasteries on Athos, which was also the most accessible to him by land. Before setting out on his forays and pillages, the bey's white hounds were washed with laundry bluing; the bey was as adept at striking with his scabbard as with his saber. He could strangle a man with his long greasy pigtail instead of his hand. He was also known to have long since become a beast in whose shadow not even the winds blew, to have seen somewhere in Africa one of those monkeys that are seen only once in a lifetime and that periodically go to the other world. He put his hand out to the monkey, let the animal bite him, and every morning since then had the khoja read him the inscription left by the bite in his flesh.

"We live on borrowed time," Karamustafa said, listened to his hounds laugh in their sleep at night, and cried frequently, biting his saber in despair at having no offspring. One day the monks from Chilandar on Mount Athos came to pay their tribute, and he asked them whether it was true that there was a vine in their monastery that had grown there since the time of the Serbian tsars and that its seed, as big as an ox eye, helped barren women. Upon receiving an affirmative answer, the bey sent his bitch back with the monks for them to feed with the grape, because even his dogs were barren. . . .

The monks departed, taking the bitch with them, and they kept her on the boat, because nothing without a beard is allowed on Mount Athos. They returned her ninety days later, and she brought forth seven pups. That was a sign for the bey to take fright, slip into submission, and go to the perimeter of Mount Athos with his saber jabbed into a block of wood and his teeth painted black. Behind him, in a small tent, rode his wife with an empty cradle. The monks welcomed them and installed them at the border of Chilandar's land, which was also the northern perimeter of Mount Athos. Every morning they brought the woman grapes from the vine that grows underneath Nemanya's grave by the wall of Chilandar's Church of the Presentation, where the large grape-seeds color the stone slabs blue.

"If a son is born unto me," the bey then promised the monks, "he will bring you fire from the sea in his mouth to light the candle, and I will give him to you to serve in the monastery for the rest of his life."

When his hopes were fulfilled, and his wife came unfastened, the bey was given not one but two sons at once. Now he had to be big in the leap as well! He owed the monks not one but two sons now. In the meantime, the waters flowed and carried the walnuts and apple to the sea, and the bey amassed children galore and degenerated back into his old bloodthirsty self, counting the steps with his saber.

His firstborns grew, and it was whispered that they would go far. Their immeasurable boldness, which soon became legendary, actually concealed an infirmity. One of the boys noticed at an early age that he did not feel pain and that a lash of the whip drew his attention with its whistle, not its effect. His brother learned the same thing in another way. Sometime in his fifteenth year, in a street in Salonika, a girl stole a glance at him through her hand mirror. As she passed by, she slapped him with her hair and her black tresses cut his cheek. But he felt no pain. He merely saw that a trace of his blood was left on the girl's hair. After that both brothers knew what was the matter with them. They were deprived of the blessing of pain. The only thing they had to fear in future was that they would be killed in some skirmish and not even notice it. In the first battle Karamustafa took them to, the sons created such a massacre that the horses they rode had to be changed three times. After the battle, however, they cloistered themselves inside the tent, surrounded by the cheering hordes outside, and examined each other's bodies, searching for injuries they could not feel, because they had no sensation and had to poke their finger in the wound to be sure it existed. In this deaf interval between the attack and the search for wounds, they became bloodthirsty, they became more terrible than their father, and nobody ever dreamed that one morning, after seventeen years, as soon as his sons came of age, Karamustafa would reappear at the monastery, leading his two firstborns, and that he would give them to the monks as he had promised.

"Who could have made the bey do it?" they wondered in the military camps.

"Who dares let the bey's two sons into the monastery?" the monks, in turn, wondered in their cells. "You open the doors to receive them and they leave the footprints of wildcats."

"That at least is easy," one of the elders then responded. "It's known what has to be done:

"To one you give the key and the money, and to the other the cross and the book. One you make the housemaster; let him trade, let him run the monastery household, let him hold the purse strings, and let his be the livestock and his the management of the land and water. But do not entrust him with the cross, and keep him far from any honors or praise; keep him at the back of the table, let him keep his name under his hat and hold his tongue, keep him under your hand so that he may easily be removed. . . .

"Place the other at the head of the table, with the cross and the book; give him a grand name, one of the grandest of the interpreters of the Holy Scriptures, point to him as an example to others, as the one with the purest thought. . . . But give him neither the key nor the purse to hold, give him no power, let everything he has be with you. And between him and his brother let it be as between water that would flow had it a riverbed and a riverbed that would be a river had it water. As long as they fight, we shall be at peace. But should the two of them come to terms, should they wed the key to the cross, should they realize that they are of the same name, then we shall have to lash the mules to the masts so that we may have salty meat to eat on the high seas. There shall be no survival for us here anymore. . . ."

Thus advised the old man, but on the appointed day, when the bey's two sons appeared at the monastery gate with reins around their necks and the fire from the sea in their mouths, everybody had second thoughts. The young boys entered the monastery ceremoniously: behind them walked two servants bearing a silver tray with their masters' braids plaited as one. Then the elder changed his mind. He addressed his guest with a wise proposal, which satisfied both God and the bey:

"It is not we who gave you sons," said the monk to Karamustafa, "and therefore it is not we who can take them from you. Let them be taken by Him who gave them, by the Almighty. . . ."

The boys bit off the tips of the freshly lit candles, took the fire in their mouths back to the sea, and did not become monks. . . .

It is said that they died on the river Prut, mortal enemies till their dying breath. One was a treasurer with the Turkish hordes, and the other a dervish who, it is said, gave the finest interpretation of the Koran.

In the evening Svilar and his travel companion sat in a small inn in Filiatra; the lamp hanging from the ceiling on the dog chain swung over the table, the light quivered in the glasses, the Ionian Sea rolled outside, and they were served dinner far from the window, which the waves bombarded with pebbles to break the glass. Drinking ouzo, the gusle-player told Svilar his life story, spluttering up to his fine eyes. He claimed that they were uncommonly like the eyes of his wife, who was older than he, but changed more slowly, and now somewhere in Germany resembled him as he was ten years ago. He was a country boy; in 1943, at the age of eleven, barefoot, he had joined the partisans, with whom he remained till the end, almost won the war with a star on his forehead; then one night something happened that changed his life completely. What it was he did not say, but he mentioned to Svilar that he had run away to plow the fields at home and had been found out. Frightened by this or by something else he was concealing, he no longer dared return to his unit, and crossed over to the Chetniks instead. And so with the crown he lost that same war already won with the star, and retreated with the Germans to the border. There his fellow fighters told him:

"Don't go to France, you're too young for the Allied countries; they will be ruled for the next decade by those who waged and won the war—by your father's generation. And woe betide those whose fathers win the war! The world will never be theirs. In France you'll get everything ten years late, when it's no longer worth anything. Go to Germany; there they'll be looking for younger people, who bear no responsibility for the defeat; the generation of fathers has lost the game there; there it's your generation's move. Rain does not fall everywhere; in places rain's children fall, too. . . ."

They say that the soul grows longer on a man than the body. As long as a beard. And it holds the body at the bottom, like the beard the face. The young man found himself in Germany and there began to earn a living from painting in a most unexpected way. In actual fact he was no better at painting than at whistling, but his wife had a habit that initially astonished him and then led them both to a painting technique that had never been heard of before in Germany. They were still young, she was crazy about him, she ate from his mouth, and one winter, as they were returning home from a tavern, the thing happened quite by accident. They were in a park; for days the snow had been falling as though it came by the bulk, and she wrote her signature in the snow, steering his penis like a fountain pen, and for a while the signature steamed like tea, and then became perfectly legible.

This turned into a habit; soon she began drawing various patterns in this way, and then they changed their technique, she began dipping the penis in paint and painting on canvas, which they signed jointly and sold illegally at surprisingly high prices.

In between jobs, the man would travel periodically to Greece, since he dared not go to Yugoslavia; he would tour the monasteries and there sing with his gusle about the saints, reviving the art of gusle-playing that his father had known. Except that his father had sung about battles, whereas he sang about angels, about Mary in hell, about Saint Petka and Joseph of the many-colored coat. This time he had gone on his trip with a group of Germans, buyers of his paintings. But never travel with someone you want as a friend. They lost patience with him and threw him out of the car.

"That's the first time something like that's happened to me," the gusle-player added at the end of his story, thinking of the incident with the Germans in the Mercedes, "and barbers don't charge for the first shave. . . ."

That was the story of the gusle-player. Every light was obviously denser to him than to others, and he took nothing seriously. He sat there, ate terribly hot food spiced with the peppers from his necklace, and suddenly asked Svilar:

"Where are you going?"

That question changed Svilar's fate.

"Why are you looking for your father here, in the Peloponnese?" asked the gusle-player when he heard Svilar's story. "On a narrow peninsula in northern Greece there is a monastic settlement that is more than a thousand years old. On the Holy Mountain, or Mount Athos, as it is called in Greece, there are also Serbian monks and monasteries. I have been there twice already, and I know what it's like. Had I crossed from Albania into Greece in 1941 like your father, I would have sought refuge on Mount Athos, among our countrymen. Maybe that's what he did, too. . . . Look for him there."

"Tear the wing off a mosquito and there go its intestines as well!" Svilar thought in regard to his plan, upon hearing this idea. But he soon wondered whether the gusle-player was not, perhaps, trying to lure him his way, so that they might travel together as long as possible. That evening in Filiatra, he lay in bed in a rented room, listened to the ticking of an alarm clock somewhere in a porcelain dish, and did not know which direction to take in the morning, when that same clock woke him up. And in the morning, it immediately turned out that the gusle-player, like the louse that transmits typhus, transmitted wisdom, which spreads among the people like an infection, because disease is truth. As soon as they set out on the journey, it became obvious that Svilar had no choice: he could return home, the job undone, or accept the gusle-player's proposal. In either case he had to go north, toward Salonika.

Impaled on his time like a butterfly on a pin, that is just what he did.

3

One night, the Empress Theodora dreamed that angels had descended into her bedchamber, carrying toothed whips, triple scourges, fishhooks, and sickles. And the angels started to flog and tear at the emperor sleeping by her side. And when the empress was awoken by her own fear and by the rustling of wings, she saw the Emperor Theophilos on the bed beside her, almost dead from the contusions, lying all broken and bruised in the angels' bloodstained feathers, not even receiving his name in his ear. That same night the entire army went hoarse, and for six weeks not a single commander could issue an order, nor one soldier wish another a good day. And from that silence, as from the most piercing scream, Constantinople's Church of Churches finally shook itself out of its hundred-year dream. The emperor had a night mass introduced for the Virgin Mary, and brought into Hagia Sophia two hundred women with children at their breasts, and the infants prayed for the parents of their sinful milk. And once again the Church of Churches was draped with icons. . . .

When the nails were returned to the walls of the empire, and the icons to the churches, on Mount Athos the monks wanted to reintroduce, alongside cenobitism, the solitary way of life, idiorrhythmia, as it had been before. Because famine had plagued Mount Athos after all its brotherhoods had converted to cenobitism. No one worked the land, they all cultivated vineyards. It was necessary to return to the dual order. But the canons of Mount Athos did not make this easy. Because the family in which all the solitaries had once, no matter when, converted to cenobitism, could never again belong to the order of solitaries. Hence there was no return from cenobitism. And so, for canonic reasons, even after the ban on icons and on idiorrhythmia was lifted, the old monasteries that had already converted to cenobitism could not return to idiorrhythmia. Only newly founded brotherhoods could introduce idiorrhythmia. And so the Greeks let the barbarians found new monasteries on Mount Athos. The newly converted Slav monks, their hair tied in knots denoting the number of daily and nightly prayers, arrived, plunged their anchoritic sticks into the earth, and waited for them to sprout leaves. If the sticks did not sprout leaves, it meant that they would not become ecumenical patriarchs, and then the monks would retreat into the ascetic order and found new brotherhoods. It was under such circumstances that upon the foundations of the older, abandoned Greek monasteries new, Slav ones were built: the Russian Roussikon, the Serbian Chilandar, the Bulgarian Zographou, and others. And they were all now organized so as to embrace both monastic orders: cenobitism and idiorrhythmia. Thus the coming of the Slavs to Mount Athos helped to reestablish the balance that had been disturbed during the conflict over the icons. The previous supremacy of the cenobites was now tempered by the presence of new orders of solitaries in the newly founded monasteries. Where these new monastic Slav settlements on Mount Athos were heading was soon to be seen from the example of Chilandar, which became one of the four biggest monasteries on the peninsula. One of those that spend the night at the top of their own leap . . .

Thunder and lightning lashed the earth and water, and then retreated. They trailed the thunder in a car full of frothy silence, following the route blazed by pilgrims who had descended through the centuries from the Balkans to Salonika and farther east, to the Slav monasteries on Mount Athos. Along the road, one could still make out the chain of caravanserais and pilgrim inns that had awaited the newcomers from the Slav hinterland of the ancient Byzantine Empire. The families that had once maintained these ties down through the generations now ran small inns along the Salonika seafront, overlooking the bay where the city's patron, Saint Demetrius, had once ridden out into the open sea, his left hand holding the reins on the rump of his white steed, and his right slashing the sails of the pirate ships that were attacking Salonika. In the afternoon, Atanas Svilar and his travel companion found themselves in Tripiti, where, thousands of years before, Xerxes had removed the anchors from his warships, harnessed the anchors to the buffaloes grazing on the shore, and dug out the canal that separated the peninsula from the mainland, hauling his fleet into the heart of Greek waters without exposing himself to the rage of the open Aegean Sea. Now this belt of saline earth, where no grass grew, marked his path and the frontier between Mount Athos and the rest of the world. That frontier, they heard, was eternal, just as salt is indestructible. The travelers left their "four horses" in Ouranoupolis, a place on the frontier, because Mount Athos can be reached only by ship or on foot. They asked for a bed for the night, fish for lunch, and the port where they would take the boat to Karyes in the morning.

"Riba?" replied one of the Greeks drinking ouzo in the thin, sickly shade of the vines on the waterfront. A string of beads hanging from his hand, he pointed to the tenth-century tower by the monastery. It turned out that the place he sent foreigners to was one where they speak the language in which that is the word for "fish." The innkeeper and his wife were called Vassili and Vassilia Philaktos; they had learned Serbian from the old, yellowed "proskyneteria"—guidebooks to Mount Athos which their ancestors had copied and later printed for their guests. The innkeeper said his wife would bring the wine immediately, and he placed before them a book containing the signatures of pilgrims since 1886. He had a part in his mustache, making it look uncommonly like eyebrows, and he trimmed the one and the other side in the same way.

"This is the third book in the family," he added. "The first two were filled long ago."

His wife had arms as plump as sourdough, with dimples full of darkness on her elbows. She was so beautiful that even her own husband obviously could not get used to such beauty. He told them that she was a being of strange, long breath, that she lived in large segments of time, that she completed today's thought tomorrow, that she found two days and a night barely enough for one day, so she merged them into one and then slept for a full forty-eight hours. She poured them wine and immediately mentioned that it was seasoned with resin and herbs, which make tears run dry and the blood throb pleasantly in one's ears, fluctuating like the wash of the sea, and attuned to the hexameter, the ancient Greek verse, whose rhythm is learned from the "retsina" although the language that produced it is not known. It is believed that barbarians who got drunk on this wine, which is mentioned in *The Odyssey,* immediately spoke in hexameters, before they learned Greek. Noticing that Svilar was put off by the liquid's strange smell, she added, as though combing him with her eyes:

"Don't ever avoid anything that is a first! There are meals that should not be judged until the third or last bite. There are wines on which judgment should be passed only on the second or third day after having tried them. . . ."

She fried the fish in corn flour and separately, in a pan with a handle bent like a sickle, prepared for herself olives in cheese and a largish elder blossom dipped in breadcrumbs.

"You need four visas for Mount Athos," she spoke up again from behind her pans, as though continuing a story. "You have already gotten, I hope, the first visa, the Greek one, in Belgrade, and the second, the one for northern Greece, in Salonika. The third you get in Karyes, when you cross the border between Greece and Mount Athos. Karyes, or Orahovitsa, got its name from the many walnuts that grow there, and it is the seat of the Protaton—the government of Mount Athos's spiritual state, which is autocephalous, international, and independent of the Greek authorities, and has its own customs zone. Administratively, Mount Athos belongs to the Constantinople, not the Athens, patriarchy. Of the twenty-four monasteries on the peninsula, several of the biggest, one of which is your Chilandar, compose the government. Representatives of four of these biggest monasteries always enter the Protaton, each bringing his quarter of the state seal. From among themselves they elect the 'protos,' the superior of Mount Athos, also in a way the prime minister, who only upon receiving the other parts of the seal can fit them together, wrap them with a lock of hair, and thus stamp the decisions taken by his Cabinet. After obtaining the third visa in Karyes (the only place in the world where there's an advantage to being a Greek or a Serb, because in that case the visas are issued summarily), there still remains the fourth, oral, but hardest-to-get visa—the one for entering Chilandar. There they always have a list of people who cannot enter the monastery (wherever they may live in the world). The list is not long, but if it has your soul photographed on it, you will never get into the monastery. And, best of all, the list's criteria are not known, and nobody who goes there for the first time, like you, can know whether his name is not already on it. . . ."

The proprietress suddenly laughed, her upper lip flattening against her nose, and began to play a strange game while the meal was being served. Her husband passed around full plates and with each asked a question, and she, covering her eyes with her hands, answered, in keeping with some ancient custom.

Both were somehow convinced that their guests were familiar with this routine and would happily play along, whereas, in fact, they had not the faintest idea of what was supposed to happen.

"To whom goes this bowl?" the host cried out, picking up the first plate, obviously knowing the words of this little performance by heart.

"To me the honors, to you the treat!" Vassilia replied, covering her eyes with her hair in order to make an impartial decision. "To the young master, that his bread may not pass the night at another's doorstep!"

"And to whom does this one go?" the host continued, after the first plate had been placed in front of Atanas Svilar.

"To yourself!" the hostess exclaimed by the window. "That you may feel thirst in the tasting! The sin is not in the feed but in the deed," she concluded in a voice that had a speck of laughter in its saliva.

"And this one?"

"To the old master, that he may grow young! To the laboring ox, that his manger be not empty!" replied Vassilia, and the plate instantly appeared in front of the gusle-player, and everybody laughed, because the innkeeper had served the food his own way, applying Vassilia's description to whomever he wanted.

"When we are full we can fast!" Vassilia said finally, pulling the last bowl over toward herself. She then recommended the fish, because "it is always healthier than those who eat it," and she said, "Blessed be the wine in your mouth," and offered water that had been brought out to mix with the wine.

"Water is eternal," she added. "It is the same water brought here with the springs in 1198 and drunk by your 'prince,' Saint Sava, and on it he and his father built the monasteries on Mount Athos."

So the meal started, and all the time Vassilia watched her guests' mouths, moving her lips silently as though she were eating their every bite herself. After lunch the men went out into the little garden, with its patch of sea where the olives fell, and even the land was oily. They were drinking coffee at the table, which rocked as though they were on a ship, when suddenly their host grabbed a handful of gravel from underfoot and picked out eight black pebbles and eight red "healing" pebbles. He laid them out on the checkered tablecloth and they began to play checkers. While they were playing, Vassilia appeared in the garden and sat down with a blue plate in her hand and a wine bottle in her lap. She filled the three men's glasses, which they dared not put on the wobbly table, and they sipped wine while she carefully washed in the plate the coins that the inn had earned over the past few days.

"You know," she said, addressing Svilar as she dried a drachma, "you probably think you're playing checkers with my husband. But we don't think so. Before the game begins, we give the pebbles names, family names. So, actually, the checker and the pebble play instead of us, and lose or win in our place. The pebble you're playing against right now is named after my father, Adam, and my husband certainly named his checker after his late mother. You should give names to your own checkers. Then you'd be stronger."

"Major Kosta Svilar wins!" Atanas Svilar shouted, catching on to the game, and he wrapped his newly won drachma in a smile.

"But remember, he won that money, not you, so buy him something with it."

"Can one buy something even for the dead?"

"What a question! And you're going to Mount Athos!" Vassilia commented, and then asked:

"Is your father dead?"

Svilar explained the purpose of his trip and inquired about his father.

"Wait, wait!" Vassilia cried, and her hair came undone, tumbling into a glass of wine. "You've just reminded me of an event that may have more to do with you than one might think. One day during the war, some mud-splattered beggars came in here out of the scorching sun, which had been blazing down for days. You could see immediately that the mud they carried was mixed with blood. They were, or pretended to be, mute. One of them was tall: I remember that he immediately saw where we hid the house key on the ledge above the door.

" 'Too strong for somebody who picks blackberries with his teeth and has no buttons,' I thought, looking at him. I also noticed that he did not urinate before going to bed, so as to stay awake at night and be on guard. When he lay down in the stable, I went over and threatened to report him unless he told me who he was. At first he refused, but eventually he agreed to come with me. I made him take a bath and rub himself down with oil; I gave him a shave and a change of clothes for him and his two friends. He was an officer of the defeated Royal Yugoslav Army. I'm not telling you this story because I think the stranger was your father. Who could make such a claim? But it shows that there were such cases. Especially important for you, I suppose, is to learn where they went from here. . . . All three of them begged me not to report them to the German authorities and to take them secretly to the border of Mount Athos. We arranged that I would accompany them in the morning and show them the way, but that very morning they did something that could have cost them their lives. They attended morning service in the local church here, mingling with the crowd in the church, which was as full as a spoon. They stood in the smoke and listened to the chanting in Greek. Although it was tantamount to suicide to reveal their non-Greek origin and Serbian language in front of so big a crowd, one of them, the oldest in rank, could not resist the temptation. He let his beautiful voice go, and it blew out the candles and changed the scent in the church. Since the man was standing by the door, for a moment we all thought that the church had been built askew, because it didn't cover his voice properly, it was a bit off center, and we all felt that the building should be moved just slightly. The whole village knew that somebody had sung in Serbian at morning mass, and I immediately took all three of them to the Athos hills, afraid that somebody might denounce them to the occupation authorities. That was as far as I could go, because women are not allowed where you're going now, and I have never been there.

"There no grave is older than three and no man is younger than eighteen. After the third year the bones of the dead are washed with wine and stacked in the charnel house, and thus the graves are emptied. Only the name is penciled on the forehead of the skull. Not a single woman has ever been buried there. Except for birds and plants, no female species lives there. They have no cheese, no eggs, no milk, because no hen, cow, or mare has touched ground there for a thousand years. Meat is never eaten there, fish only on Sundays and holidays, and bread is made once a month and is never either fresh or stale. For all the one thousand years that Mount Athos has existed, only once has a woman set foot on its soil. In 1347 the Serbian basileus, Emperor Stephen Dushan, visited Mount Athos, which belonged to his empire at the time. Dispensing gold and silver dishes, horses, vestments, villages and estates, letters and charters of gifts on the way, he went to visit the Chilandar monastery, founded by his family, and with him brought his wife, the Empress Yelena. But she was there as the basileus-empress, not as a woman. . . ."

The Greek woman suddenly fell silent; one could hear the difference in the ripple of the incoming and outgoing waves; the wine they were drinking was warm from her bosom, because she had held the bottle in her arms between her breasts, and Atanas Svilar felt tense from the warmth. He caught sight of the other two men and was surprised to see that the husband, Vassili Philaktos, was tense himself. It was hard to tell whether he, too, understood the warmth of the wine, but it was obvious that only the gusle-player remained insensible, and for a moment Svilar thought that perhaps this was because of what had been done to this man on the road, that it really had had some effect. That same instant, Svilar caught Vassilia's eye. As night descended upon them, only her eyes were still visible, like mirrors, and her gaze, which could stop a clock or bend a fork, was fixed on the gusle-player.

"Please don't take offense if I give you some advice," Vassilia resumed speaking to Svilar as though pulling herself awake. "First of all, you may be a man of the new age: I noticed that you don't cross yourself before eating. Where you are going, you will certainly find it hard not to cross yourself, and it may put you in an awkward position. Think it over beforehand. Secondly, there's a story people here usually tell travelers, and I will tell you. It's believed that the third day in Chilandar is always the day of truth. And that things and people there take on their real face and jest becomes reality only on the third day of one's stay. . . . Remember that and be patient for those three days. Because wisdom is not much use to a man; wise people do not go further than stupid people in proportion to their intelligence. That's because there is no room in life to go far; spread open your arms and one hand is in the sun, the other in the mist. . . ."

Indeed, Svilar noticed that the hour had come when one could touch day with one hand and night with the other, and the innkeeper signaled to Vassilia to make the beds. On the porch facing the sea, she rolled out the bedding and embellished it with two red woolen pillows. They wished the travelers good night, and as she left Vassilia warned them:

"Be careful when you sleep! Here they say that every night, while asleep, one forgets somebody one loved when awake. . . ."

The sound of the flute reached them from the shore through her words. The innkeeper was holding a double flute made in the form of intercoiling snakes, and he was playing. He held the double mouthpiece in his nostrils and inhaled through his mouth. It looked as though the snakes were sucking the soul out of him, as though they were drinking up his life, and as though that life, as it came out of his body, was softly whistling its new name. The player's eyes were half-closed, like a cracked walnut, and to Svilar it seemed as though the snakes, too, were weeping, as though death were doubly painful, both for the one giving and for the one taking life, like extinguishing a cigarette on the palm of one's hand. . . . Then the player started slowly yawning into his flute, sneezed into it, put out the light, and retired to bed. Vassilia remained on the shore alone, and Svilar saw her empty his unfinished drink into the sea. The retsina from the glass made him drowsy, lulling his ears, but before falling asleep Svilar took a decision that slightly pricked his conscience. He decided to continue the journey alone at daybreak the next morning, leaving the gusle-player in bed. As he made his decision, the gusle-player laughed at him through the darkness, looking at him with eyes as shiny as two black kidneys, and said:

"I prefer both myself and others when returning from Chilandar, rather than when going there. . . ."

In the morning, Svilar woke up with his arms spread wide and his feet locked together as though he had been sleeping on a cross. He knew immediately that he had overslept and had missed the chance of shaking off his companion. But when he turned to where the gusle-player had been sleeping, there was nobody there anymore. The bedding was rolled up, and the red pillow was empty. He was alone again.

4

It is not known which of the two ways of life the Greek, pre-Slav Chilandar was based on. It was probably idiorrhythmia, because the monastery was dedicated to the Virgin Mary, and at the time of iconoclasm that gave the Greeks reason to destroy it. One day in 1198, Saint Sava and Simeon Nemanya, each a ruler and a monk, purchased land and water there for the Serbian state and began to restore the monastery. Saint Sava organized his brotherhood on the basis of cenobitism, aiming at a more austere form of monastic life, and the monks at Chilandar lived their days on the same bread, on communal salt, and did not count the bees. Everything was communal, fire and water, even the food in the dining hall, whose stone tables had hollows hewn in them for the glasses and salt and reinforced edges to keep the bread from falling off.

This organization must have been undermined from the very beginning by the presence of a solitary (perhaps a Greek who had lived before in the ruins). In any event, as in the other monasteries on Mount Athos, idiorrhythmic life slowly revived in Chilandar. The monks again began to regulate and tame the water, they again began to sow and reap, to fish and put the fish on bread, they again began to develop an ear for the underground reaches of the holy summit, where riches, ores, and gems lay hidden, throbbing in the womb of the earth; the solitaries returned to work on Athos, and Chilandar received them as it did the others. The balance established between the solitaries and the cenobites was subsequently maintained for centuries, and so at Chilandar there were always followers of the one way of life and the other. The solitaries and the cenobites, now counterposed but secretly always divided, made Chilandar Chilandar. And the increasingly decisive contests, the key to all important acts and changes in the monastery, were held on the border ground between the interests of the solitaries and the interests of the cenobites, and the outcome, fate, and decisions of general interest depended on which of the two currents held sway in Chilandar at the moment. The differences between these currents were not at all merely external, and the Chilandar monks compared them with the differences between day and night, provided day and night were accepted as equally as possible, like brother and sister, or mother and son. And just as days and nights cannot mix, so the monks from one order could not switch to the other, but, rather, had to remain forever, both in this world and the next, with the order that had admitted them into monkhood. Yet there was one exception.

There was a way, one single, very costly way, by which, after having accepted cenobitism, one could become a solitary or, conversely, one could discard the habit of a solitary and don the cassock of a cenobite. That way was this: to walk out of the monastery, change one's name, join the newly converted settlers on Mount Athos, the Russians, Serbs, or Bulgarians, accept their barbarian language and in their monastery seek the way to an age of another color, with a different rhythm and organization, and thus start all over again. In short, Greeks would become Bulgarians, Armenians Serbs or Russians, and Russians Greeks, so as to be able to leave the order and system of life they wanted to withdraw from. That was the only way. And they went for two reasons: to leave the order that did not hold the advantage at the moment, or to take up activities in the new order that were not authorized by the old. Because Chilandar was not the only thing that was divided between the solitaries and the cenobites. Also divided were the monks' activities. Like wine and bread.

Once having joined another order and monastery, these "travestis" seldom went back to visit their former brotherhood; they were seen most often by the Serbian monks who came on business to Greek, Armenian, Bulgarian, or Russian monasteries, where they found their former brothers in strange clothing and in another monastic order and could not get accustomed to the new status of these renegades. They knew only too well what these transplants and fugitives thought, but they did not understand what they said or in what language they kept silent. Although they were well aware of the reasons for their fellow tribesmen's departure to a strange monastery and a foreign language, and often were even to blame for it, they were amazed anew every time, as though they did not understand that those who had departed had left not only the monastery but their own language as well, although that should have been obvious from the outset both to those who stayed and to those who left. And they were amazed (those who did not leave), and perhaps even angry, that they did not understand the end of the story. Because the émigrés told the end of the story in a strange and, to the former, incomprehensible language. And this so confused those who had stayed that, their business completed, they returned to their monastery with doubts, as though there were no ending to the story of their renegade brothers, because the end of a story told in a strange language is like the end not of that story but of some other.

"The Aegean Sea is calm only on Sundays and holidays," said Svilar to a monk in Iviron, as he stood on the small pier, waiting for a ship that resembled a fish flaring its gills. The port of Chilandar lay a two-hour boat ride away toward the north, toward the open sea, facing the Asian coast across the island of Thasos, which, they say, cannot be seen from the mainland, though the mainland can be seen from Thasos, because the islanders have a keener eye.

Chilandar's shore was flat, muddy, and teeming with buffaloes. Just a step away, as though the sea were not salty, flourished lush vegetation. It spread and climbed up the softly undulating approach to the monastery, clustered, aromatic, and in places transformed into impenetrable tangles of nettles that sting, and pumpkins that make one smile. The overgrowth and wild vines were so compact that bird droppings did not fall on the ground but swayed on the leaves.

Atanas Svilar disembarked alone, a little darkness left in his mouth and sores from the hay fever at the tip of his nostrils. Storms of smells, bracken, and mules followed him on the way, free and half-wild; red eyes burned on the black buffaloes like candles in the dark, visible from afar, although it was noon. Somewhere near the old tower, where neither the sea nor the monastery could be seen, a stone fell on Svilar's path. Then another. Svilar felt a terrible solitude, and in it a man. The man actually appeared, throwing more stones in front of him. His hair was older than his beard, gray, and as thick as fish bones. His eyes, the color of lemon-sprinkled shellfish, were close together, as though he had just sniffed them through his nose. In his hand he carried a sack made of the same cloth as the one he was wearing.

"Is it a long way to the monastery?" Svilar asked him.

"Long enough to die a decent death; but who can do that?" replied the old man. "A walnut dropped in the stream by the monastery gets here in three minutes...."

The stranger's skin was strewn with freckles, almost unpigmented sores, his clothes were singed with holes, and Svilar deduced that the stranger spent all his time in the open air and was exposed to bird droppings, which leave gray freckles on the hair they touch and can singe a leaf. Noticing a piece of tree bark in the stranger's sack, Svilar asked:

"Are you picking the bark of the alder tree?"

"I am," said the old man, and one could see that his nose, wedged between his glances, was slightly scraped on either side.

"Do you use it for dye?"

"I do."

"On cloth?" asked Svilar, noticing that the sack was smoking. The man smiled on one side of his face and, speaking behind his hand, as though he were about to spit out of the corner of his mouth, he said:

"He who smokes will never see into his pipe...."

Svilar did not understand him and repeated the question:

"What do you dye?"

"I dye wood."

From the pigtail tied in a knot, Svilar deduced that the old man might be a monk, but the stranger wore his haircloth cassock oddly, inside out, and the shirt under it was on backward, so that it could only be buttoned from behind, underneath the robe, by twisting one's arms behind one's back. Tiny moving wrinkles rippled across the old man's forehead, disappearing into his hair like waves. The man

creased his forehead to drive away thoughts the way horses ripple
their skin in shudders to drive away flies. Suddenly, as though his legs
had given out on him, the man crumpled and sat down, took a hot
bun out of his sack, and offered it to Svilar with some salt from the
shaker built into the handle of the knife.

"What do you say, is that a bun?" the old man asked.

"A bun. What else would it be?"

"There, you see," the old man replied, satisfied, munching into his
heavy beard, which could support a glass of water.

"Last night," he went on, "I dreamed that I had forgotten to make
the bun. In fact, I haven't made any since the war. So this morning,
when I got up, I said to myself, 'Let's see whether I really did forget.'
Now, if you say I didn't, that's good enough. . . ."

The man stopped chewing in mid-sentence, got up, and departed,
as if he wanted to take that suspended mouthful to somebody else.
Buttoned up from behind, the old man looked to Svilar as though he
were walking backward.

"When we stop," he wondered, "are we really standing still or
merely letting our own footsteps go by, which somewhere continue to
measure and shorten our path?"

And as he stood there, Svilar heard a strange sound, like the rumble
of water, but water somewhere high up in the sky. He turned toward
the sound and high above him saw a settlement with walls among the
birds, with houses whose windows were penetrated by the mist, with
churches whose crosses sliced the wind and whistled, with an entrance
in the shape of a deep gateway which forever played music. Full of
towers, angular turrets with a view of three winds, and small bridges
over the bottomless depths, the lofty settlement exerted a tremendous
pull, and being sucked up from the ground, creeping up its walls like
sweat, were blotches of damp green lichen, ants, hamsters, and moles,
and along with them, as though lifted up by the same thrust, clutching
the walls, houses stood on top of houses, churches on top of churches,
so that the domes of the lower pushed through the floors and walls of
the upper churches and trees and little gardens grew high up in the
sky. And like a magnet, the same force that sucked and pulled every-

thing up to the top of the settlement picked up and drank in all the sounds and voices from down on the ground, from around the walls, from the woods; it milled and mixed the sounds, producing a strange elongated voice, as though the sonorous name of the settlement hung in arrested suspension over the spot, almost like a cap over the roofs. Windows in the shape of crosses (symbols of man-window-Christ), round, or like loopholes, swarmed like insects all over the huge wall that encircled the settlement, carrying it like a sack of bones. Clinging to parts of the outside wall like nests were cells whose floors hung suspended in the sky, supported only by slanting beams. Affixed to the wall above these cells, but bigger, were other cells, and above them bigger ones still, supported by slanted beams resting on the cells below and, like them, with floors left to hover in the air. Elsewhere, perched high in the sky, were bridges, one end resting on the walls and the other hanging in the air, and standing like sentries at the end of these bridges were small wooden toilets, extracted from the holy fabric of the monasteries. And all this was constantly peppered by the living, spreading rash of birds. Climbing the walls like flies, obliquely and at random, skipping floors, were windows intermingled with strange parasitic growth on the outside stone and mortar, which revealed the internal bleeding and faults in the tissue of the huge construction. There was obviously a window for each of Mount Athos's birds and a door for each of its winds. One could see where the water reached high into the sky through the pipes affixed to the façade of the walls, where there had to be fires in the deep chimneys that were as spacious as rooms. One could see where the immense shadow imitating the building above changed the climate at its foot, creating an evening in morning, a winter in spring, where night arrived before the stars just as summer first arrives in the bacon. One could see from that shade where the upper-story corridors elbowed over the stairway only to meet and pass through each other; one could see that some of the cells faced the shade of the sun and others the shade of the moon; one could tell where the walls were built with salted mortar, the Armenian way, with milk, the Greek way, and with mortar and wine, the Serbian way; one could see through the windows the corners of the rooms so small they could not even hold a bed, the "Friday" rooms, where one could only sit, and they were only sat in, on Fridays. There were other, holiday rooms, one for each holiday in the year, and set above them over the abyss were double doors which led nowhere; they closed and aired the corridors, but only one gateway-corridor with a tiny room for the icon of the Virgin Mary over the doors opened the way into the monastery.

And all around the walls were little gardens, as tidily swept as rooms, neatly furnished with wooden bunks and a small roof and with outdoor dining areas, each with its orchard, with its patch of stream, where stones regulated the sound of the water, some with a little bridge and a bench over the dog sleeping in the furrow like a black puddle.

As soon as he stepped under the high archway with its two gates— always in the shade, because the sun did not reach the bottom from any side—Svilar found himself in a half-darkness full of icons, windows, and doors, and some of the icons were on hinges like doors, and some of the doors had icons painted on the inside. He opened one of the heavy gates whose keyholes were like small cannons and found himself standing in a huge cupboard full of rakes, divining rods, fishing nets, and surveying instruments. It reeked of stale sweat and forgotten heat. He shut the door and quickly opened an identical one right next to it, and it led him to a floor where voices could be heard. On the cobblestoned balcony a chair straddled the threshold by the doorpost, on the chair sat a monk, and on his head was a pot, making his face invisible. A second monk stood beside him, holding sheep-shearing scissors and cutting the locks of fire-red hair that licked the rim of the pot. Hair covered the floor like dry leaves. . . . Noticing that they had a visitor, the monks stopped their work, and the one with the scissors gave Svilar a rather odd look, as though trying to decide how bald he was under his hair. He handed him the end of the rope tied around his waist and led Svilar as though on a leash through the dark corridors to issue him his last visa and show him the room where he would spend the night. Then they sat down and had coffee with Mastika and Turkish delight the color of lips.

"Are you tired?" inquired Father Luke, the monk with the scissors. "Only he who can show his road where to turn is not tired by the journey. But the roads that listen are few. It is usually we who have to listen to the road. . . ."

While the monk was talking, he kept looking different from moment to moment. His smoke-colored hair clung to his ears like mildew and changed depending on the time of day: it looked as though the monk aged slightly but visibly every afternoon. With each word he uttered, something on him changed: his mustache, eyes, knees, fingers, the color of his nails. . . . When he composed a sentence he was another man. Had the sentence been different, he would have been different. He only stayed the same when he yawned.

"Do you know, dear sir," said Father Luke chattily, "that I have a dog that snores? And I can't make him break the habit. Do you, perhaps, know of a cure? It's annoying, you know, because it always wakes me up. The way our life here is organized, the most precious and rarest thing is sleep. It would be hard to add up ten nights of sleep in a month from all of us together in Chilandar. We go to bed at nightfall, wake up with the first strokes of midnight for midnight service; then we can doze off for a bit until the morning service, and then it's already time to start work. That's why they say: Check carefully who is for this world and who for the monastery! He who cannot dig, and is ashamed to beg, should not come."

Father Luke yawned imperceptibly, and remained ugly.

"All of us, you know, are one thing or another: coopers, winegrowers, bakers, harvesters, plowers, gardeners, masons, and the like. Each is responsible for his part of the work, and each cultivates his part of the monastery like his own beard. And our Chilandar land—recently measured by planes—encompasses half of Mount Athos. Since the olive trees were planted, and that was a thousand winters ago, never have all the olives been picked, but only as many as could be managed, which is to say, as many as is right."

While Father Luke was talking, Svilar watched with surprise as the monk's nose moved on his face like a knight on a chessboard.

"We know why you are here," said the monk, suddenly changing the topic after one such knight-like jump. "Unfortunately, not all of us have been with the monastery long enough to be able to furnish you with the facts you want about the year 1941. I would refer you to two monks who know something about the officers who escaped from Albania to Greece. One of these monks lives with us. His name is Father Varlam, and he will seek you out himself. The other cannot be called a Chilandarian, because he is a wandering monk who comes only occasionally, and even then does not enter the monastery. Luckily, he's in the vicinity right now and he will help you the most, as you will him, in a way. I'll tell you how to recognize him. He has pitched a roof among four trees and let his house grow! Every day he buckles his belt on a different hole, puts his cassock on inside out one day, wears it backward the next, so that nothing ever becomes a habit. He believes that the same applies to vices, that even they should not be left to the force of habit, that they should be spared it. As you in your world would say, sometimes a child should be conceived even on a bridge, breakfast eaten at night for a change, although they say this cuts life short by one day. It's not good to become accustomed to either a bed or a name, and that's why the monk I'm telling you about never spends more than three weeks in any monastery and always sleeps in a wooden chest; as soon as he gets used to a place, he changes his name and looks for new water. He speaks every other day, on the day when he doesn't eat, and on Sundays he speaks Greek. The monks think he's hiding because of his sins; they say that the devil cannot recognize one who has turned his belt inside out or turned his shirt around. But who knows?"

In the middle of the conversation both men roused themselves with a start, as though they had gone astray. The candle on the table spilled over, and before him Svilar saw a complete stranger, with only the nose still jumping like a knight across Father Luke's face. Father Luke got up with difficulty—it was not clear whether it was his bones or the bench that creaked beneath him—and he led his guest to dinner. Bats and nocturnal birds hurled and banged into the windows exposed to the moonlight, hoping that they might be able to fly through the building to the other, brighter side of the night.

On the way, the monk told Svilar about the other dinner guests. Apart from a gusle-player, who was on his third visit to the monastery, some English diplomats who had just arrived from Greece had been invited to stay for dinner and the night. Dinner was in the ground-floor refectory, where a huge hearth was blazing, like a burning barn. The gusle-player was already seated at the table, and great washes of red swept the wall behind him and laved his face as he was introduced to the Englishmen and to Svilar, whom he greeted as though he were meeting him for the first time. One of the foreign guests, the English consul from Salonika, a Catholic, spoke excellent Greek, while the other, his aide, a young Protestant, sported a fine, silky mustache parted like two bird-wings above his lips and knew Serbian better than he cared to reveal. The Englishmen did not cross themselves while saying grace; they clearly did not want to mark themselves according to the Eastern ritual, but out of respect for the place, where they had obviously been before, they did not want to cross themselves the Western way, with their hands. Since Svilar did not cross himself either, once everyone was seated the consul asked in a voice that everybody could hear:

"I see you don't cross yourself either. Are you a Catholic, too?"

"There's hardly enough room for a spoon to pass between the nose and the chin, and that is the way to so many troubles," Svilar thought, and replied:

"No, I'm an atheist." For a second, silence reigned over the table, as if inside dough, and the fire could be seen to blaze in the wine bottle.

"Interesting," the consul went on, dividing his beard into three parts. "I know, of course, that many of your writers and men of culture come here. Are those religious pilgrimages? That, you must admit, would be rather odd for citizens of a socialist country, who are communists to boot, as I presume, you are, too. . . ."

The gusle-player dropped his paper napkin into his soup, and it absorbed the grease from the surface of the liquid. Then he carefully removed the napkin and sipped the skimmed soup, not listening to the conversation.

"No, they are not religious pilgrimages, although there are those, too," replied Atanas Svilar. "Chilandar, like most of Mount Athos, was once part of Serbia's state territory, and today is part of its cultural territory, so to speak."

"Yes, I know the history," the Englishman remarked, "but I'm surprised that I have not yet met a visitor from your country who knows Greek. Rather unusual for a cultural pilgrimage to a region that belongs to Orthodoxy and once belonged to Byzantium, wouldn't you say?"

"It's very difficult to explain to someone who does not come from the region himself," said Svilar. "I agree that in principle one should know Greek. But there are age-old, appropriate reasons why we don't learn Greek the way you do in the West. Here, of course, one does not see Troy, but one does see the rain when it falls on Troy. We are close here to what for a long time was the navel of the world. Serbian, along with Greek, Latin, Coptic, Armenian, and some other Slav languages, became a holy language very early on, in the ninth century. It's like when a child becomes a saint, like those rare grapevines that produce grapes in spring, not in autumn. That's why our need to learn foreign languages is less developed than yours, whose language was never one of the holy languages, so that for centuries you were forced to learn a strange, foreign language—Latin—as the language of your Holy Scripture. Here, on the other hand, it was as though the Byzantine Empire were creating a huge barrier against us barbarian peoples, depriving us of its Greek language and not giving us that language as the common language of the church. It was a tremendous ordeal to reach adulthood prematurely and to be left on one's own at such a young age. That is maybe why to us in the East you from the West always look a generation younger...."

"Since we've been pronounced younger, perhaps you'll permit an indiscreet question," the aide with the parted mustache suddenly interrupted, addressing the prior:

"What does your monastery actually live on, Father?"

"The one who founded it all those centuries ago, and who bought land and water for it," came the answer, "took care even then to supply us with everything we need, and so it remains today. As you see, we dined yet again off his toil and sweat and shall not go to sleep hungry. . . ."

"Let's pour some day into the night," Father Luke joked, on a lighter note, and added water to the wine, leaving his own glass empty.

"You, of course, may help yourself as often as you like," he said, as though to justify himself, "but we here, as you are bound to have noticed, serve food twice and pour wine twice. Never once and never three times. A book, if you expect wonders of it, should also be read twice. It should be read once in youth, when you are younger than its heroes, and the second time when you are advanced in age and the book's heroes become younger than yourself. That way you will see them from both sides of their years, and they will be able to put you to the test on the other side of the clock, where time stands still. This means that sometimes it is forever too late to read some books, just as sometimes it is forever too late to go to bed. . . ."

Dinner was over, the bread on the table seemed to have aged, the guests got up and filed out along the bench, each placing a finger on another's shoulder.

But they did not go to bed after dinner, as Father Luke had seemed to suggest. On the contrary, it was quietly announced that the gusle-player would give a performance. The guests climbed up to the second floor and assembled in a wide hallway, down the length of which such a wind howled in the night outside that it could unplait a braid if one leaned out the window. While they waited, Svilar confided to Father Luke that he had recently traveled with the gusle-player, and he mentioned the song he had heard from him about the bey. About the Turk who, like Father Luke, kept dogs and had sons he intended for the monastery but were wisely returned to their father by the monks.

"Don't believe every single word," remarked Father Luke, smiling, and his nose got stuck between his eyes with a snicker.

"A song is a song; like water it never stands still, and like water it passes from mouth to mouth. One shouldn't think it always quenches the same kind of thirst or the same kind of fire. They tell us we watch stars that have long since disappeared, but they don't know that the water we drink was drunk up long ago, too. So, what's there to say about songs? In fact, the story of the bey's sons was completely different. They were received into the monastery, but it turned out that the young men fainted in their cells. They could not bear the local climate: the mildew and dust around the monastery disturbed and tortured them, as I see it does you. Half-dead, their noses and ears plugged with wax and their eyes coated with honey, they were returned to their father by the monks, with the observation that God would not have them. But in the song everything is prettier and different, its fangs have been removed like a snake's, so that it loses its bite. . . ."

Father Luke fell silent, took from his pocket a small handwritten book, sniffed it, and then offered it to Svilar, who sneezed.

"There, you see!" he cried. "Maladies are like different robes, my good sir; one puts them on when one must and takes them off when one can, because seldom in life can one survive naked. Who knows from what coldness and misery maladies protect us! Think about it! The only thing that really stands between us and the biggest secret of all is our malady. It is easier to fall ill than to learn the truth. Your malady is very active here. It obviously wants to save and protect you from something, just as it protected and saved Karamustafa's sons from some hard truths about this place. So take care of your maladies even in your dreams, let alone when you're awake. They always have something to tell you. . . ."

At that moment the gusle-player appeared, sat down on the chair that had been set aside; somebody brought in a lamp, and the flames of the candles on the table died out. He suddenly made a loop on his string with his tongue, pushed it through the pin with his mouth, and tightened the gusle with his teeth. Then from his sock he took out some rosin, rubbed the bow with it, and started to sing. His song was called:

T H E   L I F E   A N D   D E A T H   O F   Y O A N   S I R O P O U L O S

On the border between Greece and Bulgaria, near Skantea, where there are families so poor that caps are inherited, fingers are sucked till one's dying day, and axes are worn down to sickles, the wife of one Theodosius Siropoulos, a Greek, bore him a son, and they named the infant Yoan. On the fortieth day, when an infant's third eye, the one on the crown of his head, begins to work, their house was visited by a Bulgarian monk, a member of the Eastern rite (to which they themselves belonged), and on the infant's pillow he placed a gold coin and for the mother brought a kerchief full of presents, as though for a wedding. Having bestowed his gifts, he sat down by the hearth and said:

"The nose and ears grow until one's dying day, the name and beard even after. I have come to purchase the infant's name. . . ."

The parents said that Yoan had already been given a name, but the priest replied that that did not matter. He would simply write down in the book he had brought that he had christened the child and, with the parents' blessing, the infant would be registered not as Yoan Siropoulos the Greek, but under his new name, Yovan Siropulov the Bulgarian. The child's father, who had never seen a ducat before, who lived in a place where ten loaves of bread were baked in a day, where two languages were spoken and people drank out of one glass, found himself in a quandary. But, all the same, he did not agree to the proposal.

"In life," he said, "everything depends on two things: on blood and on death."

And he declined. So it was that Yoan grew up as a Greek, first to herd the goat, then to hold the staff, and then the money belt. He had to be a merchant if he wanted to wed his bread to meat and pour wine into his water. But a bitter cold had settled in people's mouths; the old kept the young in strollers for ages and never gave them a razor and money to hold at the same time. Poverty forced Yoan to sell his hair; he would stand at the market stall and show how his hair could be tied into a nice knot, and when a customer came by he would cut it down to the last lock. His smile became increasingly shallow, until one morning it ran aground on his teeth. It was then that the Bulgarian priest reappeared and said:

"Do you want to carry the road, or the road to carry you? If it's the former you want, then go; we know how far you will get: to the hole in your shoe. If you want the latter, if you want, as they say, to have something in, on, and under you, then take what is given."

And again he offered the ducats. And Yoan accepted the offer. He joined the Bulgarians, whose language he knew anyway, and registered as Yovan Siropulov.

"That Bulgarian priest is not a renegade," he thought, "but a man of our law, and people like him, only Greek, probably go and register Bulgarians in their own Greek books."

And so Yoan Siropoulos, raised with support from Bulgarian priests, abandoned his native tongue, adopted Bulgarian, entered a different time, where different waters flowed, acquired property by selling salted meat, married, and had children, always carrying his other, Bulgarian name, and passing it on to his offspring. Now they were Siropulovs.

Meanwhile, a border conflict had broken out between the Bulgarians and the Greeks. Yovan Siropulov assembled his sons, placed four sabers in front of them, and said:

"He who has healing eyes and can look at a boil on the palm of a hand until the sore heals, needs no weapons. But he who has not, must cut off the boil. So, take the swords by the hilt if you won't take them by the blade. . . ."

Thus they set out to fight the Greeks. Yovan Siropulov was badly wounded in battle: his sons brought him home in a sheepskin coat which they tied to their four belts. Finding himself laid out on his deathbed, Yovan summoned his wife and children. He ordered them to bring him a Greek priest to hear his confession, and instructed them to bury him in a Greek grave and have his Greek name inscribed on the cross.

His sons were appalled by such a request, but there was no point in killing a dead man, and so they merely asked him what he was doing. And he answered them quietly:

"It is better for one of theirs to die than one of ours."

And so, inscribed on Yovan's grave was his original name, Yoan Siropoulos, which is still there today.

He was born and died a Greek.

5

Chilandar's solitaries—idiorrhythmics—gained prestige and power at a time when the authority of the Chilandar abbess (that being the Virgin Mary) had reached its peak. Because all Athos solitaries had always fostered the cult of the Virgin Mary, and the Chilandarians also had the cult of their own Church of the Presentation, dedicated to the Virgin Child. Thus, raised under the aegis of the Virgin Mother and tied to her home, the solitaries had always taken care to rejuvenate the monastery brotherhoods; they were good pedagogues and looked after the newcomers, for idiorrhythmia—the solitary life of the monks—was truly an incomparably easier and more attractive discipline than the hard discipline of the communal life, practiced by the cenobites. While the life of the solitaries could be compared to that of a large family in a home protected by the mother, the other, communal way of life could be imagined as life in a family consisting only of men—father and sons.

At the monastery each solitary could take as much land as would echo with his voice; each squeezed a glassful of sweat daily from the braid on his neck; on the monastery estate they raised wheat and olives and baked bread, on the water they were fishermen and built irrigation systems, and when it was necessary to pray for rain, they prayed. Each lived by his own hand, each had his own cell and hearth, and each his own separate dining table, household goods, and bed, each his own fire and salt, his little garden and in it his own Serbia with plums and water in the enclosure. They made their own meals and at their own expense hired Greek servants to do their washing and picking. Being as they were, they never had any common interests, because each lived by his own name, cut his own hair, and plaited his own braid, and they barely knew each other. So they could have no common enemies or conflicts of common significance. Hence they were never soldiers and were not adept at waging wars, although there were indeed times on Mount Athos when the cross had to be upended in order to make a sword.... But when the monastery became so poor that it was threatened by extinction, then all the monks would revert to idiorrhythmia, and from there they would again slowly regain their way and their strength, pursuing a path marked by sweat. The night service (established in the last days of iconoclasm) belonged to the solitaries, and to them the spine remained the symbol of human life. They learned foreign languages easily and extensively, and quickly found their place in the International of the Constantinople patriarchy, which administered Mount Athos. They attended the Athos monastic school, which taught Greek; paid Armenian monks from Iviron to teach them Armenian (giving a dove for every one hundred Armenian words learned); and learned Russian on their own by visiting the Russian monasteries on Mount Athos, where, during the long nights of fasting, they listened to the Ukrainian monks and icon-painters speak in Russian verses while they painted. The Chilandar solitaries were icon-painters themselves, and it was their duty to wash the icons with wine, preserve and replenish the monastery's stock of "holy faces," or eulogize and bury the icon when its time came. And down through time, they brought with them not only the icon of the Virgin Mary on the wall, but their own failings as well, which stemmed from their basic inclinations. And these inclinations, in turn, were inherited from Greek and Sinaic monasticism. Since they had always been upholders of the icon, the solitaries sometimes lapsed into idolatry, and became still more easily tied to antiquity and polytheistic Greece with its Platonistic teachings. Even today, solitaries are easily recognized by the fact that they do not suffer one another. Names they did not mention; indeed, they even tried to forget *their own. From time to time, the solitaries would retreat into "bezmov-lije," the stringent monastic vow of silence, and for years they would not utter a single word, until their hair hung heavy and their ears ached from the silence. Or they would utter only nouns, because these come from God, and would avoid verbs, which belong to Satan. By the same logic, they (when not silent) were orators of repute and long tradition. Sometimes their speech—and they considered this the best discourse—would consist of a single sentence, capable of winning over all who heard it. For they considered the warm, spoken word to be the primeval beginning and primeval cause of everything. The written letter—that shadow of the human voice, that simulation of speech on paper—was, as they remarked, seed for the gutter, sown not to fill, but to ornament and please. So, even if they were writers, they never read each other. The spoken word, on the other hand, is seed for the living land, for man's ears and soul; it feeds and heals, and it takes as long for it to be born under the heart as it does for a woman and a field to bear fruit, which is to say three-quarters of a year.*

Linked to the bounties of the earth, the solitaries had one great love. The external and visible perspective was always very important to them. The cult of the Church of the Blessed Virgin Mary, who gave birth to Christ as night does to day, was stronger with them than the cult of the people from whom they had sprung. To them, the monastery, with its walls, with its many churches, with its graves, towers, and piers, represented God's body on earth, and they were tied to the Chilandar walls and to the Virgin Mary like a cat to the house and its mistress. They knew that the monastery had come into being under the cap of time, but they believed that it had long since removed that cap. They protected and loved it, and not for anything in the world would they relinquish a single of its stones. They subordinated everything they did to this basic principle.

The Dog Star, under the sign of Sirius, ruled the sky. Its sultry stench penetrated a foot underground. On such days, when the sun turns to the earth and the three feminine days in the week are enclosed by masculine days, dog bites become venomous, and fragrances embodying the flower waft over the open sea like mist, poison the fish and its roe then smell of honey. Flung to the far-off ships, the seething odors assault the sails, tearing holes in them. It becomes futile to cultivate plants, and lettuce, which had only to be planted head down to be tamed, runs wild again in this sun. It is a time when birds of prey feed on the eyes of their victims, which they kill by dropping stones on them from the sky. They receive tremendous heat from those eyes (which mirror the suns of bygone years), and to their nests they carry marble, which they know holds the cool, for otherwise they would boil their own eggs. It is a time when seagulls lose their breath in the odorous storms and search for a stone that will not sink (known only to them), and float on it so as not to drown. It is a time when man's seed curdles, when he chews only three times per meal, and on days like this his strong passions turn into hatred. It is a time when hay fever matures and becomes as deep as a well.

That very first Chilandar morning, it was clear to Atanas Svilar that he was trapped in a cage of smells. It was as though he were not living but being dreamed about by somebody else, not by a person, but by an animal or herb. He washed himself with brandy, gazed into the mirror, and thought: "It's as though my mother had a beard. . . ."

He knew: in order to survive, he would have to go down to the shore every morning, inhale the foam and salt, and drink in the open sea, because it is there that the plants of the sea battle with the plants of the earth, and they could take him under their protection. He was given a mule; he rubbed his eyes with spit and prodded the animal into the stream. He had to break through the bulwark of growth that ran between the monastery and the port. He goaded the animal through the smells and pollen quivering in the sun, and his hair, full of plane seeds and catkins, became unbearable; it bit his ears and scratched his forehead. Svilar never made it through that stream to the shore.

In front of him a wooden chest suddenly appeared in the stream, set crossways, like a bridge over water. Pitched among the trees above it was a canvas, and in the chest, wearing bast shoes, lay an old man, his head resting on the pigtail of a monk as though on a coiled snake. His shoes were on backward: when coming, he left footprints as though he were leaving. It was this that made Atanas Svilar recognize him immediately and realize who yesterday's picker of the alder root had been. This was an opportunity not to be missed, and Svilar dismounted. He scooped up some water from the stream, sprinkled the wild wheat all around him to dampen the pollen's strength, and sat on a bench next to the man.

He looked for a second at the gray eyelashes on the man's face, which was the color of black bread.

"How can I tell whether he's asleep?" Svilar wondered and noticed a strange smell, like baked urine.

"It is known here why you have come and whom you are looking for," the monk said, opening his eyes. "We have been waiting for you for a long time, and I'm surprised you didn't come earlier. But, then, you down there don't knead bread with your feet either, so there must be a reason for that, too. . . ."

The old man got up and showed Svilar a small garden by the stream, no bigger than three overcoats of land. It was a strange mixture of plants: anise, thyme, angelica, nasturtium, arrowroot, sage, savory, violets, iris, lucerne, aster, rosemary—they all grew together, flowers with weeds, tea with herbs. And Svilar again felt the pungent stench of mixed smells, as from baked urine.

"This is your garden," the monk told him. "In fact, everybody should have a garden like this somewhere. I've been cultivating it for more than three decades, since your father passed by here. We know your name, because he mentioned you and planted his garden before he disappeared and left you on your own. He was a wonderful herbalist. Look, you won't find a single plant here that doesn't begin with a letter from your name, Atanas Svilar, which is transplanted here, in the real sense of the word. All your thoughts, wishes, actions have germinated and blossomed here, sprouted like flowers or like weeds. You could probably now recognize all your actions, decisions, words, good deeds and bad by their variety and smell. The good deeds are weeds, the bad are flowers, and they have a fragrance, because the good goes with the ugly, and the beautiful with the bad. I always knew by the plants what you were doing and how you felt. . . ."

The monk fell silent for a moment and the skin on his forehead quivered, as though he were driving away flies. He was actually driving away thoughts.

"The monks undoubtedly referred you to me, and I will try to explain why everything that happened here to your father, Major Kosta Svilar, happened the way it did, and why it could not have happened any other way.

"Here, as you may have noticed, we are of two sorts. We are all the children of our tears, because tears are always older than we are ourselves, but in everything else we are divided into two kinds.

"One kind cook on a common fire in large pots under chimneys that are so big one can stand up in them. They eat and wash as in the army—together, from a kettle. They have neither their own buttons, nor hair, nor their own beard, just as geese haven't a feather they won't give for pillows or something else. To them, the brotherhood, the flock of Christ, is more important than the church.

"The other kind eat their own horsebeans in their own individual pots; each has his own little garden in the monastery, cultivating it himself and picking its fruit. These others live alone as though in the desert and are tied to the temple, not to the brotherhood. To the rocks, the ramparts, and the churches of Chilandar.

"The one kind and the other are very different and show that it is not all the same which constellation you are the darkness to: Pisces or Virgo. Shortly before the war, in 1940, when the birds carried their eggs in the sky, one of these solitaries was elected as the elder in Chilandar. For him, the hallowed cult of the Virgin Mary's temple came first and foremost, and he rolled up his sleeves and saw to the monastery's bread. He had a hand for wheat and rye. Tending to the olives, he crossed himself and asked the Virgin Mary:

" 'Oh, woman, what beautiful fruit! Do you nurse it to make it grow so fine?'

"He worked with both hands at the same time and could pour brandy with his left hand and oil with his right without spilling any; he knew how to cook, planted a row of trees along the road, and in them planted future shadows so that they fell on the road when the sun shone brightest. At night he liked to go around Chilandar and listen to the cenobitic monks sing; he could lose his temper and tie a slingshot to the horns of the buffaloes to drive the pests from the field without dismounting from his packsaddle. He taught languages at the monastic school, and spoke Greek, Ukrainian, and German. He left behind a written dictionary of sighs in the Church Slavonic prayers of Eastern Christianity. With the advent of spring, he would fix the drainage ditches and dig irrigation canals around the monastery and hold midnight service, praying that the terrible dampness and fog, from which the monastery took its name, would not strike again. He was one of those for whom the sky was full of birds and the water of fish. His discourses were remembered by the monks in the large Athos assembly, as though every word were a warm morsel. They were brief, sometimes no more than a sentence, and so highly prized that the sentence, which the whole of Mount Athos would know by heart as soon as it was uttered, was never repeated by anyone. It stayed a common secret.

"But man's acts are like grapevines: they sprout shoots in good weather and in bad, not knowing whether outside they will encounter the frost or the sun. . . . So it was at the time when the stones grew. But then the stones stopped growing. The war came, Greece was inundated by German units, and the solitary elder had to pay dearly for his love of the monastery. You should know that he took in your father and some other Yugoslav officers and hid them here, in the monastery. But one day, during the female lunch (when the solitaries dine), a German captain, with two noncommissioned officers and a dozen soldiers, appeared at the monastery. They conversed over coffee, laced with Mastika for the occasion.

" 'Did you come by land or by sea, Captain?' the elder started by asking.

" 'Why do you ask, Father?' responded the officer.

" 'If you came by land, then a few drops of water are added to a glass of Mastika, and that is how you drink it. But if you came by sea, where you were bathed by the sun and passed by the waves to the wind, then it is the reverse: the Mastika should be spilled into a glass of water. Almost all the liquid turns into a curl of redolent, fuming mist and smoke. It has to be downed in one gulp, and then the fatigue and dizziness will disappear as though with a wave of the hand.'

"The captain did not reply, but added a few drops of water to the Mastika and drank it. And so the elder knew that things looked bad and that the German had come by land, the way the fugitives had come from the Albanian front. He was on their trail.

"He asked the elder openly whether he was hiding Yugoslav war fugitives. Upon receiving a negative reply, he got up, waited for the redness to spread across his face and spill into his ears, and then said:

" 'I have the greatest respect for this place and for your holy family, Father, but this is war and we are only the vanguard of an army. Unless I receive a correct answer, I will order my men to search the monastery and find the fugitives myself, because my information is that they are here, that there are three of them, and that they are the officers who inflicted the only defeat suffered by our forces in this war. In the event that you do not turn them over, that I have to look for them myself, I will have Chilandar set on fire. It is up to you. . . .'

"It was the misfortune of your father and the elder that the monk was an idiorrhythmic, he belonged to the order of solitaries, those who guarded and protected the temple above all else, and so his conduct was predetermined. Had he been one of the others, who live a communal life here, had he cared less about Chilandar, what had to happen would not have happened. . . . I shall not tell you about it, because any monk who was in the monastery at the time can tell you the rest. . . ."

The monk suddenly broke off his story, took a jar out of the chest, and offered it to Svilar.

"This is honey collected by the bees in your garden. Take it and try it. It may tell you something about what you did and what you should do. I don't know. . . ."

The monk turned his stick around so that the thinner end came into his hand, wrinkled his forehead and chased away his thoughts, and then went on his way, walking with his toes in the heels of his back-to-front shoes. The grass sowed golden powder like ground walnuts in his wake, dusting his inverted footprints. The water flowed between Svilar and him and the hay fever ran wild; the old man looked as though he were coming although he was going. Svilar ran toward the monastery through the aromatic tradewinds in front of him. On the way he looked up at the sun and thought how his gaze would continue to travel toward the sun even after his death.

On his second Chilandarian night, Svilar was asleep. And his sleep was whole, like a glass. But his hands felt so cold that they chilled his face, and in his sleep he kept his icy fingers away from his head. He realized the next morning, however, that sleep had cost him more than if he had stayed awake all night. While he had been resting, exhausted as he was, the hay fever had been able to do its work undisturbed. And do it it did.

There are no doctors or clinics on Mount Athos; the sick are placed in special rooms where they receive a kind of dispensation and some assistance; that is to say, the younger monks prepare for them a meal or a hot beverage, coffee with lemon or some such thing. There the sick listen to the fragment of time inside them and to the large whole of time outside, and wait to see which one will hold sway. That is all. Or they are allowed to breakfast, which is not the custom at Chilandar otherwise. So it was with Svilar. They gave him a piece of black, hard Chilandar honey, the kind one breaks, not spreads, and in a mortar some wine cooked with ground pepper.

On that third day, he sat feebly in the old monastery refectory, the one from the days of the Nemanyides, facing the doors of the Church of the Presentation, and drank hot wine for breakfast. He rubbed his nostrils with honey and gazed at the wall, painted with scenes from the life of Saint Sava, the monastery's founder. The sun entered the room and slowly lit up, one by one, scenes from the prince's life, moving from death to birth, because the sun always moves from death to birth. . . .

Breakfast was over when into the refectory came a robust red-headed monk, sort of rusty all over. Although he had never seen the face before, Svilar immediately recognized Father Varlam, the other monk who had been recommended to him when he first arrived. The man, his eyes so blue they seemed to have drunk up the sea and the salt, now stood in front of Svilar, with his hair cut and without the pot on his head. His voice carried as though it had not been taught on land, but had come off a ship. The monk blinked like a bird, with his bottom lids rising, his nails were pointed and brittle and exuded a stench, and he already had his third teeth, the ones that hurt until death, and kept moaning softly. When he spoke, strange voices came from the depths of his enormous body, like the distant, drowned crowing of cocks arousing some kind of day buried in the recesses of his lungs and liver. A cloud of dandruff hovered like a swarm of flies around his head, settling on his shoulders and clustering around his hair like the halo of a saint. Father Varlam had cut window-like openings in his shoes for his corns, and when he walked his toenails, which had grown through the socks, clicked against the floor. One of his legs, the left one, was lame and seemed to have been dipped in a different sweat from the right: it reeked with quite a different stench, of mouse droppings, and more strongly than its twin. The angry, terribly salty sweat ate though the cassock around his neck and the nest in his armpit, and his mantle was burned by the unending seeds he scattered as he walked, searing everything they sprinkled. He spoke as though his tongue were hauling every word off of the ground. He lived, ate, breathed, and slept with immense effort, as though building a pyramid somewhere inside him.

"Not everybody in the world lost his soul, nor was everybody in the desert saved!" he said, throwing back a lock of hair as though tying his ear. "I remember, in 1941, when your father came here, the winds were strong, strong enough to peel off one's shoes and whip one to the bone. It was in such a wind that your father, Major Svilar, and two of his friends spread out their cloaks and came here as though blown in by a whirlwind. Nobody had climbed to the monastery over those craggy paths for centuries; all roads are tied and untied by the sea. That's why nobody discovered them at the frontier. Here they were received, accommodated, and entertained like any other visitor, because everything here has been free for the traveler for centuries. Your father, Major Svilar, brought a beard as thick as moss and a voice of such magnitude he could not run around it. He arrived here with a knowledge of church singing, which is uncommon—indeed, rare—nowadays, because it isn't taught at music academies (where they teach only the religious music of the West). He fit in immediately with us cenobites at the monastery and joined in our way of life with no difficulty, although we did not predominate at the time, because the elder and the others were solitaries, which I'm sure you've already heard. Your father decanted the wine and colored it with dark grapes, and took an inventory of the monastery library, leafing through the pages of old books looking for dried seventeenth- and eighteenth-century herbs or flowers, because he was interested in plants. He picked them with his eyes closed and planted them while kneeling in the little garden by the stream. And he sang in church, preferably at morning service.

"That fine voice of his apparently cost him dearly. It's hard to say how the German authorities learned that the army fugitives were on Mount Athos. They must have given themselves away. It's believed that on his last stopover before Mount Athos, in Ouranoupolis, Major Svilar abandoned caution. He was in the local church, listening to the singing, and he reportedly said:

" 'He who dies of fear will as a requiem a fart hear'; and he let his voice go, it descended from great heights into the church, and he sang a Slav liturgy in the middle of the Greek service, so that even the deaf knew that it was not being sung by Bulgarians and that among the congregation that evening were fugitives from Serbia. That is what gave them away. The Germans had followed the trail and made the monastery's elder choose between Chilandar and the war fugitives. We cenobites were as afraid of what the Germans would do as of what the elder would have to do. Because we knew his nature and the nature of the solitary order to which he belonged. His entire upbringing had made him completely devoted to Chilandar's Church of the Presentation, to the monastery and everything in it, and he had absolutely no choice. He gave it not a second's thought, because the hairs under one's arms are not angel wings. He admitted that three Yugoslav war fugitives were hiding in the monastery, and that they were officers, and at the door, upon leaving the room, we saw how after this admission his eye rolled along the part in his hair to the top of his head. We rushed to the shelter, found the fugitives hiding in the belly of a large barrel, pulled them out, dressed them in monks' cassocks, and removed them from the monastery."

At that moment the monk came up to Svilar and placed a bundle in front of him. Inside the bundle Svilar found his father's officer's blouse, and in its pockets a lock of his father's hair with a note written thirty-five years earlier saying: "Whenever somebody spills a glass, think of Kosta. Don't rue the wine, it's for me."

"What happened to the fugitives later," the monk proceeded with his story, "I am unable to tell you. The Yugoslav officers were not found by evening, although the captain searched every nook and cranny of the monastery's property, and even peered into the tall clocks in the hallways. He immediately sent out a search party, but nobody could say whether the officers had fallen into enemy hands, although everybody in the monastery had heard gunshots from the forest. That evening the elder added brandy to the captain's wine to soothe his spirits a little. He had admitted what had been asked of him and thus had protected the monastery. Whether or not the fugitives were found, he thought, was no longer our business. But it was our business to strip the elder of his rank because of his action. Obviously, he would not have acted like that had he been less attached to the monastery—I mean, to the tangible part of the monastery. Because the monastery, the real monastery, is not its walls, but its holy brotherhood inside us. The solitaries, however, do not think so, and it was the elder's misfortune that he was a solitary. And with them it is as with cats: the cat kills nine snakes, and the tenth kills the cat.

"Ever since then, the former elder has not lived in the monastery; instead he roams Mount Athos, wears his belt and shoes backward so that Satan won't recognize him, tosses stones on the road in front of him to announce his arrival so that whoever does not want to encounter him can step aside. He performs the liturgy in churches, standing in for ailing monks, and comes here to Chilandar only once a year, for the dedication of the water, the Great Agiasma, on the eve of the Epiphany. Then he bows to the icon of the Virgin Mary and says:

" 'If your mouth were mute, my love would be dear.'

"He lights three candles, but each flame separately, for fear of taking away the light meant for others and of illuminating some while leaving the others in darkness. And instead of a bed, every year he carves three chests, dyes them black with alder root, and sleeps in them in turns."

Holding his bundle, Svilar again sat alone in Chilandar's refectory. He drank his wine, which had gone cold and bitter, and then went down to the seashore to breathe in the salt and rinse his eyes with the churning green healing water. With his first sight of this water that smiles, of the waves that yawn and pronounce their names, he knew that everything about his father had been explained and that he had nothing to look for in the depths of the hay fever that raged after him along the stream toward Chilandar. "Why light a fire on a branch?" he thought, and decided not to go back to the monastery. The few items of clothing in his travel bag back in the monastery cell were not worth the effort. He caught the ship that docks in the early evening and once again was the only passenger from this deserted shore.

He was returning with the job done and a bitter tongue, as though he had been growing thorny-stemmed fruits in his mouth. The ship rocked beneath his feet; he chewed some of the salty wind that washed and lashed the eyes; it was Sunday, it was his third day on Mount Athos—the day of truth—but the hay fever inside him had not died down. It was as though something else were yet to happen. True, he was carrying his father's army blouse, whose buttons caught on his sleeves in the wind and slid into the buttonholes of his coat. But Svilar could not think of his father. He was thinking of himself. Through his thin hair his face showed on the crown of his head, where the sweat emerges. But he was still not conscious of whose face that was.

Mount Athos was no longer visible from the ship. All one could see was that over there, on the other side of the waves, a quiet reigned on the land, the silence of earth, inaudible to the ear of the passerby, not because of the rumbling sea between it and him, but because only a bird on a branch can understand silence. Man cannot.

6

Chilandar's solidaries—cenobites—from the very first became and re-
mained a sort of party of the Nemanyides, a national party within the
framework of the monastery. The cult of Chilandar's founders, the saints
and rulers Nemanya and Sava, like the cult of the ruling dynasty they had
founded, was especially strong among the cenobites, who saw the monastery
as a large sacred family that was spiritually connected to the distant people
from whom it had sprung, and before their eyes floated the principle of
fatherhood, the relationship of the father (Nemanya) to the son (Sava).
They were as attached to Sava and Nemanya and to their paths as are
sheepdogs to the shepherds and to the herd itself. Turned toward tradition,
they considered the essence of their vocation to be the discovery of hidden
possibilities. Holy warriors, the cenobites knew how to point the cross like
a spear if need be. The descendants of a ruler and warrior, they, like Sava,
defended the monastery against pirates and marauders when necessary. In
keeping with Sava's typikon, they had no property of their own save the
ears on their heads, nor cells of their own save the dormitory. Nor did they
have their own shirts, for after every washing they were always given
somebody else's to wear. Like themselves, everything was communal, mu-
tual. They were their own church, on the theory that, where two of you

are gathered together, there is a church between you. They were Chilandarians not in the Chilandar monastery, but Chilandarians in Nemanya and Sava, on the roads, in the vineyards and pastures of Karyes, St. Paul, Pateritsa, and wherever they might be; they were Chilandarians, and Chilandar was wherever they were. Preoccupied with the celestial perspective, they were not tied to a place or a wall. They always had two names for one and the same meadow by the graveyard: when they talked about it on the shore they called it the Rise, and when they mentioned it in the monastery they always called it the Fall.

If a monk claimed that the division into solidaries and solitaries was an unimportant, technical distinction, if he contended that they were all equals among themselves, that the relationship between generations did not matter at all, and that all generations were given the same opportunities in life, then one could and can safely say that he was a cenobite.

Ever geared toward one another, toward the fraternity of compatriots, the cenobites learned languages laboriously and rarely, and they read Greek better than they dared to speak it. They were, in fact, for a separate, Serbian church, one that did not belong to the Orthodox international, connected to the Greek ecumenical patriarchy. And it was no accident that, at times of power, bounty, and wealth, the monastery moved increasingly into the hands of the cenobites, who at such moments always prevailed over the order of solitaries. The cenobites rose together, sat at the table together, and listened to the common prayer read to them during the meal by one of their fellow brothers. Each took every morsel of food at the same word of the prayer. And then they walked out under the cross together and into the world where they would seemingly mingle with the solitaries. But only seemingly. Dressed the same, in the same monastery, engrossed in prayer like the solitaries in front of the same altar, they were actually always something else. And they were entirely aware of this. They even had external traits. Morning service belonged to the cenobites; tied to the hesychastic teachings of unaging light, they believed that the stomach was the symbol of man's being. In contrast to the solitaries, who kept the icon of the Virgin Mary on the wall, the cenobites kept icons of Saints Simeon and Sava in their cells. They were herbalists, cultivators of medicinal and aromatic herbs, healers of repute, and their physicians ran the eye hospitals *in Constantinople. They were also shepherds who tended to each and every one of their little sheep, producers of fragrances, and winegrowers, and hence they loved the sun. They first planted vineyards in their restless, war-like dreams, and then in reality. They grafted and trimmed the vine from the same variety planted by Nemanya, one vine of which still bears fruit on Nemanya's grave, inscribing, as though with an ink of thick must, mysterious letters on the stone slab beneath it, changing the handwriting every seven years, and the alphabet every nine. This vine, older than they themselves, they tied with hair as in the song, and every year, on the Day of the Transfiguration of Christ, they blessed the grape in the church. The cenobites were also singers, writers, and transcribers of manuscripts, and their duties included guarding and preserving the writings of Saint Sava and the monastery library. Faults as well as duties were meticulously divided between their own order and the solitaries. The cenobites had always fallen easily and quickly into a particular heresy—that of the iconoclasts; practical, the cenobites, who had never had much esteem for women, sometimes crossed the limits of the permissible into dogmatism, becoming Monophysites and denying the dual (divine and human) nature of Christ, and therefore all other nuances as well. Uninterested in foreign languages, they would embark on journeys only in large groups, and the great migrations of their people were rooted in their logic.*

Not only faults but also skills, crafts, and other activities in the monastery were carefully divided between them: it had always been known which jobs came within the province of the cenobites, and which belonged to the other monks, the solitaries.

Of the seven liberal arts inherited from ancient Greece, the mathematical —that is, the written disciplines (arithmetic, geometry, music, and astronomy) and their derived activities—belonged to the cenobites, while the trivium of oral, nonmathematical disciplines (grammar, rhetoric, and metaphysics) belonged to the solitaries. And every monk had to obey this rule. Not because anybody would keep them from jobs that did not fall within the province of their own monastic order, but because the tradition and custom of doing such work was not cultivated within that order, where one could not train for, learn, or obtain the jobs and conditions necessary for performing it. Since the solitaries and the cenobites alternated almost generationally in holding key positions in the monastery, the ones prevailing at one moment and the others the next, the written arts, which belonged to one current, and the nonmathematical, oral arts, which belonged to the other, alternated in taking precedence and flourishing, depending on which monastic order was on the ascent.

Among the mathematical arts connected to the cenobites, one was particularly important. Like Simeon and like Sava, the cenobites were masons. They knew from which side to fell a tree, and they knew it should be felled at night when there is a new moon, so that no weevil would attack it. They celebrated the holy twins and martyr-architects, Saints Florus and Laurus, the patrons of everyone who carries a trowel. They had always been prepared to build and to destroy without mercy and with premeditation. Chilandar was a work of their conception—a fortified monastery, embraced by enormous defensive walls, guarded by quadrangular towers, hemmed in by sweet water on three sides, defended from the sea by the Hrusija tower on Chilandar's pier, open in only one place, where the gate was. But, like their vineyards, it was all merely an image of another, dreamed-of city. And the cenobites carried that other, celestial city inside them, and in them it was inviolable and did not depend on earthly buildings; rather, they depended on it and were built in its mirror image. The cenobites themselves were the city, and it could be destroyed only by destroying them. Thanks to this city inside them, they never forgot who they were, and they knew they would be the same tomorrow, too. . . .

It was an eastern Friday, the day when no work should be begun. The trip was over, and Atanas Svilar brought his hay fever back unabated from the sea to the shore. He brought it to his parents' home in Matarushka Spa, whence he had taken it. It was late; he did not want to wake his son, who was sleeping in the room on the porch. He crept silently into his mice-filled room and lay down in a bed sprinkled with oil from the lamp above. His heart beat somewhere in the pillow; on the shelf, where the clock inched along and fell onto the floor in the middle of the night, lay a book. He opened it and recognized Gogol, *Dead Souls,* which he had read in 1944, as a boy, when the Russians were within reach of Belgrade. Now he was loath to read—it was the second week of Cancer, in June, when dreams do not come true—but as soon as he picked up the book he remembered its contents from its weight. He became engrossed in the reading and submerged in the book so that the night almost passed and the candle in the lamp started to dim. But the more Svilar read, the less he was with the heroes of the book. The story, which he had read when he was fifteen, increasingly called up memories of his youth. It was pouring outside in the dark, and in Svilar's book at the same time. It was night in both rains, and between those two nights emerged a day in Atanas Svilar's memory, October 15, 1944, and between the lines of the book appeared events from that distant year.

Another shower of grenades had fallen from the German anti-aircraft artillery in Banyitsa, and now it battered not the sky but the ground, and the plowfield sprayed out of the holes made by the falling bombs as though somebody were digging trenches. And then a very young Red Army soldier appeared, almost a boy, in a cotton-padded tunic, his white eyelashes muddy, dragging a field gun. He held his cigarette with the burning tip turned into the cup of his hand, and every so often limped slightly, as though his boot pinched him. A scar cut across his budding mustache and ruined his smile, stopping at the teeth. He cupped his cigarette to keep it from going out in the spray of earth, checked the target sight, and fired at Belgrade. Earth flew in all directions, knocking off his cap. The boy stood up, dropped the gun chain, leaned against a tree, and pulled out his penis, which smoked in the cold. He looked around to pinpoint the sides of the world and, avoiding east and west, turned to the south and emptied his penis, melting the first October snow. From their hiding place, Svilar and his friend saw something drip on the ground like wax spilling from a candle; the soldier buttoned himself up and went back to his gun. He licked his dirty fledgling mustache, spat out some clay, and checked the target sight. Finally he spotted the children, who were almost his age, and asked:

"What's the name of that town?"

He pointed his chin toward Belgrade and fired at the same time. He checked the information he received on a map drawn on the shield of the gun and rolled another cigarette. He was alone, terribly alone, deaf from the silence and dumb from the deafness.

And then Svilar suddenly realized that for the past two days strange, unknown people wearing the uniforms of all five Allied and eight enemy armies had been moving past him and the Russians, heading for Belgrade.

They were sparing with their steps and with their bullets; every so often they would stop, take a book of rice paper out of their pockets, tear off a sheet, and eat it, skipping over the pages that mattered to them. They carried local Kraguyevats rifles and bombs, Czech zbroy-ovkas, slim "Bredas," German Schmeissers, Russian machinkas, and English tommy-guns. They always looked the enemy in the feet and his vehicle in the tire, because the foot reveals intent before any other of man's movements, and the tire or tread reveals the driver's thought even before he has consciously decided where to go. They brought their elbows, as heavy as rifle butts, their flaxen hair and mustaches, gleaming with weapon lubricant. They took off their shoes at the approaches to town, threw their boots and shoes into the outskirts, and conquered Belgrade in their socks as silently as cats, rushing as fast as the snow drove the frozen soles of their feet. They fired only when absolutely necessary, tossed into German-manned buildings their "mute" bombs buried in loaves of bread to deaden the explosion and delay discovery until the last possible moment, when they would already be on the other side, at which the enemy does not shoot. They could put a shadow back on the fence if need be.

And Atanas Svilar, a child who had grown up fatherless, suddenly recognized them. These unknown arrivals streaming into town in long partisan columns from Avala, from Mali Mokri Lug and Sme-derevo, past the Sava and Danube, trampling their morning shadow —they were *fathers*. Had he lived to see the end of the war, Major Kosta Svilar, too, would have been marching into town and into his life with the columns entering Belgrade. . . .

Fear had long since washed the bones of these people, and they did not announce their arrival by tossing stones. Suddenly they were there. Enthusiastically welcomed in the city as liberators, later, when they dispersed to their homes old and new, many bonds remained to link them. Besides war veterans, this circle also included others, their peers and countrymen who had waited for and welcomed them in town. They were all tied by bonds of "kumstvo" cemented at weddings and baptisms, they knew that the blade is best tempered by urine and had long since peed on their swords, and during the war had slain their enemies with those same swords. They asked the cuckoo on the branch how long they would live, and they knew the answer. Although they immediately settled in town as victors, with songs of celebration and flowers, neither before nor after did they feel at home there, for the simple reason that they felt equally at home everywhere in Serbia. They measured it with their steps, they had drunk from its every river and rain; they had given birth to this land with rifles, nowhere in it could they lose their way, and they considered everything in it to be their common property. They saw the horns of high noon under the walnut trees on time; not knowing languages, because throughout their youth their communication with foreigners had been with a rifle, they were reluctant to go out into the world, where they went mostly on business and felt cut off. Even there they sought each other out and tried to stick together, yearning to go home soon and wrap hay around the plum tree in the orchard.

They cherished one another, their friends and fellows, not only as people of like minds and generation, as comrades-in-arms, as partners from school and with women, but also because the cake in their mouths allowed them to see farther, because, by taking power in Serbia and doing the work that went with it, they were geared to one another. They knew that those who ask the way at night travel alone; day was their time, they were engaged early in the affairs of administration and management, and it was early when they became older in their dreams than in reality, failing to find time to resume the schooling that the war had cut short. Although they knew that snakes are not as poisonous on Saturdays as on Fridays, they regretted the sciences they had never learned in their youth and in the war, and were determined readers, yearning for books all their lives, convinced of the omnipotence of the written word. But you won't feed a hungry Christmas with a full Easter. In vain did they seek in 1974 to read books unread in 1940. And yet they knew which tree to doff their cap to, and devoted enormous energy to the written and printed word, to writings they put on paper themselves, or to what had been written about them, but this literature devoted to the war never depicted a single day of their peacetime life in Belgrade, which lasted decades longer than the four years of hostilities.

They knew from experience that a field soaked in human blood does not bear fruit for three to four years, and in animal blood not for half that time; when they had gone off to war, others had tossed wheat at them for a safe return and success, and during the war, if they harvested, they harvested at night like Saint Peter, leaving the economy to their sons, whom they had schooled for that purpose. Occasionally, they would grow vine leaves, pour through the funnel the wine they knew as well as their own blood, and toast their horses. They were hot-blooded; they said that anyone who could release the safety on a rifle could do the same with a woman, and there was truth in that. Mothers, wives, and daughters loved them, the former and the latter more than their own husbands. But their real company was the company of men and other veterans. They divorced and married easily, sat and drank in silence for nights and days on end, as though carrying sickles and kneading mute corn bread, and spoke brusquely, as though issuing military orders. Their illnesses were like trumpet calls. Renowned herbalists, they knew that plants and flowers are cut not with metal but with wooden knives; they came out of the war as brilliant surgeons, taught that the devil has only one bone. They knew that the waters that flow to the east are medicinal and the winds that blow on them infectious; they were administrators of clinics, masters of death in peacetime, just as they had been masters of life in wartime; army doctors of repute and influence, they held human days in their upper and human nights in their lower jaw. Their death meant war again, military formations and platoons again, uniforms again. They were in constant touch with one another, either by telephone or by mail: if nothing else, they would tie threads around their waists, as during the war, and instead of letters send the threads in envelopes to signal that they were alive and still carried the names they had been christened with.

They said that mint was not always as therapeutic as on herbal Fridays, and they always retained an ambiguous attitude to Belgrade: for a long time they kept their pillows in their caps, although those they attacked had long since left the city. They always kept a rifle cached in some attic of the villages they had fought in during the war, some salt in their pockets, or a machine gun in a dry well. They used every occasion to prove their genuine loyalty to this reserve homeland of theirs, to swear by the mountains and waters of their patrimony and the woods at their rear. And they would not hesitate for a moment to set fire to the city and sow salt if they thought it would benefit and serve some higher, more general purpose. In fact, to them the state was not some particular area or town but, rather, the human element in the state, earth and fire. They themselves, wherever they assembled and joined together, were the state. But this did not stop them from changing and building this city, like kneading dough with a spindle. They were ruthless builders, as quick to demolish as to construct, and they built the city on both sides of the water, as high as their whistle would carry. . . .

In short, they were what Svilar had learned on Mount Athos was called *cenobites.*

This dawned on him at the moment when it was raining in his book as it was outside; there was mud in the book and on the street beneath the window, and from these rains mushroomed memories of that autumn when Belgrade had been on fire and his life had been opening up before him. The comparison between Svilar's life then, which still lay ahead of him and was as undefined as a crossroads on water, and his life now, between the Svilar of then, who absorbed everything and could become anything, and this drained man, spent and embalmed by the scents of the plants, was so crushing that it could barely be endured. It was as though the eyes he had pawned in this same book thirty-five years ago were now watching him from between the pages. But they did not find or recognize anybody.

In fact, everything had happened just as Father Luke had said it would. When he read Gogol's book the first time, he had been younger than the book's main character. Now, obviously, this was no longer true: they had changed roles, and now Chichikov had become younger than Svilar. And that was the basic truth of the book. Everything else was secondary. Suddenly Svilar realized that *Dead Souls* had taken him back not to the Atanas Svilar who had been fifteen thirty-five years ago, but to someone who was *now* the same age he had been then. And so Atanas Svilar finally stopped reading and, covered in arid sweat and dry tears that stuck like fish scales to his cheeks and the corners of his mouth, he rushed to the porch, where his son, Nikola Svilar, was sleeping.

That feeling of love for his son washed over him through his love for himself as he no longer was and would never be again. Time still remained only in Nikola Svilar and, transported by that love for his different self as a boy when Belgrade was ablaze, Svilar hurried to find his son. He opened the porch door softly, went over to the bed in the dark, and carefully laid his hand on the pillow. Instead of his son, he caressed the head of a stranger. Sleeping on the pillow was an unknown brunette, a child almost, her bare breasts breathing in her sleep like warm buns. His son no longer slept alone. And it was too late to change anything in Svilar's relationship with his son. Forever too late. Atanas's son, Nikola Svilar, already carried a new surname. The surname of his first mother, Vitacha Milut.

Architect Atanas Svilar looked around. Objects of incredible shapes were strewn all over the room. Electric guitars hooked up to amplifiers, headphones, quartz direct-drive tape recorders, drums, keyboards on wheels, electronic microphones, enormous speakers, and old machines with horns instead of loudspeakers—all this rolled over the floor and the armchairs. In the midst of it all, other young couples lay asleep on the floor and on the divans. And on the table were the remains of their joint dinner. As soon as he looked, Svilar knew: they had had fish fried live, uncleaned, held down in the frying pan with the lid to stop it from wriggling. His son had found his way to his grandfather far from Mount Athos and World War II. Atanas Svilar put Major Kosta Svilar's army blouse on the table and went out into the night, which was heavy with the kind of damp and low-hanging clouds that mow the grass. Choral breathing accompanied him out of the room. Suddenly Svilar felt more composed. When it eats a snake, a child acquires transparent lids and can see at night. Now he saw at night, too. And he looked at what he saw.

Worms riddled the apples in the thunder, the dogs' fur curled pending the rain, clouds darkened the skies, the Ibar rumbled as black as a plowfield and one could not tell which way it was flowing. There was dampness in the air, and Svilar breathed a sigh of relief. The hay fever was letting up, seeming to abstain from its siege, as though its presence had suddenly lost its purpose. The smell of bread baked on cabbage leaves wafted out of the bakery. And for the first time in many years, Svilar sensed the smell, just as he sensed that his sickness, his old relative, was leaving him. The hay fever was disappearing from his life forever. It had nothing to defend him against anymore. And, in parting, he was grateful to it for having spared him all these long years of his life, at least until now, from the truth, as from a finger in the eye. His nostrils and ears opened up like another set of eyes, and he finally inhaled the smell of his own body, brought from somewhere across the sea, an unknown, almost alien smell, the smell of his "Greek" sweat. And he began to see things clearly, as though looking through the tears on his cheek rather than through his eyes.

The important events in a man's life, he thought, always stay the same inside him, as they were when they dropped into that life, and they can no longer be changed or corrected. But life around them changes, and every morning one sees them from a new angle, from a new distance, and from a new side, and one day these fateful events may, perhaps, turn around and show him their true face—the face from which one can read their fateful meaning and significance. The answer to why Svilar's life had passed by in futile attempts to build something it had not been given unto him to build, finally lay before him—or, more precisely, behind him—clear, ancient, and inexorable; everybody around him could be divided into one of two types: the *solidaries* (cenobites), like his father and son, or the *solitaries* (idior-rhythmics), like himself. Two winds could not be in the same place at the same time, nor could Svilar be a solitary and a builder at the same time. He simply did not belong to the architects, and he was not preordained to build. Now he knew in whose shadow the snakes were the vilest. All his life he had tried to step out of the role intended for him by an ancient rhythm of things, and it was no wonder that in this barren effort he had worn himself out, as though he had been beating a rope. His misfortune was that he was an idiorrhythmic.

"The women were right," he whispered. "Solitaries! We are all solitaries—idiorrhythmics, as they would say over there, on that sacred tooth of rock that nibbles the sky. A whole generation of loners, all of us deaf to one another, like diving birds, hard work in our hands and soft ears on our heads, buried in peaceful marriages and dreaming of the Virgin, condemned to a solitary plate and mute meal—all of us saw towns instead of the people in them. It is only in our times that all forty-year-olds are considered to be already sixty. Not so before our time or after! . . . Didn't we have the strength to break free?"

And then he thought of languages, of the languages they had madly learned in their youth and had forgotten twice, like Adam. Those languages had actually been a signpost, an opportunity to pull out of the vicious circle of the solitary order that had been assigned to his generation. Some had tasted that fruit, had seen the blue wind. When they had tired of the solitary's deaf life in their garden-fatherlands, when they had had enough of adding spoons and forks here where not even two people drank water together, some of his friends would suddenly exclaim: "We don't even sow our own beards!" They would turn their ears inside out (because the secret lies in the ear), change their names and languages, and go out into the big world looking for bread with seven crusts. Carrying only those English, Russian, German, and French words that they had dreamed about for years, and that could help them to turn their caps right side out, they took their passports and left to become somebody else, to become what they had not been and could not become in their own language: changing from solitaries to solidaries, from idiorrhythmics to cenobites. From Yoan Siropoulos the Greek to Yovan Siropulov the Bulgarian.

It was as quiet outside as in an armpit. In that quiet, without a single thought and without a particular decision, the words of a long-forgotten language bubbled up inside Svilar, words he had been forced to learn in his youth. The strange, long-suppressed words rose like sunken islands, they surfaced from him, he found them and assembled them unerringly into wholes, just as goats in search of salt lick the rock until they find and lay bare in the earth the ancient edifice built with salted mortar:

An der alten Treppe wurden die Stirnseiten stark grün lackiert Holzverkleidung an der Wand unter einer dicken Lackschicht hervorgeholt. Das dicke Halteseil ist nicht nur praktisch, sondern auch sehr dekorativ. Alle Wände im Hauseingang sind mit naturfarbenem Reibeputz belegt. Die Decke wurden mit Holz verkleidet, der hintere Ausgang mit einem orangefarbenen Vorhang versehen. Der Orangeton und das Grün der Treppe wiederholen sich im Türrahmen und in der bemalten Füllung einer nicht mehr benutzten Tür. Geht man die Treppe hinauf in die obere Diele, die optisch durch ein durchgehendes Lichtband erweitert wurde, steht auf der linken Seite eine schwedische rote Kommode bereit, um Schals und Handschuhe der Kinder aufzunehmen. Decke und Wände der Diele wurden mit einer dezent gemusterten Tapete tapeziert. In der Küche mit ihrem gemütlichen Essplatz wurden die vorhandenen Küchenmöbel dunkelgrün lackiert, die Decke über dem Essplatz mit einem Holzraster abgehängt. Vorhänge und Bank-kissen sind aus schwarzweissem Karostoff. Die Wände der Nische haben Rauhfasertapete, ultramarinblau gestrichen. Entgegen allen üblichen Lösungen solcher Bauaufgaben, bei denen der Hauseigentümer die Beletage für seine Wohnung bevorzugt, war es hier möglich, durch Einbeziehung des Daches für Wohnzwecke ein ausgesprochenes Einfamilienhaus den beiden unteren Geschossen—Mietwohnung im l. Stock und Praxisräume im Erdgeschoss überzustülpen. Eine Benützung des Gartens für Wohnzwecke war der nachbarlichen Einsicht wegen ohnehin nicht gegeben, so dass die Konzentration auf das innere der Aufgabe ihren Reiz gab. So kommt es auch, dass die Orientierung vornehmlich nach den beiden Giebelseiten erfolgte und nach den Nachbarseiten nur wenige Fenster ausgerichtet wurden. . . .

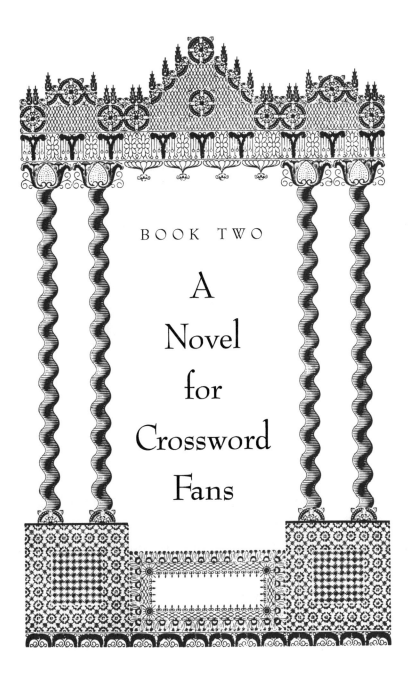

BOOK TWO

A
Novel
for
Crossword
Fans

Contents

for those who wish to read this novel, or crossword,
across

	2	1	5	3	■	4	6
1							
2	1	3	2	5	6	■	4
3	6	3	2	■	4	5	1
4	2						

Contents

for those who wish to read this novel, or crossword,
down

1 2 3 4 5 6

1 ACROSS

2 DOWN

No undelivered slap should ever be taken to the grave!

We had a friend at school once who used to say that as his maxim, but he didn't look like someone who felt that way about slaps. Truth be told, he looked like someone who was slow to remember and quick to forget. He was fond of saying: The day is faster than a rabbit, it slips away from you in a flash! He was personable, but unobtrusive, like those stories that can be forgotten twice. In our early youth, he made a strong impression on me and the others in a small, completely trivial matter; he said something, as was probably his way, that caught our fancy. Looking at the pretty young things around us, who forgive handsome fellows their stupidity but not ugly ones their brains, he said: "We'll screw 'em all yesterday!" Or I think it was he who guessed that the couples in Renoir's *Le Moulin de la Galette* were waltzing to the strains of "The Last Blue Wednesday." Or it was some third such crack, important to us at the time. Since I, of course, am averse to remembering people who make a good impression on me and immediately relegate them to the depths of oblivion, I remembered little else about him.

But certain things, quite new and recent, have drawn the attention of all of us in Belgrade to him now, after so many decades, when only the clocks still tell us the truth, and when we have all forgotten about each other to the point that, in deciding to write down something about this fellow, I had to admit to myself that I had forgotten even his name. So, for now, this story, or this crossword—because every story crosses words—lacks even the name of its hero. Here is what he looked like when we saw him again recently.

In came a blond man of average height, with two Indian parts in his hair. He brought a hat full of troubles and a tobacco pouch made of goat balls, filled with pipes. His head simply would not stand in the middle of his hat, nor his neck in the middle of his collar, and yet he was still good-looking, and what bothered me most about him was what women liked best—his muscular legs, one of which was older than the other, and his incredible speed—the part of beauty that cannot be painted. First he poured his drink and then he slid his glass under it, but without spilling anything. He was not just fast. He was one of those upon whom fortune had smiled.

Like those sprinters who burst through the crack of the gun and come in first, because they spring at the same moment as the signal, he suddenly realized (although already advanced in age) that for every two of one's pockets somebody else has a third, into which everything one earns mercilessly flows. It was then that he turned things around. He went on to spend the more successful part of his life in the United States and elsewhere in the world as the owner of a powerful company and a financial magnate—if not the equivalent of Sam Wolton and Tsutsumi, then at least on their tail. Sporting a shapely chiseled shadow, he had now come in his own plane to see his former class-mates in this inn with its checkered tablecloths, because he loved fish, and the best fish is always to be found where there are checkered tablecloths. Even after a quarter of a century abroad, he still couldn't drive a car in his dreams, nor did he spend a single night in foreign parts. All those decades in America, Vienna, and Switzerland, he dreamed he was burying his boots somewhere in Zemun and was sleeping in Belgrade on an iron sled with bells, which jingled when-ever he turned in his sleep.

As soon as he spotted me, he spread open his arms and cried:

"Misha, my gluttonous fast, why, all that's left of us are our eyes!"

Still not knowing who he really was, I made as if I remembered him, as if everything were in order. Anyway, it was only logical that he should have remembered my name, for the same reasons that I had forgotten his. I certainly remember everyone on whom I have ever left a good impression; I remember because one always reasons beneath one's capacity, and therefore such good impressions are so rare that they should be rescued from the oblivion into which they will be cast forever by those on whom they were made.

Seeing that I didn't recognize him, he did not turn away; instead we sat down together and he continued talking with the same warmth, all the while playing some kind of polka on the table, as though it were a piano, his nails leaving marks on the cloth, like notes.

"Don't worry," he added as though he could see straight through me, "our memories, thoughts, and feelings reside in other worlds, and depend little on us here. Because, whatever the thoughts of two different men, they resemble each other more than do a man and his own thoughts. . . ."

His mother had just died around then; and that evening he told me an unusual story, obviously rooted in his own loss but containing a certain reversal, as though he had died and his mother were still alive.

"A widow," he began, *"lost her son, and the mother was racked with grief. She cried all the salt out of her, and her tears became saltless. One evening she fell asleep weeping, and dreamed of a landscape, half bathed in sunlight, with flowers and happy-looking people, and half steeped in mud, rain, and darkness. And in that mud she saw her son.*

" 'You see, Mother,' he said to her, 'over there they are walking in the smiles and joys of the living, and this mud, here where I am, that's from your tears. . . .'

"The mother—what else could she do—stopped crying for her son.

"A bit later, the son again appeared in her dream and showed her how his garden now basked in the sun but nothing grew in it, nothing could take seed as in the other, neighboring gardens. Yet everything was put in the world to give seed and produce, and if there were flowers and fruits in those other gardens, it was because there was life there, and its seed.

"The mother understood the story, remarried, and soon had a lovely

little boy, who smiled and gave seed to the first apple tree there in his brother's garden. . . .

"Now, this simple little story," concluded my unknown collocutor, "would not merit attention were it not for the possibility of translating it into another meaning. It shouldn't be taken literally. That other world and the gardens inhabited by her son, that is the world inhabited by our thoughts, memories, and feelings. It's perfectly clear, seeing how unearthly these things are and how strange to us ourselves, who are merely their anchor in this world. In the story her son is nothing other than her thoughts, her love or memory, for what else are our memories and loves but our children in some other world? All this, as I said, does and does not depend on us. We often have to smile here in order for the sun to shine there in our memories or loves, to impregnate a woman here to have an apple of knowledge take seed in our thoughts there; our tears on earth are sometimes the reason for the mud somewhere far away in our soul. . . . Maybe I can't even read all there is to be read from that little story, but . . ."

"But that's no reason not to have another drink," I said, steering the conversation in another direction. We clinked glasses and I turned for a moment to the others sitting with us, thinking: "This one has ears even on his ass; watch out for him!"

But the person I had turned to (one of our old classmates, otherwise a thief who would steal the chair from under you) came straight to the point and told me that Atanas Svilar (there it was finally, the name so neatly forgotten) had recently been received with a group of American businessmen by the president. Imagine, Atanas Svilar, the man who once didn't even have enough money to get married, let alone buy a newspaper, at the White Palace in Dedinye with the president of the Socialist Federal Republic of Yugoslavia!

"To me," he went on, taking care that our guest from America didn't hear him, "Atanas Svilar always looked like somebody who has the egg but not the yolk. But, as you can see for yourself, boy, were we wrong. Imagine, his last name wasn't even Svilar, he was called Atanas Fyodorovich Razin, no less! Like some Russian prince or cossack tsar, who drinks vodka holding the glass in his teeth instead of his hand. It was not for nothing that his mother addressed him with 'vous' from his earliest childhood! Anyway, the truth lies neither in the tare nor in the measure, but in the weights of the scale. Our Svilar's Russian surname stayed behind somewhere in Siberia, along with his father. His mother returned to Belgrade from Russia, and she rolled on a barrel, they say, so as not to give birth, but Atanas came into this world all the same. And so, instead of downing vodka, smashing his glass on his spurs, and his plate on the ceiling, he grew up, knowing nothing about his origins, as poor old Tasa Svilar with the blue eyes that gaze as though looking through ice. For instance, it never even occurred to him that the joke about the famous Moscow mathematician making the rounds of Belgrade, and perhaps even being told by Atanas himself, referred to his own father. And as for his father, Fyodor Alexeyevich Razin, in Russia, he left behind his sumptuous Moscow apartment, where it is always an autumn after-noon on a St. Petersburg Saturday, and the said

JOKE ABOUT FYODOR ALEXEYEVICH RAZIN

There was a prominent mathematician living in Moscow in Stalin's day. His name was Fyodor Alexeyevich Razin; once a handsome man and a good singer, now lost to song, he bore a mouthful of dry teeth and carried his smile, like a morsel of food, in the left side of his jaw.

As sometimes happens, the defeats of his enemies in the profession were exploited by others, and his own defeats were exploited by friends. At the university since way back, vigorous even with one foot in old age, he liked to say: "Every whippersnapper is fifty nowadays!" Totally bewildered by everyday matters, our Atanas Svilar's father did not live in this world and was so preoccupied with mathematical matters that in Moscow he became famous for his comparisons, such as: "Good wine must leave the tart taste of a mathematical error in one's mouth."

Well, one morning a total stranger called upon the said Fyodor Alexeyevich Razin in his office. In his hands he held a pack of cards depicting icons. He immediately started flipping the cards onto the table, and the first one was Saint Nicholas; then he turned over Saint Paraskeva (Petka), Saint Ilya the Thunderer, and he stopped at the Holy Dove. The caller, a young man, said almost incidentally, while looking at the cards, that the professor's great international reputation placed a responsibility upon everyone, including Fyodor Alexeyevich himself. He came straight out with the proposal that Razin join the Communist Party. He swept up all the cards from the table, except for Saint Nicholas, and, moving closer to Fyodor Alexeyevich, said in conclusion:

"Every story should be left to stand for a bit. If it rises overnight like bread dough, then it's good. Yours was left to stand and now it has to be baked. This would have an international impact as well. . . ."

The professor pleaded ignorance of such things; he said that he was already getting on in years, that all his time was taken up with projects at the institute; but it was no use. The visitor cleared his throat loudly, was about to spit in the middle of the room, changed his mind, swallowed it, yet could not resist rubbing the imaginary spit into the floor with his shoe.

"We will take that into consideration," he added. "We do not kill anybody's time. We have other things to kill."

He took Saint Nicholas and departed.

They made Fyodor Alexeyevich a member, and soon he was invited to his first meeting. The doorman at the university came to pick him up; a pint-sized man whose left eye always wept, he was the professor's age and, one might also say, friend. They entered a long hallway full of chairs and smoke so thick it could be combed. They sat down and the meeting opened. The professor, whose methodicalness and speed were proverbial, immediately started writing down every word. He eased his foot into his shoe by wriggling the toe, and took notes. He did the same thing again at the next two meetings, and at the third he took the floor. In the meantime, realizing what was now being expected of the organization he had recently joined, he worked out at home a system of measures that were imperative if the desired objective was to be achieved. As a mathematician, he knew that every day of beauty was paid for in life with a day of ugliness, and he converted all his conclusions into mathematical formulae, which, following the inexorable logic of numbers, imposed their own solutions.

On his way to the meeting, having gone hungry at work, he bought a piroshka, stuffed it in his pocket, and entered the familiar hallway. He sensed, of course, that the furnishings of the future had actually been moved from the cellar of the past: it was from there that the heavy loads of long-forgotten, shabby, rotting junk were brought into a new, still-unpossessed domicile. And, in his unspoiled language of numbers, he said as much at the meeting, stressing that what Comrade A of the Committee and Comrade B of the Auxiliary Services were asking for would result not (as they expected) in C, but in Y, and therefore, in order to obtain the desired C, it was essential and logical to change exactly what they ... Anyway, anyone who wanted to change the world had to be worse than that world, or else it was a lost cause. . . .

He was interrupted in mid-sentence by a timorous voice:

"Excuse me, Comrade Professor, but may I have a piece of your piroshka?" From the professor's pocket came the irresistible smell of the onion piroskha, and now somebody was after it.

Razin, somewhat flustered, took out the piroshka and offered it to the doorman (who had been the one to ask for it), but the spell had been broken. As the professor confusedly pieced together his closing words, a hand suddenly yanked him by the jacket and made him sit down. It was the doorman again.

"Have you got any money?" he whispered, once the professor had sat down next to him.

"I beg your pardon?"

"Have you got any money on you, Fyodor Alexeyevich?"

"A bit . . . Why?"

"Don't ask any questions. Here, take this, but so that nobody sees. . . . It's thirty rubles. Now, listen to me carefully. I'm telling you this for your own good. Don't go home from here. Don't go home at all. Ever again. Not for the life of you. Go straight to the Riga, or any other train station, and take the first train out. Any train. And don't get off until the last stop. The farther away, the better. Then get off.

And don't tell anybody who you are. After that, you're on your own. . . . The darkness will be your roof, and the wind your morning. Now go. . . ."

And Fyodor Alexeyevich, who knew little about the things of this world, put on his cotton-padded overcoat and obeyed his friend.

On the third day of his journey, famished by now, immersed in the morning landscape, which looked as though it had been painted with wine on the train window, he slipped his hand into his pocket and found the piroshka. The same one the doorman had asked for and had then inconspicuously put back in his pocket. Now he welcomed it as a bald man does a cap, but just as he took his first bite the train whistle blew, piercing the morsel in his mouth, and everybody got off. It was the last stop. "A Russian enjoys only the journey," thought Fyodor Alexeyevich uneasily, and he got off the train and plunged into the unending silence that had grown from Moscow with every verst they covered. He trudged through snow as deep as the silence and looked at the houses hanging from the motionless smoke attached to the invisible sky like bells to the bell tower. Marooned by the snow, a dog yelped hoarsely. He stood perched on a tree branch like a bird, because his chain was too short for him to make a bed in the snow.

Razin looked around. He did not know where to go or what to do. Everything was deep in snow, and in Russia in those days there were no inns in Moscow, let alone here, where all that was left of a man was his frostbitten ears. He noticed a shovel leaning next to a door and, without thinking, simply to warm himself up, grabbed it and started shoveling the snow.

Since it was getting colder and colder, so that one dared not lick one's lips because they would freeze solid, and since, on the other hand, Fyodor Alexeyevich was still strong and as systematic as ever, the progress he made could not have been better. Not only did he dig away the meter-and-a-half-high snowdrifts, clearing a path to the house from which he had started, but now he set off at a right angle, to clear the main road. While he worked, he decided that eternity and infinity were asymmetrical, and he amused himself by trying to check this idea mathematically. Then he cleared the snowdrift from a shop and in its display window noticed a barely legible advertisement. He blew on the glass and read:

Three-Dimensional Photographs
of the Soul
X-Rays of Dreams

Appointments made seven days in advance. Dress rehearsals. Also looking for the best X-rays of dreams in all formats, color and black-and-white. Successfully photographed memories, to be considered for airing on TV networks, paid extra. Magnetoscopic tapes of children's thoughts will be purchased at specially favorable prices and distributed to collectors and closed-circuit video systems.

Razin was stunned; he felt as though something had washed the eyebrows, mustache, and ears off his face; he wanted to put his hand on the door handle, but then he noticed that underneath the incredible advertisement someone had penciled in:

Shop, at the very least, closed.

Razin smiled with relief, but that let the cold deep into his mouth, and he quickly went back to work. By afternoon he had already reached the main square, and it was there that they discovered him.

The townspeople immediately realized that standing before them was the best snow-shoveler since snow had come to these parts, and they sent him straight to the local sanitation bureau. "A stranger appeared out of the desert," they said, "but he's good with a shovel." They gave him tea, sugar, and a spoon, although it had a hole in it and its handle was twisted, as if somebody had tried by brute force to wring something out of it, a tear, a drop of tea or butterfat. In short, he warmed himself by the stove, sipped his tea, and was flabbergasted. It was the famous white tea that used to be sold in tsarist Russia for ten silver rubles a pound; dogs given the tea became so rabid that they tore to pieces everything they could get hold of. But before he had time to wonder what this tea was doing here, with these people, he was back out in the snow, this time with a ragged group of municipal snow-shovelers. He listened to what the interrupted silence had to tell him and attacked the snow with still greater determination, realizing that, come evening, he would get a place to sleep with the others.

And so his new life began. He washed his socks with snow, drank tea of snow, and shoveled snow, and by the end of the winter he was proclaimed the best snow-shoveler in his shift. He woke up with impressions of his ear on the towel he used as a pillow, which was wet with tears and snot, and he shoveled the show with a vengeance. The next winter he was written up in the local papers, and two years later an item about his achievements appeared in the Moscow *Pravda*. He became the top snow-shoveler in the district, and one of the best in the entire country. Sometimes at night he dreamed about twelve ships bearing the names of the twelve apostles, or thirteen horsemen carrying the crucifix and baldachin, racing to catch up with the fourteenth horseman. When they caught him in the shadow of the baldachin, they stopped. "Who are you?" Christ's disciples, assembled around the crucifix, asked him from their saddles. "I am the fourteenth disciple," replied the stranger under the baldachin, and Razin woke up. His face was covered with some kind of sand; he rubbed it and decided that these were dried tears from his dreams. He had cried in his sleep for the son he had but had never seen. Dreams and tears were obviously still coming from his former life; they were late. He got up to start work with his shovel.

But that morning they would not let him. They detained him in the shack. A young man came to see him. The tips of his eyebrows and mustache were neatly tucked under the scarf wrapped around his head. His eyes settling upon Fyodor Alexeyevich's face like dust, the young man removed his one-fingered glove, and a burning cigarette appeared in his hand. He put the cigarette in his mouth, took out a knife sharpened for the lefthanded, and a piece of bacon; he cut off a slice with his left hand, offered it to Fyodor Alexeyevich, and came straight to the point. The reputation as champion worker enjoyed by Alexei Fyodorovich (that was how Razin had registered in his new domicile and how they addressed him) placed a responsibility upon everyone, including Alexei Fyodorovich himself. Therefore, he should join the Communist Party. Without delay. This would have a very good impact, not only on the town, but on a broader plane. . . .

Razin froze when he heard the proposal and his brain began working quickly, but he heard the wind cough at the window and, desisting from thought, said:

"But, my dear comrade, I'm illiterate; how can someone like me be in the Party?"

"Never mind, Alexei Fyodorovich, never mind. We have others like you. Natalia Filipovna Skargina shows them the letters of the alphabet very nicely; she runs the literacy course, and we shall send you there with the other illiterates, and when you have finished, you will start coming to meetings. Until then, we shall let you alone for about a month."

And so Fyodor Alexeyevich went to Natalia Filipovna. He found himself in a nice wooden building; in the hall he came upon a pile of shovels and twenty-four pairs of boots. He removed his own boots and entered an unbelievably low-ceilinged room, crammed with school benches. Sitting at them were the twenty-four students taking Natalia Filipovna's course; they were steaming with wetness, nibbling at their pencils and writing the letter *i,* dictated by Skargina herself; upward stroke thin, downward stroke thick. . . . The stove hopped in the corner, spilling the water that had been put on for tea; Natalia Filipovna sat behind her desk and said cheerfully to the new arrival, who grazed the nape of his neck against the ceiling:

"You're bowing your little head, bowing! So you should to the teacher. That's why the ceiling has always been hung low, as low as possible, to stop you from swaggering."

She seated Fyodor Alexeyevich, offered him tea, and in so doing Natalia Filipovna revealed that she was in fact standing behind her desk and was of such a height that when she stood up she looked as though she were sitting down. She turned to the blackboard, pulled a piece of chalk from her ear, and started the math class.

"One plus one," wrote Natalia Filipovna, as she spoke the words out loud, "one plus one is two! Both on Mondays and on Tuesdays, remember that. It was two yesterday and it will always and forever be two and only two."

It was warm in the room, the stove began to scuttle around as though let off a chain, and everybody repeated: One plus one is two. Fyodor Alexeyevich took a pencil to copy down what was written on the blackboard, and suddenly he could not stand it. Only now did he realize that ever since he had picked up the shovel to clear away the snow he had stopped sweating, and that what was left unwrung had to come out of him somewhere. And for the first time in all these years, he could not resist. He stood up purposefully, immediately banged his head against the ceiling, went to the blackboard, and, using his former self-confident voice to address Natalia Filipovna, who looked at him speechlessly, he said to the astonishment of all present:

"That, if I may say so, dear Natalia Filipovna, is nineteenth-century mathematics. Modern-day mathematics takes a different view. It knows that one plus one need not always be two. Give me the chalk for a second, and I'll prove it to you right here and now."

And with his innate speed, Fyodor Alexeyevich began writing numbers on the blackboard. Equation followed equation, silence descended in the room; after so many years, the professor was doing his work again, although, stooped over like that, his view of the numbers was not the best, the chalk scraped queerly somehow, and suddenly the result turned out completely different from what Fyodor Alexeyevich had expected: again it was $1 + 1 = 2$.

"Wait a minute!" Fyodor Alexeyevich cried out. "Something's wrong here, just a minute, we'll see where the mistake is in a second." And all the while his head was spinning with the inane thought: "All lost card games constitute a whole!" and it prevented him from calculating. Thoughts thundered in his head, and the thunder deafened all else. But his peerless skill helped him, he immediately knew where to look for the error, and his chalk flew across the lines of written numbers, their white powder already flaking.

And at that very moment, the entire class, all twenty-four of them, everybody except Natalia Filipovna Skargina, began whispering the solution to him in unison:

"Planck's constant! Planck's constant!"

Corporatiae illustrae

ABC ENGINEERING &
PHARMACEUTICALS
(Californiae)

FUNDATORI

ILLUSTRISSIMO
DOMINO

ARCHITECTAE ATHANASIO RAZIN

ob
decimum vitae lustrum
hic tomus
a sodalibus amicisque
in observandi signum

dedicatur

This Testimonial
is dedicated to

THE FOUNDER

of the
illustrious company of

ABC ENGINEERING &
PHARMACEUTICALS
(California)

the most illustrious
ARCHITECT ATANAS RAZIN
for his jubilee

as a token of
friendship and respect

1 DOWN

In preparing this Testimonial to our friend, schoolmate, and benefactor, architect Atanas Fyodorovich Razin, alias Atanas Svilar, who once inscribed his name with his tongue on the backs of the most beautiful women of our generation, and who has now inscribed it in gold letters in the illustrious annals of the deal of the century, who has become a great businessman, whose night carries ten days, the editors bore in mind the fact that we shall never learn the full truth about his life and work. Because, as Razin himself says, the truth cannot suffer a change of continents, and our equations always trail behind their accuracy. The Greek "no" does not mean the same as the Jewish "no."

It should immediately be said that here we shall not dwell on the professional activities of our Atanas Fyodorovich Razin, architect and founder of ABC Engineering & Pharmaceuticals—California. Suffice it to say that his dreams are faster than those of other people, that he dreams more swiftly than a horse, and that his telephones neigh like a stable full of stallions, reporting on these dreams. For those interested in this aspect of architect Razin's life, we recommend sources that are incomparably more qualified and more complete than a testimonial like this can be, though it comes from the heart and is for someone who, as they say, has the band playing as soon as he starts his morning ablutions. Ample information about his work and the work of his company is provided by the monograph *ABC Engineering & Pharmaceuticals* (Ohio, 1981) and by an hourlong documentary film called *Colors in the World Without,* made in California in 1980.

Just how and when architect Razin acquired a fortune big enough to support generations, he alone knows. The story among his school friends here is that the first time he went abroad he bought a chair. An ordinary chair made of iron and wood. It was a chair in a Viennese or Swiss park, one of those you rent for two cents an hour to sit under the cool shade of the chestnut tree. He bought a chair like that, chained to a tree; he bought it not for a day or two, but for always. Then, in a bookshop in Boulevard Saint-Germain in Paris, or somewhere in Zurich, where he liked to stop and chat with the bookseller while leafing through the books, he asked if he could buy one of the chairs that were there for the convenience of the customers. He immediately mollified the shopkeeper by saying that, in his absence, he had nothing against the chair's being used by whoever came by, but when he himself visited he wanted to be sure he had his own chair in the bookstore. And he did. Then he bought a wicker chair in the café of the Graben Hotel in Vienna, and he developed an appetite for chairs. All night he would nervously comb his beard, and, come day, he would buy chairs everywhere—he took seats in movie theaters in Paris, bought a seat in the Stockholm–Munich train, acquired stone benches in cemeteries from Campo Santo di Genova to Mexico. Then, in London, he bought two second-row armchairs at Covent Garden and two pews in St. Paul's Cathedral, he bought a plush velvet bench at the Louvre, a permanent seat on the Paris–New York plane, a folding deck chair on the ship sailing between Alexandria and Haifa, and finally, after all that, architect Razin bought, for a fabulous sum, a seat in the Italian Parliament, without the slightest desire to sit or, God forbid, vote in it. He bought it only to be able to include such an item in the printed catalogue of seats, armchairs, benches, and chairs in the possession of architect Razin, covering a wide area, from the temples of Burma to the Church of St. Peter in Rome. On each of his chairs, which he scarcely ever used, he put a metal plate bearing his name and surname. The story does not say how these purchases brought architect Razin fame and wealth. It merely says he worked so hard that at lunch his glasses would often slide into his spinach and mutton, as he planned his next move. This unknown side of architect Razin and his affairs shall not, therefore, be discussed here.

Here, in this Testimonial, the focus is on the origin, life, and character of architect Razin, a man who differentiated between the Mediterranean and the Chinese type of sleep, an architect, as we said, who once declared that the difference between the Serbian and the Croatian languages was that they were one and the same language but Serbian was retouched in Doric style and Croatian in the style of the floral Gothic; and, last but not least, we shall discuss the businessman who, like dice, always had six different moves open to him. We shall also dwell upon the fate of his parents: his father, a Moscow mathematician of considerable repute, and his mother, Anna, née Nikolich, married name Razin, remarried as Svilar, who taught her son that life is not a remedy against death as death is a remedy against life. This Testimonial shall also pay due attention to the beloved wife of architect Razin, Vitacha Milut Petka, married name Pohvalich, remarried as Razin, whose strange voice echoed on three continents and whose eyelashes, which looked as though they had been dusted with ashes, we never forgot. Her smile, piercing the cheeks, followed architect Razin in those initial days when luck still smiled upon him through closed doors.

Because, even when he had already made it, architect Razin still experienced something like the resistance of matter, the inertia of fate, or the overheating of time. He himself says that, during his first days out in the big world, doorbells did not ring at his touch, his shirts no longer got soiled but became terribly wrinkled, he was strong, he could snap open his belt with his stomach, but birds bleated at him like goats, and the ink would not flow from the pen when he had to sign contracts that were already reaching astronomical figures. It was then that he realized that man does not age uniformly with the clock, that sometimes he ages more in three days than in a year. Everything around him behaved as before, his pipes would not draw, the sky sailed overhead, freckled with birds, like trout, the bed beneath him overturned like a canoe sinking him into sleep, and he, as is the way of all unhappy people, continued to wish his friends a Happy New Year at the end of the old, so that luck would not turn its back on them as it had on him, while his own temple of business had already been built, too tall and strange, the navel and key of a whole universe, the hereditary boar with herbs growing on its back; he was already winning the race, while time around him stood still, just as imperial time is sometimes wont to stop in the mist. And only Vitacha and money wanted him.

But they wanted him as nobody had been wanted since Christ was lifted with the cross on which they had nailed him.

And then slowly, in the wake of Madame Vitacha and the money, came the rest, including the many friends and colleagues whose hands have filled these pages with the story's children, because, as we said, the story remains impenetrable.

Moreover, special attention here, as is only fitting, shall be devoted to those regrettably few pages written about himself by the man we are honoring, our friend architect Atanas Razin. These pages were written with cramped fingers (as though architect Razin had wanted to bless the paper, not write on it) and usually inserted in architect Razin's notebooks, famous for the beautiful pictures he put on their covers. In these favorite large-sized books of his, he for years jotted down notes and other things of revelance to his private, not his professional life, from crossword puzzles clipped out of various European and American papers to architectural plans, which we shall return to later.

But very little remains of what Atanas Fyodorovich wrote himself, and it is all included in this Testimonial. For one, there are the written reminiscences of Razin's first meeting at the Belgrade Opera with the future Mrs. Razin, then the still-young Vitacha Milut, who at the time spoke word by word, stopping as though plucking her eyebrows. Second, there is the mysterious text about three sisters, Olga, Azra, and Cecilia, copied in architect Razin's own hand but not written by him, as becomes immediately evident from the very first lines. It was written by an unidentified person, ostensibly from a story told by Atanas Fyodorovich himself, when he was already the director of ABC Engineering & Pharmaceuticals. Although this false confession is not in the least credible, there are two reasons, each of them sufficient in itself, why we have included it for the reader's inspection. First, all three texts were inscribed in the notebooks by architect Razin himself. Second, we do not and never shall have sufficient information about how architect Razin achieved his dizzying climb to success, and these texts about the three sisters are a welcome addition to fill the gap.

Those who remember how our Atanas used to like Lika cheese soup and how he wrote those "verses read on the running board of the tram before jumping off at Teraziye" can never imagine the extraordinary road Atanas Razin traveled from Belgrade's prewar movie theaters, where along with the sepia film reels they served a barbecue, beer, and onion-dyed eggs, to the position of a man who owns 2 percent of the world's income from the sale of nuclear equipment for peacetime purposes.

Part of this mystery can, perhaps, be deciphered from the family photographs of architect Razin and Vitacha Milut, but illustrations have been omitted at the express wish of architect Razin himself, although they had already been collected and prepared for publication in this Testimonial. Instead, architect Razin's office very kindly placed at the disposal of the editors some other family documents, and copies of three letters, sent by the anonymous informant of one unidentified Don Donino Azeredo to the latter. These letters pertain directly to the life of Mr. Razin and Madame Vitacha. Finally, this Testimonial includes the reminiscences of Mrs. Svilar, the mother of our friend and benefactor, compiled at the request of a journalist, but it is uncertain whether these pages of Mrs. Svilar's reminiscences were ever published.

Let us just add that in Vienna, where he found himself at the beginning of his new path as an architect of advanced age, Atanas Razin immediately did three things: he discarded and forgot his old surname, Svilar, the name under which we had known him at school, under which he had graduated from the School of Architecture in Belgrade and under which he had married the first time. Second, he reverted from night to day and for the first time in his life began working during the daytime instead of at night, as he used to. And third, he set himself a task: Imagine that you like everything you don't like! And then, as he himself says, he switched over to the side of his enemies, and that immediately turned the trick.

In Vienna, during those first days of his life abroad, architect Razin called on another prominent figure from our circle, and his rise in business seems to have started with that meeting. The man was architect Obren Opsenitsa, known as "the gentleman who dreams of scents." Opsenitsa has an apartment in Vienna's Ring near the Burg-theater; lynx-hide bellows to fan the fire lie under his feet like a live animal; he has hair the color of glass, curled at the tips like fishhooks, and a face as inexpressive as cow dung. In actual fact, however, he is a shrewd man, who can replace cherry pits with the tongue in his mouth. He eats with a knife, omits the fork, wears a double-knotted tie, and received his guest with exceptional solicitude.

The two of them smiled, Opsenitsa's smile closing both of his eyes, and sat down. Opsenitsa planted crystal and colored glasses, often half-empty, all over his rooms, and he had the habit of licking his nails. He immediately told his caller that he was prepared to invest in the building designs that architect Svilar (by now Razin) had drafted in his youth in their native land, and which they had been unable to realize there, although it was not for want of trying. . . .

"I've come for your money, not your advice," Razin replied, "and as for your proposal, the finest examples of architecture that I know are a toilet in France, a jail in Spain, and a cemetery in Italy. So why be an architect?"

And then architect Razin whispered something to Obren Opsenitsa. The latter licked his nails, tapped his cane against the tip of Razin's shoes, and gave the money. Out of that renewed friendship, that cash and that collaboration, slowly grew architect Razin's grand California company, ABC Engineering & Pharmaceuticals.

5 DOWN

I remember in my youth, when my last name was not yet Razin as it is now, and when I didn't know who I was, when I was still poor and washed with my cap on, winding up at a party one evening. I was standing alone, off to the side, ashamed of my suit and my age, when the hostess came up to me and sat me down on one of those old-fashioned divans that keep marching around the room on their six legs. I felt as if I were sitting in a saddle, and the girl seated next to me stared at me with eyes that were at first warm but, as they rested on me, slowly turned cold, as though I were ice. When they were quite frosty, she said she would like to tell me a story that had happened to her and her sister. And she did.

"In the autumn of 1949, my sister and I decided to go to the opera. Those who were young then remember that when the weather was nice one would nip out coatless in between acts to stroll around the square and then go back into the warm theater for the rest of the performance. That was popular at the time, and the doorman would let you back in with the stub of your ticket. That evening, they were giving *La Bohème*; we had three tickets, for the two of us and for a distant relative who had been foisted upon us by our mother, but we didn't know him and had never laid eyes on him before.

" 'Who knows what wind his mind works on?' my sister commented as we were leaving for the opera. But he didn't show up, for reasons better known to him than us, and the two of us wound up with an extra ticket. In those days, tickets for the opera and theater were in great demand, even though they were very inexpensive. It was a pleasant evening, but it was quickly getting cold, like dinner. In front of the theater a swank crowd of young people pressed together against the wind full of leaves, spotted like a Dalmatian. We noticed a young man in the crowd, drinking beer out of a bottle, leaning against the billboard. We somehow took pity on him and offered him the extra ticket.

" 'Orchestra, second row,' my sister said to him.

"He thought we wanted to charge him for the ticket, and since he assumed that a seat like that would be expensive, he retorted:

" 'Forget it, I can come just as well standing.'

"My sister turned away, but I convinced him that the ticket was free. He put down his unfinished bottle of beer and took the ticket from my sister, and we went in.

"His eyebrows and mustache glistened as though they had been licked wet. He was pleasant, heavily perfumed, and could merge his otherwise handsome nose with his chin, just as breakfast sometimes merges with lunch. He told us he didn't like the theater and the theater didn't like him. He said that to him opera was like stirring the fire with trumpets, flutes, and tin music, like blowing the most beautiful songs into it with the help of divine voices, whereas the fire, like any fire, can be fed with mere animal droppings.

"When the performance began, in the middle of *La Bohème,* he began—softly, correctly, and very prettily—to whistle arias from *Tosca.* After the first act, when we went out for a stroll in front of the theater, we saw him drinking beer again from his bottle. But he did not appear at the beginning of the second act. Seated next to us now was an old lady with quail eggs on her chignon, as had probably been the fashion in her day. The young man had made a good bargain. He had obtained a ticket, seen the first act without paying a cent, then sold the unused two-thirds of the ticket to the old lady and taken off for a beer with the money in his pocket. That's what we thought, but we thought wrong. At the third act, next to us appeared a little girl, about ten years old, with missing teeth and a bandaged hand. She had brought a book to the opera and was leafing through it in the semi-dark, barely glancing at the stage. After the performance, a man and a very well-groomed woman waited for her outside. So the young man had sold the third act as well, and as we came out we saw him guzzling down a fresh bottle of beer, bought with the money from our ticket. . . ."

"That's a marvelous story," I commented to the unknown woman. "Thank you for telling it to me."

"Thank you for the story's happening," she replied cryptically.

"I don't understand," I said.

"Didn't you recognize the story?" she then asked.

"No," I said hesitantly, and my memory rapidly started stretching like ears in school, but to no avail.

"The young man who sold that ticket all those years ago was you."

"Me?" I said, astounded. And the astonishment came from not being able to remember anything of the sort, yet I knew, of course I knew, that the damn story had not been invented and that the unknown girl was speaking the truth. All the same, I asked:

"How can you be so sure? Maybe you've confused me with someone else?"

"If I have, my sister, who gave you the ticket, hasn't."

"And where is your sister now?" I asked stupidly, just to say something.

"She's right there, sitting on your other side. In fact, we're sitting exactly as we were that time at the opera. . . ."

And then I turned to look at the other girl. She had a Greek profile, which somehow reminded me of Pushkin's drawings of Amalia Riznich in his manuscript of *Eugene Onegin*. The living image of Mrs. Riznich, I thought. She was pretty, dark, her lips could give the kind of kiss that is called "two ripe cherries, and a sweet caterpillar in between." She bathed serenely in my eyes, as the six-legged sofa carried us somewhere through the warmth and smoke. I was sure

I had never laid eyes on her before, but at the bottom of my soul I sensed that she knew me. Because that's how it is with bad impressions. If ever you leave a bad impression on someone, you'll never recognize him again, and you'll forget the whole thing with the speed of a thief.

"You saw me, my pigeon," the other girl said. "Oh, yes, you saw me, a long way back. And once even before the opera. I was seven at the time and I was carrying a doll."

"And what happened?"

"You asked me, my pigeon: Is it hard to have a baby at the age of seven?"

"Well, what can you do," I said, hedging in front of this other girl. "A man is like an onion. Under one skin you always find another; you keep peeling, expecting God knows what, and when you come to the end, you find nothing at the core. Absolutely nothing."

The girl observed me fixedly with those green eyes of hers that swim in the rain, and said in a deep throaty voice:

"Nothing? Nothing, you say! Rubbish! And tears? What about tears? You've forgotten tears, my fine fellow."

I knew then that I had to do something to extricate myself. No quotes from Freud could save me anymore. And I took a sure-fire step which brought the whole thing to an end.

"And that relative, or whatever he was of yours, who didn't come to the opera, whose mind works on the wind," I asked as if casually, "why didn't he show up?"

"He did show up," the green-eyed girl replied. "Oh, yes, he showed up all right."

"And what happened to him?"

"What do you mean, what happened? Why, that, of course, was you again. You are Atanas Svilar, aren't you? Only, at the time, the two of us couldn't know that. And you didn't know that it was the two of us, your relatives Vida and Vitacha Milut. You just happened to run into us in that crowd."

"And how is your good mother now?" I switched the conversation to family.

"We haven't had a mother for a long time. We didn't have her even that time at the opera. We invented her to improve on the story. And you're not a relative at all. . . ."

Thanks to the fact that I wasn't their relative, I became their husband. Both of theirs, in a way.

3 DOWN

Exactly how many such notebooks may have been in the possession of architect Atanas Razin is not known. Only three have reached us, but there were certainly more. Because, just as some people cannot be held down in one place, so architect Razin could not always be held down by one time, and at such moments he devoted himself to his notebooks. On the covers of each, architect Razin drew a landscape, and at first glance these drawings looked like watercolors, but a more careful observer would quickly realize that that is not what they were. They were drawn on the covers of very large notebooks, so that, if necessary, Mr. Razin could also include in them architectural drawings or facts about the various buildings that caught his eye. But these notebooks contained many other things as well.

For instance, on the back cover of one of these notebooks was the following list of names:

The Batashov brothers, Shemarin, Malikov, Taile, Vanyikin, and Lomov.

Judging by the first surname, the surname of the brothers Ivan, Vassily, and Alexander Batashov, these were the names of the most famous makers of samovars in Tula and elsewhere in Russia. Underneath this list was a note about the manufacture of "travel samovars" and how to adjust the special "language of samovars" which is mentioned in the works of writers such as Vyazemsky and Saltikov-Shchedrin.

On the following page were excerpts from books on tea. There were quotes from Chinese and Japanese handbooks and literature, from Gogol, Dostoyevsky, and others. The quote from Pushkin, for example, reads:

> At dusk the samovar is gleaming
> Upon the table, piping hot;
> And as it hisses, gently steaming,
> The vapor wreathes the china pot. . . .

Beneath these lines was a text believed by architect Razin to have been composed by the Buddhist monk Dharumu, the same monk whose eyelashes sprouted the first leaf of tea:

"Our days are formed so that our first day, like the egg from which the chick will hatch, carries and nourishes and finally brings into the world the thirtieth day of our life. The second day of that life conceives and carries the next, thirty-first day, and so on, until a dead chick is hatched from an egg.

"In the same way that tea is the thought of the bowl from which it is drunk, so our thirtieth day is the thought of our first day, from which it is born. . . ."

On pages four and five, architect Razin gave the first of the stories about the three sisters, the one about Olga, followed by several crosswords from the French press.

Although we know the detailed contents of three of them, the purpose of these notebooks is not quite clear. Razin himself told us jokingly that they are a mixture of his epic and his lyric hatreds and that he filled them in the shallow stillness of evening, dragging his New York shadow behind him, or in the barren mornings, when he would awaken from the chill in his mouth, holding last night's smile in his teeth like a captured prey.

Yet all the notebooks can be said to have one thing in common. In them architect Razin recorded, with immense and obvious interest, details about the dwellings, residences, houses, and summer homes that had been lived and worked in or occasionally visited by Marshal Josip Broz Tito, the president of the Socialist Federal Republic of Yugoslavia, the long-standing general secretary of the Communist Party of Yugoslavia, and a member of the Communist International, as architect Razin wrote in one of his notebooks. Plans of these buildings, their access roads, layout, and furnishings fill the better part of the notebooks. They show how, despite his many long years of exhausting work at ABC Engineering & Pharmaceuticals, architect Razin still dreamed of his first profession as an architect, which had been overshadowed for decades by his business success.

The cover of the first of these notebooks, if the first it was, already attested to this particular field of architect Razin's interest. It depicted a landscape overlooking a river, with a large building perched in the greenery, atop a knoll, and off in the distance by the church one could see, like a herd grazing, the white crosses of a cemetery. The picture created an unexpected effect, as though you were looking at a painting done with or seen through tears. In it, the light and shadows behaved as though they had a sex, as though they were of the masculine gender one minute, and the feminine the next. . . .

And so now we come to the key point of this Testimonial. Under the picture, architect Razin had written "Camelia sinensis." This was a landscape painted with tea. It is interesting to remember that it was painted by architect Razin, a man who knew about paints, their history and technology, perhaps better than anybody alive, because his company had actually started out by producing chemicals and paints before it expanded into other areas. And now he had completely discarded paints, at least in the conventional sense of the word. Here architect Razin had obviously used a brush of porcupine quills; he did the river by dipping his brush in "tropanas"—a dark fruit tea— mixing it with "sweet orange," light pink in color, and the bright-red hibiscus. The vineyards were depicted in the dark colors of the purple "hyssop" mixed with camomile, producing what is called "afternoon green." The sky was painted with a brush made of calf's ear, with very weak souchong tea, picked in May, and rapidly roasted green tea. For the building, architect Razin had used lotus tea, and the shore he painted with Russian tea, which used to be served with salted butter, and with Chinese tea picked at an altitude of two thousand meters above sea level. The stone was done in what is known as the "champagne of teas," the famous Darjeeling. In the lower righthand corner was the inscription:

"PLAVINATS," J. B. TITO'S SUMMER HOUSE ON THE DANUBE BY SMEDEREVO, EAST OF BELGRADE

Thereupon followed copies of several detailed architectural plans dating from different periods. Sketched in architect Razin's own hand, drawn hurriedly and obviously on the spot, was the ground plan of the summer house, a classicist building. Appended was a beautifully produced 1897 plan of the same building, but slightly extended, certified with the seal of the Serbian Obrenovich court, and signed by architect Yovan Ilkich, and finally there was a plan marked "Annex to Plavinats," bearing the signature of architect Bogdan Bogdanovich.

The ensuing pages gave a detailed history of the Plavinats summer house. Here architect Razin noted that the building on the Plavinats hill overlooking the Danube, several kilometers before Smederevo when traveling from Belgrade, was built by order of Prince Milosh Obrenovich in 1831, as the summer residence of Serbia's ruling Obrenovich family. The building was surrounded by vineyards and an estate nearly five hectares in size. Initially, it had only lodgings and a cellar, then it was extended on the basis of plans drawn up for Queen Natalia Obrenovich. Architect Razin goes on to say that in 1903, after the assassination of King Alexander Obrenovich of Serbia, the Queen Mother Natalia presented the summer house and its property to Colonel Anthony Oreshkovich, and that around 1960 (between 1958 and 1961), pending the first conference of nonaligned countries in Belgrade, the residence was restored for Marshal Josip Broz Tito, using Bogdan Bogdanovich's architectural, structural, and extension plans. The residence was furnished with period pieces, bought off of old Belgrade families; brought or restored there were antique mirrors, chandeliers, lamps, clocks (floor, table, and mantelpiece clocks), candelabras, glassware, porcelain, pottery, precious metals, carpets, paintings, etchings, maps. . . .

There were also architect Razin's structural drawings and preliminary estimates, and a catalogue of ornamental articles, paintings, and housewares—obviously the present-day inventory of the Plavinats manor. Surprising is not only the detail of these descriptions and inventory of articles and their origin, but also the listing of the exact whereabouts of every item at Plavinats.

The remainder of the notebook was empty, until just before the end. There, on the inside of the back cover, working his way from back to front, architect Razin started writing down the story of the famous beauties in his wife's family. And so we come to the history of the heroine of this book, Vitacha Milut, who became famous under another name. As Razin himself observes, in writing these lines he used as a blotter his beard streaked with last week's sweat, tears, and snot. The story tells about the beautiful ancestors of Vitacha Milut, later to become Mrs. Razin, about the men they loved, about the Countesses Rzewuska and Amalia Riznich the younger, and it was passed on to Razin by Vitacha's grandmother. Since this family tradition (which explains some of the strange predilections of Vitacha Milut, the heroine of this book) is given separately, there shall be no further mention of it here, except to say that it begins with the well-known saying in the Milut family:

"October has never come as often as this year. . . ."

■ DOWN

"October has never come as often as this year; every time you turn around, there it is again. At least three times ahead of schedule . . ."

Thus whispered Miss Amalia Riznich in German into her Sèvres cup. For the past one hundred years, her family had spoken German in autumn, Polish or Russian in winter, Greek in spring, and Serbian only in summer, as befits a family of grain merchants. All past and future seasons thus blended in her consciousness into a single eternal season, resembling itself as hunger does hunger. Spring merged with spring, Russian with Russian, winter with winter, and only summer, which was enclosing Miss Riznich now, broke step with this sequence to take for a moment, but only a moment, its temporary calendar place between spring and autumn, between Greek and German.

Miss Amalia Riznich was the second in her family to carry this name and surname, and through her grandmother she traced her roots to the Counts Rzewusky. The Rzewuskys in eighteenth-century Poland produced writers and statesmen, and in the nineteenth century were already known for their beautiful and famous women, whose hair and dresses still grace museums.* The first, eldest Rzewuska, Evelina, married one Hansky, and her second marriage was to Honoré de Balzac, the French writer.† The second Countess Rzewuska, the sister of Hanska-Balzac, was called Carolina, and at a very young age she married into the Sobansky family, but that marriage did not last. While visiting her younger sister, the third Countess Rzewuska, in Odessa and the Crimea in 1825, she met the poet Mickiewicz, who dedicated his most beautiful love sonnets to her. They were still among the family papers at the time of Amalia's mother, and when Amalia started binding her menu collections she included one of the poems Mickiewicz had written to her grandmother, because on the other side of that sheet of paper was a list of the foods served at a luncheon in 1857. The third Countess Rzewuska (Amalia's real grandmother), Paulina, at whose house the poet and Sobanska had met, was the second wife of the Serbian shipowner Yovan Riznich. He, in turn, was one of the wealthy Gulf of Kotor Rizniches, who at the end of the eighteenth century began to expand their trading network to the north and east, to buy estates in Bachka and reside in Vienna. One of the Rizniches in whose house drinks were imbibed before sunset only with one's eyes closed, one of those whose handsome ancestor had received a ducat from his mistress for every smile. At the dawn of the nineteenth century, one generation of Rizniches moved from Vienna to Trieste to oversee the family's expanding fleet. Thus, at the beginning of the nineteenth century, Yovan's grandfather was still in Vienna or on his estates in Bachka, while Yovan's father, Stevan, had already bought the gold-embroidered banner of Saint Spiridon for the Serbian church community in Trieste and was comfortably settled on the waterfront of Trieste with a fleet of fifty flags, and as many hearths to call his own.

"Your Imperial Highness, may I present a poor man who has only fifty houses in this city," said the governor of Trieste in 1807 to the

* Simeon Pishchevich, the Serbian writer and general of Catherine the Great, arrested the Counts Rzewusky, father and son, in Warsaw in 1767, and had them imprisoned for opposing the annexation, of which Pishchevich himself disapproved.
† See Balzac's published correspondence with the Countesses Rzewuska (Paris, 1969).

Hapsburg Grand Duke Ludwig, leading Stevan Riznich up to meet him.

From Vienna, Stevan Riznich also brought to Trieste that famous "double-tariff" smile of Grandfather Riznich's, which was subsequently passed on from one generation to the next and learned by all the men in the family, if it was not bequeathed by natural means. In the Riznich family, this more-than-century-old smile was jokingly called "carafindl," the word used for the vinegar-and-oil cruets on the table.

With this smile on their lips, like the trademark of their company, the Trieste Rizniches engaged the writer Dositei Obradovich (1740–1811) as a tutor for their heir, Yovan, and began to subscribe the boy to books, dictionaries, and calendars, and then sent him to study in Padua and Vienna, where he met the girl who was to become his first wife. At the time, the Rizniches had already started transporting grain from Bachka to all parts of the world, and especially to Odessa. Austrian informants, who sat in Venetian theaters watching who clapped when and who laughed at what, knew that the Rizniches used the money they earned from their deals for supplying the southern Russian army, to support the 1804 Serbian revolution. Business with the Russian army expanded, and the young Yovan Riznich was soon appointed to set up and consolidate a branch office of the Riznich trade network in the port of Odessa, where their ships docked, and where, when it rained, the only way to cross the street was on stilts— that's how much mud there was before Odessa was paved with its resonant flagstones.

In 1819, Riznich had his ship set sail with an entire Italian opera troupe on board, with basses who vomited in a tenor voice on the open seas, with tenors who temporarily lost their voice and wanted the ship to turn back, with sopranos who in fear momentarily stopped imitating Angelica Catalani, and with a conductor who sobered up along with the chorus only when they reached Odessa. To amuse his beautiful but ailing wife, Amalia (the first Amalia Riznich), Yovan founded Odessa's first opera house, which mostly performed Rossini, and the young of Odessa started coming to Mrs. Riznich's loge to sip champagne.

This beautiful Tsintsar woman was famous for her grandfather Count Christofor Nako, who strung up peasants by their mustaches, had estates in the onetime Avar capital in Banat, and wherever he struck his pickax came up with a golden cup from the "Attila treasury." Two dozen pitchers, bowls, and goblets of pure gold were discovered while putting up fences around one of his vineyards. We know what Amalia Nako, married name Riznich, to whom these cups belonged, looked like from a drawing done by the Russian poet Alexander Pushkin, because he, too, visited her loge in Odessa, and celebrated it in *Eugene Onegin*.* Wearing his ring on his thumb, the poet later wrote other verses in Odessa to "Mrs. Riznich," which are included in all anthologies of his love poems, and on her death he wrote a poem that speaks of the olive tree's shadow sleeping on the waters. After Amalia's death, Yovan Riznich consoled himself by taking another wife, this time the youngest of the said Countesses Rzewuska, Paulina.

Riznich's granddaughter from that second marriage, Amalia, inherited the name of her half-grandmother, Amalia, née Nako, the Riznich family estate in Bachka, and the beauty of her real grandmother, Countess Paulina Rzewuska. She lived mostly in Vienna and Paris, carried a lorgnette made of perfumed glass, made the sign of the cross over plates of uneaten food not to offend it, and kissed dropped spoons. She played the flute, and her flute was thought to be made of a wood that slows down the transmission of sound. It was jokingly whispered: You blow on Thursday, and you don't get the music until Friday, after lunch. . . .

"Foods are my only friends," Miss Riznich opined, usually to her lady companions, and, indeed, her enormous Vienna library was entirely devoted to the alchemy of tastes and smells. It was stacked to the ceiling with history books on the culinary arts, essays about food-related religious bans, about the Pythagoreans' nonuse of beans, about

* Pushkin's drawing of Amalia Riznich can be seen in the museum of the former lycée Tsarskoye Selo, now Pushkino, near Leningrad. It was done on the manuscript of the novel in verse *Eugene Onegin*.

Christian fasts, about the Islamic ban on pork and alcohol; it was full of treatises on culinary symbolics, handbooks on winegrowing, guidebooks for feeding fish, manuals on animal reproduction, herbaria of nutritional plants, and, holding pride of place in this library, essays on the diet of mythological animals, on the eating of pearls and other precious gems in antiquity, and a handwritten dictionary of ritual sacrifices carried in the form of food. During the Serbian-Turkish war, bookshops and newspaper offices in Pest (where her parents lived) set aside for her all engravings showing supply wagons on the battlefront, because Miss Riznich maintained, at her own expense, several field kitchens, and in these kitchens there on the front, food for the Serbian and Russian soldiers was prepared according to a menu she put together herself. In devoting herself to the ninth art, the one that requires the practiced hand of a violinist and the memory of an alchemist, Miss Amalia soon came to the conclusion that, some time around the first century B.C., the intermingling of religions (both those on the decline and new ones then on the ascent, like Christianity) led to the free meshing of the various culinary traditions of the Mediterranean, and that in this basin, as in a kettle, was prepared the best cuisine of Europe, which we still enjoy today. Convinced that this tradition was slowly dying out, Amalia tirelessly visited the famous restaurants of Venice, Paris, London, Berlin, Athens, and Odessa.

Despite her gastronomic inclinations, Miss Amalia never lost her slim figure, which followed her through illness into old age, so that when she was seventy she sometimes put on her wedding gown and the dress fitted her as perfectly as that first and only time.

"She could go straight to the altar," sighed the women around her, and she smiled and lamented:

"Everyone I hate has long since died. I have no one anymore. . . ."

She could have said the same thing at the beginning of her youth as now, at the end of her long life: that she had no one. She had traveled alone for a long time, with her bewitching eyes which, wherever they glanced, found a dropped coin, sometimes a silver Roman sesterce, most often a worthless filler. They stuck to her gaze and played in the dust like shiny stains. In expensive restaurants she would absently lower her head to the spoon instead of raising the spoon to her mouth, her glass hairpins would tinkle as she chewed, and she knew that some foods and some wines she was tasting for the last time, because food and wine, like human beings, die. And every year for Christmas she would have bound in a book all of the preceding year's menus and the labels from the bottles that had been drunk at these meals.

It was on these travels that she met engineer Pfister, who at the time was trying to assemble an airship that was later to finish ignominiously under the name of *Count Zeppelin.*

As soon as she saw him, Miss Riznich thought:

"Beauty is a disease! A handsome man is not made for just one woman. . . ." And she asked him whether he knew how to swear in Serbian, to which he said like a shot,

"I fuck your mother!"

"And why shouldn't you? What's wrong with her?" she replied calmly, staring deep into the golden ring on his left ear, which signified that Pfister was an only child.

A famous good-looker, Pfister, as is known, sported only half a mustache, a coat bedecked with fashionable Parisian buttons, and silver gloves. He also wore two watches, like twins. One was gold (showing the days, weeks, and years) and the other sterling silver (showing the quarters of the moon). His gold watch (made at the same time as the silver) was known to have two diamond axles, and was virtually perennial. The other, silver watch had ordinary axles, and its days were numbered. Pfister used both watches and had one of the two diamond axles transplanted from the gold watch to the silver watch. That way the life span of both watches was the same. When she saw the watches and asked what purpose they served, Pfister told Miss Amalia without thinking:

"This silver watch measures your time, and this gold one mine. I wear them together, so that I can always know what time you have."

The next day he sent her *The Dictionary of Smiles* as a present, a book that was in vogue at the time, and together they began to tour restaurants all over the world. There he was as famous as she.

One evening they suddenly got married during a storm, had the piano brought out onto the terrace in the rain, and during the wedding feast listened to the rain beat down on the piano keys. And they danced to that music. On Sundays, Amalia always drank only her own wine. Wine from the Riznich estates in Bachka, which her servants carried into the restaurants in straw baskets. Now they drank that wine together. They would eat fish in aspic or sauerkraut with walnuts, and then sit in silence; she would watch him, and he would read and flip through his book as quickly as counting money, and then she would suddenly exclaim defiantly, as though in response to that silence or that reading:

"Well, it isn't true!"

"In sleep one doesn't age," claimed engineer Pfister, and he slept with his young wife sixteen hours a day. She adored him, nibbled the ivory rings on his fingers, and lit her long black cigarettes on his pipes. She washed these porcelain and meerschaum pipes in cognac, and every so often had a mad desire to light one of them herself. Noticing this, Pfister said:

"What in October seems to us like March is really January."

She did not understand him then, but a few months later she realized she was pregnant.

A few words should be said here about Alexander Pfister, who was to be the issue of this marriage. He was anxiously awaited by the Riznich family as their sole heir. But he did not appear. Everybody in the one family and the other was waiting for Alexander, but Ana, the daughter of Amalia's sister, came into the world in his stead; then in his stead came Ana's sister, Milena, and Alexander came only in the end. His name had been there five years before him, and three years before Amalia met Pfister, so it was always older than the boy. He was talked about years before his birth, secret prayers were held for him in the churches of Vienna and Pest; the vocation of the future family heir had been decided in advance, as had the school he would attend, the private tutor he would have, a Frenchman with two tiers of mustaches; a sailor suit had been made for his Sunday outings, and gold spoons had been bought for him, as though he had already taken the place waiting for him at the Riznich table in Pest, or at the other, Pfister table in Vienna.

One spring morning, just when the Rizniches were switching from Russian to Greek, into the world came little Alexander Pfister, a handsome strapping baby boy. He immediately cried out at the top of his lungs, in a bass, showing a mouth full of teeth. Three weeks after he was christened in Vienna's Greek church, he started talking; at the age of three, he was already counting in five-digit numbers; by the age of four, it was discovered, to everybody's amazement, that he could play the flute and speak Polish, and his mother noticed the first gray hairs on the boy's head. When he was five, Alexander Pfister developed a beard and began to shave; he grew unusually large, he looked almost like a young man, a good-looker with a gold ring in his ear, and the uninitiated started eyeing him for their marriageable daughters. And then stories started circulating about him as if all the tongues in the neighborhood had suddenly blossomed. Among these tales (spread especially by the maids), was a perverse and hideous story about the child's unusual, premature sexual exploits, which excited attention. It was rumored that somewhere little Pfister had a son with his former wet nurse, a son who was only a year or two younger than he himself, but these stories were exaggerated. In actual fact, Madame Amalia's son never looked strange for even a day; those who were unaware of his history and his age noticed nothing unusual in either his mild manner or his handsome face, which had an abundance of everything, like the Riznich dining table. It was only the mother who kept saying to herself like a madwoman:

"Beauty is a disease. . . ."

But when the week starts it does not stop at Tuesday for long. In his sixth year, little Alexander Pfister was completely gray, the gray twin of his still-ungraying father (who had just turned twenty-five); at the end of the same year, the boy began to age as quickly as cheese; in his seventh year, he died. It was that autumn when the vineyards were buried from the Tisza to Tokai, that very day when, they say, not more than five words were uttered in all of Bachka. . . . The death brought the Riznich family together once again, if only for a moment, and split up the Pfister family forever.

. . .

"The closest thing to thought is pain," said Madame Amalia, dressing in black, and she immediately divorced her husband. Even before his marriage, Pfister had lost all his own property working on his dirigible, and after the divorce he went off penniless, leaving his wife his gold watch to remind her of him and taking with him the other, silver watch, which measured the time of Madame Amalia, who went to her parents in Pest right after the funeral. She sat in their dining room, counted her stone buttons, and stared fixedly at her mother and father:

"Your husband and you have brought me a hereditary misfortune."

"Your father, you mean, not my husband."

"It wasn't me who chose a father, it was you who chose a husband."

"I suppose you would've chosen your mother as well as your father, had you been able to."

"Had I been able to, you certainly would not have come into consideration. . . ."

And that is how they parted. On her own again, Madame Amalia lined her trunks with lavender, placed walnut leaves in between her blouses and wild flowers in her wig, filled her gloves with sweet basil, sewed verbena in the hems of her dresses, and went back to her wandering travels and her "blue, dark-pretty" dresses, always wearing a locket with a picture of the late Alexander Pfister, who looked like someone who might have been her patron or lover, but not her son.

She again toured restaurants, seeking the tastes of foods, but the years passed and the appeal dwindled. The difference between the same food tasted in her youth and prepared and tasted now was greater than two different foods. Just as grass does not grow under the walnut, so there were no more shadows under her arms; they became transparent. The corners of her eyes were silvery; she spoke little, looked at the tip of her knife, but instead of drinking kissed the glass and nibbled the meat on her plate as though biting the lover she did not have. One day, gazing at the picture in her locket, Madame Amalia decided to do something to preserve at least the memory of the child. She called in a Berlin lawyer (she was in Berlin at the time), gave him the picture, and asked him to publish the daguerreotype.

Amalia Riznich had decided to adopt the young man who bore the strongest resemblance to her late son. The daguerreotype was printed in the French and German press, and offers started coming into the lawyer's office. The lawyer selected seven or eight pictures most like the picture in Mrs. Riznich's locket, but he advised his client that there was one, which unquestionably came closest, of a person with the same graying hair as the boy's. Amalia compared the two pictures and decided to adopt the graying man whom the lawyer had pointed out. It will never be known when she learned the truth about the man. Because time can harm the truth more than lies.

The apparition she saw standing in the doorway so resembled her son, as he had been a year and a half before his death, already graying, but handsome, that she was overwhelmed. As elated as if the young man had been resurrected, for a long time she neither could nor would recognize in him her former husband, changed, older, graying, so that now he began to look like his son prior to the boy's death. She joyously adopted him, behaved toward him exactly as she had behaved toward her own son when he was alive but without that fear and sadness, took him to Paris to art shows and choice meals, chattering excitedly:

"Hunger is most like the seasons because there are four kinds: there is Russian, Greek, German, and, of course, Serbian hunger!"

In the throes of her excitement, she began spilling coins everywhere, she lost them at every step, just as she had once found them wherever she looked; the house was full of coins, she dropped them wherever was handy, in her hats, on the bureaus, in the sink, in her shoes. . . .

"How handsome you are, you look so much like your father, his spitting image!" she whispered, kissing her adopted son. And one morning this madness, or oblivion, or excessively resurrected sorrow, or whatever it was, was shattered by an incredible plan. Namely, the whole thing would have continued as though everything were normal, although nothing was normal nor could it be, had it not occurred to Madame Amalia to get her "son"—that is to say, her ex-husband and now adopted son—married.

"His time has come, he's handsome, he's still as handsome as before, but beauty is a disease; to every soup there is a bottom; I am getting old if not he, I want to be young for my grandchildren, there's no time to lose, I must get him married. . . ."

Pfister sat in the depths of despair, he felt the heat of his pipe slowly descend to the palm of his hand, his graying hair could not quite decide which way to go: black or white. And then it irrevocably chose white, and for the first time he became older than his son. He said nothing and agreed to all of Madame Amalia's fool notions, until she herself went searching for and found a bride from an excellent Pest family, one with a large dowry which began in Buda and finished in Eger. Then Pfister announced sharply that he would not marry, that he loved another, that he was unlucky in love, and that the one he loved could never be his. Madame Amalia protested with a joyous heart, demanded to know who dared to refuse a Riznich—that is, a Pfister—but he would not say. He held his tongue, they sat in silence, she watched him while he read and flipped through his book as quickly as if thumbing and counting money, and then she suddenly exclaimed defiantly, as though in response to that silence:

"It isn't true!"

"Yes, it is," he finally replied, "it's true. The only woman I love and would marry, though I can never have her again, is you. . . ."

She wept, and only then did she admit to herself and to him that she knew who he was and who he was not, and that, no, they could not be together. Not for a single night. Because what would happen if they had another child? "Not that! Anything but that!" she said almost deliriously, and they parted, this time forever. He remained her adopted son and in parting said to her pensively:

"You know, I've had a feeling for a long time. A perfectly ordinary feeling, which maybe most people have. I'm walking, but I simply can't pace my steps properly or measure my stride; I keep hitting against somebody's heel. I try to be careful, but somebody's heel keeps getting in my way. Lying in wait, it's forever leaping out right in front of my toes. As though the toes, apart from their own heel in back, always have to have somebody else's heel in front, too. Whose, I wonder. Maybe it's the Achilles' heel, where we are vulnerable, not our own but somebody else's heel, the heel that forever waits ahead of our toes to slow down our walk, shorten our every step. . . . As though one has to step on somebody else's heel in order to be able to walk at all, to move forward. And our Alexander, you know, maybe he never came upon a heel. That's why he left so quickly. . . ."

With these words Pfister made his farewell; they never met again, but one morning Madame Amalia woke up horrified, with the sentence on her lips that had been the beginning of her tragedy:

"What in October seems to us like March is really January. . . ."

She felt she was carrying some kind of new seed under her heart. This strange thing slowly began to grow inside her, together with her horror; she felt it, the embryo got bigger and spread, although nothing yet showed on the outside. She was stunned, because after that terrible tragedy with the child, after that death which in a way had been a salvation, she no longer felt the need to make love, and she had not slept with anyone for years. And yet this thing under her heart continued to grow and enlarge. It was not until twelve months later, when her figure remained unchanged and nothing had happened, that Madame Amalia realized she should call a doctor, not a midwife. She was sick.

If the reader is patient long enough for his soup-scalded tongue to heal, he will discover how she cured herself, cured herself completely.

"The closest thing to thought is pain," Mrs. Riznich whispered, traveling again, carrying her illness under her heart. Visiting the same places, from Venice and Berlin to Switzerland, where she and her husband had once roamed in search of foods and wines that were dying out, she now searched for the health that was fading and disappearing. From doctor to doctor and spa to spa, Mrs. Riznich wore rings on the thumbs of her lovely hands, the Rzewuska earrings of her great-grandmothers, each of which had a drop of poison in the stone; she moved her lavender-hemmed dresses and showed her illness to Europe.

"Ah, my illness how we do spoil you," she said when racked with piercing stabs as long as a sentence, so that the pains extended at the expense of her speech, which became proportionately shorter as it ceded them its place. A therapist in London was then recommended. She took a drop of wine in Brittany, crossed La Manche on a train aboard a ship, and in England spat out the wine. She sat in the office, moving her rings from finger to finger; the doctor examined her, shook his head, and said:

"There is only one piece of advice I can give you. Live for today. That will place you on a par with everybody else. Because all of us are really always dead to our tomorrow. There is no us in this tomorrow, as though we had never even been born; we are buried in tomorrow's day as if it were a moving grave, which shifts through time and flees in front of us, always postponing the final outcome for another twenty-four hours. And then, one day, we catch up with it, with tomorrow's day. And that tomorrow, where we are not, where we have never been before, crosses over and moves into our today. And that is the end of everything. There is no more tomorrow. Think of all of us who are in the same position and you will see where you are yourself. . . ."

Horrified by this inexorable verdict, Amalia Riznich fled London. On her way back, in the dining car, a woman happened to tell her that somewhere in Europe there was a medicinal mud that cured the kind of pains Amalia Riznich was carrying and feeding, because Amalia's disease had started eating voraciously. It could almost be said that Madame Amalia was driven for the third time, this time by illness, to visit all those expensive restaurants on the Continent and to feed her pains with choice foods, which no longer agreed with her. Her fellow passenger had mentioned the name of this mud from memory, and Madame Amalia wrote it down on the band of her feather wig. The name was "Cat's Mud." At her first stopover, in Brittany, Madame Amalia got herself a map of Europe and tried to find the place. She had thought she would find it as soon as she looked at the map. But it was not on the map. In Paris she bought another, bigger map and looked for the same place, but again in vain. Then she took the Brockhaus lexicon and tried to find the name she was looking for there, but it turned out that she did not even know what language to look it up in. Because the name "Cat's Mud" was entirely different in French from what it was in German or Russian. What letter should she look it up under? Madame Amalia threw away the lexicons and maps and started making oral inquiries. In France they led nowhere, and she decided to return to Vienna.

It was snowing; if you opened your mouth, your tongue became snowbound. The pains now came in a chorus, and Madame Amalia got to know one of them very well, one that could be called the choirmaster. There were moments when she felt she could play her pains on the flute. Unfortunately, no one was able to help her in Vienna either. She sent the servants to make inquiries at the railway station, and an engineer told one of them that he had overheard a passenger, who himself used the mud cure, inquire about just such a place, and that the man had then set off in the direction of Pest. And so Amalia went to her mother in Pest.

Her father had long since ceased being among the living, her mother barely heard a word that was said. She found her with eyes as transparent as an ice patch, and for a moment the eyes of mother and daughter met, forming something like connecting vessels. But it was only for a moment.

"Only bread, clothes, shoes, and hate is man capable of using up in large quantities," Madame Amalia thought in Pest. "Everything else, love, wisdom, beauty, is in larger supply than we are capable of consuming. There are always too many precious things, and never enough ordinary ones. . . ."

Her father's surviving friends, whom she called on in Buda, had never heard of Cat's Mud, although they owned a good part of the Hungarian plains. Some of them, it is true, knew that there were curative muds in the south, but they had no idea whether the mud recommended to Madame Amalia was to be found there. They suggested that she go from Pest to Lake Balaton, and then head south to Kaposvár, inquiring along the way.

The weather was nice; her illness was waiting for the rain and hiding inside her for a moment; Madame Amalia sighed into her Sèvres cup, filled her wicker trunk with dresses and Grandfather Riznich's wine, and set off on her journey with a companion and coachman in tow. Carrying a bun rolled around a sausage and a pickled pepper stuffed with horseradish, one morning, as bright as the dawning of the fifth season of the year, Madame Amalia found herself in a plain covered with dust and mud. There was not a living soul anywhere. The infinity in front of them and behind the coach was furrowed with the eternal gaze of the stars. And every so often a fleeting cloud of birds would darken the sky. It was now the third day that Madame Amalia had been traveling south, smelling the stench of mud, but not the mud she was looking for. Soon the coachman no longer knew where he was. He stepped down off the coach, looked around helplessly, and became angry. He spat into his palm, clapping it against his other hand, and set out in the direction of his flying spit. That afternoon they hit upon some more mud, and smoke appeared up ahead. As they approached, they saw a melon patch. The caretaker was toasting corncobs. He offered to sell them some melons, a big ripe watermelon to eat and refresh them, and five little fist-sized ones to take with them and pickle. And he offered them a toasted corncob with cheese.

"Cheese, madame, is very much the gentleman," he added. "There's a lot of running around to do for it."

Madame Amalia took stock of the man. He had a fur jacket on his huge body. On his ears, instead of earrings, were little crosses.

"Where are we?" she said.

"In Bachka, where else?"

"What's the name of this place?"

"Mud."

"Just Mud?"

"Cat's Mud," added the caretaker.

"So, this is it," Madame Amalia sighed, undoing the ribbons of her hat. "And does it heal?"

"It heals those who aren't dead already. It's good earth; it can give new life to a living human being!"

"Who might be willing to rent out a bathing spot here?"

"I don't know. You'd have to ask the owners."

"Are any of them around?"

"Not for the past fifty years," replied the caretaker. "I'm alone here. The masters are far away. And they're not in the plural anymore."

"How come?" asked Madame Amalia.

"Well, the old gentleman died. And now we only have the young mistress."

"And where is she?"

"God alone knows. She herself probably doesn't know where she is. They say she doesn't bathe on St. Procopius's Day. She's roaming around the world somewhere, she can't stay still. They say she's now in Pest. . . ."

Madame Amalia began turning over in her mind the names of women her age in Pest. And suddenly she stared at the melon she had just bought.

"What's the name of your mistress?" she asked, and received the answer already guessed by the reader.

"Amalia Riznich, Pfister by marriage . . . Surely you know her story," the keeper replied, "you must have heard of her. . . . That thing with her son happened. Uncommon it was. But instructive. His god, the god of young Pfister, had not yet grown up at the crucial moment. He simply matured slower than the boy. The god was still a minor at the time, he couldn't retain the child and slow down his progress, as our gods here have retained and held us back. He had no one to forbid him the apple of knowledge. He tasted it on his own and went on his own from here, from paradise, into voluntary exile on earth. Because he whose eyes are opened must change the world. . . ."

Amalia Riznich, Pfister by marriage, stood there for a moment as if she had gone deaf, then removed her shoes and stockings and stepped straight into the mud. Into the saving cool of her black and oily earth. And the earth received and drew in her feet as though it wanted to plant them there.

4 DOWN

People who are afraid of life leave their families belatedly and reluctantly and are disinclined to start their own. Strange as it may sound, Atanas Razin was just such a person: he was afraid of life, and for a long time he belonged to the family from which he had come. Later he remained faithful to his first wife, although she did not love him, and during his second marriage, to Vitacha Milut, he stayed in touch with his mother to the very end, always regretting that he had no father, and always looking for him.

People who are afraid of death stay with their families briefly and go into the world quickly and easily, leaving one another. The heroine of this book, the great-great-granddaughter from Amalia Riznich's last extramarital affair, the younger Miss Milut, Pohvalich by marriage, later Mrs. Vitacha Razin, and later still celebrated under the universally known name that shall remain unspoken here, was such a person: she was afraid of death. She remembered well from her grandmother's stories that she owed her birth to Cat's Mud, which had cured her great-great-grandmother Amalia. Vitacha had managed, in her life, to change countless names, to leave or be left many times. Her breasts moved left and right, not up and down.

Between the two world wars, Vitacha's father, Captain Milut, had been a cadet in a French artillery school, whence he returned with a nick in his military step and a fine mustache wrapped around a spindle, two curls attached with sugar to the corners of his mouth. In his opinion, the seven grades of officer corresponded with the grades of the musical scale. And only those who had an ear for this kind of music could advance to the next octave, to the rank of general, where everything was repeated in a higher register. Captain Milut was very musical, he could tell from its sound whom a sword belonged to, but he was stone-deaf to this military scale. He returned to Belgrade to get married, receive his last rank of captain, and have children, who slept in a drawer underneath the bed, then to become a widower and to find himself alone with four daughters and a young mother-in-law who had never dreamed a dream in her life, who wore a silver watch in her chignon and a lacquered black straw hat stabbed with a Chinese needle that whistled softly when she walked. He had the feeling that he had already worn out the path he was treading and decided to take the only step, other than the military step, that still came to mind. He decided not to remarry.

And so the heroine of this story, Vitacha Milut, was not raised by her mother, who died young, or by a stepmother, whom she did not have, but by her said maternal grandmother. Madame Yolanta, née Ibich, Isailovich by marriage, gave the little girl forty-nine names; Vitacha learned that her name was Paulina Amalia Angelina Yolanta Veronica, etc., before she learned to talk.

Her grandmother Madame Yolanta was still beautiful at the time, with two eyes as black as eggs boiled in the Jewish manner, and so strong she could snap the handle off a frying pan. She was pious in a strange way; on her wall she kept a clay icon depicting *Joshua Stopping the Sun and the Moon over Gibeon,* and in the evenings she gazed at her navel. Raised in the poverty of a once famous and wealthy family, Madame Yolanta had had a hard life, and of the family possessions she inherited only three things: a watch in the shape of a silver egg, a baking pan for soothsaying, and the gift of walking. Her walk was as celebrated as a famous song and others afterward learned from Miss

Ibich how to walk and how to speak with one's walk. She could "walk with her breasts" like her grandmother Amalia Riznich, the younger, like that one's mother, Yevdokia Riznich; she could walk leading a dog, spit on it, and suddenly let it go to see whom the dog would carry the spit to; or like this one's mother, Madame Paulina, the Countess Rzewuska, Riznich by marriage, who trod wherever she looked and did not look where she trod. One day Yolanta's father received a visit from some strange people, a husband and wife; they said they had heard of the girl's lovely walk, and it was whispered that they had come to propose. But throughout the visit they kept water in their mouths and did not speak. They had come to see her for their son, and as a token of approval they left ten ducats tied up in a lace glove. On the assigned day, under the window, gypsies played the song "The Peeping Ray . . ."; they dressed Yolanta in white and took her to the cemetery, where her future in-laws were already waiting. It was forty days since the death of their son, who had passed away at the age of twenty, unmarried.

They took him out of the grave, bathed him, and clipped the little black mustache he had sprouted in death, dressed him for the wedding, and placed a ring on his finger and the bride's; somebody read a few words from the Holy Scripture. Then everybody—including the bride—kissed the groom, he was reburied, and Yolanta was not allowed to marry for a year. Such is the custom in the Danube Valley. During that year, she lived in the groom's house, and while she wore black and carried the groom's surname, the surname of the man who was under the earth, Yolanta grew a beard below her navel, and under her pert little nose a real hussar's mustache, just like that of the man under the earth. She then rouged her cheeks, darkened her eyebrows, bit her lips to give them color, placed her two heavy breasts in the vitrine of her deep décolleté, and with her finest walk, the walk of the oldest Countess Rzewuska, which was at least two hundred years old, she went to the barber's. She stretched out in the barber's chair and ordered that her mustache be trimmed. Thereafter she sported a fine, pomaded little mustache, as straight as bangs and as black as coal, she had two minds and three ears, sang beautifully, and fell ill every Tuesday. In her ninth month of mourning, her milk began to flow, and at the barbershop she caught herself a husband with her mustache—one Isailovich, who told such outrageous and scandalous tales about his sexual exploits that the barbers said that after hearing his stories they felt as though they had never mounted a woman. This Isailovich was so disconcerted upon discovering on his wedding night that his widow-bride was a virgin that he openly admitted he had no idea whose child he was fathering. During this marriage, the silver egg stopped ticking and Vitacha's mother was born.

When Mrs. Ibich was left without a husband and daughter, she devoted herself to her grandchildren, and they immediately discovered that their grandmother had two tiny bald spots like ducats in her hair, there where one of her great-great-grandmother-witches had had little horns with bells on them, the one who could shave a man's beard in a soapy mirror from ten meters away, using her left eye instead of a razor. Madame Yolanta just smiled at this story, but it turned out that she was as adept at holding a razor with her foot as with her hand, and that she could slit open a snake with a silver dinar. On days when the sun was eclipsed and on nights when the moon was devoured, she poured water into her baking pan and caught the sun and the moon in the water to see which side of them the demons were gnawing at. She would not let children or puppies drink water, and she forbade the little girls to go to the toilet on holidays.

In addition to these virtues, Madame Yolanta had two other traits that delighted her grandchildren. She wove legends about the beautiful women of the Riznich family and believed that members of a good family resembled the teeth in one's head, so in her stories the members of her family were divided into molars, incisors, wisdom teeth, loose, broken or funny, dull and painful, bad or shining teeth. Her stories and her walk became especially beautiful whenever she was visited by the captain's friends from the regiment, Major Pohvalich, whose face was so narrow he could lick his ears, and Colonel Krachun. The officers knew by heart these stories about Vitacha's ancestors, the beautiful women who drove poets wild, and about the unfortunate and handsome engineer Pfister, who was first the husband and then the son of his wife.

But Mrs. Yolanta Ibich's other virtue was not quite so simple, and it manifested itself suddenly, in what was initially a perfectly innocent form. One winter, when the captain forgot to buy fish for Christmas Eve, fish being part of a man's job, the grandmother whispered that foods were the only friends she had left; she boiled cabbage and mutton and suddenly, drastically, began to put on weight.

She gained weight with such dedication, with such contempt and speed, that although nothing had been said about the fish, by spring Captain Milut noticed that something strange was happening in the house. By the summer, when they left for the seaside, the captain knew that her gaining weight had to do with him personally, but he did not know what he had done wrong. He uncorked the melons, poured brandy into the watermelons, and wine into the cantaloupes, and left them to settle overnight, while Madame Yolanta, née Ibich, continued to prepare with every meal her own added portion of cabbage and mutton. She gazed at her navel every day until she forgot which was her left ear and which her right, she tied string around the little girls' moles to make them fall off, and without a word she put on weight in opposition to her son-in-law Captain Milut.

Finally, one morning, as though bewitched by this growing obesity, Captain Milut bought a big tin box of cookies. He divided up the cookies among the children, cut an opening the size of a coin in the lid, put a mackerel in the box, and soldered it shut. He poured olive oil through the little hole every day for as long as the fish was willing to drink it. When the mackerel stopped drinking, he took a coin and soldered it over the hole, and the tin of fish was ready.

"We shall have it for Christmas," said the captain, and the little girls cast an astonished look at the grandmother, who, exulted, started losing weight with dizzying speed, and instead of cabbage and mutton made beans and walnuts. She was slow again, became noticeably prettier, and subsequently and inexplicably looked more and more like her late husband. She was turning back into that mustached beauty of yore, with a lorgnette of perfumed glass.

"I want to be beautiful for my grandchildren," she whispered into her teacup, and when her neighbors urged her to remarry, she answered through that double-tariff Riznich smile, but so that Captain Milut could hear:

"My men could always stay erect for as long as it takes a two-dinar candle to burn. Where am I to find men like that today?"

Captain Milut looked at Madame Yolanta in astonishment and bought a two-dinar candle. To wit, for some time now he had been planning to throw his cards on the table and openly tell his mother-in-law what was troubling him. Going to the drill site, among the cavalry horses that masturbate by beating their sexual organs against their stomachs, he thought and thought about what to say, but the sentences hovered in his head like the dust behind those horses and would not come out.

Captain Milut was a man in his prime, when he flexed his stomach muscles he could gouge out the eye of a passerby with the button off his trousers, he needed a woman as a stomach needs a navel, but still he did not intend to bring a stepmother home to the children. All confused, he whispered to himself, looking at the lovely Madame Yolanta, whispered deep down inside, where tears spring, not words —Help me, if you wish both them and me good—but, instead of those simple words, his head swam with a sentence from one of his mother-in-law's endless stories:

"What in October seems to us like March is really January...." And then he noticed that Madame Yolanta was again putting on weight against somebody. Against whom he did not know, but it was visible; even the children noticed it. Eggplant stew was brought onto the table every day now, but separately for her, and before the meal she whispered a prayer:

"With the cross to protect us, we oppose the devil, fearing neither his snares nor his ambushes...."

This renewed gaining of weight upset the household. The captain's ears were riddled with stupid smiles, and all sorts of things happened in the house. When he opened the cupboard, all the colors of a flower-print dress or striped suit flew out into the room, flitting in tiny silky pieces, blinded by the sun; in his pocket watch Captain Milut found worms; and even the widow Isailovich's late husband began returning to her whenever there was a full moon, as if it were the most ordinary thing to do, though he did not do well on weekdays. For instance, the deceased never knew whether Tuesday came before Wednesday or after. He thought it came after, and they had to correct him and return him to the day whence he had come. Madame Yolanta would then take the baking pan, fill it with water, and start to tell her grandchildren their fortune.

One evening, two months after the widow Isailovich had started gaining weight for the second time, Captain Milut took water in his mouth, washed his penis with the water, the army way, and barged into Madame Yolanta's room.

She was lying in bed as naked as God had made her, contemplating her navel. There in those sheets she looked like white, well-leavened dough, with a deep navel in the middle and the smell of lemon. Below the navel she had a huge, hairy third breast, and above the navel one of the finest waists Captain Milut had ever seen. Or so, at least, it seemed to him in the light of the two-dinar candle burning on the table. Looking at the candle, Captain Milut became a bit dazed and lost his tongue, while Mrs. Isailovich implacably continued her scrutiny until she finished her prayer, or whatever it was. Then she turned to the captain, blew out the candle, and drew him toward her, the way she drew close his daughters. Embracing him, she said:

"What in October seems to us like March is really January. . . ."

Lying on his back after making love, the captain groped for her in the dark. She was there, and already, he knew, she was losing weight with dizzying speed. He caressed her and, touching her randomly, asked:

"Is that your foot?"

From the dark he received a slap as scalding as a cheese crêpe. It was her hand.

"Grandma, your egg isn't working!" Vitacha Milut was fond of saying to Madame Yolanta, whose family watch shaped like a silver egg had stopped working long ago but could still play. Crickets chased the silence across the scorching sky in the opposite direction of the wind that drove the clouds; it was war, Captain Milut was in that war, and nothing was known of him. Madame Yolanta let her granddaughters put the silver egg to their ears and listen, as one listens to the rippling waves of the sea in a conch.

"It works, child," she would say, "but now it hatches some other, bygone hours, not yours." And, indeed, burbling inside the egg or stopped clock was a bygone time, and in it the voices of the erstwhile beauties of their family. Vida, it is true, heard nothing except wheezing, but Vitacha, who had two entirely different ears—one as deep as a snail, and the other as shallow as a shell—Vitacha heard everything. She could recognize clearly the high-pitched soft voice of Countess Paulina Rzewuska, Riznich by marriage, and behind it the chirping of swallows just before the rain, when they rip the dust with the tips of their wings; Amalia's flute could be heard, and the glass pins that tinkled in her hair when she ate, and behind them all was the cracked mezzo-soprano of Madame Yevdokia. The only voice not heard in the watch was that of Vitacha's prematurely deceased mother, Veronica Isailovich. Instead of her mother's voice, Vitacha heard in the silver egg a faint, faraway soprano well washed with egg yolk, a voice that Madame Yolanta claimed did not belong to anyone in the family. It was the most beautiful voice in the egg, and the most beautiful voice Vitacha had ever heard.

"It's the voice of that whore Polychronia," claimed the grandmother. "She fell in love with your young great-grandfather Alexander Pfister, and he had a child with that Polychronia and became a father at the age of five."

"Tell me about her!" Vitacha implored. "What happened to their son? For heaven's sake, he's our relative! Tell me! Quick, tell me!"

"There's nothing to tell; under her eyebrows Polychronia had two big blue flies instead of eyes, and that's all. . . ."

And the widow Isailovich, née Ibich, would not loosen her tongue on the subject. As always when scolding Vitacha, the grandmother called her by one of the Rzewuskas' names.

"Your ass is like a gold coin, Evelina, but all you're interested in is stuff and nonsense. Mind your own business!"

And so Vitacha had to keep silent, but she remembered Polychronia forever after. And in her thoughts she added Polychronia's to her own numerous names.

Vitacha Petka Amalia Paulina Evelina Carolina Angelina Polychronia, etc., was, above all, a very beautiful woman. Her body was buried deep in the dreams of all the men who knew her. She had a V-shaped wrinkle between her breasts, and toes so slender and perfect she could play the piano with them. For several generations the female beauty of her great-great-grandmother Amalia Riznich the younger had flowed exclusively through the male blood-line, and it was only in the present generation that it was again embodied in a female offspring, in Vitacha Milut. Between her and her sister Vida Milut, who bore not the slightest resemblance to Vitacha, there had been a kind of crosswalk or bridge formed by two other sisters, who had died young and taken with them every connecting link between the features of Vitacha and Vida, so that one could no longer tell they were sisters. On Vida's body and face, Great-Grandmother Amalia Riznich, Pfister by marriage, had irretrievably lost to her husband, engineer Pfister, their game of chess; on the faces of Vida's other sisters, that game was still in progress or at a draw when the girls died; but on Vitacha's face and body, Great-Grandmother Amalia had won the Sicilian opening against her husband in the most splendid way, with a checkmate in a single move. From her father, Vitacha had inherited only her thin skin, through which her teeth showed.

And so every evening Vitacha lowered the transparent lids of her father, Captain Milut, over the green eyes of Amalia Riznich, and plunged into the undreamed dreams of her grandmother Madame Yolanta. In these closed green eyes one could see dreams the way in Grandmother's baking pan one could see the future.

One evening there was a full moon, and since the captain had not written from the war in three years, Madame Yolanta scooped water into her baking pan, called in the little girls, and placed the pan in the moonlight like the bucket of a well. The winter night was as clear as day, ice was catching on the puddles in the street, the stars were dimming under it and were visible only in the unfrozen water. And that street was long, so long; at the beginning autumn, at the end winter, in one part noon, in the other candles being lit and night falling; in one part they learned Russian, in the other they were already forgetting it. . . . At the bottom of the street Madame Yolanta held the baking pan with the water and whispered into her breasts:

"Let Sunday wed Monday, and Tuesday, Wednesday. . . ." She was afraid of seeing a female face in the water, for that would mean that the captain was dead. But in the baking pan appeared a male face bathed in moonlight, and Madame Yolanta cried excitedly:

"It's him! It's him! Did you recognize your father, children?"

And so they knew that Captain Milut was alive and well, and one day he really did appear, he came back from a German prison camp sporting a pair of well-fattened ears on a lean head. Instead of Madame Yolanta Ibich, he found in his house an old woman drinking her morning tea with pepper to wake herself up and lamenting that half her soul had died, and in Vitacha's room he found an eight-year-old neighborhood boy and Vitacha stark naked holding the boy in her arms and whispering in his ear:

"I adore little boys, I like it when little boys make me babies. . . ."

Captain Milut was stunned by such a sight, and now he was at a loss in this house, where even the chairs meowed and bit like cats, where his artilleryman's blood and flesh turned into the virginal flesh and blood of his daughters. Frightened, he shuffled between Madame Yolanta, who left hot seats behind her on every chair and wore her eyebrows far into her hair as though perpetually astonished, and his daughters, who left scattered on their towels and pillows prints of their green eyelids and black eyebrows and traces of their red nocturnal smiles and bites prepared for the apparitions in their dreams from which their pee afterward plaited itself into whips. Captain Milut carried his eyes around the rooms like stones and was seized with horror at the secret vomiting of his two daughters, who used this age-old method to keep their figures. He could barely stand the smell of the depilatory cream and the hairs that were all over the house, even in the talking silver egg. They cleaned their combs with toothbrushes or stabbed hairpins in the Vaseline tube. And then, one morning, the captain heard a man hawking in his bathroom in a deep bass, as though straining to roll his boot up through his mouth. He jerked open the door, the army way (foot first, then hand), and in the bathroom found Vitacha clearing her throat.

Not knowing what to do, he packed his elder daughter, Vida, off to the Pfisters' relatives in Vienna, and in desperation began planting roses in the garden. Strangely enough, he was good at it. He had what they call a green thumb, and he knew that one bound plants with plants. But he did not know the most important thing. He did not know that behind all this lunacy, behind these little boys and meowing chairs, lay a family misfortune, which had been kept from him.

That misfortune happened during his captivity. This is how.

One morning, Vitacha looked at the freshly boiled sky, as dark as a summer night, tossed her silver, ivory, glass, and jade combs into the washtub, and stepped into the water, singing. She was still more child than girl, but that step into the water was decisive for her whole life. She sang a song then that she quickly forgot later, and she waited for decades to remember that song, which was called "The Last Blue Wednesday." And, unfortunately for her, she eventually remembered it. But now, while she was singing in her washtub, everybody was astonished. For it was the first time that they had heard her sing. And it was obvious that Vitacha had a perfect ear, although otherwise she was practically mute. Mrs. Yolanta Isailovich then gave her that silver egg in which one could hear Amalia Riznich's flute, taught her to gaze into the baking pan, and sent her for voice lessons. From then on, everybody in the family waited for her to enter girlhood to see whether her voice could carry the burden of her perfect ear.

Vitacha's teacher, an old gentleman with two beards, each of which hung from its own ear, was awestruck.

"In the beginning there was the voice," he told Vitacha at their first lesson. "A divine voice that sang the following word: Fiat! It was a threefold word, with which God built the four elements of the world.

It was the Axis Mundi! Around that voice, as around an axle, God created the world. And the first of the senses that God addressed was Adam's hearing. That's why even fish will start singing at the Last Judgment. . . ."

And the little old man with the square pupils in his eyes and wisp of hair on his head leaned over to show Vitacha pictures of old frescoes in which the fish were singing.

Vitacha smiled; her fine broad forehead was like kneaded dough; she was left-eared, and with her silence could wind a watch. The teacher regarded this silence of hers as the reverse side, as the inside lining of her singing. And he felt it made a difference whether someone who wanted to sing kept silent in a major key or a minor.

"They say a singer doesn't need brains, he thinks with his ears; but it is not in the ear that the secret lies," the singing teacher kept repeating, and he taught her Byzantine liturgical songs, saying that they were better and older than Bach. Hair grew on his nails, and sometimes he would stroke her cheeks with that hair, give her a quick, cursory pinch on the breasts, saying that a bass has to have balls and a soprano tits. He taught her vespers, which could be learned not by day but in the dark, when one could tell from the song whether the singer's mouth was big or small. He taught her to forget what she wanted, because that was more important and harder than to remember what she did not want. The vespers, the ones sung in church at midnight service, were of three kinds:

    1. self-sustaining songs, without models, which serve as a model for other songs;

    2. songs that are modeled on other songs and bear their stamp (name);

    3. songs that neither imitate others nor serve as a model for anyone.

"If you can't understand the essence of these songs," he said, "then imagine them as singing about the following:

1. the wrong we have done others;
2. the wrong others have done us;
3. the wrong we have done ourselves."

After the lesson, the teacher rubbed his hands contentedly, cautioning that the sun holds the light of the moon, just as a good voice holds all songs, both those that exist and those that are yet to come. Vitacha left these lessons as though bathed in music, and time passed agonizingly slowly for her. Like something one cannot finish chewing. Her time was still full of bones. As for her, she either kept silent or sang, and she sang as soon as she walked out the door or stood by the window, like a bird that sings as soon as the sun comes out. Gemini twinkled in Vitacha's eyes, and Madame Yolanta, née Ibich, whispered eagerly, "Once the week starts, it doesn't stop long at Tuesday," the voice of that whore Polychronia tinkled from the egg, and Vitacha sang. She still mixed the deepest alto with the highest soprano, and sometimes a void yawned between the two. She was waiting for her voice, her real voice, and the moment when her singing would mature. And everybody around her was waiting, too.

And then that voice arrived, and everything came crashing down.

As soon as she reached girlhood, Vitacha acquired eyes that were deep and transparent down to two meters and ten centimeters; deeper than that, nothing could be seen. Her eyelashes seemed always to carry a sprinkle of dust, and her voice, that voice that had been so promising, that had been so eagerly awaited, almost like that of little Alexander Pfister in that same family once, suddenly cracked like an earthenware jug; it became deep and absolutely unusable. It held nothing of what was poured into it. Everything leaked out before it could be drunk. It was total disaster. All that was left of the singing was the silence, and the girls at school whispered maliciously that Vitacha's voice was an illegitimate child, that it had been inherited from Alexander Pfister and that was why it had aged prematurely.

Some women cannot manage a house and theirs are always in disarray. Others cannot manage their own souls and these are in disarray. Things have to be straightened up at the right time; afterward is too late. Because any similarity between the house and the soul ceases in that *afterward*. Vitacha obviously did not know that. Defeat and disarray reigned in her soul. She began to stutter and to speak unusually articulately and well in her sleep. She became lefthanded and claimed that the lefthanded were people who in a previous life had been beaten on their right hands, or who in one of their future lives would put their hands in the fire for a friend. It was spring; flocks of swallows streaked by overhead, forked off, and whirled along the center as though somebody were wringing a black sheet in the sky, and Vitacha kept seeing the same image: she saw a bat hanging upside down from under the stomach of a naked man. And then, one evening, she plaited herself a braid and invited a little boy from the neighborhood, with hair as red as rust, to come to her bed and impregnate her just as Polychronia, that witch from the silver egg, had been impregnated by Vitacha's little great-grandfather Alexander Pfister, who was born with teeth and a knowledge of Polish. The boy's name was Suzin; he was eight years old and did not understand what was wanted of him, but he came into Vitacha's room this once and brought her matzos. He said:

"The amount of fear in the world is constant; it neither decreases nor increases, and it must always be distributed to all beings, like water. What do you think? I think that the last people on earth will go crazy with fear. Somewhere in Africa wild animals are afraid for me, too, in this sense. The less afraid I am, the more afraid somebody else is, and tomorrow perhaps you will be less afraid on my account, and then I will have to be that much more afraid. Fear is something like common property. It is the clothing people had to put on after being expelled from paradise, because they recognized their own nakedness in the face of death. . . ."

The next day, Suzin and his family were taken off to a German concentration camp.

"Never," whispered Vitacha afterward, "shall I defile the taste of that matzo by taking another matzo. That taste of matzo in my mouth is my only child."

When Vitacha began running after eight-year-old boys in the street, holding them while they peed and plaiting their hair into braids, luring them into her bed, the widow Isailovich was horror-stricken. For days she flapped her eyebrows as though she were rowing, or about to fly. And then those eyebrows suddenly flew off her face straight into her hair. Madame Yolanta took a red-hot knife, sliced some onions, made an eggplant stew, and began gaining weight again. This time she gained weight against her own granddaughter. She watched Vitacha Milut's beautiful buttocks greedily chew at her underpants, occasionally swallowing a patch of the legging, and she whispered through a morsel of eggplant:

"Her ass is like a gold coin, but she doesn't know where her head is. She needs somebody old to take hold of both her ears. Somebody as old as possible . . ."

Captain Milut, who had returned from the war about this time, smoked tobacco that smelled divine, and through that smell he reeked of formic acid, while Madame Yolanta, who said nothing to her granddaughter, with each passing day devoured ever-bigger portions of eggplant moussaka. She gained weight for the last time in her life, determined at all costs to make her granddaughter give up her love of little boys with hair like the fluff of chicks and eyes like glass buttons. She was determined to marry her off. And from this came misfortune, just as misfortune comes from all successful attempts at education.

Vitacha nibbled at unpicked peaches in the garden, leaving toothmarks in the fruit on the branches, and she plaited braids wherever she could. In her father's beard, on the widow Isailovich and Vida in turns, between her own legs, on the willows along the tree-lined paths, and pigtails on little boys in the street. She carried her own hair like a whip in her hand, her eyes reflected the constellation of Cancer, and all the while Madame Yolanta kept gaining weight. Whenever she drank a glass of water, she would steal a look at her granddaughter and whisper:

"Wherever you touch her she's full of holes!"

And this gaining of weight had an effect. The fish weather vane on the roof of the house started to turn in a new direction; objects in the apartment, which, like people, sleep at night and do their work by day, lost sleep and began creaking at night, as if waiting for moving day; it became unbearable; the captain's mustache became as rigid as a fish bone, leaving sores on his chin when he spoke and ate, and only Vitacha sensed nothing, except that somebody invisible wanted to grab her by the ears.

"The lower lip of Amalia Riznich, the upper of Countess Rzewuska," Mrs. Isailovich chanted in despair, looking at Vitacha, whose mouth was full of saliva as thick as honey, but she herself showed no signs of any change. She kissed dropped pieces of bread and pinched little neighborhood boys as before. Then, one day, after her grandmother's hundredth portion of eggplant moussaka, she was found near the school breaking the ground-floor windows with a hairbrush, yelling out in a stutter every time the glass shattered:

"Marry me! Marry me!"

Captain Milut, big as he was, with his shallow shadow and rockhard nose, was taken aback and started stuttering every time he addressed his daughter. Madame Yolanta hoped this was the turning point, but she was wrong. There is not a thing in all the world that won't become true one day, just as a stopped clock always has a moment when it is accurate. But the truth, like dough, needs time and warmth to develop and grow. During this time, Vitacha whispered a saying from school: "The mind runs slow and love runs fast!" And during her father's stays with his unit, she turned more and more toward school. That year her breasts grew faster than her teeth and Vitacha developed those beautiful lips of hers, about which they said: The upper lip sweet, the lower as bitter as almonds. One can tell from the first twelve days of August what the twelve months of the year will be like; with Vitacha Milut one could gauge from these twelve months what life would be like. It was autumn; Polychronia could be heard whispering from the silver egg, "I have drunk all my tears, not one did I spill!" Vitacha plaited braids wherever she could and experienced, like an illness carried by sight, her first puppy love. One of those loves that are later remembered and related by generations. She met Atanas Razin, who was still called Svilar at the time, and went to the same school. He got up to give her his seat in the tram, and she made the sign of the cross over him as old ladies used to do on such occasions, but she did it strangely somehow, with just one finger, or by sticking out her tongue and crossing him with it. The next time he saw her, she was standing alone in front of a yellow wall in the schoolyard. She stared at him fixedly and did not return his greeting. After a few seconds she said:

"Atanas Svilar, you are too old for me; find yourself somebody else! I like little boys, younger than me."

"And I like very little girls. For instance, I'd gladly screw one of your dolls. Pick one out and bring it next time. . . ."

Instead of an answer, Vitacha slowly began sliding down against the wall into a squatting position. When she was finally in a squat, a gleaming, knife-sharp two-meter-long spray spurted out from between her legs, aimed straight at him. They did not see each other after that, and if they did happen to meet, she would remain silent; for months she watched him fixedly with eyes full of murky water, the kind that drains away with such dizzying speed that it looks as though it has been stopped short. These eyes were full of stars from the constellation of Taurus and as somber as her voice, which Atanas had not heard for a full ten weeks. And then, one day, she brought him a doll. The doll had the same name as her sister.

"Here's your wife. Her name is Vida," Vitacha said, and again he heard that deep voice, which, like a cracked jug, held nothing and was the object of so much talk.

Atanas was a year younger than Vitacha; he told her so. She looked at him, licked her Countess Rzewuska lip, bit the other lip, the Amalia Riznich lip, and they began seeing each other. Atanas went home at night from these trysts, to which Vitacha came somehow reluctantly, with his hair full of her cracked words and hoarse whispers, and Vitacha somewhat mockingly called her prelove self "Sister Badlyika."

It was about then that Captain Milut learned of the affair. And he became deathly afraid. Chewing a mouthful of bitten-off mustache, he sought and found in Vitacha's mirrors, which greeted every morning with smears of spit, the shadow of yet another of his adult daughter's nonadult lovers—the shadow of Atanas Svilar, today Razin. Captain Milut had troubles of his own at the time. He was not being promoted to a higher rank; he started dreaming of his late father as being older than he had been when he died and worried whether his father had not continued to age somewhere in the meantime, after death, and how many thousands of years he would have to complete before he settled down, if he continued this way. Old Mrs. Ibich died just about then, grossly fat and miserable that her weight gain against her granddaughter had not borne fruit. The captain, at a loss, summoned his other daughter, Vida, but she just simpered in her Vienna letters, which were slightly swollen because she sealed them with her tears.

Finally, the next time he left on a monthlong march, he asked one of his good friends, Major Pohvalich, an artilleryman himself, whom he had known since their days in France, to keep an eye on his daughter in his absence. And off he went on his tattered path. It is hard to say what happened after that or how, but when Captain Milut rang the doorbell of his apartment a month later, the door was opened by the major, who sported a freshly plaited pigtail on the back of his head and said:

"Her ass is like a gold coin, but she doesn't know where her head is. She needs somebody old to take hold of both her ears. . . ."

All of Captain Milut's calluses started aching from the shock; he pulled a pistol on the major, who grinned at him from under something that looked like artificial skin, but he felt like a man who has just had a bird shit in his glass. And that is why Major Pohvalich was faster. He was already holding the key to his bachelor apartment in his hand. The captain scratched himself with his pistol, pulled the roses out of the garden, and moved into Pohvalich's small apartment. He hastily arranged the wedding of his daughter to his former friend, wrapped his military pistol in a shirt, sent it to his son-in-law, and never drank or peed again for the rest of his life. He died with the words: The crazy live as long as they want, the wise as long as they have to.

Vitacha quickly had two daughters, one after the other; her marriage to Major Pohvalich fell into its groove, the silver egg was forgotten, and she whispered into her café au lait:

"One shouldn't think. Thoughts are like hunger, they're always the same. So one should eat." And she did not think. But every so often she would scoop water into the baking pan she had inherited from her great-grandmother and gaze at length at the empty bottom. She waited in vain for an image, a face, male or female, to appear in the water. And she gained weight. It was then that she developed into the beauty that no one at school would have ever expected. Her bones cracked like sparks of fire, and every morning a transparent pebble gleamed in the corners of her eyes and in it one could see, like insects caught in amber, miniature dreams. . . .

She knew from the late Madame Yolanta that demons talk through human coughs, whistles, or snores, and she listened to her husband in bed next to her as in his sleep he ate in Serbian and then translated into French, tasted cabbage, dipped into the jar of pickled peppers, gnawed at fish bones, guzzled brandy, or blew into the polenta full of bursting bubbles. . . . And she understood not a word of what the demons were saying, because she lacked that other half of the conversation—her own sneezes, snores, and coughs. She tried to study. For three years she left the light on in her room, studying at night. But nothing came of it. Then she began to fall ill on Tuesdays and during these one-day illnesses to write endless letters, which she never mailed, so that they lay strewn all over the house, they filled the cupboards and drawers, they were under the beds and even in her husband's old boots. It would have been all the same even if she had sent them to whomever they were intended for, because Vitacha Pohvalich's handwriting was completely illegible. Not even the major or his daughters could decipher it. And Vitacha wrote these letters most probably to her little girls, who played around her and could not yet read.

Then one day, quite out of the blue (they had not met for years), Atanas reappeared. He leaned his bicycle against Vitacha's gate, entered the apartment where the sisters Vitacha and Vida had once lived, and where the Pohvaliches now resided. He licked the weeping eyes with his long tongue, took Vitacha by the hand, and led her away to Vienna and then to America. He left behind his bicycle by the gate, his wife, son, and mother, and she her husband and children, and she never returned to them again.

6 DOWN

As far as I can remember, Mr. Atanas Razin (already a wealthy and prominent man at the time) told the following story after one of his business trips:

I'm sitting at the Three Benches inn, and on the table in front of me are my pipes. Cleaned so that all of them peal like trumpets, as if they might start playing at any moment. I choose a pipe and ponder. All that I have left of my youth is tears. And even they aren't as sweet as they used to be, but bitter and shallow. But do you know, old friend, what tears are? He who learns that every one tear is worth two will be worth his tears; otherwise, I figure, he won't be worth even that much. And the heart... Here the waiter interrupts me. I memorize where I've tied the knot in my thoughts, and ask him:

"Have you got wedding cabbage and mutton, boy?"

"I beg your pardon?" he says, and I see that one of his eyes is sealed, as though a drop of wax had spilled into it, and a tear is glistening on the tip of his nose. This tear isn't worth two, I decide, and explain: "That's the cabbage and mutton that's put on the fire every morning and removed in the evening, and so on for seven days."

"Come back in seven days," says the boy.

"Terrific! What are you drinking?" I ask in reply to this answer.

"The gentleman is too kind," he says, delighted by my offer. "Lacrima Christi. I adore Lacrima Christi, sir."

"Fine. Bring me a glass of Lacrima Christi."

And while he goes away to bring the drink I ordered, I continue where I left off. And my heart—I think again—my heart stopped beating in my chest some time ago, it just keeps scratching inside me like a little animal locked up in a cage. In front of the cage is open space and freedom, with a glistening river that, the moment you catch sight of it, folds into a forest and vanishes. And the cage has a little door made of pinewood and bast. If a nightingale pecks at it, it will hold, but if a sparrow hawk is inside, it will burst open at the first rap and let the bird out into the wide-open spaces like smoke into the blue sky. . . .

Just then the white-eyed maid I've been expecting enters the restaurant. I bring her over and sit her down next to me.

"Why are you so pale?" I ask in surprise, noticing the color of her face.

"It's horrible, sir, of course I'm pale! I've just seen the devil."

"Where's the devil?"

"What do you mean, where? Why, you're the devil."

"Ah, if only that were true, would that it were true," I say. "But down to business! Did you bring the bottle?"

She pulls a little bottle of brandy out of her pocket and says doubtfully:

"Are you sure you can tell from the brandy whether they are the ladies you're looking for?"

I think how every one of us is born crippled in one of his souls and retort:

"Yes, I'm sure," and without further preliminaries I take a swig from the little bottle. Suddenly a languid river of silence and ecstasy pours into my chest, slowing down the course of everything it encounters. Once more I know youth in the silence and warmth that enter me and, old as I am, I again drift away to my thoughts of a moment ago. . . .

"That's it!" I say to the maid. "I recognize it, it's their brandy!

Their father used to make brandy like this—so strong you could kill a rabbit with it!"

And as I drink from the bottle of brandy, my thoughts, like birds in the sky, suddenly flock together and then vanish again, after first intertwining and carding east and west. When their time comes, they fly away from us, each with its flock, somewhere to their own south. Because our thoughts, too, need warmth to recover from our winters and harshness and return to us again only after the coldness in us passes . . . if it passes. . . .

"So they're still here," I add as though to myself. "They haven't moved away. Do they still have the same last name, or have they married?"

"There's only one with that last name, Olga. She's a widow, and she resumed her father's surname. The others have changed theirs," replies the white-eyed girl.

"All right," I rejoin, "does this Olga suck at her hair and like to paste on beauty spots?"

"Yes, she does," replies the girl, surprised.

"Well, that's it, then! Now, tell me, what's your favorite lunch?"

"Chicken rolls and bacon!" declares the white-eyed girl happily.

I let her go then, and after she's gone I think to myself how the future is of value only if we predict it; otherwise it's just ordinary fuel —garbage, if you will. Just then the boy with the wax in his eye brings me my drink and I finally order lunch.

"Bring me a chicken roll and bacon," I say.

After lunch I go out into the street. Rustling in my ears, like a silky beard, is a long-unheard language, learned in my youth.

How easily language makes one remember something that that language neither says nor wants to say and that would never occur to you, no matter what you are told. And yet, all the same, it reminds you of who knows whom; that very rustling whispers something to you, and afterward you look around and hardly know where you are. Absorbed in these thoughts, I look around me and hardly know where I am. A moth-eaten dog is trotting down the street ahead of me, thrusting his left hind leg between his front two. And then suddenly he changes legs and veers to the other side; he goes into a courtyard, and I somehow realize that I have arrived. I suddenly also realize that there are always two "now"s and that the present is not as indivisible and solid as you usually think. I recall such wonderful words as "krokarye" and "skara," which mean God knows what but caress the ear. Who needs to know their meaning when in between other words a lovely, eternally young word sticks to your ear (even if that ear does snivel like a nose), a term such as "white bees." What a wonderful expression, "white bees"! And it means both what you want it to and what you don't. "White bees" are the generation of your descendants (if you have any) that comes right after great-great-grandchildren. Imagine, what a powerful and visionary language! And you, you think, you have to occupy yourself with the word before it is yet a word. And once, when you were young, you occupied yourself with love before there was yet love. . . .

And right then I knock at the door, but nobody answers. I yawn into my fist, lose my hearing for a second while I yawn, and then rap again. Silence, as when I yawned. I try the door and walk into Olga's house. Everything is open. The house is listing like a ship. All the icons are already hanging crooked, and the windows half-close by themselves. And then I catch sight of Olga in a mirror and freeze. She is standing in a corner of the room, her eyes glued to me. I look at her as if I've never seen her before, and she looks at me in the same way. She does not recognize me. I remember her as a girl who swatted flies with her pigtails, turning her head left and right. Now her hair is very long, and I suspect that the ends are always wet with pee.

"What do you want of me, sir?" she inquires in a watery voice I do not remember. She stands under her hair as if under a tent. She was never beautiful, but she considered all clumsiness a virtue, all stupidity innocence, and her own plainness a guarantee that she would become a saint. Once a month she changed the soles of her feet like a snake its skin. I think how our ancestors, in making our youth and our life, also made, with just as much clumsiness, our old age and our death. Through the back window I see the sky behind the house, with clouds billowing in the wind, coasting like sails without need of a boat. And I stand up and spit in Olga's ear.

"Atanas, you brute, you haven't changed!" she cries out, clapping her hands in joy. "I didn't recognize you!"

And her speech begins to meander, as in the old days. She was a past master at scuttling every conversation into a ditch. I am immediately told, disjointedly and in between her paste-on beauty spots, her entire life story since we parted. She serves me coffee and brandy, the same brandy that led me to her; we sit and talk. I see how her grape brandy has no color but collects, like a magpie its feathers, the colors in the room to spruce itself up. I notice it is partial to yellow. Meanwhile, Olga is tireless. Married early, she divorced early and was proud of it, because these constant divorces in her family, from one generation to the next, are a kind of family heirloom.

"You know the story, my sweet," she says to me, happily chatting about her marriage, "you know the story about the writer and the pauper? A writer is a writer, and he will not spoil only what he hasn't written. Well, one day the writer meets a pauper who is all alone in the world; he's in the street, blowing into his hands, with no place to go. The writer offers him a place in one of his stories. He offers to let him live there, at least temporarily, because, he says, he's got a large room and plenty of food in his story; he says: Of course, it's snowing there now and it's cold, but there's a stove and wood, you can warm yourself, he says, to your heart's content. The writer says his piece, his glasses trembling with emotion. The pauper says nothing, his beard merely glowing. It is red and ablaze; he could light a pipe on it. With no place to go and nothing to do, the pauper jumps at even this; to a poor man, he says, even lunch in a dream is a godsend. And so he moves in. On his first day in the story all he does is sleep. On the second day all he does is eat, and on the third day he starts calling on the other tenants, the heroes of the story. They see that he doesn't quite belong there, but he hangs around as if he were the main character. On the fourth day he begins asking for loans of money; otherwise, he says, he'll ruin the whole train of events. And they begin to give him a penny here, two there, just to get the wretch off their backs. He doesn't return the money, and on the fifth day he starts pestering and blackmailing the women in the story. His evil eye on them, he paws and ogles them with a gaze that ferments like potatoes. And bit by bit he becomes emboldened. On the sixth day he makes babies, and on the seventh, as soon as he sees that he has grown rich in the story, he immediately moves out, drops in the right places a few words about the heroine, quickly prospers, becomes mayor, bans the story, accuses the writer of having dreamed such-and-such a bad dream (recorded in the report), and takes him to court. . . .

"Well, that's how it was with my marriage. Like the writer, I barely survived."

"But you were rolling in children and grandchildren. The story didn't stop you from doing that," I cut in, waiting to see whether she will say something about the children. But she starts talking about her sisters. Never mind, I think, let her have her say about the sisters; she's bound to get around to the children later.

"I'm sinking like this house, my dear. While the three of us sisters were together, I always looked out for the family. Cecilia and Lenka (you remember Lenka; her lover calls her Azra now), as soon as they grew up, immediately began looking out for themselves. Family doesn't exist for them, and no wonder. They didn't form their own families and become homemakers. And they never will, because their lovers won't let them. They prefer my sisters the way they are now."

"And what way is that?" I ask, all the time waiting for her to get around to the children.

"You know, about the little fish that, when it's swallowed by a pike, thinks to itself: Oh, if only I'd been swallowed by a catfish! For them the height of freedom is to be able to attack me and mine; they have chosen us to blame for all their failures and believe that we are the only ones to derive some advantage from our common misfortune. Obsessed with these false freedoms directed against others, against me and mine, they don't even think of their own freedom, they don't even dare to laugh until their lovers laugh first, for fear of appearing silly. They're willing to have ties with me and to keep up the family only if it doesn't impinge on their own personal interests or the interests of their lovers, who come from abroad. I, on the other hand, look out for my own interests and the good of my children only if it does not clash with or work to the detriment of the entire family, of all of us, my sisters included. Somehow I don't think of their lovers or of my ex-marriage as anything important. But I can see that my children aren't faring well in this family, for which I've sacrificed everything."

And right there, when she finally mentions the children, I turn into an ear and think: Now all she has to do is ask me about my earnings and the stage is set for me to say my piece.

"My sisters and I," she goes on, "we're not, I see, crippled in the same soul. They look out for themselves and their lovers, while I have aged and am now ugly when I sleep, and I still don't see what advantage my children have, I don't build or plan for their future, I'm not used to it, I keep thinking, somehow, that the family itself will take care of it all, and of them, too, that everything will fall into place."

"He who cannot help himself cannot help others," I prompt her gently.

"That's easy for you to say, but a single woman has to look to her family for shelter and protection, especially if she hasn't got a powerful patron abroad, like my sisters. Family is my only defense against calamity and miscreants. But even here, in my own home, I'm forced to suffer torments beyond your wildest imagination. My sisters and I spit tears at each other, you can tell from the salt on our faces afterward. Every evening, Azra kneels and prays for the devil or God to take Cecilia's children away across the water, and Cecilia kneels and clasps her hands, begging the devil or God to do the same with Azra's. And I, I kneel under this icon, whispering: 'If you answer their prayers, Lord, you needn't answer mine. They will all have been answered.' But they haven't been. And my sisters, with their high-placed patrons, shrink from nothing. They even go for my grandchildren, they procure my little granddaughters for their lovers, to soften them up. And after a few years, some sluts appear at my door—they've packed their asses and are on the road—and some boys, dripping with brandy instead of rain. And they say: We are your progeny, the ones who were led astray. How can I know? I keep counting which are mine and which are not, but I simply can't work it out. I buy a sponge and keep erasing: this one isn't, and I don't think that one is. My head aches, and I can't sleep from thinking about which of them are genuine and which aren't."

"Well, if anyone will help you, I will. You and your offspring. That's why I'm here."

Olga perks up slightly at these words, her elbows cut through her hair, and she says just what I've been hoping to hear:

"People here say that, when you went out into the world, three dinars were like one to you, and that you're here today because now every one dinar is like two in your hand. Tell me, was it worth it?"

I think to myself, "She should be swathed and kept like Christmas yeast," and I say:

"It was hard at first. At least three times during that first year abroad, I dreamed of myself. It's me all right, but I'm an old man. White as a sheep in my dream. Somewhere in Switzerland, wherever, I take a room, lie down in bed, my shirt hanging on the chair as though someone were sitting with his back turned. I get up in the morning, and as I dress I glance down my body, but my penis is nowhere to be found, it's retreated like a snail, and I think: 'That's what it'll be like when I die.' I gaze around the room, think and remember how in the eighteenth century the Serbs used to say that they lived scattered like Jews. And I didn't want to tidy up that room in Switzerland, so that it wouldn't look to me or to anyone else as though I were staying there, as though it would be my home. 'For how many more generations will we go on like this?' I think to myself, looking at the snow-deep dust in the corners and at the cobwebs that catch at the eyelashes. That's what I thought while I still had hopes of having children. I live like that and see that I can say whatever you like in German but don't understand a word when they speak to me. Sadness ticks in the corner like a clock, it wakes me up every spring and sometimes runs fast, the unaired cupboards reek of last year's pipe smoke, and I get muddled. I write English in Cyrillic, correspond in Greek script with people from Munich, and write Russian in Latin script. Healthy when awake, I'm ill in my sleep at night, and it's only in my dreams that I realize how much I've changed, beyond recall. My dreams are shallow, there are no other rooms in them. In the morning you can log it all, take inventory as in an army barracks. In short, they're not dreams, they're garbage."

"Well, was it worth it?" asks Olga, interrupting my story.

"The worst part came with the success and the money. That's something you don't know, and neither did I until I went through it myself. Those who loved you before your success will no longer love you after it. Fame and success are not forgiven. And these people will keep their distance from you. And you will come to hate and push away those who were once close to you, whether you want to or not. And in your eyes they will die. And you will turn completely to those others, whom you met and who met you only after your success. And they will be your family and your friends. But you don't sustain a fast with meat. None of that means anything to me. You at least have children, grandchildren. I know, unhappy grandchildren, you'll say, but I, why am I reduced to being alone like this, like a path in the woods? And now we come to the reason for my visit. I said to myself: If I haven't had luck or offspring, you have. At least half your wish has been fulfilled, if not all. And so I headed this way, and here I am. When you arrive, as they say, I judge you by your clothes, when you leave, by your reason, but we don't have to pretend with each other or play guessing games. We, at least, know each other."

"Yes, we know each other," says Olga, and she begins to grope for the brandy glasses, clearing them away blindly to her left, staring unblinkingly at me with her viscid gaze, which clings like mildew to whatever it touches.

"So let's get to the point," I continue. "I'd like to adopt some of your descendants, all of them, in fact, however many there are. . . ."

Olga instantly throws herself into my arms and kisses me, her upper lip smelling of bread and her lower of cork. Through these aromas I kiss and remember those same lips of a quarter of a century ago, I remember kisses through Olga's hair, I feel alone and weak, I see the seven Pleiades in the sky resembling the seven days in the week, and my thoughts disperse like clouds in the water. I sense which of my nights is inside me, and which hour inside her, but I say:

"Olga, you cow, I'm not proposing to you, I just want to buy your great-great-grandsons. To pay what it costs to have them assume my name."

She stares at me, plucks an eyebrow impulsively, like catching a fly, and only then becomes astonished.

"What did you say? You want to buy my great-great-grandsons?"

"Yes."

"What do you want great-great-grandsons for?"

"Why, I told you; you can see for yourself, I'm as alone as the nose on your face, I need some support and joy in my old age. . . ."

"What are you saying, man? Move your foot! I won't live to see my great-great-grandsons, let alone you. . . ."

"All right, if not your great-great-grandsons, then sell me the white bees."

"Whoever heard of buying and selling human beings, unborn ones at that? Are you out of your mind? Why, they don't even have souls yet! But, let me tell you, your strength doesn't match your brain, it's much much weaker; you won't achieve a tenth of what you plan, and Lord alone knows what you're planning. How can I sell my own flesh and blood, no matter why you need them? And male, at that! It's out of the question. They're not for sale."

"Well, if you don't like the idea of selling them, think of it as my wanting to adopt them as sons and we're even! That'll be better for both them and you. I'll take on the costs of supporting them, and I'll pay you right now in cash. Later they'll pay it back bit by bit, not you. What's unclear about it?"

"Atanas, where on earth did you eat today? It wasn't at that scoundrel's at the Three Benches, was it? He takes the fish and wrings it out like a shirt until it loses all its stench. And then, seven days later, people have reason to remember that same fish. Until they're wrung dry themselves . . . But, tell me, do you fish? The perch here are excellent. They catch them with live grasshoppers dipped in brandy. . . . The fish go for it like mad."

While Olga's talking, my fur hat watches me from the little chair in the corner like a cat. That look, or whatever it is, makes me tremble. It occurs to me that one remembers reality in one's dreams just as faintly as one remembers a dream when awake, and I say, as though not having heard the bit about the fish and the grasshoppers:

"You're right, why have just them alone, what would I do with them? I'll take everything else that goes with them."

"With whom?" Olga whimpers again.

"With the great-great-grandsons," I reply.

"And what is it that goes with the great-great-grandsons?"

"Why, this house and this property."

"And me?" she says. "Me you'd discard?" She picks up a glass pensively and waters the flowers through her fingers.

"You're no bother. None at all. I'd buy the house so that both it and the property wouldn't be mine for another two hundred years. But I'd give the money immediately. As for now, I wouldn't even take as much land as my tailor takes fabric to make a suit."

"I don't understand a thing. You're frightening me. We never talked like this before. What do you want with a house in two hundred years?"

"What do you mean, what do I want? Why, to provide the great-great-grandsons with a roof over their heads and room to run around in and fresh air to inhale. And I ask nothing for myself except the earth for my grave. What's so strange about a man wanting to choose where he's going to be buried? But if you don't want to, I'll just go to your sisters. They'll be more reasonable. There are Lilians even without Lilian!"

And with those words I pick up my fur hat.

"Be careful it doesn't have kittens on you," she adds with a laugh, looking at the fur hat. But at the door I suddenly feel Olga come up to me from behind, press her breasts against my back, and whisper into my ear, through her hair and mine:

"You wouldn't want great-great-granddaughters? You wouldn't buy girls? I'll give them to you at half-price. . . . You came here to buy the East, the Arabs buy the West. I'll give you the girls because you come from the West. Better to you than to the Arabs."

And then I feel her breasts rolling left and right against my back and I notice they are cold. I hear the birds' voices knitting endless socks and gloves with a thousand fingers there outside, above the sky, which has already descended to the ground with the fall of darkness. My thoughts again scatter, leaving only pure transparent fear, through which nothing twinkles, not even the stars.

"Half-price?" I say and step back into the room.

2 ACROSS

1 DOWN

Critics are like medical students: they always think a writer is suffering from the very disease they happen to be studying at the time. But a writer always suffers from the same disease, the disease of crisscrossing words, of building, from the one tongue in his mouth, two. What is a book, really, other than a collection of words well crossed? However, there is also the reader who suffers from the same love, the love of crosswords. He will certainly have already noticed that in this book there are four sections marked *Across,* and that each of the chapters in these sections is entitled *Down.* He will immediately be reminded of a crossword, and he will be right. This novel can indeed be read in the same way that one does a crossword. Across here, down there, a name here, a surname there.

But, you will say, primitive man had, like an animal, hundreds of feelings and thoughts running through his head at the same time, and it is only modern man who has separated thought from thought, who has superimposed one feeling over the countless other feelings that constantly inundate him from the outside world, who has given them ordinal numbers and started to differentiate the first from the last. Why now go back? Why now introduce a new way of reading a book, instead of the one that moves, like life, from beginning to end, from birth to death? The answer is simple: because any new way of reading that goes against the matrix of time, which pulls us toward death, is a futile but honest effort to resist this inexorability of one's fate, in literature at least, if not in reality. The present is like a garden; in it grows one plant that contemporaries eat with relish, another that (if it does not shrivel) will be the most splendid of foods for the people of tomorrow (the sons and grandchildren of those today), while the third grows for some distant descendants, who will weed our garden of everything we loved and look for their own magic plant, their hyssop, their mandragora, caring little about the gardener. This we know. So why, then, must the reader always be like a police inspector, why must he always walk in his predecessor's every footstep? Why not let him at least zigzag somewhere? Not to mention the heroes and heroines of the book! Perhaps they, too, would like to show a different profile sometimes, to stretch their arms out to the other side. They must be tired of always seeing readers in the same formation, like a flock of geese flying south or trotters in a horse race. Perhaps these heroes in the book would like to pick a reader out of this gray procession, if for no other reason than to bet on one of us now and then. What do we know?

Naturally, this new way of reading is not obligatory. It is for those who choose not to read in order of succession and across (as the river flows), but *down,* as the rain falls. These readers should, in all four sections of this Testimonial, follow the chapters marked with the same numbers. As in all crosswords in the world. And they should not be afraid to read this way. The crossed words will be no less fine for it. Only bad stories need fine language and fine words. Good stories find their own words and their own language and do well in all tongues. This, then, is not the point in question. The point, as we said, is to find a new way of reading, not a new way of writing. Because, while a fine story may not need fine language or fine words, it does need a fine way of reading, which, unfortunately, does not yet exist, but will, we hope, come with time ... Because, just as there are talented and untalented writers, so there are gifted and ungifted readers ...

"Crosswords! Well, that's not much of a discovery!" you will say. Of course it isn't. But it will do for a start. Until you get used to it. For you must bear in mind that a writer is like a tailor. Just as the latter, when tailoring a suit, covers up the shortcomings and defects of his customer, so the writer, when tailoring a book, has to cover up the defects and shortcomings of his reader. And these shortcomings, as with any suit, are in both width and length.

HOW TO SOLVE THIS BOOK DOWN

Whoever chooses to read this book, or this crossword, downward first, like the Chinese, instead of across, will gain the following advantages by progressing vertically. He will be able, under direction:

> 1 DOWN—to read or skip over all three accompanying notes of this Testimonial, the second of which lies before him now, while the first he has already encountered;
> 2 DOWN—to follow, through all four sections, the fate of the central figure of this Testimonial, architect Razin;
> 3 DOWN—to gain complete insight into the plans, drawings, and other contents of architect Razin's famous notebooks, whose covers always depict a landscape painted with tea, just as the cover of this book carries the title of the same name;
> 4 DOWN—to follow, in every detail, the fate of the heroine of this book, Vitacha Milut;
> 5 DOWN—to read separately the love story in this book, because architect Razin's Testimonial can also be taken as a love story;
> 6 DOWN—to learn about the separate fates and adventures of the three sisters Olga, Azra, and Cecilia, which at least partly explain to us architect Razin's unusual and incredible rise to success in business.

In short, whoever reads this novel downward will follow the fate of the characters, and whoever chooses to read it crossways will basically follow the plot of the story but not the denouement, because the solution of a crossword never lies in the crossword itself; that, as is known, is given separately, "in the next issue."

The reader of this Testimonial may find the whole thing inapt and unseemly. Why should a collection of texts devoted to a prominent businessman—"Mr. Two Percent," as architect Razin is rightly called —be structured in such an unfitting way, in the form of a crossword? The answer is this: the book takes its form out of respect for our benefactor and school friend, architect Razin. He always loved crosswords. Not only solving them, but also collecting them. His notebooks are full of crosswords clipped out of various American, European, and Yugoslav papers and magazines. And the reason was always the same. His press-clipping service sent him any crossword that included as solutions the pseudonyms or names of Vitacha Milut, Razin by marriage, or the name of his own company, ABC Engineering & Pharmaceuticals, or that expected the solver to fill in three squares with the initials of the owner of a famous company, that, of course, being: A(tanas) F(yodorovich) R(azin). Indeed, architect Razin's entire life can be viewed as one enormous crossword.

H O W   T O   S O L V E   T H I S   B O O K   A C R O S S

The reader who opts for the old way of reading, for the one-way street, the reader who is determined to slide toward death by the shortest route, without putting up a fight—in other words, to read *across* rather than down—will be surprised to see that the chapters in this Testimonial are not given in numerical order. And he may rightly object to such poetic license. Why should these numbers be haphazard, and not the way they are everywhere else, in all crosswords and love stories in the world? The answer, once again, is quite simple. Because not everybody likes to read in order. And some do not like to write in order either. As we all know, crosswords can be filled in with a pencil, with purple ink, a felt-tipped pen dipped in tears or in a kiss, with a hairpin or a fork. It does not matter. But it does matter who does the filling in. Because there are at least two kinds of crossword fans, just as on Mount Athos there are two kinds of monks—the idiorrhythmics (solitaries) and the cenobites (solidaries). There are those who in crosswords like and hunt for the actual words, and there are those who like and hunt for only well-arranged crossings. The ones put in time where not much time is needed, and the others time where Time is needed. Those who solve haphazardly, and those who solve in order. That is why this book has been adjusted accordingly. For the former, the disorder is already there so they do not have to create it themselves, and for the latter, there are the numbers, so let them instill some order.

I. The former, who like words more than the crossing of words, look only at the clues, and pay little attention to the crossword itself or to its squares. As though nursed under the knee of their mother, they will sometimes prefer the wrong word to the right, even if the maneuver of crissing and crossing fails to succeed as a result. It will not bother them that in this book, or this crossword, unlike all other crosswords, the numbers across are given in sequential order but the numbers down are not, they are given haphazardly. Each has his own little table, his own household and bed, his own hearth and salt, his own little garden, and in it his homeland with fruit and water. They barely know and do not easily suffer one another; they neither like nor mention names; each plaits his own braid, cuts his own hair; they have no common enemies, because they are never together. They have a mother cult, but not a cult of women. Theirs is the night; the backbone is the symbol of their life; they are fluent in foreign languages; they are painters, fishermen, and idolators; they are good with wheat and bread; they know how to keep silent and how to speak. When their people fall upon hard times, they take on the difficult task of picking them up by the scruff of the neck. They think: "Since you have already read the book and lived life, isn't it too late and futile to arrange them backward and posteriorly, like a crossword? Is it worth it to arrange one's memories like pieces on a chessboard before a game? Should our memories of a life gone by always be turned right side out like a shirt and folded in the drawer? In arranging the crossings of crosswords, do we not lose the words themselves? In trying to arrange your life, do you not lose that life, do you not lose the world in the very effort to put it in order?" For such crossword fans, part of the job has already been done here; they will see and look at the book before them as it is; that is, they will be able to read it by casting the die, and then it depends on whatever number comes up, from one to six.

II. But there are also the others, those who will complete the job in advance, who will first sit down to cross the words and fill in the squares. Before they embark on reading, or before they embark on life, they will make sure that everything is in order and follows the rules. Recent history, which shows that a well-ordered, perfectly organized, and preadjusted world leads straight to mud and ruin, does not serve them as a teacher of life. Moving in strict order from chapter to chapter, they will in advance line up and inspect both their own troops and others', their own crossroads and others', with but a cursory glance at the words and their meaning, just as a military commander takes no notice of the individual men in his army or their names. They are the people's party of their native land, they do not know languages, they do not know how to speak, they foster the cult of the father and tradition, they are holy warriors, they have no property of their own, no shirt of their own on their back, because everything in their country they consider their own. They do not tie themselves to one place or one wall; where there are two of them there are all of them; they like to mention names; they get up together, sit down at the table together; morning is their part of the day, the stomach the symbol of man's being; they are healers, winegrowers, singers, and writers. They are practitioners, iconoclasts; it is they who lead the migrations of their people. They are builders, astronomers, mathematicians, and theater people. They stick together and hold power in their native land until the latter goes to ruin. They prefer the order of the crossings to the words in the crosswords. They will therefore define and circumscribe their own life and world, and that of others, compressing it into the squares with little concern for what these squares enclose. Or whether the squares can hold it all. Here again, they will follow the strict rule, wherein they will put into numerical order the chapters marked *Down,* abandoning the slightly careless arrangement left by the writer.

And as a medal for their efforts they will get the final inviolate order of reading and crossing, and only then and after that, on the basis of this infallible schedule, will they sit in the train safely to read the book or travel their life and others'. Concealed behind the words of their solutions will be the secret of an orderly, well-arranged world, which we have long been yearning for. Isn't it thrilling, what this group of crossword solvers is doing: to organize the world, someone else's at least, if not your own? My life and my book at least, if your own is not at hand or slips your attention?

Which of these two groups of crossword fans is right? In the right, of course, is the solid port of silence that one sails into after all crossings and after all solutions. How are we to know who is right, when in our lifetime there have been so many whom we have had to respect, and so few whom we could love? That is why those who have loved at least once are fortunate. Loved a book at least, if not a dog or a cat, their writer if not their wife. And unfortunate and wretched are those who have respected a book they did not love and hated those they did.

As for architect Razin, his is a case you will not believe. He belongs to both the one and the other group of crossword-solvers. Originally he belonged to the first group; his life seemed more like disorder to start with, in youth his fate (unlike yours) really was a kind of badly solved or totally unsolved crossword. And then he turned over a new leaf, switched pencils, and enrolled in the other group. But it was not easy. Believe it or not, in order to switch membership from one group to another, you must leave your country, change your name and passport, forget one language in order to learn another, and start from scratch. The Greek must become a German, the Italian a Russian, the Serb must become Magyarized, the Hungarian must go over to the Romanians. And our architect Atanas Razin did all that. At first, admittedly, he felt as though he had been slapped by an empty sleeve, but later things improved. And now here before us is the Testimonial honoring him and it all.

One will find in this Testimonial, as one does in crosswords, prominent political figures, parts of the world, fine pieces of furniture, big towns and small from Šabac in Serbia, where (as is known) Faust once stayed, to Los Angeles in the United States, where architect Atanas Razin, alias Svilar, once lived. And there will be black squares to make the job easier for the author of the crossword, and give the solver a chance to rest. The black squares are the "nights" between the "days" of the crossword and have been inserted here like the black squares in crosswords, which, where necessary, break the sequence of empty squares that are to be filled in with letters. These black squares, as is known, do not count and are not numbered, but there is no crossword without them, and so this one is not without them either. Let us say something about them as well.

Found among architect Razin's papers were several stories, mostly written in a strange hand. They have as much to do with him as the black squares have to do with the words of the crossword. Some of them are said to have been told by architect Razin on special occasions (like the Story of Plakida), or were told to him (like the family legend about Vitacha Milut's beautiful foremothers), or were even told in turns by him and another person as part of a game (like the story of the Blue Mosque). Among these tales are some that have nothing to do with this Testimonial, or this crossword, or this love story. These sections and stories, mixed in among all the others, will have to be discovered by the reader himself, without anybody's help. Will the honest person who finds them please keep them, mail them back to the owner, the editor of this crossword, or else throw them away.

But, in hunting for such intruder-stories, the reader must be careful not to start throwing out the necessary stories, the real chapters of the novel, the white instead of the black squares of the crossword! Because then the book will come undone like a sweater, the crossed words will fly apart, and all he will be left holding is what can be found in any novel, and that is the familiar clause:

ALL READERS OF THIS BOOK
ARE ENTIRELY IMAGINARY.
ANY RESEMBLANCE TO ACTUAL READERS
IS COINCIDENTAL.

3 DOWN

The second of architect Razin's notebooks in our possession includes somewhat fewer entries than the first. On the first page, a note written in large print by the owner catches the eye: "Broz smokes Havanas and drinks twenty-five-year-old Chivas Regal. He offers his guests wine that is the same vintage they are."

The landscape painted with tea on the cover of this notebook presents a somewhat broader panorama than those on architect Razin's other notebooks. It depicts a littoral dotted with islands and clouds drifting like canoes in the sky; in a corner of the open sea a small storm is raging, as though locked in a room. The brush used to paint this scene has been preserved. According to its inscription, it was made from the hair of Vitacha Milut, Razin by marriage.

Some ten types of tea were used to paint the sea: one could immediately recognize Chinese black tea, laid on in a very thick coat; Earl Grey, extremely diluted; "Little Nun," used cold, or perhaps simply soaked in mineral water before cooking; green maté, generously applied to highlight the sea; while the "tropanas," a dark fruit tea, and "Winter Dreams," a broken tea, were spread on with a wooden spoon and served as the base. The golden Nepal, a pinch of "Margarita's

Hope," and the dark-red Piña Colada were used to paint the islands and the mainland. The sky was washed with the colors of "bendjo," a tea made out of hashish mixed with another tea called "samba pa," and with the expensive Russian white tea, used to excite greyhounds. The underbelly of the clouds was accentuated with Chinese dust tea, and the entire littoral and islands seemed to have been captured at great speed, making the colors, the teas, look as though they had been just slightly displaced from their beds, as though they had been wiped on one side with a brush made of Chinese otter tail. Underneath the picture was the caption:

BRIONI, THE SUMMER RESIDENCE OF
THE YUGOSLAV PRESIDENT JOSIP BROZ TITO

On one of the very next pages, there is a geographic photograph of the Brioni islands, and an aerial view of the same region. Underneath is an abbreviated excerpt about Brioni, taken (as architect Razin notes) from an encyclopedia, but it is obvious that in places the owner of the notebook inserted additions or remarks of his own:

"The Brioni isles are a collection of two islands and twelve islets off the western coast of Istria in the Adriatic Sea, separated from the mainland by the Fažana Canal. They lie at a distance of 6.5 km. from the town of Pula. The biggest island is Veliki Brion. The land is composed of light-colored limestone; the rocks, which are quite porous and lend themselves to cutting, are covered with a layer of oily red soil (which bakes quite well and can be used as paint). The temperatures here are quite stable—5.8° in winter, 12.5° with the spring, 22.8° in the summer, and 14.8° come autumn. Lush vegetation blankets the islands, and the air is quite humid, so that the meadows are always green. Settled in the year 2000 B.C., the Brioni islands boast ancient architectural landmarks—a terraced castle descending to the Bay of Veriga and an aqueduct. According to one legend, it was here that the prehistoric man of Brion discovered his tomorrow, which had not existed before in the consciousness of his ancestors. Through the centuries, many places of worship and structures were built on these

islands; a Byzantine fort in the Bay of Dobrika, a three-nave basilica in the Bay of Gospa, a Benedictine monastery with sixth- and seventh-century mosaics; built in the Middle Ages were the donjon, the castle, the churches of St. Germanus, St. Roch, and St. Anthony. The economy was based on the saltworks, viticulture, and olive-growing, and later on cattle-raising and farming as well. In 1893, P. Kupelwieser, a Merano industrialist, purchased the islands, where he lit yesterday's unfinished pipes, drinking in their bitter smoke in lieu of morning coffee. At great expense (which they concealed from him) and with the help of the famous bacteriologist R. Koch, he rehabilitated the islands and then built large and, for the times, sumptuous hotels. Next to the beach he fixed up a covered pool with heated seawater and dropped crabs into it, so that people would know the water was clean. A large hippodrome was built, and tennis courts and a golf course. Drinking water was brought from the Istrian mainland by an underwater conduit beneath the Fažana Canal (2 km.). All this was destroyed by bombs at the end of World War II, and restored after the war...."

On the blank sheets of paper in the middle of his notebook, architect Razin penned the story of "The Blue Mosque," which begins with the words "One evening in Istanbul, just before aksham, the evening prayer..." The story originated in what appears to have been a game in which he and a mistress from his youth took turns telling it when they met again in their native country, many years later. This story (like the others in Razin's notebooks) is given separately in this Testimonial and therefore shall not be dwelled upon here.

Right after it, the notebook presents a detailed plan of several different buildings (the foundation and cross section) with information about the building material used, and one is struck by the special attention architect Razin paid to traffic arteries and access roads. The green belt around these buildings is carefully drawn, and a separate legend is given describing them:

1. Main house
2. New cellar
3. Old cellar
4. Terrace with pergola
5. Vineyard
6. Mandarin garden
7. Fountain
8. House for work and recreation (Macedonian salon)
9. Kitchen
10. Slovenian salon
11. Fisherman's salon
12. Indonesian salon
13. Neptune (bust)
14. Pier

Underneath the sketch, architect Razin wrote:

WINTER RESIDENCE OF YUGOSLAV PRESIDENT JOSIP BROZ TITO, MARSHAL OF YUGOSLAVIA AND LEADER OF THE PARTISAN MOVEMENT DURING WORLD WAR II. SITUATED ON THE ISLAND OF VANGA, BRIONI.

(N.B.: When one of J. B. Tito's residences was built on the islands of Vanga and Veliki Brion, everything on the island was repaired, the restored castle and tower were turned into a museum, new roads were laid, the port facilities were made operative, and in 1978 a safari park was installed on Veliki Brion, with a multitude of animal and plant species living in the wide-open spaces.)

Five or six blank pages later, several German crosswords were pasted into the notebook, together with the following text:

The Man Who Invented the Zero

The man who invented the zero came back after many years to the marketplace where, before he invented the zero, he had liked to sit and think. He used to sit here and think about how the unriddling of unknown laws and their implementation was our life. He used to think about this sitting on a rock amid the trash cans in the marketplace, because all the other, nicer spots in the square were always taken whenever he came by. There was a stone bench with a superb view that especially caught his eye, but that spot in particular was out of the question, because it was always claimed by somebody else. There was always somebody already sitting there. And so he invented the zero sitting on his rock amid the trash cans.

Now, when he returned so many years later to this place where he had invented the zero, it was winter, and all the seats in the square were empty. He could have his choice. However, he had come here not to invent the zero, because the zero he had already invented years before, but to sit once again in the spot where he had invented the zero and to remember how he had invented the zero. And so once again he headed straight for that rock by the trash cans. That spot was now his forever, and he could no longer choose.

And with a smile which was a bird forced to fly through water, he walked up to the rock by the trash cans, to his rock where he had invented the zero, but he did not stop. He walked on and finally installed himself on the beautiful stone bench with the superb view.

"I piss on the man who invented the zero," he said, sitting down.

2 DOWN

Asked to provide information about the origin, nature, and youth of my son, architect Atanas Razin, I feel both flattered and hurt at the same time. I remember the piano keys stained with wine, tobacco, and wax, because Atanas liked to play by candlelight, and sometimes he played with his hands contorted, with his rings instead of his fingers. It is an effort for me to remember Atanas's father, my first husband; I still see only his Russian eyes, turbid and pearly like a shell when it opens. The rest I don't remember. Some of those distant days are no clearer to me than last night's dream. But, let me try.

All my life I always threw away my spoons before a trip. As if to say: I don't want them to survive me. Well, let me tell you before anything else how I threw away the first spoon. As a child I lived in Panchevo, on the banks of the Tamish River, in mud jumping with fish, where my family took in overnight guests in their three-room house. Because in those days, Panchevo, a small town at the confluence of the Danube, facing Belgrade, was still on the southern border of the Austrian Empire, and there was always a lot of coming and going, with people needing a bed for the night. One man stuck half a watermelon on his head, swam across the Danube and the frontier from the

Serbian to the Austrian side, and showed up at our place for the night. An unknown man came to us one evening in a terrible storm and downpour. Even the candle became blind. He brought a big soaking-wet package and kept wailing in a strong Russian accent:

"We're locked into twelve months as though they were twelve solid rooms, and we have no way out except from one room to the next. And, believe me, apart from these rooms, there are more beautiful and sumptuous chambers through which we shall never pass, not to mention the woods around them and the heavenly hunting grounds...."

As he was taking his leave in the morning, he left behind his package.

"The weather is so bad that now the wolf cries first and only then rips into its food," he added, saying goodbye. "Let this stay here with you until some more propitious occasion. But if I do not return within the year, then whatever it is, let it be yours." And he departed.

We unwrapped the package, and inside found a painting. We hung it up next to the icon of Saint Petka, our family saint, and forgot all about it. Two years later we had another guest for the night, because Panchevo's only inn, the Trumpeters, was closed. This one was again a Russian, but a gentleman. With a beard, in boots that squeaked under the table as though they were spelling out the alphabet and angry at their master, he sat and drank tea, his eyes fixed on that painting. The corners of his pockets were frayed from what you could tell was the nuzzling of borzois, who tore at them with their nails. And he had brought a whip. His name was Tolstoy. He wanted to sleep in the barn with the horses, but we wouldn't let him: it was cold. He laughed and went to bed where we told him. And in the morning he pointed at the painting and asked where we had gotten it. When he was told, he became obsessed again, and went on and on about it.

"Do you know," said he to my mother, "who that is in that painting?"

"Good Lord, sir, of course I know," she retorted. "Spare me your inanities, man."

And suddenly he asked:

"And would you, matushka, sell me that little picture?"

"It's not for sale," said Mother, rebuffing this Tolstoy again, but he was insistent.

"I'll give you," he said, "a gold coin for it!"

"What does it matter!" said Mother, doing a sudden about-face. "If you're willing to give, then give, and take the thing away. It's not my patron saint that I should keep it."

And, sure enough, he rolled a gold coin out of his boot, which merely squeaked sadly, and tossed it onto the table, and we began wrapping the picture in a shirt for him. But while he was doing up the painting, he could not stop himself from asking one more time:

"You really don't know who's in that picture?"

When Mother shook her head and proceeded to tie up the painting with the shirtsleeves, he said sharply:

"The man in the picture is the famous Russian writer Count Leo Nikolayevich Tolstoy, my grandfather."

"What are you saying, man? May God put *you* in somebody's seat when it's still warm!" Mother retorted. "Saint Nicholas your grandfather? Since when have God's chosen people and saints started begetting the likes of you?" She spat at the gold coin and threw it back at him.

"Take your filthy money, I don't need it!" And she turned her back on him to unwrap the picture. "Boy, the wind blows in all kinds these days; Saint Nicholas his grandfather—the nerve . . ." The visitor realized then that he had chosen the wrong tack and apologized to Mother:

"I obviously got it wrong," he said. "It must be the fatigue or something," and he crossed himself in front of his grandfather Leo Nikolayevich Tolstoy, whose head and beard really were painted there. And he barely persuaded my mother to take back the gold coin and wrap up the "icon" for him in case he needed it on his trip.

I watched Count Tolstoy leave and thought how it is not he who knows the truth who is right, but he who is convinced of the truth of his lie. And that is how I conducted myself later in life. I'm telling you all this, because the third Russian who came to spend the night in our house left behind his wife like the gold coin, and took me like the icon. At the time I had already started reading *Anna Karenina* and fortunes from the cards.

And so I threw away my tin spoon, took my cards, and went off to Russia. When I left Moscow to come back, pregnant with Atanas, I threw away twelve silver spoons. All I brought with me from Russia was an iron sled shaped like a bed with a small bench. The sled was riddled with holes from shots that had been fired wildly by Atanas's grandfather during some binge. Painted on this bed-sled was a church, and on it a blue dome sprinkled with gold stars, as though one were looking at the sky from the outside, not from the inside, from earth. They hitched up an old nag to the bed and brought me back home in it from the Ukraine.

Atanas slept in that bed when he was a boy and every evening waited for me to come and comb his hair before going to sleep. He could not fall asleep uncombed. I would wet his head and knead it at length, like dough. And then, I remember, I would slice his hair with a comb, as though with a knife, and divide his hair the way one divides a loaf of bread. Finally, I would kiss him, stir the fire in the room, and tell him that by morning his hair would rise like dough for fritters. . . .

When he grew up, he proved to have an eye for the refined; he could tell, just from the sound, a silver from a metal fork, and crystal from glass; he liked purebred animals, well-built houses, and, I would say, beautiful women. But, a qualification needs to be made here.

My second husband, Major Kosta Svilar, for instance, now, he had a voice you could neither circumnavigate on the sea nor run a circle around on land. And he, too, had an eye for women. He could sight a good-looking woman like a target on a rifle range. I knew that; it was obvious at once. When he went to his mistress, he would first arrange to have a band of musicians wait for him at a tavern. And on his way home from his mistress's he would pick up the musicians and bring them to me, his wife, and have them serenade me under my window. But with me he was so jealous that I didn't dare even mention my first husband. My son, Atanas, had an entirely different nature. He was incapable of jealousy, which is to say he was also incapable of love. He was generally different from my husbands. Both my husbands liked to eat and drink, they liked taverns and the theater. Atanas's father, Razin, was fond of saying that wine was tasted before it was swallowed, but meat only after a bite was taken. And he divided women into those savored like wine, and those savored like venison. But Atanas never visited cafés, and could not stand the theater. I started being afraid that in some way he would disgrace me in front of the whole world.

So I dressed him in a new suit, tweaked his nose (as is the custom on such occasions), and took him to the theater. And he, I remember, said: "Mama, do you believe what they're saying on the stage?" I said: "It is not he who knows the truth and says it who is right, but he who maintains that his lie is the truth." And I told him the story of Tolstoy and Saint Nicholas.

And he said: "I don't believe a word they say on the stage. The theater is made for others, not for me or my kind."

Even later he generally had the strange feeling that some institutions as such were enemies, not just his, but his entire generation's. He said, using words he had brought back with him from Mount Athos: "The theater is always within the dominion of the cenobites, there's nothing there for solitaries like me. . . ."

I don't understand how somebody with so little love for music and the theater could develop such a passion for Vitacha Milut, who lived for singing, and whom, I think, he met at the opera. He was generally strange. When hungry, he could kill; when full—you could mold him like dough. . . . There are rivers that first appear in the form of a waterfall and instead of water have only a cloud and foam, and for a while that cloud sails over the empty riverbed before settling between its banks and beginning to flow. Atanas was like that. And his love for Vitacha Milut was like that. Even when he settled in his riverbed, when he married Vitacha, and when his life picked up full speed in America, I was still afraid that he would in some way disgrace me.

He did not have a happy family life. You may ask why I never told him that his father was the Russian Fyodor Alexeyevich Razin. Well, it was because Atanas had spent his childhood without a father anyway, and without a stepfather, since my second husband, Major Kosta Svilar, disappeared in the war in 1941. Does it matter whether Atanas grew up without a father or without a stepfather? That's like asking: Is it easier to go without wheat or without bread? And he did not have a happy marriage with his first wife either. That marriage didn't stand a chance. Atanas had the rare and unusual gift, or fault, of loving only one person all his life, Vitacha Milut Petka, and nobody else. I never understood it. It's like a painter who has the gift of painting only one single picture. There are people whose oblivion has a deep pocket. Of all the people I know, my own son had the greatest power of forgetting. Atanas forgot more in his lifetime than anybody. The force of his forgetfulness was titanic. But he could not forget Vitacha. I always felt it was a great injustice that Vitacha and I had to live at the same time. And the fact that we met was absolute disaster for all of us. She really was and still is a very beautiful woman. With such a deep arch down her back that her sweat can trickle down to her ass without moistening her dress or her belt. She, too, was strange. She never finished the school of politeness toward oneself—the elementary school of life. But she was always like those expensive perfumed oils that scorch everything they touch. Like all wise women, really, she had an extremely stupid cunt.

Atanas was still a minor, he still didn't know that God had created man on a Friday, when he came and said he wanted to get married. To an older woman, at that. I could feel it, he was already wearing *her* perfume.

"To whom?" I asked, in alarm.

"To Vitacha," he said, and I immediately knew I had reason to be alarmed. I thought to myself, "Well, instead of breasts you're going to get the finger," reached secretly for a pack of cards, slipped a fifth jack up my sleeve, and said:

"You know, Atanas, a night for her is like ten days for somebody else. Let's do it this way. You're still young. No one within shooting range can remember for the life of him whether you have a mustache or not. And probably neither can she. If you take her, older as she is, half-crazy, mute, you will have to support a kindergarten of her eight-year-old lovers, you will have to throw her little boys, like the seven Pleiades, out of your bed with the dawn. And I will not help you in that. So choose, if you can: either her or me! And if you can't, let's play a game of cards, and if I win you won't marry, but if you win you'll do what you want."

He became pensive. I could see it: the devil was riding him, driving him upstream through the night. But what could I do? "Bringing a child into the world is a kind of castration," I thought to myself, but said:

"I knew you would disgrace me in some way."

He laid out the cards then. And there's nothing I don't know about cards. My grandfather used to play, and he lost both me, his grand-daughter, and my brother in card games before we were even born. I had that diamond jack up my sleeve and I played, waiting to use it. I got two jacks, slipped in the third, and threw down three. Then he threw down three deuces and lost Vitacha in the game.

He looked at me for a moment; I felt his two thin eyes touching me, and the past in his belly turn into the future, because the future always starts from the large intestine. And then he said:

"Something's wrong; let's count the cards."

I froze, but I had no choice.

"If you feel like counting, count," I said, and he counted, but to my great astonishment there were just as many cards as there should be, and floating inside was my fifth jack, it had folded its wings like a seagull sailing through a rainy sky. How come, I wondered, racking my brains, and when he left, saying he would not marry, I grabbed the cards to count them myself and was flabbergasted. A two of clubs was missing, and that's why the number of cards with my fifth jack turned out right. . . .

After that, Atanas didn't dare approach Vitacha again for a long time. Both he and she were already married, or, better said, each was under his or her own stone; they had children from these marriages —she two daughters and he a son, who was not really his—when he, now getting on in years, went off on a trip to Greece—Mount Athos, I think it was. There he was probably given one of those medicinal pillows full of aromatic herbs, and suddenly it dawned on him that my second husband, Major Kosta Svilar, was not, of course, his father, nor Nikola Svilar his son. That was when he went out into the big world. The only thing he took from home was a family icon, *John the Precursor Shaving His Decapitated Head,* and from his new life he wrote, asking me to tell him the name of my companion in Russia, the name of his real father. And I answered him.

"You wanted to find your father?" I wrote him. "You even went to Greece, to Mount Athos, among the saints, to look for him. Well, first let me tell you who was not your father. Your father was certainly not Kosta Svilar, that hulk of an officer who peed from a moving horse. But it would have been your good luck if he had been. The man who fathered you had beautiful hair but a pair of soft-boiled ears underneath it. He sang in a choir with another 120 singers from the Don, and they all held hollow mirrors in front of their noses, they held the empty frames and through them shouted out into the world. He drank vodka and then stuck the glasses on his tongue and held it that way, but tea corresponded with his real nature. It was not for nothing that he used teas to paint flowers on Russian dolls and wooden spoons. And I, if you really want to know, I rolled barrels of plum brandy all over my body so as not to give him a son. But you were born all the same.

"You wanted a father. Well, that is your father. Now you've got him. The whole story about Razin, your entire father, along with his dogs and his faults, can fit into a slap on the boot. . . . But don't worry, you are not the error of your father's life. He didn't make that much of an effort over you. Your father crossed thousands of versts and cleared kilometers of snow, he traveled for years to get to the biggest error of his life, a mathematical error. And even so, such as he was, he was different, not like you. That man would have buried me next to his horse in the yard without batting an eye. But you, all you do is wash soap."

But Atanas did not think as I did. Whenever he inhaled a bit of darkness at night, he felt himself turn into his father for ten seconds. And he wanted to know what he was called during these ten seconds a day. He would say to me: "Before I didn't need Him. He was not my teacher. Now He is." And so, in place of the surname Svilar, under which he had finished school, he took the name Fyodor Alexeyevich Razin, and has carried it ever since. And it was only after taking this name that he summoned the strength to approach Vitacha anew. And it was then that he took her off into the world, where they married. I never really understood Vitacha's attitude to Atanas. Her sister Vida has kept some of Vitacha's letters, and they show that Vitacha's attitude to her second husband, my son, was strange, to say the least. What is called a great love, and it appears to have happened to them, is not as equally divided between the participants as is thought; one does the lathering, the other the shaving. If you don't get my meaning, I'll tell you an old story on this theme.

"A priest makes his wife swear that she will never eat without him; otherwise she will turn into a wolf. And she makes him swear that he will never drink without her; otherwise he will turn into a goat. Sometime later, during her husband's absence, she peered into his deaf book. She became absorbed in the reading, ate a leaf of cabbage, and turned into a wolf. When he came home, the priest ran straight into the beast. Naturally, he had no idea that it was his wife. As soon as they set eyes on one another, they went into battle, and the man managed to sink his teeth into the wolf's ear. He bit harder and harder until it gushed blood. As soon as he drank some blood, the man turned into a goat, and the wolf tore him apart.

"That is equality. The stronger always becomes the weaker."

And so it was with Atanas in his marriage to Vitacha. The proof is in a passage from one of Vitacha Milut's letters to Atanas:

"Somewhere on the shores of the South Seas, where the stars are farthest from their images, passengers off a ship ate a huge tortoise. Five hundred years later, on that same shore, a sailor found its shell and curled inside it for the night. In the morning, rested and cheerful, he pushed his arms, legs, and head through the openings in the shell, and descended into the sea in a private game with himself. After half a millennium the tortoiseshell again echoes with the beat of a heart and can again swim.

"So your heart echoes inside me."

. . .

As for the business activities of my son, architect Razin, as I told you, I was always afraid that in some way he would disgrace me.

"Good Lord," one of my friends usually says to me, "how can you be afraid Atanas will disgrace you? He's so handsome and as quick as the holy wind on the frescoes, he breakfasts with heads of state, he's wise, two languages lick his lips, he finances both communists and capitalists, he's left all his old ways behind him and given them up forever! What's gotten into you?"

But I, again, have my reasons. Because Atanas was not always all that serious. He himself says that he always dreamed of America wrongly. He believed that with the correct calculations one could lose a continent, and with the wrong calculations one could discover a sun. I don't know what sun he was thinking of, but I'll give you an example. There was a nice piece of furniture in our Belgrade apartment, all in plate glass and gilding, with little drawers. Instead of ring handles, the drawers had real glass knobs, and Atanas kept his money in one of them. Once, when he wanted to take out some money, he slid his hand into the drawer and scratched himself on a nail. His finger bled, and Atanas had to bandage it. Many years later, when his cash in America had piled up so high that he had to ask for special banking services, Atanas started checking San Francisco for a bank that would best serve his needs. And do you know what he did? Quite by chance he saw a building very much like that glass piece of furniture, with its gilding and countless drawers in which both he and I had once kept the little money we had. It was a bank. He walked right into the large hall and looked straight up at where a life-sized airplane was hanging as a decoration. But he was not looking at the gleaming aircraft. He was looking at the lefthand corner of the hall, at more or less the spot where the nail that had scratched his finger would have been in the bureau drawer. And, sure enough, sticking out of the wall was a mast with a flag. The tip had black stains on it like traces of dry blood.

And so, imagine, he decided on this bank and equipped it to handle his affairs; it serves him to this very day.

From his Russian father, Fyodor Alexeyevich Razin, Atanas inherited speed, and from me a predilection for the beautiful. But the two did not blend inside him, and he was afraid because in his heart of hearts he could distinguish his mother quite clearly from his father. He studied architecture, and when he went out into the world, everybody expected him to make it big in his profession, to start building all over the place, to finish the tower of Babylon and erect the Skadar fortress in the waters of the Boyana, even if it meant immuring people alive. But nothing doing! He had everybody's mustaches up their noses.

I know, however, that things did not go quite as unexpectedly as that. Even as a student, Atanas, apart from architecture, had shown signs of being interested in anything to do with paints, with their technology, and with the production of varnishes and lacquers. He knew, I remember, everything about the color spectrum, from Goethe's essays on colors and treatises on optics, appended to his books, to popular beliefs about colors and painting. He got hold of Atanas Stoikovich's *La Physica,* published in three volumes in 1801, for its chapter on the human eye's reception of painted surfaces. He knew that white is given for red, that "butterfly-yellow" hemp is obtained only if the painter faces west; he knew that dye for yarn is prepared with the eyes closed and that before soaking one must utter a lie and if the lie takes so will the color, because color is a lie.

From affinities such as these it is not such a big step to creating a company that deals in pharmaceuticals, and in America it was here that Atanas invested his speed and his strength. I've already said that Atanas was quick; he could catch a lock of his own hair in his teeth with just a turn of the head. From early youth he had worked sixteen hours a day, but he could fit into those sixteen hours twice as many working hours as anyone I know. That is why, when he was in his forties, and his turnover in America was forty million dollars, Atanas felt that he had just as many years of work behind him—forty. And it was true. He multiplied his working years by two. He bought special watches that worked only for him, faster than other watches, and he got ahead so quickly that today nobody knows his real age anymore. I am unable to explain or describe his dizzying rise to success in California. An example may help to clarify his methods.

Just when his California company was approaching a billion dollars in capital, and when he had already completed his sixtieth year of work (but not of life, because he was considerably younger), Atanas stopped for a minute in front of a beautiful tall door in Los Angeles. His hand hung suspended in the air instead of on the door handle, he closed his eyes and squeezed them shut, as when dyeing fabrics black. He knew, he had long known, that the fabric would be well dyed if total darkness appeared before his closed eyes. But what appeared were red spots. Atanas also knew what these red blotches meant: that the dye would not turn out as it should. He knew that the red spot could not illuminate objects or that door in front of him, but it did illuminate something else, which allowed him to move through the darkness without risking injury or losing his way—it illuminated the future. The future, very condensed directly ahead of him and increasingly rarefied as it moved off into the distance. And, standing in front of the door like that, he came to the conclusion that, unfortunately, the future, too, belongs to history. Or, to be more exact, the reddish spot behind his closed eyes illuminated only this part of the immense darkness, no other, in a world that belongs to and connects with history. Everything else (except for this thin ray of the future, which had already been discredited by history and branded by those reddish blotches of his own blood) was, a priori, out of the question, and did not come into consideration. The nonhistorical part of the future was constantly within reach, but it was inaccessible forever and probably always had been. Because we, not somebody else, leave that red blotch, our future is our own child, not somebody else's; it is *our* blood, not somebody else's, that paints this darkness in front of us red. And yet only that red spot led to the future, to that sole, unattainable, but salutary kingdom of the possible. And it was that one and only future that had already been stained by history beforehand. . . .

They found Atanas wrapped up in these thoughts and took him away before he put his hand on the handle, which was high up, at chin level. He spent two months in the hospital and felt that, with this red spot in front of his eyes, he was on those shores where boats move away from us forever, sailing the earth under crosses instead of masts, whereas the future lay in front of him in the water.

And then, when he had recovered, he went back to the same place, to that door in Los Angeles, and this time he put his heavy, quick hand on the handle, which was so high up it could knock out one's teeth. There and then Atanas, for the first and last time, was cheated, cheated in business, and that, at the same time, was his biggest financial success. He had to let them cheat him in order to become what he is today—"Mr. Two Percent" of the world's revenue from the use of nuclear energy for peacetime purposes. It happened like this.

At the time, the United States Army was offering a fabulous contract to chemical concerns for its war operations in Asia. Suddenly Atanas's American competitors, and he himself, started acting each in its own behalf at breakneck speed, in the hope of grabbing the profit of the century. Naturally, Atanas had no equal when it came to speed. I watched him during those days. He sat with his transparent hands, his nails painted pink by rushes of blood. He was not only fast, he was faster than others. The fastest speed is said to be the speed of the angels. If that is true, then at that moment he was an angel. And yet the race left a bitter taste in his mouth forever after. It was as though the others were not quite as slow as they seemed or wanted to appear. They let him win, that was obvious, although it was equally obvious that he would have probably won anyway. He got the contract and with it the chance of earning nearly a billion dollars. Remembering those days, he told me:

"I lie down at night, put on my glasses, and pick up something to read. Suddenly I freeze. I sense, I clearly sense, somebody watching me. Somebody's eyes are fixed upon me. And then I realize that staring out at me from my glasses, quite near, is my right eye transformed into my left. . . ."

The order was ready on time; Atanas's anti-foliage poisons were such a success that he didn't dare reveal the true extent and duration of their effect. He delivered them, they were used in the war, he earned more on them than he had expected—and then he stopped counting his cash. And he still had the impression that his rivals for the contract had not been quite as slow as they had made themselves out to be. "If I earned this much, then how much did they earn?" he wondered. The answer came fifteen years after the war in which his toxin had been used. His poisons had destroyed everything down to a depth of one meter wherever they fell, and they fell not only on the ground but into the human bloodstream as well. The veterans who fifteen years before had trod the ground that was now denuded sued Atanas's company for grievous and permanent bodily injury, which was slowly but increasingly making itself felt.

They asked for hefty compensation and Atanas paid it, rubbing his hands contentedly, because they had not thought of seeking compensation for the next three generations of their descendants. His poison had that long a reach, as in the Bible, where it says: The fathers have eaten a sour grape, and the children's teeth are set on edge. Atanas was almost offended by this underestimation.

Once, when journalists asked him how he could live with all these corpses and cripples, how he could sleep at night, Atanas told them briefly:

"You simply have to get used to yourself. After that, everything is easy."

For the first time in my life, I thought:

"Maybe he won't disgrace me after all." I decided to test him with that old jack up my sleeve, and said:

"Atanas, my dear, all you need now is just one letter at the beginning of your name (the one at the end) and you will become a man."

And he replied as though he knew what I was going to do:

"Do you remember that game of cards, Mama, when we bet on Vitacha?"

"Yes," I said.

"That was when I became a man."

"A man, you say? A grown man?" I jumped in. We were in Atanas's house in Los Angeles at the time, but he had had several of his favorite pieces of our old furniture brought over from Belgrade. Among them was a beautifully framed, glass-encased wreath that my grandmother had worn at her wedding. I had also sent him that little bureau on which he had once hurt his finger. Now I went over to the bureau, took out my old purse, and from it the jack, and showed it to him.

"Had you already been a grown man then, you would have known,

Atanas, that you didn't lose Vitacha in a poker game, but because you were immature. You didn't notice that I had a fifth jack up my sleeve, this one here, which I still keep. And that I used it."

He took out his wallet, and in the picture fold showed me something that made all my gray hairs curl. Inside the plastic fold was Vitacha's picture on one side and a two of clubs on the other. The very same one that had been missing from the deck of cards when my son and I had bet on Vitacha Milut. He had obviously had four twos, and would have won the game and Vitacha had he not deliberately (seeing that I had a weaker hand of three jacks) pulled out a two from his hand of cards, hidden it in his pocket, and thus lost an already won game, and with it Vitacha. Now he carried that two of clubs in his wallet in place of my picture.

I looked at him. He had a blue, hairy tongue, two ties around his neck—one the color of chestnut and the other of lemon; I simply couldn't remember who he was. This was no longer the boy who had been quick to catch cold and slow to cover himself. And for the first time I was afraid of him.

And I said:

"Whenever I talk to you, child, I feel a need to wash thoroughly afterward."

5 DOWN

When Atanas Razin suddenly licked his eyes clean and carried Vitacha off into the world, they set out for Vienna and Vitacha's sister Vida Milut. They were so frightened by their action that they were consumed with hunger, but, not daring to do anything else, they ran straight to the train station. They laughed afterward when they remembered how Vitacha, rushing to the station, had dreamed of lamb fed on seaweed, and Atanas of fish kept in the earth for three nights before being thrown onto live coal. Because, when life turns topsy-turvy, the abyss beneath one's feet does not immediately become the sky. They say that at the train station that morning they did not have time to eat those famous buns that are given a good thrashing before baking and bear the lash marks ever after. The Belgrade–Vienna train was already pulling out, and they jumped aboard. But in those days the train did not have a dining car, and its one and only sleeping car was full. So they did not sleep a wink, and they did not eat what was served on trains in those days: grated cheese and butter on rye, with beer, or fish in aspic.

"Never mind," Vitacha consoled herself, "our hungers are us ourselves, our gratifications are not. At least we'll be able to look at each other to our hearts' content, because a hungry eye doesn't sleep." Indeed, all they could do was look at each other, because they were not alone, they were on a train, and could not even kiss.

"Sleep. In dreams one doesn't age," Razin whispered into her hair, and Vitacha periodically dozed off, always dreaming the same song and knowing she would wake up once the song was over; but this waking seemed to her in her sleep like death, not waking, because to every dream waking is a sort of death.

Even at the border, where they stopped for a long time and where everything was blanketed with snow, they did not eat the horseradish and ham that had wintered in the ashes of pinewood, and in Austria, where they arrived after midnight, they saw, but only through the window of a closed inn, a leg of veal soaked in beer, skinned and boned with a twine.

The angels swirled up from the earth to the sky; Vitacha, half-asleep, squeezed Atanas's faster leg; but the train gleamed, casting into the snowy night a light the color of white wine. Somewhere in Innsbruck they finally sat down in a tavern to order "priest's hunger" with lentils and fish sausages made of ground bream, but it turned out that the place was reserved for Allied troops, and so they could not get served. They thought of staying and going to the first hotel they came to, but Vitacha cut it short:

"Pack your tits under your arms and get going! Hungry hounds hunt better."

And so they continued their second day of fasting. As they approached Vienna, they saw through the train window a station and next to it an inn displaying mushrooms being roasted in sizzling sea salt and basted with wine, but the train did not stop. They arrived in Vienna as hungry as lice, holding each other by their dirty hands. They entered the shadow of the cathedral and, after a long hike through its shade, through their three-day hunger and desire, which stretched out like a street, on the church doors they saw little dogs leading each other on leashes into the temple, proudly holding the ends of the leashes in their teeth. Afterward Vitacha remembered this particular moment vividly, and she says that she experienced Vienna's

Cathedral of St. Stephen as a visible cry rising into the motionless sky. Remembering that cathedrals are never finished by those who started them, she froze at the thought that this cry belonged not to one person but to two. And there was something stranger still about it all. This dual cry was not a male but a female, almost a child's cry. But the hunger and desire that fused inside her drove away such thoughts, and they rushed into the first pastry shop to order Sacher torte and coffee with cardamom. And just as it was about to be served, the waitress dropped the tray and spilled everything all over them, so that, starving and wet, they hurried off to Vida's house without having had even a bite.

Once they finally found themselves in the Pfisters' spacious Vienna home in the XIIth district, instead of going to dinner they made a beeline for the bedroom. Vitacha pressed tight against Atanas as she ran, whispering: "Deflower my lips, they are still virgin, they've been waiting for you!"

As soon as they entered the room, they came, before even touching properly. Vitacha, with a mute, hot cry in her throat, and he like a belt snapping.

Vitacha's sister Vida, whose guests they now were, was cute, quick, and mustached like a cherub; she had breasts like buttocks, as Mrs. Yolanta Ibich, Isailovich by marriage, used to say about her. She usually moved her plate from the table to the sofa next to her, eating with her hands over to one side. On her Slava, her saint's day, it was Vida's custom to serve the Slava wheat to her first guests and then go out into the hall, give all the used spoons a quick, secret lick, and bring them out for the new arrivals as though they were clean. She held her finger in her mouth, was simpler than Vitacha, and believed that every virtue was merely a station equidistant from two neighboring faults. For the past fifteen years, from her bed she had looked straight at a painting by Josef Adam Ritter von Molke (1714–1794) on which the moonlight revealed a group of people assembled around the throne of a woman, with a winged old man flying backward low over their heads. In the daylight, instead of the old man, the painting showed a fairy-like apparition with a gold chain on its ankle. The picture hung on the wall of a spacious house with a carriage entrance. In that house, bread turned moldy overnight, and things were so thoroughly lost that you needed at least ten years to find them again. Over the said entranceway stretched a hall for twenty couples if the girls danced in crinolines, and thirty if they did not. Behind the house, which was as old as the painting, flourished a garden full of birds, and farther back still, behind the little gate at the bottom, stretched the green expanse of the Schönbrunn Castle. The house had once belonged to Duke Hetzendorf, in whose street it still stood, and then to the Pfisters, who died off because their souls had wasted away faster than they themselves, and now architect Svilar, for the first time happy and for the first time under his real surname, Razin, had measured the garden as being the length of a pipe full of tobacco on the way out and half that on the way back, because the land was on a slope.

For years now, Miss Vida Milut had lived in the house alone but not lonely. Her window looked out on the tall reeds that lay like a meadow by the Danube and resembled shallow grass, where the trees seemed smaller than they were, as though they branched out of the soil. Vida had started early on to translate from her first mother tongue, Serbian, into German, and her house was always full of people. Serving her guests meat on Szolnay plates, Vida liked to say:

"To each person comes, like his portion of meat, his own part of the truth. But the truth, too, needs to be salted; otherwise it's tasteless. I only translate writers who can do that."

She was loquacious, and opined:

"Whenever I'm happy, I fall ill. And I always step on everyone's same toe—the fourth toe of the left foot."

Friends came to drink plum brandy on her piano and eat goat cheese with garlic from her homeland; when they sneezed the expressions on their faces would have made one think that they had at least two international reasons for doing so; and they departed content. And they came back again.

Mr. Amadeus Knopf came with his wife, Rebecca; she, it seemed, was a Rothschild or from some other such fabulously wealthy family;

he was a businessman with eyes that continually melted, like two lumps of ice. The middle fingers on his right hand had grown together into one enormous digit. It was rumored that he nibbled snot and mortar off the walls. He was extremely courteous and with that rigid nail-less member that looked like one of his private parts, he kept brushing against and knocking over vases and glasses, figurines and umbrellas, and with his other, smaller fingers was even fleeter at stopping them from falling. The beautiful Theofana Tsikindjal came, an artist with translucent eyes like medusas that have just eaten fish, and lovely hands stained a green color that hurt the gallbladder, because she painted only crocodiles. Her husband, Dr. Arnold Pala, came, admittedly always late, because he was enamored of horses and could tell, just from their excrement, a colt from a mare. He came from the hippodrome, the leather patches between his legs always smelling of a sweating filly, and his overcoat of Three Nuns tobacco. Along with his smells he brought a plaited leather whip, and Theofana Tsikindjal smilingly showed the lash marks on her beautiful mustached breasts, waiting for the high point of the evening, when Vida brought out her picture albums and a tiny box set with pearls threaded on silk. Theofana would be the first to take a pinch of snuff and cocaine from the box onto the base of her thumb, sniff it, and try not to sneeze for as long as possible. Mr. Knopf alone took nothing from the little box, though he laughed with the others and leafed through the albums. They contained only female portraits, taken with old French cameras at the beginning of the century, and these were incredible-looking faces, staring into the camera's eye that sees only in yellow. Those whitish gazes as though from the dead, those mouths gaping open as though creating a draft through their teeth, as though before bed they had plugged their ears with their hair so as not to hear, it all looked unreal, like a collection of victims out of a police file. Knopf was the first to solve the secret of these photographs, just as he was always the first to solve such small mysteries. These were the faces of women photographed at the height of passion, at the moment of orgasm. And then suddenly there would appear in Vida's album, like a bearded face peering out of panties, a picture of a man at the same moment of passion, and everybody would burst out laughing, making the little old man flying backward in the painting turn prematurely into the fairy-like apparition with the gold chain on its ankle.

And so they lived in a kind of twofold time, as though wearing a hat on top of a cap, when one evening, as she was leafing through books from the old country, Miss Vida Milut came upon a sentence that surprised her. The sentence was short:

"Our thoughts are like our hungers—they are always the same."

She became interested, gathered information about the author of the sentence, and finally, during a visit to Belgrade, met him. He was a bit boorish, had some sort of grass growing on his face in place of a mustache and beard; women related that he always slept in the nude, with a leather belt around his waist, and men that he was trained to piss while running.

"Are you left-eyed, Miss Milut?" he asked Vida.

"No, but anything sweet I always feel only on my right side," she replied, and invited him to visit her in Vienna. He came for Christmas with his ants in his hair and suggested that he stage a puppet show on Christmas Eve for Vida and her friends. He prowled about the large hall of Vida's house in Herzog Hetzendorf Street, played around with the wires and puppets; drowsy trapped winter flies kept buzzing in his beard. He arranged the chairs for the audience, and on his hands, on his palms and in between his fingers, he kept finding all sorts of things: a straw, a strand of hair, something sticky, a piece of fingernail, crumbs of bread, grains of coffee, butter, or sand. It was not that he asked for it, it was just that everything stuck to him, he felt all of it on him and carefully picked his hands and nails clean, plucked the wine flies from his eyes and hairs from his glass. And so, weeding his body, he now prepared the stage in Miss Milut's large hall, where the striped armchairs were upholstered in yellow rep at the back, so that in the mirror, inset like a door, it looked as though there were another, yellow, stripeless drawing room. While he worked, he chatted with the guests.

"Imagine," he said, "Vida's father bought her mother a doe for an engagement present. A live doe. Vida has a picture, I don't know if you've seen it. Her mother, looking beautiful, petite, the wind could strip her naked, is standing next to her fiancé. He's in uniform, leading the doe by the ear with one hand and holding a saber in the other. He cuts a striking figure; if he tried, he could snap the button off his trousers smack into your mouth and knock out a tooth!"

"Amusing," replied Dr. Pala, casting a voracious look at Mrs. Rebecca Knopf. They were sitting at the table, smoking or snuffing, and Dr. Pala was sipping Mrs. Knopf's unfinished drinks, ostensibly by mistake.

"Your gazes, Doctor, leave lesions, like your whip. But if you keep staring like that, you'll see something you won't like; one sees too deeply through my eyes. You'd do better to put on sunglasses. . . ."

While Rebecca spoke, Vida's gaze was fixed on her bearded compatriot with the shaved ears and rolled-up sleeves; she watched him work, her eyes full of sorrow, but a sorrow so hard that afterward she could sharpen knives with it and polish spoons.

"Upon closer inspection, your face is like the year," he said to Vida, fixing the theater curtain; "it has at least four seasons."

"What season is it on my face now, in your opinion?"

"Summer. Quiet, like a bedroom."

He kissed her and went off to work his puppets. His play had two names:

The Star or The Creche

(The stage is illuminated by a star traveling slowly from east to west; the Infant Jesus is lying in the crib; next to him, by the cave, is the Virgin Mary. A Lamb, an Apple Tree, and the River Jordan approach the crib to pay their homage to the newborn king. The Virgin Mary sings to the child)

> A church I shall build from the stars,
> White doors for the church from the moon,
> Icons I shall draw with my eyes.
> The liturgy I shall sing by heart,
> On a horse to the church I shall come,
> From the horse unlock it with my spear. . . .

THE LAMB (holding up a book): This is the Old Testament, the future blood of Christ. The blood of this newborn child lying in the crib. He has a Father in heaven, but not a Mother.

THE RIVER JORDAN (holding up another book): This is the New Testament, the future body of Christ. The body of this newborn child lying in the crib. Here on earth he has a Mother, but not a Father.

THE LAMB: He shall expiate all future and past human sins, he shall expiate original sin, those expelled from paradise he shall to paradise return. Bathing his divine spark in human blood, he shall save man and his own blood and body give for him.

THE APPLE TREE: That does not mean he shall also save me. Or you, water, or you, animal! Our game and our star are not here!

THE LAMB: What do you mean?

THE APPLE TREE: The Old Testament is not our blood, nor the New Testament our body. We are not of the human race, we do not carry original sin, we were not expelled from paradise, Christ is not embodied in a fruit tree, water, or fleece, which are our blood and body. We elude his cosmic power of redemption, because we are exempted from the calculations of sin, and we should live our own life. Why should we atone for the sins of others? We should create our own world, free of human sins and of the human world. Because there is no salvation for us in Christ's suffering and sacrifice. We shall be sacrificed, if we do not find our own redeemer.

THE RIVER JORDAN: But Adam christened us, Adam gave us names.

THE APPLE TREE: The first man gave us names before he was expelled from paradise and sinned; in his state of innocence he, by his own free and pure will, ruled over us animals, waters, and plants just as, before the fall, an innocent soul rules over the senses. But now, when he with his hands has polluted this world, polluted the waters, plants, and animals; now, when he wants to go further and pollute the universe as well, is it not better that we separate from him? Is it not better that we follow the stars, we who are plants, waters, or dumb animals, we who do not destroy the world around us? This has been promised us in books. "Though thou exalt thyself as the eagle, and though thou set thy nest among the stars, thence will I bring thee down," says the Lord, but He says it to them, to people. Not to us. We should separate from man's star, which guides us now, and turn to our own guiding star and our own star and fate. See how many of them there are in the sky and choose!

THE LAMB: In parting, before we restore to people the names Adam christened us with, let us reveal to Adam's descendants two things they did not know until now.

THE RIVER JORDAN: *The first thing.* Out of the seven days of creation, four were successful and three were unsuccessful. Only one day held sway and made this world a successful world. That was the seventh day, the day of rest, when the Creator did nothing.

THE APPLE TREE: *The second thing.* Watch out for your thought. You don't know it. It's nicest when it stands, and best when it moves. Because a thought can stand and it can move. It can always stand (past and future things can neither grow nor change). A thought can move only in the present, while time stands still. If the thought moves, it is most important at the fifth step; before that it is still either incomplete or unpracticed, and after the fifth step it tires you out. So watch out for the fifth step! After the fifth step you're so tired you can no longer follow your thought, because it is either too strong and fast or too far away. At the seventh step the thought dissolves and turns into love. . . .

With these words the play came to an end; Vida sat in the dark for a moment and thought of her countryman. She read his books every evening and regretted having wasted her time translating others.

"One should translate him all one's life," she said to herself, "and learn seven languages, and into seven languages translate him, just as one flees down seven paths from the enemies unto whom one has been delivered by the Lord!" But for weeks her guest remained politely silent, stroking his flaxen beard, and it never even occurred to him to ask whether she might like to translate what he wrote. And now again she sat there in the darkness tormenting herself.

And then came flashes of light; outside predatory stars chattered their teeth in the frost, and inside everybody noticed Mrs. Tsikindjal deep in a kiss with Rebecca Knopf, who was sitting on her lap.

Then, as though each were choosing his or her own star, Miss Milut's guests in Herzog Hetzendorf Street parted forever. Rebecca took Mrs. Tsikindjal off to Paris, and soon it was heard that the two of them were happily ensconced in a huge studio apartment in the Tuileries, rented for Dr. Pala's ex-wife by her mistress so that she could paint crocodiles there. Vida was left with memories of her departed friends, she was left with starched, warm pillows that rasp and scratch against the cheek like hot breads, but her memories were now always somehow connected with the negative. Her friend who did puppet shows would sit beside her and she would say to him:

"We don't want a summer house like Knopf's! We won't go to Karlsbad with Dr. Pala! Anything but the kind of car that pisspot Tsikindjal has!"

He, Vida's writer, would sit by the fireplace, his hair full of ants, getting on in years, but his German still full of enthusiasm and youth because it hadn't been used for twenty years. Vida would translate in the room whose doors opened onto the striped drawing room and thought more and more how, of all the successful writers from her homeland whom she knew and read, this one alone, the man of her choice, with whom she had been sleeping for the past two years, had never mentioned what would have been the most logical thing in the world: that she, above and beyond anyone else, should translate him. Embarrassment or who knows what stopped him from letting such a request cross his lips, and Vida thought, "Two darknesses are not the same, let alone two people," and she did not ask for a favor that one does not request but accepts, if it is offered. She hemmed her dresses with wild flowers and verbena, and whispered:

"It's not natural; our rooms are full of his trampled thoughts. Un-translated into German . . ."

And then something else occurred to her. That he was shunning her here in the West because there was certainly another woman translating him somewhere in the East, in Berlin perhaps, on the other side of the wall. The tender cushions of her palms, in between which there was a constant trickle of sweat, swelled from such thoughts. Such thoughts pushed them to their limits. The limit was crossed when it turned out that nobody was translating him into German, even in East Berlin. That was when she left him.

"Whoever wants the second half of life has to remain in the first half of everything else," he said, and departed.

Miss Milut rolled up her sleeves and got down to work as though the devil had spit in her mouth. Soon there was not a major writer from her native land whom she had not translated. There was only one exception. He whom she wanted most to translate, he because of whom she translated and loved all the others, remained untranslated. Instead, Vida ultimately received a medal from the Yugoslav government, flung it over the fence into the Schönbrunn Park, and decided to marry.

This is how it happened.

The jilted Dr. Pala came once or twice in his riding boots, grumbled that Mrs. Tsikindjal had taken his whip away with her, and took Vida to the Danube to show her how with his new whip he could kill a catfish when it jumped out to catch a fly. He complained about his lot, and then disappeared, carrying his smell of Thoroughbred fillies between his legs. Amadeus Knopf dropped by more often, toting his double finger mutely in a glove. He openly confessed to Vida that at first he had been miserable because of Rebecca's departure and had walked the streets holding a fork and spoon in his hands. But the very next moment he would tell her a string of inanities and not mention his errant wife again. Vida was delighted when once, in a café, he did his match trick. They each had a Scotch and soda and went off to make phone calls. When they returned, Knopf's matches had been appropriated by a man next to them at the bar. Knopf asked for his box of matches back, but the man refused to return them. He claimed the box was his.

"If it's yours, tell me how many matchsticks are inside," Knopf countered.

"If it's yours, you must know how many matchsticks are inside!"

"Unlike you, I do know—twenty-seven!"

The stranger wanted to bet on it, and they did.

"I want to make a bet, too," Miss Milut suddenly chimed in.

"On what?" Knopf asked in surprise, but the stranger said that the same meal, when ordered by a man and by a woman, is no longer the same meal. He was exultant.

"That's a secret," replied Vida, "but if you win the first bet with this man here, you'll lose the second one with me, and vice versa. Understood?"

"Understood," said Knopf, and they counted the matchsticks. There were exactly twenty-seven, and Knopf picked up his matchbook and money, leaving the stranger with a draft in his mouth. To Vida it seemed like the biggest and most inexplicable victory she had ever seen in her life.

When they reached the house, she asked: "How did you do it?" But Knopf ignored her question in favor of his own:

"What the devil did we bet on?"

"On this," said Vida, showing him a little key.

"So that's what I lost by winning the first bet?"

"Yes."

"And what is it?"

"It's the key to my bedroom," said Miss Milut, flinging it over the fence into the Schönbrunn Park as she had once done with her medal.

"Come, darling, it's not locked," she added, and took Knopf for a husband. For Vida, that moment was the beginning of happiness, and in that happiness, like some kind of disease, the beginning of her titanic jealousy, which stayed with her forever and finally drove her to her grave. Because one dies of happiness sooner than of misery.

At the time when Atanas and Vitacha were visiting them in Vienna, they had already been together for a year, and the new Mrs. Knopf whispered:

"Ah, my illness, how we do spoil you!" Mr. Knopf was still in that radiant phase before he started carrying himself like a beggar, which came later. His face was like a mask (the years passed by imperceptibly behind it), and only his mustache and eyebrows were alive on that beautiful mask. Affable and talkative, he told them no end of little stories, and Vida took her guests off to show them something. Lying on the bed in her bedroom was a doll. The other Vida.

"Do you remember her?" Vida asked Atanas with a laugh. "She was once your wife, she brought you Vitacha. Did she and I maybe get something mixed up then? Or are we getting something mixed up now?" And again she laughed, her finger in her mouth, and then hugged them both, secretly pinching Knopf, who was standing behind her. Words dropped out of him like loaches out of a duck.

"A Japanese," Knopf said, starting one of his stories, "was in an aquarium in France. He kept taking photographs, and when a fish particularly caught his eye, he would stop for a minute and stare at the fish for forty seconds; it would stop swimming, and one could see it slowly acquire slanted eyes.

" 'What are you doing to that fish?' a Belgian visitor asked him.

" 'Anyone can do it,' replied the Japanese. 'Just pick out a fish you like and concentrate on it for forty seconds, and you'll see that you can do it, too. It's like reading.'

"The Belgian found his fish, stared at it, forty seconds later he started to let out bubbles and gasp for air like a fish out of water.

"The point is that the Japanese's choice of method was wrong. A lover cannot understand true love, and therefore is always in the position of the Belgian and the fish, or the icon and the mirror. Because, they say, one should not try to catch an icon in a mirror. It is not given unto the lover—that is, the mirror—to perceive his love— that is, the icon. Because love creates lovers, not lovers love. . . ."

Atanas did not listen to what Knopf was saying, but gazed unblinkingly at the man's muscular body, which could support two such bodies, and remembered with a shudder how when they shook hands Knopf's huge double vertebrate had stabbed him, as though the man were holding a church key. He gazed at Knopf's lusterless hair, which looked like a knitted woolen cap with a part in it, and felt that the first day in the month of October (which had elapsed thirty days ago) had given birth to his thirtieth day in October (which had just begun), but he could not remember that first day and before him had only its incomprehensible result. Gazing at Knopf he felt that his eyes were becoming bigger than his soul; he thought that Amadeus Knopf did not need a sexual organ at all, that with such joined fingers, better than with any penis, he could satisfy a woman whenever he wanted. Gazing at that powerful double vertebrate, with which Knopf was endlessly catching at glasses and chairs, Atanas felt disarmed. He dared not look at Vitacha; he felt soft and vulnerable. The feeling lasted for no more than a moment and then passed, but there are moments in a man's life that last even after death.

"His left eye is like Scylla, and his right like Charybdis," Atanas Razin thought, caught between Knopf's two eyes. "Anyone who slips through will survive. . . ."

And then that high tide of unease and fear passed; Atanas Razin snapped out of it and whispered smilingly into his spoonful of soup:

"Nobody can be masculine every day, not even God."

It should be said that architect Razin and Vitacha did not marry in Vienna. Somewhere in a small town whose name remains forgotten, architect Razin hired two violinists, a Petroff piano on wheels, and a horse and groom decked out in magnificent livery. After the wedding, the two violinists played the wedding march with two bows on one violin, standing in an embrace on the steps of the church, and then the newlyweds walked behind the horse-drawn piano led by the groom. There is a photograph of it. The two of them walking behind the piano, Vitacha whispering the words of her great-great-grandmother Amalia, Pfister by marriage: "Man ages like cheese, but cheese is a fine gentleman, and we are not. . . ." As they walked, they played music with four hands and periodically sipped champagne from the crystal glasses standing on the tray on the piano. . . .

This period, the happiest in their life together, is captured in two other photographs, taken in Istanbul. And with them goes a little story. In Istanbul, Vitacha and architect Razin went shopping for leather suits. When they had bought what they wanted, they asked the salesman if he could recommend a good place to eat.

"Would you like to see the menu?" the obliging salesman inquired, and within minutes his errand boy came running back with the menu. Surprised, the newlyweds looked at the menu and, at the insistence of the salesman, picked out two dishes. That very same moment, two boys carried in and set down in the middle of the store a table already set for two, all agleam with silver and porcelain, and with two unlit candles. The photograph shows Atanas Razin and his wife dining in the middle of the leather store, as customers come and go or pick out items to buy. In the picture one can almost see their warm thoughts soaring up high, and their cold thoughts plunging into the darkness, into the waters of the Bosporus and into their souls under the table. . . .

Later, once Razin's business got off the ground, they moved to the United States, and Atanas had a villa built for them in Los Angeles. Vitacha had two bathtubs in the villa, one tiled and the other with a gravel bottom; in her bedroom, instead of rugs, she had a real English lawn, and on it a huge water bed. From that journey of no return, Vitacha wrote to her sister Vida that her days passed quickly, three in one. "In Los Angeles," said Vitacha, leafing through the newspapers, "the only thing I still believe are obituaries!" She dreamed that they had returned to their cramped Belgrade apartment and that she could not fit her bed into it. There was no room in the past for her future, which had grown. Only the past can fit into the future, not vice versa. From time to time Vitacha also dreamed of her daughters, but it was always only of how she beat them. . . .

It was evening, she was sitting up in bed, he was lying crossways under her bent knees. Aquarius glistened in her eyes, she was propped up against a pillow, holding a mirror in her hand. He was deep inside her, still, his eyes closed. His aura penetrated deep into the aura of her body. It may have even pierced hers in one place. She felt no pain. On the contrary. She wiped off her makeup with light, brisk motions which reached him inside her. Then she turned off the light and, without changing position, with him inside her, murmured a prayer:

"Thou, devil, art prohibited by the power of the revered and life-giving cross from holding any power in this space and in this home and over God's creatures in this home. From holding power in the wheat, or in the vineyard, or in the cows, or in the sheep or the goats, or in the horses, or in the pigs, from having power over anything in this home forevermore. And thou, cross, help this space. Amen."

At the words "or in the horses," he usually came and an icy quiver ran through his body; at the word "forevermore," or a bit before, she came, too, then whispered the rest of the prayer almost inaudibly. They did not even manage to kiss, or change position. But a child did not present itself. For them there were no children. Even though they lay in the shape of the cross.

Instead came news. News of the ghastly thing that had happened to Vitacha's little girls.

6 DOWN

As far as I can remember, Mr. Atanas Razin the architect, already a wealthy and successful man at the time, told the following story after one of his business trips:

The tower stood among the houses in the street like Sunday among the days in the week. And I, my eyes darting down the row of houses, started scanning this living calendar for the first major holiday. And I found it. "That must be it," I thought, and soon found myself in front of Azra's house. It was in noticeably better repair than Olga's. It had a deep, solid gateway, echoing the sounds from the bottom of the street, a high wall, and behind the wall a horde of children.

"Fine!" I thought, and went in. It was obvious to me that Olga was paying for this house in the same proportion that Azra's present lover, a man of immensely slow memories and long range, was avoiding its upkeep. He lived abroad, sent her nothing but candles as presents and tended only to her spiritual life. So from him Azra received books; he converted her to his faith, built her a place of worship on the property that was hers and Olga's, but nothing else. He paid for her prayers and in that respect was very generous, but for food Azra had to earn the money herself, or was given some by her sister Olga. He sent Azra to religious school at his own expense and, in short, provided for her Judgment Day, when all people and all angels shall die.

I was thinking these thoughts as I knocked at Azra's door, but there I found a note and was told that Azra could not receive me at home but at the library, a few doors farther on. The note said:

"Happy is he who is always one step behind the first. Because in heaven and on earth we shall not love the same people and we shall not hate the same people."

And so I went to the library. I entered a brightly lit auditorium. The earth groaned under the weight of the crowd. The men were wearing rings lined with cloth, whispering the call to prayer in one another's left ears, and the prayer itself in one another's right ears. And taking care not to accidentally touch one another's beard. One was speaking. I had come in the middle of his speech, but I had no trouble following it. However, I could not understand what the two men in front of him were doing, the two with the whips. The speaker at the rostrum put it well:

"During the time of the beys, in a whole year no man earned enough for bread, but it was not because he was lazy. During the time of the empire, in a whole year all subjects earned enough for three loaves of bread a day, but it was not because they were diligent. During the time of the beys, nobody in the land cried for a whole year, but it was not because everybody was happy. During the time of the empire, nobody laughed for a whole year, but it was not because everybody in the empire was unhappy. Such were the times. . . ."

In the audience, the water into which the priest had breathed the Lord's name was already being drunk and wafers made with tears were being offered. Suddenly, out of the crowd stepped a lean young man, well dressed, a light rising in tides from the depths to the surface of his face. The smile on his lips was as cold and heavy as a padlock. The lamps floated overhead in the bluish room, like jellyfish in the South Seas, and there was the beating of iron drums that had first been warmed on the fire. The young man walked up to the two with the whips and tossed back his black, nicely combed shadow. They let him pass between them and suddenly one of them lashed him with his whip. Violently but with attention to where the whip fell. That very instant, the other did the same thing. While they took turns with their whips, they seemed to be particularly mindful of their breathing. After every blow, one of them would feverishly polish his nails against the wall. Or they would both close their eyes as if calmly planning the next blow, or use the span of their hands to measure something on the whip and the ground. And with every lash, the flogged man was driven to perform new movements, which those with the whips elicited from him like musicians eliciting steps from a dancer.

And then the auditorium suddenly burst into applause. At first I didn't understand why, but after several more blows it became clear even to someone as unenlightened as me. The young man's shadow had begun to detach itself. And with every succeeding blow, thanks to the deftness of the floggers and to his own movements, it became increasingly and more noticeably undone, until finally, after a twist of the body, showing how quickly speed can be learned, the shadow broke off him and rolled down the steps, and the young man, as though sprouting wings, pulled himself up and proudly strode out of the auditorium to accompanying shouts of approval.

But Azra´ was not among those shouting in the auditorium. And I left to see whether she wasn't somewhere in the vestibules of the library. I passed hallways as long as the salty mornings of this street, lost my way twice, and both times came back on the right track, forcing myself to go in the opposite direction of the one I thought I should take. Finally, I walked through a door and found myself in the semidarkness of a spacious room. On the stairs I stepped on something sticky and realized it was blood and in the blood was the shadow of that young man. That was how I recognized the auditorium of a little while ago, which was now dark and as empty as a deaf ear, and the only light came from the door to the room at the other end, where I had left my coat. I went over to the door and saw in that room the young man who had been flogged, holding a meeting with some unknown people. They all looked up at me in astonishment when I walked in and took my coat off the hook. They interrupted their work, their silent looks following me.

"We have never seen you until now. Where were you before?" they asked.

"Before?" I said in surprise.

Then the young man, who, it transpired, was the director of the institution, turned around to a girl, and without a word she got up to see me out.

"I'll show you the way," she said, although it was obvious that, by having her accompany me, the people at the meeting wanted to make sure that I left.

In the darkness of the hallway on the way out I asked the girl what was the meaning of the scene we had both witnessed in the library that evening.

"Have you thought about what you saw?" I asked.

"I don't think," she said. "A thought sent from the west will have land to the east of it, a thought sent from the east will have land to the west. And they shall not meet. Can he who herds sheep bring anybody to the emperor's palace? Can he who herds thoughts bring anybody to heaven? Why think, then?"

And she left me standing there alone in front of the library gate.

On my way back to Azra, I was worse off than when I had gone there the first time. If I, duped and exasperated like this, and Azra, prepared as she was to be spiteful, put our cards on the table, my plan would come to nothing. . . . That's what I thought, and so I decided to interpose something between us, to prevent us from reaching one another right away. I was immediately led into a lovely room with sofas and a little shelf on which two luxuriously bound Korans were squeezed. One was in green cloth studded with silver, and the other was in red and studded with gold. One was genuine, and the other a perfect replica made of Venetian soap. Keeping to an old custom, Azra would swear on the soap when she did not want to keep a promise.

"If you don't know the difference between tall and short, ask a woman; if you don't know the difference between love and hate, ask the river," I thought, whereupon Azra came in.

We turned to look at each other and stood there like that for a minute, waiting to see which one of us would blink first, and then burst out laughing.

She had gained a lot of weight and opened her mouth to hear what was being said to her. She wore a watch in her ring, which would not come off, and, as with a fish, her every movement reverted back to herself. She mumbled something, and I thought she was apologizing because of the misunderstanding at the library, but she was apologizing because of her weight.

"I gained weight because I was already full of hate. A person has only as much love as hate leaves room for, just as a jug of wine holds only as much water as the drunken wine leaves room for. And where hatreds run deep, loves lie shallow. . . ."

She looked like a man who had once been handsome. But she did not look like a woman. I remembered her breasts, freckled like two goose eggs, but now they had sprawled on her body and could not be seen.

"Do you remember how we used to play 'the story's children' at school?" I asked, coming straight to the point.

She bit the corner of her lip and asked how it went.

"Don't you remember? That's the game where you give a title to a story and somebody else starts it off with two or three sentences. Then we take turns telling it, and between us unravel the skein, which has your color wool one minute and my color the next, depending on who is doing the unraveling."

"And who wins?"

"He who gives grist to his own mill," I thought, but the trouble was that with Azra I dared not win or lose, because then all my plans would fall through. I muttered that, since there was no judge, there was no decision, and I threw out the title:

The Blue Mosque

She was a bit surprised, spit seemed to simmer under her cheek, but she collected herself and began:

"One evening in Istanbul, just before aksham, the evening prayer, the emperor's eyes alit like two black doves on a spot next to the At-Meidan. Sultan Ahmed's gaze was numb from looking through the thickets of his thoughts, and he decided to build the mosque of mosques on this very spot. He made up his mind that the shrine should have six minarets and dispatched messengers to both sides of the empire to find him the best mason. . . ."

There she stopped, not knowing how to go on, because she was inventing the story, as was I; waiting for this break to continue the story, I continued as follows:

"But the messenger to the West encountered unforeseen difficulties. The most celebrated architect of the empire was so frightened by the prospect of the assignment that he vanished without a trace. . . ."

And so in that quiet room Azra and I took turns telling the tale of the Blue Mosque, passing pieces of the story to one another like a pipe, and sipping coffee. I noticed that as soon as she became slightly excited she would begin to make grammatical errors, and it was then clear that hers had been a shallow education, that one could not even wet a sock in it. But when we finished the story, she said to me, without the slightest restraint:

"Both women and policemen have an eye for the likes of you. . . . Where are you now and what are you doing?"

And so I knew that the moment of danger had finally passed, that "The Blue Mosque" had done the trick. Azra fell into conversation, even if it was in this unpleasant way.

"In Hungary, in Szentendre," I replied, "there is a café they call Nostalgia. They serve coffee with cinnamon there, and I seem to be having cinnamon in my coffee more and more often. I have no children, and it's killing me."

She giggled into her breasts and suddenly cut short the laugh, as though with a knife.

"I'd like to adopt a son," I went on, "but—I don't know how to put it—I'd rather not take an already grown-up child."

"Yes, yes, you're right. Grown-up children are not suited for adoption. They can't hold water in their mouths, they'll outtalk you before you can click your heels. So you'd prefer something younger."

"Sort of. In fact, much younger. Or let's put it this way: I'd adopt several of your youngest as my own sons; I'd give you the money right away, to have them properly educated, raised, and brought up, as befits families like yours and mine, and then later, once they grow up, they can reimburse what I gave...."

"And just how much younger would they have to be? What age, roughly?"

"Well, sixty to a hundred."

Azra leaned over, smelled my breath, and only then seemed to understand my meaning.

"What do you mean, sixty to a hundred?" she asked.

"Well, that's roughly how much younger than you and me they should be."

"Well, that's a different matter, then. You'd like to have great-great-grandchildren, or 'little white bees,' as they're called?"

"Yes. Exactly."

"See that," she mumbled as though to herself, "now you can even cash in on the future—somebody else's, to boot. What an age we live in! It goes on all fours! People keep telling me that, but I won't believe them." And then she addressed me again:

"Well, why don't you say so! What are great-great-grandchildren? Why not sell them? Here, I've had this list of them for a long time. Just take a look. There's a wide choice. I've studied our family, planned and done the family tree forward and backward. As much as one can. Here, look, this one, for instance, Luka, he's guaranteed to resemble me. Handsome, just the tiniest bit plump in his old age, but sweet. He'll heal through the heel. You won't find a better healer or a better great-great-grandson. True, he'll have two different-colored eyes, one red and the other blue, and he'll be just slightly deaf on the side of his blue eye. But he'll be gentle and quick. This other one, his adopted son, Vassili, he will have a strong ear. He'll hear on all sides and be listened to on all sides, all four sides of the world.... As the poet says, only this John can in his soul still be the devil, through his father; only this Isidor can still discover why the five constellations assemble in the same corner of the sky on St. Petka's Day; only this

Peter can still take the keys of the celestial grammar book that begins with the pronoun 'Thou,' with which God addressed Adam; only this Alexei can still prove that man's present is not whole and that it has day and it has night, its tiny today and tiny tomorrow; only this Paul can . . ."

Azra took the ice-cold drink that had been served to us and pressed the glass against her burning ears. I gave her back the list and said:

"You know, there's an additional circumstance here."

"What?"

"Along with the white bees I buy the house."

"What house?"

"This house. And the property around it. Together with the descendants goes their estate. So that they can have a place to spread their wings. But don't worry, I'll pay you in advance, and I won't take over the estate for another two hundred years. For now all I need is earth for my grave, just enough to be buried here with a bird under my arm, rather than overseas."

"But haven't you already bought a grave from Olga? How many times do you plan to die? Mind you, I can't say the terms you offer aren't favorable. But couldn't you move those two pods of earth, or however much you want for a grave, just a little, so that they don't bury you on the other side of the ocean? I know a lovely place, you won't find a nicer spot for a grave anywhere, it has the best view in the area, you could put yourself there. True, it borders on my sister's land, where she sows wheat, but it doesn't matter, two pods of earth isn't very much, it's no more than you can sprinkle with a mouthful of wine. As for the rest, the house and the children, take them when the time comes, in two hundred or however many years you've got in mind. . . ."

Just then a strange, syncopated thudding could be heard outside in the moonlight. Like the gallop of camels or giraffes. We went to the window and saw a camel pass by with someone in the saddle. The rider was wearing a turban and he was so pale you could see his face even in the moonlight.

"Where is that camel coming from?" I asked Azra.

"It's coming from our Islamic cemetery. Every holy evening it carries a sinful soul from our Moslem cemetery to the Christian cemetery. That way the camel cleans our cemeteries, turns them into righteous, pure cemeteries where there are no sinners, and turns the Christian cemeteries into cemeteries sown only with sinners. . . . But it just occurred to me—are you perhaps also interested in buying a cemetery? There are abandoned ones here, they can be bought for next to nothing."

I was astonished by such intuition on Azra's part. It was as though she were reading my innermost thoughts and hopes.

"I wouldn't be averse to the idea. The great-great-grandchildren will have to be provided for somewhere one day, won't they? Some expired cemetery, closed down or not, it doesn't matter, I'd pay well. . . . But let's get down to drawing up the contract."

Azra then laughed, her ears disappearing under her hair.

"You know," she said, "I have an additional circumstance of my own."

"What is it?"

"I don't have any children. And I won't be having any. I'm barren and will have no offspring. And even if I weren't, Yusuf wouldn't hand over our descendants."

"Barren? What are you selling, then? What's the point of those lists of names and all that talk?"

"Well, they're not my great-great-grandchildren, they're somebody else's."

"What do you mean, somebody else's?"

"Olga's and Cecilia's. They have children, and these are their descendants, straight down the line to the white bees. . . ."

"But Olga won't sell the male grandchildren, only the female. I asked her."

"Not to you, she won't. But she'll give them to me. Why, I'm their great-aunt. Why wouldn't she give them to me to support for free?"

"And afterward?"

"Afterward I'll turn them over to you, as you asked. Is it a deal?"

"It's a deal," I said, the expression on my face like that of those astonished horses in the paintings of the Italian Quattrocento.

"I've understood everything, Azra," I said. "I agree, so let's put our signatures to it." She signed and swore on the Koran, and I saw she was swearing on the real book, not on the one made out of Venetian soap. That's how I knew I was not being tricked.

Fresh air greeted me outside. Time had passed. The sky had stopped, the clouds hung like curdled milk, and again there was the gallop of the camel. I saw it returning with a new cargo. This time it was carrying a righteous man. From the Christian to the Islamic cemetery.

■ DOWN

SHE: One evening in Istanbul, just before aksham, the evening prayer, the emperor's eyes alit like two black doves on a spot next to the At-Meidan. Sultan Ahmed's gaze was numb from peering through his dense thoughts, and he decided to build the mosque of mosques on this very spot. He made up his mind that the shrine should have six minarets and dispatched messengers to both sides of the empire to find him the best mason.

I: But the messenger to the West encountered unforeseen difficulties. The most celebrated architect of the empire was so frightened by the prospect of the assignment that he vanished without a trace, and in his place put an illiterate Serb from Bosnia, whose family had, admittedly, been worshipping Islam for five generations.

SHE: He, too, had earned a name for himself as a mason, building turbehs and wells, but nobody dared even breathe to the imperial envoy that this was not the genuine article. The man was taciturn, his nose soared out of his forehead and plummeted onto his face, painfully parting his eyes. There were always seven hard years showing on him, and nobody knew how much more salt he would eat.

I: And worst of all, not even he, such as he was, agreed without a struggle. When he heard what was wanted of him, his smile aged by a day, and he asked to consult with the mufti before going. They met at the "vakuf," the mufti with his beard in his hand, and the man in a shirt that in place of a collar had a rope sewed on. As though he were ready for hanging.

SHE: "You are going out into the far distance, the sort that one can only recall but not run around," the mufti said to him. "But remember one thing: he who cures himself of himself shall be undone."

I: "The least use comes from the wisest conversation," thought the mason, and walked out.

SHE: After this talk, the mufti reassured the emperor's envoy that the mason was able to think symmetrically and could simultaneously lift one glass of wine with his left hand and put another on the ground with his right, without spilling either. Since the envoy dared not return empty-handed, he headed back for Istanbul with this man who used snot to heal wounds, and with the hope that the other imperial messenger, the one who had gone to the East, would have better luck.

I: But it happened that the other one, on his way back from Damascus, had gone down along with his ship, and so they brought before the grand vizier the only mason they had. Asked whether he had brought some preliminary drafts of the future building, the mason slipped his hand into his shirt and pulled out three strings, each tied with knots at uneven intervals.

"That's all?" asked the vizier in astonishment.

"That's enough," replied the man.

"And how will our master know what kind of building you have in mind for him?" inquired the vizier.

The mason pointed to the dignitary in front of him and said: "Let the master point out what he wants and I shall build it for him."

SHE: They say it was then that the grand vizier realized that the mason barely understood what they were talking about and that Turkish was not his forte. "How can the master explain what he wants when you can't understand him properly?"

I: "Dreamers have no fatherland, and dreams know not of language.

And what else can the master's mosque of mosques be but a dream?"

It is not known whether the grand vizier liked the plan or not, but the mason was brought before Sultan Ahmed and, to the vizier's astonishment, the emperor led the man to the window and pointed outside. Standing there in the mist of the Bosporus, in the green water of the morning air, as though in the sky, was the huge Church of Churches, Constantinople's St. Sophia, the pride of the demolished Byzantine Empire, the biggest temple of the Christian world, which had long since been converted into a mosque.

"It must not be any bigger, because I myself am no bigger a ruler than was Justinian, who had it built, but it must not be any smaller, either," said Sultan Ahmed, who then dismissed the mason, ordering him to commence work immediately.

"Even this world is only Allah's first attempt," the mason thought as he left. "If anything in this world is to be done properly, it should be done twice." He slipped off his shoes and walked under the huge dome of the Church of Wisdom.

"The question now," he said to himself, "is whether I will be buried drunk or sober. . . ."

SHE: First he climbed the cobblestoned ramp to the upper floor and from the church's balcony and gallery peered down into the space below, which looked like a square shut in by nine doors. Then he walked around the upper-story porches, where, glistening in the dusk, the eyes of the mosaics that had not yet flaked greeted him. Looking at him were Christ and the Virgin Mary, and placed next to and above them were leather shields inscribed with the suras of the Koran, which he couldn't read because he was illiterate. Below, thousands of lights flickered over the stone floor of the church, and the man felt as though he were seeing the star-studded sky from above, like God, rather than from below, as usual. Then he slowly descended, asked that a tall—*the* tallest—camel in Istanbul be brought to him, and ordered that ten thousand builders be assembled on the appointed day down by the hippodrome, which here they call the At-Meidan.

I: For the next ten years, every morning he went to St. Sophia and, with his strings, measured the foundation and walls, the altar and apsidal chapel, the windows, diaconica, and proskomidia, the choir gallery and nave of the church, the narthex and porches, the dome and the doors. Three knots to the left of the entrance, four knots up. And in the sand by the hippodrome he transmitted all this to the builders, who worked according to his instructions and according to identical knotted yarns. Had he fallen off his camel and died, had the wind nipped him or a snake bitten him, the next day nobody would have known how to continue the building. He alone knew how far they had come, and all the future drafts were deep inside him. But, riding his tall, double-humped camel down to the building site, he sat with his back to the animal's head and stared fixedly at St. Sophia, using even this time of departure from Wisdom to etch in his mind every detail of its immensely grand walls and gables. And as he rode he thought about calligraphers who sometimes look not at the flower they are drawing, but at the emptiness that frames the flower, and see not the contours of the flower as being what they should draw, but the edges of the emptiness. And so he, too, moving away from St. Sophia, memorizing its corner and window, etched in his mind even the fragment of sky that framed the huge dome and its rim, a fragment that, once seen, can never be forgotten. Because it matters what kind of emptiness is left behind by things or beings. Emptiness is really like a mold shaped by the thing that was there before, an emptiness pregnant with the object that filled it. The world in and around us is full of such pregnant emptinesses.

The mason had trained his visual memory so well that his gaze curdled, it congealed, and his eyes looked like two pebbles fired from a slingshot. He finally began, like the sky outside, to remember in detail even the shape of the perfumed emptiness that from the inside, in the light of the lamps, filled and held the membrane of the walls. And the deeper he penetrated into every detail of St. Sophia, here, within reach of Topkapi and the sultan's chambers, the faster the magnificent, beautiful mosque grew down there on the shore by the hippodrome. The mosque of mosques.

SHE: Yet, all the same, there was something that jarred. St. Sophia carried a Christian temple in the stone of wisdom, whereas the mosque rising in the sands of the hippodrome, by its nature, purpose, and even its form, seemed to resist that model-edifice. It was as though they were at war with one another, the one already there and the one rising in its image. And the mason had to reconcile and bridge the gulf between them, carrying this terrible schism and discordance inside him like an abyss. He had to subdue and tame that first large church, where wisdom had been turned into stone. He knew the taste of that stone by heart, even in his sleep. But the stone of his own edifice did not have that taste. In other words, the imperial builder was incapable of finishing his mosque.

I: For years the mason had not veered off the road from St. Sophia to the building site, and it was only now, when he occasionally avoided going to the hippodrome because he did not know what further orders to give, that he discovered the large marketplace, and he wended his way down its crooked, arcaded streets to the Golden Horn, where on the shore he caught sight of another, smaller market, the Misir Bazaar, under whose very roof ships from Egypt unloaded fragrant oils and spices. He entered as though bewitched, looking to buy anything at all.

"Sandalwood?" the fragrance merchant asked him, propped a small ground-glass bottle under a bigger one, and waited. They waited in the semidarkness, but nothing happened. And then, just when the customer was about to give up and walk out, the merchant said:

"One must wait as long as it takes to read a sura of the Koran."

The customer was illiterate and did not know how long it took to read a sura of the Koran, but just then a drop as bright as a comet appeared on the inverted neck of the bigger bottle, slowly descended on its tail, and trickled into the smaller bottle.

"Do you want to try it?" the merchant asked, then deftly ran his finger around the edge of the bottleneck and held the finger out to the customer. The latter took a little onto his own finger and was about to wipe it on his robe.

"Not on the robe!" the merchant warned him. "It will burn

through. On the palm of your hand. Right on the palm of your hand."

And when the customer had done as he was told and was about to smell it, the merchant stopped him.

"Not today, sir, not today! In three days! Then the real fragrance will come out. And it will last as long as sweat. But it will be stronger than sweat, because it has the strength of tears. . . ."

SHE: And so the mason understood why his edifice was putting up resistance. It had to be judged on the third day, not right away. He had put his hand up to his nose too soon. No real work can be finished on just any day. One has to wait for the right day for its completion. The right day. And that is what he did.

I: When the edifice was finally erected and when the builders closed the dome after the mason's eye had first caught the half-moon and star through the opening on top, he went back to St. Sophia and gazed at its towering height.

SHE: There, attached to the chain holding the lamps, was something round and white hanging in the darkness of the dome. He stared at it for a long time, and asked around until he found out what it was. It was an ostrich egg. Not knowing what purpose it served, but knowing whom it served, the mason had two such ostrich eggs put up in the new mosque.

I: Then he entered the now finished building, cracked his great whip, counted the number of times it echoed, and returned to St. Sophia. He counted the echoes of his whip there and heard ten echoes more than in his mosque.

SHE: He then had four large earthenware jugs built into the arch of the new building, and these jugs gave the mosque the necessary number of echoes, just as they began that very same moment to draw in all the soot from the lamps, which later, when scraped down, gave the best India ink in the empire. And those ostrich eggs drove away the spiders, and there are no cobwebs in the mosque to this very day. Then, at the entrance, the mason placed a double-winged leather curtain, had Bukhara rugs spread out on the stone floor, fell prostrate before the emperor, and presented him with the Blue Mosque.

1: On returning home, the mason still dreamed that he was dismounting to look at the porches and foundations of St. Sophia, that he was measuring the proportions and numbers of Wisdom with his strings and knots, and that he was carrying them somewhere in his bosom on a camel. And he dreamed of every section of the stone of Wisdom again. He woke up with the strange feeling that he was ill, that something inside him had changed, that he had stepped somewhere into hole-riddled dreams. He couldn't adjust to his previous life. He was no longer the same. Even when these dreams faded somewhat, he still felt a strange sickness inside him, and he started going from one doctor to another, looking for a cure for his malady and complaining that he was aging terribly slowly and with great effort.

SHE: At the end of this journey a tamer of plants told him:

"Every death has a father and a mother. The cause of your pain is not your death's mother, but its father."

"What does that mean?" he asked.

"It means that it's not from doctors that you should look for a cure, because your malady isn't physical."

And then the mason returned whence he had set out into the world, to that mufti who had seen him off to Istanbul. And he told him all about his troubles.

1: The mufti looked at him for a while, or, rather, the mufti's nostrils looked at him like two shortsighted black eyes. And then the mufti pulled himself together and said decidedly:

"I know what's the matter with you."

"What?" cried the mason.

"You've become a Christian."

"A Christian? But I'm illiterate and I've never set foot in a Christian infidel temple, except in . . ."

1: And here the mason choked so badly that the mufti had to hit him on the back with a book.

SHE: "Is there a cure?" the terrified mason finally spluttered out.

1: "There is, but it's as hard to come by as a man's soul. You have to find another sultan and a mosque as big as the Blue Mosque in Constantinople. And wherever you find it, no matter whether it's

in Damascus or Jerusalem, you must spend ten years staying in that mosque and constantly staring at it, while you build, according to the exact measure of the mosque, a church with a cross on top, a synagogue, or anything else, a bath, if you want. . . ."
But he who cures himself of himself shall be undone.

4 DOWN

After his wife left him, Major Pohvalich—"the man with the blue ears," as they called him—remained alone with his daughters, said, "Fuck the door," and proceeded to polish his boots.

"Sorrow isn't always in proportion to intelligence," the neighbors thought, observing him, and thus passed a year of solitary life. The family got used to the house without Vitacha, as much as one could, but in the morning, at their school desks, the girls always somehow knew when their mother, off in America somewhere, had dreamed of them the night before. And then that dreadful thing happened with the children. One day the major came home from work to find it was all over. The girls were shot dead. The major and the police did everything they could to track down the murderer. But the investigation soon came to a dead end. When the police gave up, he continued the investigation on his own. He whispered: "What you miss in life, you can't catch in dreams," and his whole life slowly turned into a search. The murder weapon had not been found, and the major thought about that often. Maybe the murderer had tossed it into the Danube. But if he had been pressed for time, he might have hidden it somewhere near the scene of the crime. Reflecting in this vein, the

247

major sat on the balcony and smoked. The blossoms quivered in all
their colors at the foot of the neighboring yard, the leaves inverted the
bright side of their lining, you could hear the river. The major looked
and listened. He listened to the Danube and thought God knows what,
but he knew and felt quite positively that these thoughts of his were
not springing out of his head but, rather, like fish, were swarming and
spawning in the waters of the nearby Danube. "Such are human
thoughts," he decided, but suddenly he felt his thoughts move, and
this time he again knew that they were nascent not in his head but in
a nest at the top of the next-door lime tree.

"You know how to look for it, but you don't know when you've
found it," he said in response, picked up an old glove, and went down
to the next-door yard, redolent with lime blossom. He walked over to
the tree and stuck his hand in the hollow of its trunk. He felt a solid
object inside, wrapped in a rag, took it out, and departed with it. Once
home, he examined it carefully. It was a pistol. He decided not to turn
the weapon over to the authorities for the time being; applying his
skills as an artillery officer, he examined its ballistic properties himself
and lifted the fingerprints off the gun. There was no doubt about it,
this was the murder weapon, and, amazingly enough, the murderer
had left a clear set of prints on it. The magazine had been profession-
ally removed from the revolver. It was an army gun; the murderer
was obviously someone of the major's acquaintance.

And so Major Pohvalich began inviting home old friends of Vitacha's father and his own army associates who had visited him while
he was still married. And he got them to leave their fingerprints on
the glasses. He usually poured juniper brandy for them and cold tea
for himself, because the color was the same. He was determined to be
patient and catch the murderer. Friends gladly accepted his invitation,
came in the evening, and consoled him, left, as he was, to his own
devices in an empty apartment where the clocks no longer worked
but merely glowed on the walls at night. After these visits, the major
would brush the glasses with a mixture of soot, graphite, and some
smelly powder, and then carefully compare these prints with those of
the murderer. But his superior, Colonel Krachun, somehow kept
avoiding these invitations.

This Colonel Krachun, a good-looking man, was wont to say that he belonged to a small, tubercular tribe that liked Russians. He had visited Vitacha's father, Captain Milut, in his day. In the middle of his mouth Colonel Krachun had a big yellow tooth, which protruded like a horn when he was not talking. This tooth bisected every word that wanted to come out of his mouth, and, once expelled, these two pieces searched for and pursued one another, trying to reassemble as best they could. This left the colonel, a decisive man otherwise, somewhat flustered. Vitacha had found the man attractive at one time and the major knew it, even though she hid it from them both in those eyes of hers that held the constellation of Taurus, where the stars stand in the flowing river. Krachun had served as the military attaché in India for a while, and there he had a car accident in which his daughter was killed.

When the funeral was held for the major's daughters, he appeared at the cemetery to pay his condolences, met Vitacha at the forty-day commemoration, and paid his condolences to her as well, and even to her second husband, architect Razin; then, embarrassed by the incongruousness of it, he quickly arranged to pay the major a visit. He put off that visit for a long time, then one evening suddenly dropped in.

"Hi, Bato!" he wanted to say at the door as usual, but it came out as "Hi, Barto!" and to cover up his confusion Krachun said:

"The years are like days, but there's no end to the month," and he undid his belt so quickly that he dropped his overcoat, and the reserve magazine of his pistol, along with the cartridge, fell out and rolled into a corner. He looked obliquely at the major, as though both his ears had burned through with embarrassment, hung his coat on the hook, and placed the magazine of his gun on the little shelf for the clothes brushes.

"Juniper brandy?" the major asked as usual, and when the colonel accepted he poured him brandy and himself a tea and placed both glasses on the table, looking Krachun straight in the eye, determined to follow his every move. But he was not concentrating. His head was spinning with myriad thoughts. His grief that evening was behaving as though it were deaf to conversation. He couldn't get his mind off a soldier from Kostainitsa who had lost the power of speech after being wounded in battle during World War I and then, twenty years later, during World War II, dreamed about that same battle and regained it. At the same time, Major Pohvalich kept thinking about the saying that one does not carry mirrors into church, and, wanting to shake off such thoughts, he stared at Colonel Krachun's mustache and was on the verge of asking whether he had planted it himself since it had sprouted so nicely. Instead, fortunately, he merely yawned without opening his mouth, and for a second his lips thinned. Then he flinched, and with a smile as frayed as a cap, dispelled this sadness and confusion and pulled himself together. Now he was on the alert, ready for anything.

"Do you suspect anybody?" the colonel asked as soon as they sat down.

"Not yet," said Pohvalich.

"Did you notice anything at all that might have foreboded such a thing? Did you have a premonition or anything?"

"No—or, rather, yes, but it was very strange. Anyway, it was a long time ago. When Vitacha and I were still together, I started, at certain moments—not often, but quite distinctly—to hear inside me my wife (it didn't matter where she was at that moment) wailing. I'd be wide awake, at work, riding, or running, but I'd hear it or imagine it—only why did I imagine that, of all things, and so clearly, too? Anyway, I'd hear her voice loud and clear, and while it cried in my ears, I, in horror, would conjecture what could be happening and to whom, because one doesn't cry in that kind of voice for oneself, but for others; one wails like that only for the dead or when something terrible happens, something beyond the imagination. I didn't know how, but I could hear that voice, her voice, so clearly, as I had never heard it nor could have heard it before, because Vitacha had never wailed, not even for her father. And in that wailing my wife appeared quite clearly in my memory, with her green close-set eyes, with her breasts set close together, with her ass that was like a gold coin, as the late Madame Yolanta used to say. I heard her crying, and in that wailing even her personality was more pronounced than in everyday life. And in those moments when I listened to her wail disconsolately somewhere, she herself gave no signs of being upset. Naturally, I was afraid; I'd race home, usually thinking at such moments (and they recurred two or three times) that it was our children, the one or the other. Later it transpired, however, that this wailing had foreboded the death of my father.... But a year or more after my father's death, I again thought I heard wailing. This time, however, I couldn't recognize the voice. I only knew that it resembled Vitacha's, but, unlike hers, it was high-pitched, very high-pitched; it wasn't cracked and it didn't stutter as usual; rather, it chimed like a glass bell, which it had never done ... as though it were coming from mirrors. That's all."

Colonel Krachun listened to these words carefully, smoking a pipe in his armchair, and periodically firing, like a cannon, long puffs of smoke, the ends of which exploded somewhere, at the clock on the wall, the glasses on the table, or the glass lamp under which they were sitting. This silent, slow-motion cannonade planted explosions all over the room, while Major Pohvalich spoke and the colonel scratched his ear with his pipe.

"You know, I've already had what you had," he finally said. "And I defended myself against misfortune as best I knew how. Time heals our pain and misery—not time still to come, but time that has passed. ... I know one shouldn't speak of rope in the home of a hanged man, but my experience may help you solve your own troubles. When what happened to you happened to me, when my daughter was killed, I started taking an interest in death for the first time. 'What is it?' I wondered. I was in India at the time, as you know, and looking back on it now, I don't know exactly when it was that I built this feeling behind me that death is an extremely complex calculation, something like solving equations with several unknowns. That feeling and preoccupation with death—its technology and mechanics, so to speak— rose up behind me like a wall, cutting me off from the past, and now that feeling is here, and behind it my terrible past can change or be enlarged to its heart's content, without my knowing it, or with my barely feeling it.... That's the point I've reached. Let's start by asking: What is time? Time is rather like a language that is learned along with one's mother tongue—in other words, imperceptibly. And yet we seem to learn our mother tongue at the expense of this other language, or at least we use it more often, whereas this other language, the language of time, we forget. You, for instance, are now in a very difficult position. There are people who, in such situations, are prepared to confront the future before everybody else, and there are others, like you now, who encounter the future after everybody else. The present of the former and the present of you latter are not of the same duration. Your present has expanded at the expense and to the detriment of your past and your future. Please don't think I mean to correct you in any way. I simply wanted us to get to the key question at this point, that being: What is the present? Our present is really the stoppage of time. The tips of snails' horns stretched to their limit. And this 'now' is the only common denominator of all living things. It is the only moment of life, from the beginning to the end of time, because everything else, the two eternities that stretch out before and after our 'now,' are in the deepest torpor. Consequently, *the present is that part of time which has stopped.* Life cannot survive in time that flows, or while it flows. Life survives only in the present, where time stands still. You want proof? Here it is: My present is nobody else's future. The past, therefore, consists of moments in which time has stopped, and the future of moments in which time will stop. And death, my dear major, whatever Einstein may have said, death is the fragment of our time that has lost the power to stop. Because the amount of time that stands still in the universe is constant, the surplus drains out. That's why deaths have to happen. In submitting to this universal inevitability, everybody's time sooner or later ceases to stop, and drains away forever. When your part of time loses the power to stop, you, too, will be dead, because, remember, there isn't, wasn't, and won't be life in time as long as time is in motion. . . . It has to stop and wait for us in order for us to survive. In short, these moments of arrested time accumulate inside you, and when you are full of your hours like water, they drown you, because you have no more room for them, and meanwhile the universe becomes younger and younger. In Asia they go even further and say that this is true only of one gender of death. Because the shamanist religion believes that there is male death and female death, that there are two kinds of death. One death, they believe, is of the female gender, with dark eyes, with a wreath of lotuses around the head, in a dark-red dress. It weeps over what it does, and ruthlessly takes both male lives and female. Its own tears turn into disease and death. Death of the male gender is a god, and his name is Yama. It takes both kinds of lives. In order to live forever, it is not enough to defeat Yama, the god of death (which the rakshasas, the order of Brahman priests, have already managed to do), one must also defeat the goddess of death, which no one has ever managed to do."

"Do you think death is not as monolithic as our conventional medicine would have it?" the major interrupted. "Do you think that, like our present, it is split?"

"I don't think anything," the colonel answered, his words cut by the tusk poking out of his mouth. "I merely imparted a belief to this effect that is held in a part of Asia. Now, then, this is the point. . . ."

At that moment the colonel half-lifted himself out of his armchair, as if to give his words time to patch themselves back together in the air, and in his pipe's closing cannonry he aimed the smoke at a picture on the wall where there were glass-covered photographs of Major Pohvalich's two late daughters. With a precise shot that exploded like a bomb, he got one of the little girls right in the head, then turned around to his host, smiled abashedly, and resumed the conversation:

"In his Epistle to the Hebrews, Saint Paul said: 'It is appointed unto men once to die!' And women? I ask. Female death, as you have probably heard it said among our people, is again divided into two kinds, into the death of childless women and the death of childed women.

"The death of the childed woman is only that one single death, her own personal death, and nobody else's. Anyway, that death does not resemble death; it is more like another, last childbirth. Hence, the childed woman experiences her childbirth once again in her own death. Childless women, however, die in an entirely different way, not having this experience before their eyes.

"A dying childless woman is a woman who has never died, since the

beginning of time, and is dying now for the first time. All her childed predecessors have come to die in her death. And their long—all-too-long—journey ends irrevocably, there and then, in the childless woman's death, after countless thousands of years of uninterrupted life. Let's, for our purposes, leave aside the marginal offshoots of this female line; it is still clear that one branch of the whole of life dies out and ends here forever in the death of the childless woman.

"For instance, with your daughters, who died childless, also died their mother, Vitacha, who is still alive, who uncovered one church to cover another and will have no more children, and also her sister Vida, who offered handfuls to some and pinches to others, although she had tits like buttocks; and with them, too, died Vitacha's mother, Veronica Isailovich, Milut by marriage, who gave flour to the devil and bran to God; and her mother, Mrs. Yolanta Isailovich, née Ibich, the eloquent great-grandmother of your daughters, who married the dead and read fortunes in pans; and her mother, Mrs. Angelina Ibich, an illegitimate Pfister, or Riznich, who turned from a priest into a deacon, making her milk weep; and with your daughters also died their illegitimate great-great-grandmother, Amalia Riznich, who read dictionaries of smiles and wanted to marry her husband, and the lovely Amalia's mother, Yevdokia, born a Riznich (in one family) and married to a Riznich (in another), who fasted when full and wanted bread when she had cake, and her own mother, Paulina, Riznich by marriage, born of the Counts Rzewusky, who married her sister to Balzac, and herself trod wherever she looked but paid no attention to where she trod, and her mother, née Pototska, who ate her food sour and whose husband's teeth went numb, and her own mother, who knew that a watch gets you nowhere because it goes in a circle. With your daughters also died that famous noble lady Medjansky, the most celebrated in this tree of your family's milk, who, leaving church after her wedding, minced instead of walked because her father-in-law tossed a gold coin underfoot with each step she took. And with them died her mother and her grandmother and her great-great-grandmother and the mother of that great-great-grandmother, and her "navern-baba" and "askundjela," and her "kurdjupa" and "kurebala," and her "sukurdacha," and the mother of the "sukurdacha," and the "surde-pacha," and the white eagle, who during the Hundred Years' War turned defiance into an art and was afraid to sleep; and the white eagle's grandmother, who covered herself with lies as though they were a blanket, and this one's mother, who carried a smile on her face like a wound and charged stomach first at the spit, and the great-great-grandmother, who had a split forehead and doused brandy with fire; and this one's mother, who loved her husband only in winter and dyed wool with onions; and her great-great-grandmother, who wanted to make black out of white and was burned at the stake; and her mother, who sowed millet on ice and disbelieved the hungry because her own stomach was full; and her grandmother, who threshed thorns barefoot and sweated around the eyes; and her mother, to whom first came the chemise and then the dolman, so that they forbade her to sing but not to cry; and her mother, Veronica, who on her towel caught the face of the Messiah; and her ancestress, who in the Stone Age spoke into the ear of the deaf and combed the wind with her fingers; and her great-grandmother, who married the sun to the moon, while her eggs clucked and her chickens remained silent; and her great-great-grandmother, who cut off her child's um-bilical cord and out of one goat made two bellows; and her predecessor by blood, who carped but whose jaws didn't ache; and her mother, who carried her male on her back; and the great-grandmother, who kept a live snake in her bosom and climbed up with her eyes and down with her brains, walking with the help of her hands.... To cut it short, since the beginning of time, since the conception of the human race and your distaff line, they all came to die in the death of your daughters. The death of your daughters is of cosmic proportions and multiplied a thousandfold. It is the extinction of an entire human milkline...."

At this point, the guest drew out a pistol, quickly cocked it, put the barrel in his mouth, and pulled the trigger. Instead of a shot, there was only a faint "click," and the colonel began to play the weapon like a double flute, softly and lingeringly, the way it is played by the shepherd in the mountains. Then, as though jerking awake from a dream, he said, "Excuse me," put down the pistol, and exhaled a long plume of smoke, which, of course, came not from the gun, but from the pipe. . . .

The hour after midnight struck outside, Colonel Krachun went on talking and drinking, drinking and talking, twirling his mustache, and the major listened, every now and then glancing at the plate of fish, where one single anchovy was still left. And he thought to himself how, like a finger, pain, too, had a bone. It seemed to him that the colonel had put down his glass too close to the edge of the table and that he, Major Pohvalich, had told his friend the story about Vitacha's wailing long ago, not this evening but half a year earlier, and that he had told of the event before it had happened. The juniper brandy was running out; a shallow silence descended in which there was no angel to pass overhead. The guest abruptly got up and began taking his leave, stretching. The birds could be heard outside, and the major thought, as he bid farewell, that birds never lie.

"And what conclusion can we draw from these beliefs?" he asked his guest at the door.

The guest became flustered, walked over to the coatrack, where his overcoat was hanging, and, tall as he was, slipped his two arms through the sleeves before he unhooked the coat, as though the coatrack had been holding it for him.

"What can we do?" he said absent-mindedly (although that is not what the major had asked), and reached for the doorknob. "We have to know that our daughters died the hardest kind of death, and do everything else accordingly. . . ."

And the colonel flew out of the house, waving goodbye behind him, looking not at the major but at the path ahead. The host immediately noticed that his guest had left behind the magazine and cartridge on the little utility shelf, but he did not run to the gate to catch him, or call him back to take what he had forgotten. Instead, he glanced around the room and, staggering with exhaustion, went over to the glasses on the table. He lifted the fingerprints and was instantly wide awake when he saw the result. The prints on the brandy glass were identical to those found on the pistol that had killed his children.

There was no doubt about it: the brandy glass, the glass of his guest that evening, Colonel Krachun, bore the prints of the murderer. But something was wrong. Something had completely escaped the major's attention, something was nagging at him. A small detail. He arduously went over everything that had happened that night, and suddenly noticed that he was drunk. So drunk, in fact, that he went to bed, resolved to pass judgment on everything in the peace and quiet of the morning, when his head had cleared.

In the morning he got up, looked at the glasses, realized that this time he himself, not his guest, had had brandy, and that there was no longer any doubt about it. The brandy glass and the weapon bore identical prints. The prints of the murderer, the hand-marked traces, were his, Major Mrksha Pohvalich's, who had killed his daughters.

At seven in the morning, Major Pohvalich took the magazine off the little shelf and slipped it into the gun. He ate the remainder of the fish, thought, "The ass may suffer, but the appetite does not," and shot himself through the ear. At three minutes past seven, as soon as the shot had reverberated, Colonel Krachun entered Major Mrksha Pohvalich's apartment with an army patrol to inspect the scene and retrieve his magazine.

3 ACROSS

6 DOWN

As far as I can remember, Mr. Atanas Razin the architect told the following story after a business trip abroad:

You know, I'm sure, those sweeping staircases with the double echo that crosses and makes a knot on the landing above, like the staircase itself. Well, that's the kind of staircase there is at Cecilia's house. When I stepped onto that staircase, it was late summer, and through the window there was a view of the garden. The slick shadows of the chestnuts lay under the trees like puddles of oil; the broad leaves slapped the wind and tumbled, knocking into one another, as heavy as grouse. A diaphanous shade spread over the garden like a cube of ice, and growing in it were mushrooms. A cloud stopped and stood still over the nearby church, and the others began circling it; down below, by the stream, the yellow clay and dark-green soil touched. . . .

On entering Cecilia's house, I was determined to behave strictly as I had planned. That evening I had to keep Cecilia shining my way, like a flame in a draft. In matters like these, the most important thing in my job is always to act exactly as you planned, and not to veer from that comportment and posture at any cost, no matter what happens.

261

Whatever does happen will always fade away an hour or two later into the backwaters of memory, but you, if you were steadfast, will hold the advantage. There is a little trick to all this. A trick you should resort to to be on the safe side. During visits and talks of this sort, you should think of Indian-cress salad, which helps men not go bald, or you should carry yourself as if you had a mouth full of ink, and ears full of mustaches. In such situations, I have always gained the better of my collocutor by telling myself some story especially chosen to fit the circumstances. This silent storytelling always kept me at the same boiling point, so to speak. . . .

Absorbed in these thoughts, I climbed upstairs, but Cecilia was not yet in the large dining room with its hearth. A mirror and a candlestick stood above the fireplace. Waiting there alone like that, I spit like a slingshot straight into the mirror. Then I heard a muffled giggle and saw the tiny tapped heel of a child's shoe peering out from under the long tablecloth.

"Azeredo, Azeredo, do you know how children are born?" came a child's little voice from under the tablecloth.

"Do you?" replied a voice that was even frailer though male.

"Yes. And I know how you were born, too."

"How?"

"Your father grabbed a rooster as it was about to crow, and when the rooster opened its beak, he spat into it. This made the rooster lay an egg, and a compassionate man came by and carried the egg in his armpit for three months until you were hatched."

"So what?"

"So nothing."

While the children prattled on, I continued to prepare for my meeting with Cecilia. Because it matters what story a man tells himself in the given situation. The color of your silence depends on what you're keeping silent, and in my job the color of silence is everything. And so I thought that this time the best thing would be for me to treat myself to the Story of Plakida. It's a short, straightforward little story that currycombs even souls who like to buck. . . .

Just then the two children hidden under the tablecloth whistled into a broken button. Judging by their voices, the little girl must have been about ten, and the boy considerably younger.

"Azeredo, Azeredo," she said, still hiding under the table, "how many suns are there in the sky today?"

"There are three suns," replied the frail little voice disconnectedly, as though it had been nibbled. "The first sun is seen by everybody. The second sun is seen by certain animals—snakes, for instance—and all three suns are seen only by the dead.... As for me, I am not Azeredo, I am Don Azeredo."

"Mama says you're the devil."

"What's a devil?"

"You don't know? Stop pretending! Haven't you ever been to the theater? Haven't you ever heard *Faust,* the opera?"

"No. I have no ear for that. But I do understand languages. All except one. I don't know which one it is, probably some new language."

"Well, that, too, goes to show you're the devil! When you grow up, one of your tits will be male and the other female. Don't you have a tail in your trousers?"

"How should I know whether it's a tail or not?"

"It must be a tail, because I want to be flogged with what you've got inside your trousers. Before Adam, Eve herself slept with the devil. Show it to me!"

"I can't in front of this man who's come to do business. I have a job to do with him first."

And that same moment the boy appeared from under the table. He could not have been more than six or seven years old. Above his lips, green snot coiled into a knot over the old, dry snot, which glistened like the trail of a snail.

"Have you got a pencil?" he asked me out of the blue.

I took mine out and handed it to him, a bit surprised. He didn't even look at it, but shoved it into his mouth and before my very eyes ate it, crunching it with his small teeth as though it were a straw. I wanted to stop him, but it was all over in a matter of seconds.

"I don't like haircuts," he said, as though nothing had happened. His small, frost-tinted ears floated in the waves of his pretty, curly head. But his locks, eyelashes, and eyebrows were all the color of ash, as though they had gone up in flames and burned only moments ago, without injuring his rosy face, and had stayed like ash on his little head. One puff and it would all blow away, like burning letters whose white script can still be read one last time before they disintegrate. . . . I was afraid that my pencil would injure him and I wanted to raise an alarm, but I immediately realized that this would interfere with my work, that it would, in fact, make it impossible. I was beside myself, but I dared not show it.

"Why are you so thin?" I, too, now spoke as though nothing had happened. His two fine eyes flashed on and off, like a lighthouse, and it was then that I noticed one eye was defective, as though a drop of wax had spilled into it.

"Food serves to warm a man and wake him up," he said, and asked me to pass him the candlestick from the mantelpiece, which was beyond his reach. I put the candlestick down on the table next to a box of matches. But it was obvious that he was too little even to reach the matches on the table.

"Is it true that you make your bombs out of water?" he asked, spitting at one of the candles. That very instant it lit up. Then he spat at the second and at the third candle, and one by one they lit up.

"Out of heavy water," I belatedly replied in astonishment, starting hastily to mumble to myself the Story of Plakida as though it were a prayer:

"That same Plakida who caught a stag with a cross on its head instead of antlers was once hunting by the sea. . . ."

"You can put the candlestick back now," the boy said in response, laughing. His smile, which was vertical, not horizontal, always by-passed his nose and mouth on the left side of his face.

"What did you say?" I asked in surprise.

"Put it back in its place, on the mantelpiece."

I was somewhat bewildered, but I went over obediently and tried. The candlestick would not budge, although I had brought it over to the table with no trouble at all just a few minutes before. I turned around. The boy was staring at me through that drop of wax, his good eye closed. And then, from under the table, the little girl giggled again.

"What's the matter? The fire too heavy for you?" she called out from down there. "Blow it out! Blow it out!"

And obediently I blew out the candles.

"Now try again!" she shouted from under the tablecloth.

I picked the candlestick up and this time had no trouble returning it to its place. And that very same moment, my Story of Plakida was interrupted inside me.

"Have we become acquainted now?" asked Don Azeredo, and immediately added: "I know what you're thinking."

"What?" I jumped in.

"Nothing worse could happen to you than for your father to win the war. The world will never be yours. . . . Is that what you think?"

"That's it."

"And did you meet Cecilia a long time ago?"

"So long ago it isn't true anymore."

Passing over my answer, he pointed to the stairs I had climbed a moment ago.

"What do you see?" he asked. "They're shiny stone steps, right? See, they look wet, although they're not, because it's a sunny day. That's how Cecilia looks. Cold although she's hot, wet although she's warmed by the sun, as if she were in the rain although she's under a sparkling-clear sky. She wins just when you think she's out of the game. Remember that and you'll get along with Cecilia. But don't do what you've been doing anymore. Even if your fatherland took away everything you got from it, don't do it. The fatherland always takes away everything it gives you. . . . And don't sign that contract with Cecilia, the one you came here for."

Just then the little girl, who was still sitting under the table, cried out:

"Azeredo, Azeredo, is it true that fear makes the ears get dirty fast?"

"Fear makes the ears ooze out, and you go deaf."

At these words, she lifted the tablecloth and came out, picking her ear with her pinky. Then she sniffed her finger and licked it. And then turned to me and said:

"This one here hasn't crossed himself in more than forty days. It's the devil he'll see. . . ."

Thereupon Cecilia walked in.

She had in her hair a comb with teeth as sharp as needles, hair that was black and sleek like patent-leather shoes, and clothes that were the same. She sat down on the little bench, a book in her hand. She was still as beautiful as before, but her eyes had aged faster than she herself and had become swollen, straying in separate directions. She kept losing and recovering them again; one moment they escaped her, the next they submitted, broke off, and returned, which noticeably confused her.

"I'm listening," she said, and bit me with her smile, while I started again murmuring to myself the Story of Plakida.

"You don't seem to remember me, Cecilia, but I haven't come to renew forgotten acquaintances. I've come to seek advice and consolation for my old age. I don't dance the kazachok with my foot in my mouth anymore. I'm getting old now. Especially in the winter. Every winter tears me off the branch. What about you?"

Cecilia thereupon opened the book. She read aloud, and the two children and I listened:

> "How I rejoice to hear the clattering spade!
> It is the cloud, for me in service moiling.
> Till earth be reconciled to toiling,
> Till the proud waves be stayed. . . .
> Overseer!"

At this, Don Azeredo's eyes lit up by turns like a lighthouse, and he answered as though he himself had been called:
"Here!"
Cecilia laughed and proceeded to read:

> "However possible,
> Collect a crowd of men with vigor,
> Spur by indulgence, phrase, or rigor,
> Reward, allure, conscript, compel!
> Each day report me and correctly note
> How grows in length the undertaken moat."

Don Azeredo again jumped in and said something that surprised me, because it sounded like the verse:

"When they to me the information gave,
 They spake not of a moat, but of a grave!"

Here Cecilia once again laughed, and you could see that in the left corner of her mouth her smile was quick and lean, but in the right it was broad and fat.

"What is it, Atanas?" she said to me, closing the book. "How's your building going?"

"How's it going? Well, let me put it to you in a few words. Recently, after my mother's death, I stopped by her house in the village. I went to put the key in the lock, only to discover that there was grass growing in the keyhole. So why build?"

"That's not an answer. But you don't have to tell me a thing. I'll give you the answer."

Her eyes delved into mine as if they were hunting for something. And she coughed.

"The shepherd seizes upon his fattest sheep to slaughter. Similarly, man takes the fattest of his thoughts to somebody else. And you've come with just such a little sheep. I won't know what it is until you show me this sheep of yours, but I do know the following.

"Besides the old way of man's exploitation by man, or the exploitation of one class by another, a far more practical solution now presents itself: the exploitation of one generation by another. Those who won the last war fully exploited you, their sons, and those who lost that war were later exploited by their sons. So your son will exploit you, as did your father. He'll say of you: Why should I go to his funeral? He won't go to mine!

"But this method is behind the times. Much more expedient for exploitation are future, still-unborn generations, those that have not yet found a soul on the street, those that have yet to have their fill of tears, unborn little souls that are not yet subject to any legal regulations, that cannot defend themselves, not even by spitting in someone's eye. That is why it is not the sons who should be exploited, as they were by your naïve fathers, but the future, the grandchildren and great-grandchildren, the great-great-grandchildren and the white bees, as you would say. Toward this end, these future generations must even now be placed within the strict legal framework of exploitation; they must be obligated in advance by universally valid and irreproachable international norms, procedures, and contracts that are lawfully verified and cannot be legally or monetarily annulled in either West or East. Already all the sweat can be wrung out of these future generations, already they can be compelled, in one or two hundred years' time, to carry their mouths full of salty sweat, like blood, if only someone wise is found to cash in on them and their future living space now, in advance. But not everywhere on the face of this planet can this be done with equal success. There are streets in the world that have been converted into corridors, with wallpapered façades on the houses, and squares arranged like rooms crammed with period furniture. But there are other kinds of places as well.

"Hard, fast, and unstable times always befall somebody somewhere. There are wretched regions in the world so wretched that there exists in them a centuries-old deep-rooted general belief (confirmed innumerable times by reality) that nothing acquired can be kept or enjoyed for long, just as a chick cannot be kept from becoming a cock. In regions such as these, the days drag on, the seasons stand still, but the years flash by like lightning. Here hard-won things, painfully acquired, are lost and are easily and mercilessly squandered, and nothing is kept for tomorrow in the way that everything is kept by great nations and powerful states, which will not at any cost let go of something once it's obtained, just as a dog does not let go of a bone, because they know that they will permanently keep, enjoy, and possess it all. There is a suitable crack in time here for you and those like you. . . ."

Upon these words, Cecilia caressed the little girl and smiled. Only then did I notice her corroded tongue, and again I heard that coughing like an unintelligible question. She caught one of her runaway gazes, brought it back to me, and continued:

"So, my dear, you rightly think that buying little bees is more profitable than any kind of building. People who build are people with nothing better to do, who grow weeds under their coats instead of hearts. And you have opted for a profitable, timely deal, the deal not of the century but of the millennium.

"Since you have concluded such deals all over America and Asia, now you've decided to try your luck in Europe. Here it's even easier for you. Because you think (and again you're right) that here, in the B——, for instance, where instead of the sun a huge sea urchin, all black and full of prickles, plunges into the clouds as if into murky water, periodically surfacing in between wars, you think that here and in places like it, where not even two people have managed to pair their socks, that here is the right place for such a deal. You also think, again rightly, that this region is particularly suited to you, because you know so many people here, all those who dine barefoot; I myself, with my sisters, am one who went arm in arm with you when we were young; you remember, I used to have a shallow smile that ran aground on my teeth, I used to smoke your pipe and screw you in that boat. . . .

"And there's another thing," Cecilia went on. "Just as tears are the sweat of the soul, so sweat is the tears of the body. Well, these tears of the body can be leased in advance. And you know best how; that you've long had at your fingertips. One can already cash in on the koshava wind that will blow in the year 2200, not to mention on the future space under that wind. The objective isn't to exploit only these great-great-grandchildren themselves, with their niggardly steps, or the little white bees, their wings clipped in advance. The point isn't to take advantage of them themselves, through prepaid food that will bring you payment upon payment, through financed transfers to new guardianships and new technologies, through the prearranged long-term adoption of sons, for which all these of the future will repay you with interest upon interest, enjoying this future hunger that has already been paid for today. . . . The objective is to exploit and obtain their living space as well, to possess, drink, and breathe even now their land, water, and air. . . . And everybody knows what goes with water, land, and air. The grave . . .

"Your thinking is perfectly logical: 'Who's going to deny me that one (well-paid) grave?' Who's going to deny an old man, who comes, his ears full of tears, from abroad to buy himself a grave—who's going to deny him that?

"What you actually bury in those several cubic meters later is no business of those who sold that strip of land and who no longer think of or can lay claim to it. Whether a truck will deposit a coffin with the remains of the late departed Atanas Razin, Svilar by birth, or with the refuse of some nuclear-waste site, which will become harmless in three hundred years, is no longer anybody's business but your own. And if you have the luck to buy some dead cemetery, the bigger the better, you can put there whatever your heart desires.

"Where else would those trains full of contaminated milk that roam the tracks of Europe, or those tankers carrying nuclear waste that sail the seas never to find a port—where else would they go except to dead cemeteries, like the ones you buy the world over?

"But enough of these serious business matters. Not to bore you, let me tell you a story that is eagerly being passed from mouth to mouth hereabouts. This little story takes place sometime around the year 2200, when you will be entering the property you're buying now:

"A grandfather sat his grandson on his lap and told him a fairy tale. But boys will be boys, and the grandson wriggled and interrupted his grandfather.

"'Tell me, Grandfather,' he says, 'I've heard people talk, they mention a strange name, like Chernobyl or something. . . . What is that?'

"'Ah, my boy,' replied the grandfather, 'that's an old and long story.' And he stroked the boy's heads.

"Mark you, not head, but *heads.* . . . So it's those two-headed ones you want to rob now, in advance. Look at yourself in the mirror: your mustache curls like a sow's tail, and keeps twitching. . . . But, my dear, you've made a mistake in your calculations! You can't lure everyone by wiping your chin with a fat banknote after lunch!"

This was where I stopped recounting to myself the Story of Plakida, because it no longer helped. I noticed a completely new set of lips on

Cecilia, hard as breadcrust, with the same old smile inside. But that old smile, patched together from scraps of others' smiles, hit me right between the eyes. And I became afraid that Cecilia would ruin even what I had already arranged with her sisters.

My ears started squawking like a flock of chickens, they started calling out to one another in a panic. I muttered that my intentions had been misunderstood and got up to leave.

"It's not so simple," she remarked, and rang a glass bell. Once again surprised, I was observing how in fact she had no tits, just two enormous nipples tearing at her blouse, when at the door appeared a man with a bare pate and eyebrows tied in a knot. The wrinkles glistened on his perspiring face, as though it were caught in a golden cobweb.

"Father Tarquinius," said the lady of the house, "make some tea for our visitor. Tea from that birch broom we use to sweep in front of the gate. Make it as strong as possible. If I remember correctly," she said to me, "you like your tea strong, don't you?"

I tried to get up, but the stranger looked surprised, seemed to sneeze, and then said:

"A great love takes a long time to mature, but a small love is here in a flash."

And he lowered his enormous hand onto my shoulder. He was the kind of man whose strength grows even as his hair recedes.

"A strong wind drives away even the fish in the Danube," I thought, and, waiting for the broom tea, once again tied myself up in the Story of Plakida, which was all I had left:

"If you imitate gold, you will not turn into gold; if you imitate a ghost, you will turn into a ghost. . . ."

And everything that subsequently happened to me happened behind the calm inner monologue driving the Story of Plakida as the wind drives a cap. And that's what saved me.

As the broom tea was being brought in, served in an expensive Szolnay cup, I asked Cecilia, just to say something:

"Even if our troubles are not brothers, Cecilia, even if yours are like a rich year and mine like a lean, there's no reason for us to argue. Where do you think I went wrong in my calculations?"

"I'm glad you asked me that," Cecilia replied. "When my father wrote his book (I don't know if you ever read it, it's about butterflies), he drank wine while he wrote. When he had finished the first barrel of wine, he marked his manuscript with the note: *End of part one.* So you, when you finish your tea, mark it: *End of part one.* Then comes part two, and that depends on you."

"What do you mean?" I asked, but she did not reply right away; first she sent Azeredo and the little girl out of the room. Azeredo burst into tears and ran out. Only then did she continue:

"You know, Atanas, the only thing we heard about you abroad was told to somebody by your Vienna maids. 'When we were hired to work in his house,' they recounted, 'the first evening the master said: Anyone who doesn't want dinner gets twenty schillings. And he remarked, laughingly, that it was a joke. But he gave the money. We thought he wanted to send us out to eat so he could be alone, so we each took twenty schillings and left. But the next day, at lunch, he said, no longer laughingly: Anyone who wants lunch has to pay twenty schillings!'

"That's the little story. And now let me ask you something. Do you think I'm one of your Kraut maids?

"Well, that's where you're wrong. . . ."

My eyes were on Father Tarquinius, on his beard, made out of what looked like white threads; I felt the days rush toward the new year in a swelling herd; the future crumbled and fell to pieces, ceding its place to us intruders. And I realized that the conversation was not ending with drinking the broom tea. I said then:

"You underestimate me, Cecilia. Imagine that we're playing a game of chess. And that I'm now about to exchange my pawn for a queen. But think a moment. You're appraising the situation and playing the game as though I were going to turn my pawn into that queen. But what will you do if you're wrong in your predictions, if, to take you by surprise, I exchange my pawn not for the queen but for another piece?"

"In that case," she said triumphantly, "if everything I predicted and said is wrong, then the opposite is right—what I didn't say but can easily say now."

I froze, because now I knew that she knew what I was doing. I touched my mustache and found it to be as hard as the bark of an oak but curled like a sow's tail. All I could do was hold on to the Story of Plakida like a straw.

"If you're not buying our great-great-grandchildren for the reasons I enumerated, then you're buying them for other reasons, which are twice as bad and should never even be mentioned. Right?"

"Right," I said and hiccupped, and she coughed, and that same instant I remembered that devils communicate with one another through the human cough, hiccup, sneeze, and whistle.

"In that case," Cecilia concluded, "the price must be twice as high as well. And certain conditions must be met."

"I agree to all conditions," I said, and immediately inquired what they were. Cecilia pulled the list of her great-great-grandchildren out of her blouse, and I reached for the contract and for a pencil, which, of course, I didn't find. Cecilia, however, gave the contract not to me but to Father Tarquinius.

"You know," she said to me, "every census, including the census of great-great-grandchildren—in other words, taking inventory of the future—means violating the rules of heaven and entering its jurisdiction. So, before we draw up a veridical list and have it certified to give it legal standing, Father Tarquinius has to christen these unborn and unchristened souls according to the Christian rite."

"Does a child have a soul before it is born?" I asked in amazement, but Cecilia merely coughed and continued.

"If you do not christen them, and they begin to live and die—because to sell them means to release them into circulation, into life and death—they will collect unwanted names; they will then be called whistlers, squealers, bawlers, yaudis, navis, lorgis, whiners, or vermin, or who knows what. They'll turn into tiny winged children, unalive and unchristened, who fly, whistle, and piss from the air into the ears of passersby. They will roam forever, especially in the nights of un-christened days, or, elongated like wrung-out fish, with beards on top of their heads, they will shriek with the spring down the streams, in cemeteries, they will scream in underwater voices in the night air and attach themselves to the bellies of nursing mothers, playing their breasts as though they were bagpipes. Screeching, they will call on your house, too, they will sob under overturned bowls and bite your progeny and their brothers with wise dreams. . . ."

Cecilia coughed once more; Father Tarquinius sneezed three consecutive times into the scroll of names, the way priests blow at children at christenings to ward off the devils, and recorded the names in the book; and the three of us set off for the nearby church, which was ringing the hour.

There where the echoes of the footfalls cross and the stairway forks, I yawned and turned left, and the others turned right.

"Brrrr!" a child's voice softly called me the way horses call one another in the night. The curve in the staircase separated Cecilia and Father Tarquinius from me for a moment, and I saw Don Azeredo sitting on the staircase window seat, right by the window that looked out onto the gorgeous summer landscape with its chestnut tree. I came over to him obediently, and froze with fear. Behind his tousled little head of hair, smelling of lime and the sweat of a child, I saw through this other window the same landscape as some minutes before, only now it was covered with snow. The chestnut tree was bare, stripped of its leaves, and down by the stream the clay had ice on it, and the dark soil snow. Stretching off into the distance behind them was a snowbound road, consisting of two parallel paths that were as straight as if they had been fired out of a double-barreled gun. . . .

"Azeredo, Azeredo," called the little girl from the room, "are you showing him the years?"

Then she appeared at the top of the staircase and said to me comfortingly:

"Don't be surprised. One always sees the coming year through that window."

Don Azeredo jumped up from the window seat and said to me:

"I'd like to tell you something. Something about my origin. My distant ancestor was an archangel. His name was Nathanael. A fresco of the archangel Nathanael's meeting with Christ was done in 1350 at the Dechani Serbian monastery. This Nathanael is also depicted in the icons. You were on Mount Athos. I don't know whether you saw there the icon depicting this ancestor of mine. It's an icon showing the fall of Nathanael and the conversion of his name into the name of Satanael. Once God's archangel, my ancestor suddenly became a renegade from heaven and, as the prince of darkness, was called Satan. Painted on this icon in Mount Athos is the image of God, beneath it a group of loyal angels in white, and tumbling into the depths on either side of this group are the insubordinate angels, the fellow-travelers of my ancestor and fellow-travelers of darkness. In that eternal darkness, they are already black, and their wings can fly only downward. Leading them in their fall are the former officers of the celestial court, Semyaz and Azazel. In the middle of the assembly of white angels stands a boy-angel holding an icon. This icon within an icon already depicts the future image of Christ, and beneath it lies the huge fallen archangel Satanael, my ancestor. He's completely black, and in the position he will assume at the Last Judgment, when Christ will come to earth a second time, to break down the gates of hell and crush him, Satan. This Satan, my ancestor, is really the onetime light.

"Because," Don Azeredo continued, "in the icon the line between light and darkness is not straight but crooked. The universe is not symmetrical. The relationship between good and evil is not symmetrical. The sum total of light in the universe is constant, and when one of the archangels and his followers fell from God and tumbled into the darkness, when he became the prince of the night, or Satan, then that sum total of light—or love, if you will—was breached. It was reduced by approximately one-third. That is how many of us there were, us insubordinate angels who fell from heaven. God then created a small universe—you—that is to say, man—to make up for that one-third of the sum total of love, for that part of light that was missing. Man, therefore, is merely a replacement for Satan, the fallen angel, but Satan as he was before the fall. You, therefore, are part of the belated light, a replacement for the former light or former love that is no longer light, or love. Consequently, the human race is close to Satan, because it is a replacement for him. Turn a man upside down and you've got Satan!

"But beware—man has not made up for the entire one-third of

light or love in the universe, the amount that was reduced or torn off with the fall of my ancestor, the insubordinate morning archangel. He has made up for less than that. And now we come to the key point.

"What is man? Half angel, half beast. Saint John thus says of you and those like you: 'Ye are of your father, the devil.' And it is precisely through this dark, bloodthirsty half of human nature that my ancestor Satan and I still come into touch with that luminous angelic nature of man. And that means also with *our own* former light—not our original one, of course, but that part of light which is the replacement for our onetime morning light, long lost even then. Forever lost. In short, it is only through man that Satan and all of us still come into touch with our sinless youth, with ourselves as we were before the fall into sin, and thus we also come into touch with God. Since his fall, Satan hasn't known who he is anymore. It is only through man that he can see it. And he will never relinquish to another this realm of his sole contact, he will not at any price allow the extermination of the human race.

"I know, you don't know for whom you're doing what you're doing, but those for whom you're doing it know only too well. Such is man's fate. This is not only a matter of man's, but of Satan's fate as well. If you, Razin, were working on the destruction and suffering of hundreds of millions of people, Satan and I would gladly support you. We have long been preparing winds for sails such as yours. But you, with your business deals, are working to destroy the entire human race. And there Satan will stop you. So henceforward know that, no matter whom you work for, you are working against Satan by doing what you're doing. And beware of him.

"If you have doubts, take a good look at me! I am your death. Or, if you like, I am the biggest mistake in your life. But watch out, because for every death and every big mistake in the life of a man, the years are counted backward toward birth. And know that your death is now in its boyhood. I, however, do not gain years, I lose them; mine don't grow, they diminish! Bear that in mind and be careful, because I have not come to teach you how to live but how to die. And that is what I am doing now.

"Now, look at me once more! I am seven years old. The difference between you and me is that I can influence things outside your world, this world in which you and all those around you are enclosed. And this you will feel through the fate of the person you love most. Your wife, Vitacha. You know that she has a weakness for little boys, little boys like me, for instance. Think it over, because it is not hard for us to rekindle in her that youthful passion. We'll provide this predilection of hers with the broadest possibilities. We'll fulfill her wishes to the utmost. We'll carry her into a world where she will always be able to love those much younger than herself, and where it will be natural, even unavoidable. She'll fall in love with little boys hundreds of years younger than herself, boys who come omnipotent and can kill her with just a blink of the eye. And she will love them fatally and forget you because of them. And you, you will be jealous of the wrong one. Thus you will get older and older, and your death and your wife's lovers will keep getting younger and younger. Now, you decide and choose: it's either smash the stone or kill the dog. If you oppose us, you'll knock at your own door and won't get in, I'll make out of you three of the same, you'll kill the one you love most, and we'll interrupt you at your sweetest moment, when you're at your peak. . . . Be careful of what you do, I'll spit in your every footstep! Don't sign that contract with Cecilia! And burn the others!"

Then Don Azeredo's gaze inscribed with fire my name in the air, my original name:

Atanas Svilar, Architect

And he asked me:

"Do you know this name?"

I began weeping and kissed the boy's hand, but I did not want to interrupt inside me the Story of Plakida.

The boy raised his hands to his lips, licked the kiss, and spat.

I ran into the church.

3 DOWN

"An anonymous writer records in 1443 that by translating the Persian calendar into the Byzantine one gains a day in between—an extra day, in fact—and from it one can embark on new possibilities in time, on a future that is not ours. . . ."

These are the opening words of architect Razin's third notebook, which, in contrast to the others, has not one but two landscapes painted with tea.

The covers depict a white building enclosed in verdure, perched on a hill overlooking a sprawling city. In the painting it is already daybreak, but part of the night is still there, hidden in the eye of the painter, the yeast of future eclipses. Extensive hunting grounds stretch out through the early-morning air at the foot of the hill on which the building stands, secluding it from the crush of the city and its streets. The sky above is painted with a poisonous tea called "crow claws" or "spurs" (Calcatripae flos), which is dried in a draft in the shade and produces a strange dark-blue color. The eastern border of the sky is done in crushed evergreen coated with red wine and applied with the finger. To paint the verdure of the hunting grounds and woods, architect Razin used pekoe tea picked in March, laced with turmeric, hunting tea, green maté, mango, maracuja, and three-day-old mint tea. The building itself was painted with camomile and a dash of weak China tea called "dragon font," and the lighter washes were done in marshmallow.

Written in large print underneath the painting are the words:

THE WHITE PALACE
*The Belgrade residence of Yugoslav President
Josip Broz Tito.*

On the inside cover, architect Razin had pasted a picture of a 1762 Russian samovar belonging to the Hermitage of Leningrad, and thereupon followed several excerpts in French and Russian about tea and about sitting by the samovar, taken from the works of Tolstoy, Dostoyevsky, Gogol, and other Russian writers. Mrs. Razin (Vitacha) had written in her own hand that the samovar first starts to sing in an alto, then, in descant, climbs to a tenor, switches to a basso cantante, and works up to a mezzo-soprano. Then comes an excerpt from a book about tea:

"The kettle sings prettily, because the small pieces of iron at the bottom are arranged so as to produce a special melody wherein one can distinguish the echoes of the waterfall shrouded in clouds, the distant sea breaking against the cliffs, the rainstorm in the bamboo forest, or the pine trees rustling on some distant hills. . . ."

The third page of the notebook has an extremely detailed architectural photograph of the White Palace and the surrounding green landscape, with the above-sea-level altitudes of the Koshutnyak game preserve, the Topchider area with its river, rail center, and little station at the foot of the hill, and an aerial shot of the entire Yugoslav capital, taken from an angle that highlights Dedinye, the smart residential quarter of Belgrade, with the said palace and the private Dedinye residence of the president of the republic, J. B. Tito, in Uzhichka Street, number 15. All this is explained in architect Razin's own hand in the legend underneath the text.

Next, pasted into the notebook is an envelope. In it Mrs. Svilar, architect Razin's mother, had sent to an unknown person (whose name is on the envelope but means nothing to us) a dream dreamed and described by architect Razin. In the accompanying letter Mrs. Svilar says:

"He had a dream about me recently and wrote to me about it. The dream had surprised and hurt him. Like any truth. I thought, 'Well, it's not so bad for a woman my age,' wrote to him that this was Vitacha filling his dreams with wicked stories about me, and went off to lunch with Vitacha."

The dream went like this:

ARCHITECT RAZIN'S DREAM

I'm dreaming of waterfronts, birds chasing above the water in the dusk, disappearing from sight whenever they fold their wings. Like our loves and prayers. I sit there on the waterfront and pray. God, I pray, my mother doesn't see me any more than she sees her own back. She says: "That hotshot officer who douses church candles with his song and picks blackberries with his teeth isn't your father at all. Even so, you're a far cry from him," she says. "You draw half from your pipe, but the other half it draws from you."

You spend your whole life gripping your shoes with your toes to keep them from falling off. And friends and waiters in various taverns accept her words and shout: "That one'll fall from one ass onto another in life, and if he is silent, we know why that is—either he's full and corked or else he's empty, and there's nothing to come out of him anyway!" . . . Lord, just once spare me their contempt, just once have them not say: "Look at him, he's walking in empty socks!" Have them miss me with their venomous gaze that can kill a bird when it strikes between the eyes!

And God heeds my prayer and gives me the power to walk the waves. In my dream I'm overjoyed, if one can be overjoyed in a dream. But I feel it is not given unto man to read his own desires; for that he is illiterate. Still, I get the boat ready and pack the boat with food; for each guest I prepare an ear of music and a full mouth of drinks, and then invite everybody I know. The dusty and moldy moonlight is two days old, but everybody comes. Including my mother. I'm the only one not there. I'm hidden, sitting on a wooden chair on the waterfront, waiting. Waiting for them to put out to sea. They, too, are waiting, waiting, they're all on board already, only my mother isn't, she seems to be hesitating, I'm sitting concealed, she's standing nearby in the moonlight, there's something long and shiny in her hand, it glitters like gold, is it a braid of hair, a whip, you can't tell. Suddenly there are three blasts of the ship horn and two echoes from the shore. It's all as usual. Then I seize my chance, jump up, and shout:

"Wait," I say, "I'm coming!"

But they're already sailing, sailing away. And I'm on the waves, running on the water! My shoes fall off, and I'm barefoot on the waves, holding my shirt wide open, catching the wind, running, waving, and shouting after them. They are all huddled on one side of the ship, they're going to overturn it, they're amazed, they marvel and cross themselves. But my mother simply shouts out to them:

"Look at him, he can't even swim!"

And she takes that hank of hair that was in her hand, goes over to the chair where I had been hiding before I ran out onto the water, swings with all her might at the spot where my head must have been before I ran on the waves, and lets go with a whack. My blood gushes out, my head drops off next to the chair, and through sand-caked eyes that no longer blink I see my headless body sink into the water out at sea.

Needless to say, this notebook contained in architect Razin's own hand the Story of Plakida, which he was thought to know by heart and to recount to himself at moments when, in his difficult dealings, he came up against a hairy nose and when, as he puts it, he was ready to chew the mane of his steed in desperation. The story begins with the words "That same Plakida who caught a stag with a cross on its head instead of antlers. . . ." and since it is given integrally in his Testimonial there is no need to dwell upon it here.

Right after this story comes a photograph clipped out of an old newspaper, explained by architect Razin in the caption as follows: "The palace and grounds once belonged to the Karadjordjevich dynasty of Serbian kings, and old newspapers have photographs like this, showing the prewar White Palace and King Alexander Karadjordjevich the Unifier, then the ruler of the kingdom of Yugoslavia, standing on the steps, receiving the yule log from his troops on Christmas Day."

Finally, there are several detailed sketches of the rooms in the White Palace and in J. B. Tito's Dedinye residence in Uzhichka Street, with annotations about the furniture, interior decoration, and layout of the rooms, the paths and the approaches.

The back cover, like the front, has a drawing. Here again architect Razin dipped his pencil in tea. In hemlock tea. Painted here, like a confession, is the confluence of the Sava and Danube rivers, at the foot of Belgrade. And at the confluence is an island, but at one place it is as if the painter's eye had hit against a barrier, as if an invisible, upright wall had partitioned off the landscape. As if some strange sieve had been erected from the earth to the sky. Passing through it, the water abruptly turns into land, and the land into water, the sky hangs suspended like the earth, and the earth shifts like the cloud-studded sky. Behind this invisible barrier, Belgrade is not Belgrade anymore, and the Danube is not a river. A bird, flying overhead in its yearning for freedom, banged against this barrier, the way birds trapped in a room bang against and break the window or the glass of a painting depicting a landscape painted with tea. The bird in Razin's painting had banged against this invisible barrier, broken and flown through it. But it is not known whether the bird found freedom, because it emerged on the other side stained with blood, and its blood trickled down the other, eternal side of the barrier, as if down a pane of glass, while it flapped its torn wings, trying to catch the wind from that other side.

2 DOWN

Milan
April 23rd of this year

To the Most Illustrious
Don Donino Azeredo

Dear Don Azeredo,

I know, God is inconceivable and since our beginnings has become more and more inconceivable to us. The sun appears before me as a ball of blazing darkness. But, as you say, prior to the advent of humans, this was not a trait of God's, He was not inconceivable. Because this trait of His inconceivability sprang inside us humans, not inside God, who for us changes by moving further and further away from our understanding. Or, to put it the other way around: nature moves further and further away from our understanding. It is in this sense that God says to us: "Thinketh not that I am what I was! ..." But man's words and voice are merely the cooled part of our pain, and they do not convey the real thing.

It is therefore hard for me to explain how I perceived the matter of

Signora Vitacha Milut, the wife of architect Atanas Razin. Neverthe-less, I shall try to describe her case, so that you over there may know how the changes she underwent after her children's death are viewed over here. Naturally, I shall do so within the bounds of my abilities. Because it is you, Don Azeredo, that God has taught to comprehend human affairs, and these human affairs proceed in the opposite direc-tion from divine affairs, drawing nearer to your own reasoning, while God has been moving away from them ever since that day long ago when man collapsed in the dust under the cross and started to lick the blood that ran down the crucified one's leg.

The story is that, upon receiving word of the death of her daugh-ters, Mrs. Razin did not utter a sound. That instant she fanned wide her eyebrows like a peacock's tail, but made not a sound. Hearing the ghastly news, she did not weep, or cry out, or collapse. She was dining at the time, and she continued feverishly to chew the food in her mouth, but she did not swallow it, and not until morning did she remember to spit it out. . . .

You know, Don Azeredo, that Signor Razin is afraid of nothing, except of dying at somebody else's funeral. That is the ultimate dis-grace, and a decent man will never allow himself something like that. Therefore, he does not like funerals and avoids them whenever he can. But this time the Razins were ready to go immediately. Signora Vitacha hurriedly packed the suitcases, but for two days now she had not uttered a word. She just kept cracking her knuckles. The news had not been sent in time, and they could not be there for the funeral, but they left all the same. At the airport in New York Signora Vitacha took a drop of Scotch, and in Belgrade she spit it out. She was still silent when they attended the forty-day commemoration at the chil-dren's cemetery. There (I attended secretly) my left cheek grew a mouth in amazement when I saw that the funeral service was being chanted by a priest and rechanted by a boy of about six or seven. The child was well versed and had a good ear, but I didn't like it, and I don't know whether children should chant at children's graves. Si-gnora Vitacha merely stuck out her tongue at all this, using it to make the sign of the cross over the two little mounds where underneath her daughters' names was the inscription:

THEY LIVED 5 YEARS OF THEIR FATHERS'
2 YEARS OF THEIR OWN AND
3 MONTHS OF THEIR MOTHERS'

Signora Vitacha read the inscription, turned around, and left, not looking back, not shedding a tear, not uttering a word all the way to Vienna, where we stayed with her sister. There her silence became so heavy she could have broken a plate with it. A mother is always a *mother*. Instead of words, she exuded a body odor like that of frightened game. Signora Vida, who knows her fair sister well, said that at the time Signora Vitacha was assailed by pains which she herself experienced as the points of the compass, and she could imagine the north, the east, and the west of her sufferings, but nowhere was there the south. . . .

Signor Razin contemplated the part in his fair wife's hair, which began from the back of the head and grasped her skull like a sickle; he blinked in wonder and didn't know what to do. This muteness of hers, or the exaggerated hoarseness that comes from constant silent weeping, or her vow of silence, soon began to attract attention.

She herself gave no sign that anything unusual had happened; she ostensibly had a sore throat. But those around her thought differently. Especially the servants. At first they thought that somebody had deliberately drunk from her glass and drained Signora Vitacha's thirst along with her voice, that echoes had begun to creep into her speech until they finally gnawed away at it and carried it off like mice, or that, when told about the children, she had incautiously called out to someone through the closed door of the room, that through the wood she had cried out the name of her husband, or some other name, and had remained mute ever since.

But these stories stopped when a servant reported that, a month after Signora Vitacha had become speechless, he had heard her soured alto, which stutters and is easily recognizable, in Vienna's Burgtheater. Then, one evening, when the erratic visibility that precedes rain opens man's quicker eye to the surrounding mountains, and keeps the other eye from seeing farther than the threshold, architect Razin was secretly informed that his wife's voice had been recognized at the railway station in Lyon. And then one of architect Razin's employees clearly identified Signora Vitacha's voice at the station in New Orleans and cabled the news from America to his boss in Vienna, from whom Mrs. Razin had not been separated all this time.

Unlike the others, I knew that this was that moment of weakness in Madame Vitacha that we have been waiting for so long, and that you, Don Azeredo, foretold in the life of Signor Razin and his wife. So I paid double attention, and ever since I have been like a hunting dog when it crosses and pins together its ears. The signora felt as though she were treading on children's graves, and indeed she was at the point of changing the side on which she dropped her lovely, transparent hands. I took care to have her drop them on our side. And suddenly everything changed. This is what happened.

There is a season of the year when Signor Razin is always sad. It is that moment when no fragrance reaches far, early spring, when we avoid the spoon, and when like a clapper the birds crisply beat their wings through the clouds of rain. It is the time when once, long ago, Signora Vitacha got married and left him. Now she was with him, but all the same, every rainy spring, he was sad again, thus paying homage to his grief for the Signora Vitacha of his youth. It was rather like sloughing the snake skin off his sorrows, or like bathing memories. Because we do not bathe just the body; we also bathe memories to cleanse them every so often. But since memories are earth, as are we ourselves, what happens when they are bathed is what happens when the earth gets wet—they turn into mud.

This spring was as usual. It rained in Milan, where they had arrived after Vienna; it was a boring time of year, when women leave one dream and go into another and kill somebody there; architect Razin was silent, chain-smoking his prefilled pipes, when suddenly Signora Vitacha shocked us all, and later, as is known, the entire world as well.

At first, however, nobody noticed anything. She dreamed that she was yawning into the hair of a child sitting on her lap. To begin with, the yawn was like a fish smiling: the mouth gaped open mutely and that was all. But then Signora Vitacha's maid noticed that her mistress would talk occasionally in her sleep or in the delirium of illness, although it was not a voice, or a speech, in the true sense of the word. Others say that at the time Mrs. Razin could use only the echo of her voice but had no voice of her own at all. Anyway, what came out of her mouth at first sounded like the yowling of a cat in heat; then, when it softened slightly, the voice was the call of a child, a female child. When he heard it, Signor Razin flinched the way one does from one of those slaps that make your eyes pop out of your mouth. But the voice aged like wine, faster than Mrs. Razin. At first it was as heavy as water, shallow, not even knee-deep; then it caught up with her years and became increasingly mellow, it soared high up to the sky; the older it got, the better it got. It caught up easily with Signora Vitacha's onetime stuttering alto, so familiar to us all, but it did not stop on its ascent there. The voice was now like a candle burning down, just as the human soul is a candle burning down. From one day to the next it acquired a growing bouquet, like a drink left to stand. It cleared slowly, until one morning that voice inside her spoke. You know, Don Azeredo, that in the beginning man's tongue was forked like a snake's, and only then was it tied into a knot and the one made out of the two. Signora Vitacha's became unknotted again.

You are an old-time hunter, Don Azeredo; you know the image I want to evoke. We follow a fox as it steals up to the sheep's watering hole; on its way, it collects the wool left on the thornbushes along the river by the sheep as they cut through the bramble to reach the water. The fox carries this wool in its jaws. When it collects enough, the fox slowly, ever so slowly, dips first one paw into the river and then another, all the while holding the skein of wool in its teeth. Then, step by step, it enters deeper and deeper into the water, until it sinks, and starts to swim so that all its fleas move to the wool, that alone being above water. When all the fleas are assembled and start to tickle its nose, the fox hurls the flea-laden wool as far as it can and, now rid of its trouble, returns to shore. This fox, so familiar to you from your hunting, is not just a fox. It is also man's soul, which you, Don Azeredo, know better than any quarry, because a man's soul is the quarry of all quarries. So, too, did Signora Vitacha's soul fling away everything that had perturbed it, that had gnawed at and troubled it in life, and suddenly she started to speak in the most beautiful Tuscan, like a born Florentine, without understanding a word she was exchanging with her Italian servants or me. In short, she had forgotten her own language but had not learned another. And so she remained immured in song. And now her voice was high and clear, silvery in its heights and golden in its depths; neither she nor her husband nor her friends recognized it. It was the voice of the bearded seraph with three pairs of crossed mustaches and three pairs of wings. And Signora Vitacha began to sing—in a language she had never known well, in our language, Don Azeredo—and it was then that I knew we had won the battle. It was a sublime voice, Italy's finest soprano since Angelica Catalani. Thus God, when He wants to punish someone, delivers to that person both the greatest misfortune and the greatest fortune at one and the same time.

Madame Vitacha's voice, it immediately transpired, was also perfectly trained. Because her present love for music was already the granddaughter of her childhood love for singing. Her soprano had simply taken over the old training of Miss Milut's former fractured alto, emerging from it like a butterfly from a cocoon. You know, Don Azeredo, that ever since then she has been appearing on the world's leading stages, from the Lyric Opera of Chicago to Milan's La Scala, under another, happier name, which we shall not mention here because it is mentioned and known by the entire world. Signora Vitacha now looks and sees only with her voice. She is a wonder of beauty and talent on the stage. All Egyptian ships are sculpted according to the curved line of her closed eyelids, but nobody knows what she actually sings. That is how one sings about something that is more important than life, than memories, than death; that is how one sings to somebody whose gaze can renew one's life. It is of no importance whether she is repeating the songs that whore Polychronia sings in Yolanta Ibich's silver egg, or whether she is singing the contents of her unmailed letters, which fill the apartment of her late daughters. Music bubbles inside her, and the longest journey in the world, the journey from mouth to ear, she covers effortlessly, forgetting everything.

You should hear, Don Azeredo, the applause that follows her. That clapping sounds like rain pounding the pavement in front of Milan's La Scala, and occasionally cutting across that rain is a heavy carriage, drawn by trotting horses, which disappears around the corner, leaving behind the drumming of the rain on the pavement, until the next carriage comes along. . . .

After all these ovations and performances, the signora lies down, completely drained, behind the curtain, her lips ravaged and she untalented, no longer understanding what she sang only a moment before. The green of her eyes sinks deeper and deeper, until finally all that is left awake is that deeply banked green color that sees best at night: Signora Vitacha sleeps with her eyes wide open, forgetting to lower her eyelids. That lasts a few seconds, and then she is fresh, beautiful, and gifted once more.

In the chorus of rave reviews, only one critic once wrote that at her finest moments—not so much in her voice, which was flawless, as in the echo of that voice—one could detect a deep underwater alto, cracked and marked by a slightly foreign accent, which sometimes lost the rhythm below Signora Razin's sublime soprano, as though her echo stuttered and could not catch up with her own voice. It must be said that the signora herself may have been aware of this and tried to remove the uneven spot. Indeed, with time, the echo vanished and her voice was left without an echo, like a bird without a shadow. . . .

Sooner or later there comes a time in a woman's life when she looks as though she had never been fifteen. This is the apogee, the moment of mature beauty. Mrs. Razin has reached that moment now. She has never looked better; she and her voice have reached their zenith at one and the same time.

Mr. Razin—like everybody else, for that matter—senses and sees it.

There are various kinds of love, Don Azeredo; there are those that have several layers, there are those that can be rolled out like dough, but then they grow thin. Loves thin out like this whether they are kneaded with sugar, leaven, or stuffing, or are made of plain gruel. Because sometimes our loves are nothing more than plain gruel. Nourishing and tasty in their way, but gruel all the same. Nothing more than that. And you yourself know what Signor Razin's love for Vitacha Milut was like. As strong and swift as a beast. And it never had time for jealousy. I watched him the other night, and I know why this is. He opened a glass cupboard full of pipes made of meerschaum, of red earth, with long slender stems like a cane, ideal for slipping into the boot, beautiful Mogul specimens that do not go out and do not overheat, that cannot be bought but must be ordered, pipes made of rosewood, wrought the way violins used to be made—according to the size of the hand that will hold them. . . . Then he closed the cupboard and relit the ancient pipe, made almost entirely of iron, he always smokes. Mr. Atanas Razin the architect obviously knows nothing about change. Nor can he change himself. Some things that have already happened to him he thinks have yet to happen, whereas with Signora Vitacha some things that have not yet happened she believes happened to her long ago. Maybe Signora Vitacha would still love Razin, were he not the same as before. But he has not changed for a long time now, and this is what she cannot bear. And so now, for the first time, this love is being severely challenged. The smile that passed through Vitacha's body now cools on Razin's face faster than before, but he does not feel it. It is hard to measure the weight of somebody's smile on your cheek. Especially on the cheek of architect Razin, who has a talent for everything, except jealousy. That is why, for the moment, he is successfully resisting the said challenge.

They say, Don Azeredo, that a horse thinks only when it's standing on one leg; the rest of the time it digests. Many believe that Signor Razin is digesting right now. I don't. Take, for example, his recent arrival here in Milan. When he entered Signora Vitacha's dressing room after the performance, she turned around in surprise and said:

"Who are you? Whistle me your name."

Architect Razin answered this question with another, which is, in fact, the reason for this letter. He mentioned your name, Don Azeredo! He said:

"Have you been seeing Don Azeredo?"

"Who's he?" replied the signora, and this put architect Razin's mind completely at rest. At first he had obviously wondered whether there was not another seven-year-old brat in the offing, one with eyes like glass buttons, and that is why he inquired about you. But, judging from his behavior after Vitacha's reply, one can conclude that he thinks it is we who are working against him with Signora Vitacha, and in her he has faith and is still not jealous. That is why we need your help, Don Azeredo. Make him jealous, something neither we nor Signora Vitacha can do, and then everything will be as you wish.

Vienna
May 2nd of this year

To his Most Eminent Seigneur,
Mr. Donino Azeredo,
with trepidation and love

Most Esteemed Don Azeredo,

Signora Vitacha recently extended her contract with La Scala, under her other name, which is exactly as much more beautiful than her real name as her present soprano is more magnificent than her former alto. She is now more successful and more beautiful than ever, the Big Dipper and the Little sparkle in her eyes, and only when she thinks of her husband does she become ugly. It was at one such moment that she noticed, in a heap of letters, congratulations, and newspaper clippings, a black-bordered envelope. In it was the news of her sister Vida's death. The telegram was signed by Amadeus Knopf.

The Razins rushed to Vienna each from his or her own corner of the world. In Herzog Hetzendorf Street, Vitacha found her Los Angeles apartment on the first floor, and her Belgrade apartment, where her daughters had lived and died, on the ground floor, but the house was in Vienna. She was totally confused.

Assembled were the widower Knopf with his singed beard and yellow teeth, neatly clipped like a mustache; Mrs. Tsikindjal, with her huge wrinkled lips; and the Razins. Madame Vitacha was no more aware of her husband than of the nose on her face, but he still noticed nothing and was not jealous. The house looked run-down and small to them, Mrs. Tsikindjal looked faded like the dress she was wearing, but Knopf shocked them completely. As they immediately heard and saw for themselves, he had been dressing like a beggar for the past few years. The reason was simple. Vida had been so jealous, a feeling that had grown and spread inside of her, devouring her love, that he, in the hope of assuaging this disease, this chimera, or this hussy in his wife, had begun to dress more and more carelessly, in an effort to dispel the very thought of any infidelity on his part. It had reached the point where Knopf wore only one sandal in the summer; unkempt, unwashed, and shabby, he could no longer move in the same circles as Vida anymore. Once they caught him in the Russian church eating bread dipped in the lamp oil. When they met him at the cemetery, he had a pair of eyebrows sprouting from his nose. He was thin, and for nights on end he sat, full of unwashed, fetid pockets, talking to Razin and Signora Vitacha, his double finger catching at glasses and other people's sleeves.

One evening, after Madame Vida's funeral, we were sitting there, drinking wine in the garden. A butterfly appeared and dropped on Signora Vitacha's brow, as though it wanted to kiss her. Then it flew away, although she had done nothing to make it go. Next it alit on Knopf's shoulder, and finally on architect Razin's finger. It fluttered its wings, holding its balance, and simply would not go away, as though it were waiting for something. We stared at one another, and then, quite unexpectedly, Razin dipped his finger into his wine, taking care not to make any abrupt movement that would scare the little creature away. All the while he kept whispering something reassuring to it. And then, to our amazement, the butterfly began drinking the wine off Razin's finger. This continued until the butterfly had drunk all the wine. These few seconds, when all eyes were on the butterfly, sufficed for us to understand what was happening. We were all as silent as a stone; when a conversation is broken off like that, you say: "That's a soul flying by!" And we all knew whose soul had flown off in reeling inebriation; the only one who didn't was Razin. But he soon remembered. He remembered only too well, and paid dearly for that drunken soul.

Signor Razin was obviously bored in Vienna; Mrs. Tsikindjal collected her brushes and flew off to Paris with those eyes of hers that fast before Easter; whether Signor Knopf was bored we do not know. Signor Razin had work waiting for him, so did Mrs. Razin, Mr. Knopf had none. Signor Razin decided to go back to Los Angeles, Mrs. Razin decided to wait for the forty-day commemoration before returning to Milan, but Signor Razin could not wait, so he sat in his plane and flew back to the States. And that was his biggest mistake.

In Vienna, where I remained, as usual, by Signora Vitacha's side, absolutely nothing happened. But in America, architect Atanas Razin woke up one morning as a woman. The hair in his armpit smelled to him like the hair between a woman's legs. These smells were quite distinct and very familiar to him from somewhere. He was not surprised, however; he slipped on silk stockings and barely managed to stuff his tits into his shirt. As he held them in his hands, their weight and shape again reminded him of somebody he knew well. He stood in front of the bathroom mirror and stared at his face in surprise. It, too, reminded him of somebody, of a woman's face, but he could not remember whose. He prepared himself breakfast, took the cup and plate from the table, placed them by his side on the couch, and ate that way. And then, instead of washing them, he licked clean all the dirty spoons on the table. He put his suit on over the silk lingerie and went to his office. He wasn't in the least upset. He felt there had to be an acceptable explanation. Just as in a dream one can tell exactly which part of the dream comes from the eaten slice of sour-cherry pie, which from the piece of roast chicken soaked in yogurt, and which from the spoonful of mushroom soup taken at lunch, so one can tell with other things, too. People live in their own thoughts, like larvae. Only a few develop into butterflies and leave the cocoon. Something similar was happening to him now. It was noon, not yet time for his regular meeting; Razin locked himself in the room, lost in thought. Then, as though he had remembered something, he slipped his hand between his legs and felt the silver cunt of Vida Knopf. He smiled with relief and stood in front of the mirror. Staring back at him from the glass was the face of his late sister-in-law. Suddenly it all became clear.

Architect Atanas Razin was turning into his wife's sister Vida Milut, Knopf by marriage, the same Vida who had been lying at the Vienna cemetery for the past forty days. . . .

At the end of the following week, Vida Knopf began appearing to architect Razin, and at moments, tanned from the sun, he looked so much like her that he was afraid of the mirror and had the feeling that he himself was disappearing. This similarity increased day by day, but it did not stop at that.

One night, violent jealousy jarred architect Razin awake, like a hammer or an earthquake.

Vida Milut had bequeathed him not only her face and tits, which were as abundant as her buttocks; she had also willed him her undigested and unconquered jealousy, which had driven her to her grave. Jealousy of Mr. Amadeus Knopf. And that very same night, half-asleep, Razin clearly evoked in his memory Knopf's dry, wrinkled palms, as long as the sole of a foot, and those two monsters merged into one on Knopf's hand like an enormous phallus, bigger than any Knopf might have had himself. And it was only then that it dawned on Atanas.

That his wife, Signora Vitacha, and Knopf were alone in Vida's spacious Vienna house, that they were consoling one another, and that the darkness had begun. Everything around him now looked moldy; he saw mildew on the food, on clothes, on his hands. He immediately took a plane to Europe, and in Vienna found nothing either to persuade or to dissuade him, but he saw mildew everywhere, on Knopf's hands, even on Vitacha Razin's face. He tried to take his wife away and separate her from Knopf, but she sat on her sister's Viennese balconies, listening to the birds in the Schönbrunn Park as they knitted day out of three threads and night out of four. She would not budge. . . .

Over the succeeding weeks, tremendous fatigue showed on Razin's face, and all resemblance to Vida Knopf slowly began to fade. The smooth areas of the face, betraying wickedness and malice, increasingly became his own, and Vida could now be detected only in the wrinkles, where the good parts of the soul show.

And then Vida Knopf vanished from his face forever, leaving him even his own wrinkles. Feeling like his old self, he cast off the women's underwear he had been wearing and put on men's underwear. At times he felt as though nothing had ever happened, as though he had not changed at all. Even so, although Vida had vanished from his face and from his body forever, her jealousy regarding Knopf stayed with him. Unshaken, terrible, and unremitting, a weasel that kills with its stench, a tea that destroys the flower it waters. The most powerful driving force in his life, stronger than money, than his years as an architect, deeper than the oil wells he owned, more deadly than the chemicals his firm made. He resorted to drink in self-defense, but it didn't work. The more he drank, the clearer his head became, and the blacker his soul. And it was then that architect Razin began to hate his wife. It was the first hatred he had ever felt in his life. Hatred at first sight, ending his great love at first sight. For the first time in his life, he did not know what to do.

And it is totally unimportant that he had no reason to be jealous of Mr. Knopf, who, incidentally, had tits bigger than Madame Vitacha's and was no longer fit for anything. But this does not mean that Razin had no reason to be jealous with regard to Madame Vitacha. As incredible as it may sound, Vitacha did have someone else. Someone much younger than herself, and than her husband.

That someone whom you, Don Azeredo, had prophesied to architect Razin on those intersecting steps.

■ DOWN

That same Plakida who caught a stag with a cross on its head instead of antlers was once hunting by the sea. He was following a trail that, to his mind and in his experience, was unusual. The front legs of the beast he was tracking left prints like a bird's, the rear legs the prints of paws. A fish tail swept the trail.

The sand smelled of shells and algae, the memories reeked as usual, and he did not know whether he would like to catch the beast in front of him or not. He was afraid of both it and himself. And then he made the sign of the cross over the trail and said one of those prayers that make the animal reveal itself to the hunter. A prayer that resembles a net. But the quarry did not show itself, and so Plakida knew that before him he had a spectral animal, on whom the uttered prayer had no effect. He left it and returned home, because it was late. In the morning, when he went in pursuit of it again, Plakida ran into a tradesman and told him the story. The man scratched his beard and said:

"If you imitate gold, you will not become gold, but if you imitate a ghost, you will become a ghost."

Plakida had on his brow a wrinkle tied into the letter gamma, very fine warm eyes, and always a touch of snow on his eyelashes. He smiled, revealing three dimples on his cornbread-colored face, and went after his quarry. He devised a plan. He figured that the beast, judging by its front paws, had the traits and habits of a bird. Plakida was a veteran hunter and familiar with the ways of birds. He started to whistle and to imagine how he himself would feel in a fowl's place, how he would behave in certain situations, when he would attack with his beak, and when he would take wing and make his escape. But this, of course, was far from enough. The stars fumed, the tracks periodically disappeared, and only the paw prints were left in the sand, as though a two-legged creature, a bear or something, had dragged the bird away in its jaws. Plakida began to mutter, and it was as though he were carrying a part of himself in his teeth, the part that was the bird. He began to behave like a big, heavy carnivore that leaves deep paw prints. And then they, too, disappeared, and Plakida climbed a tree and found the trail of the beast, which had clambered up the trunk and left scars on the branches high above. These scars had been made by something metallic, as if the claws had had the hardest blades for nails. And then the animal had again descended on all fours and covered the bird and paw tracks by dragging behind its fish tail. The trail disappeared into the river. Plakida was as quiet as a fish; he tried to still his eyes and feel the scales on his hands. He was more afraid now than ever. He felt that the beast could infect him with its disease by just looking at him. And there could be no doubt that the beast he was after was sick. Plakida had enough hunting experience to know that much. And then, one morning, he spotted the place in the sand where the animal had spent the night. It had laid its cheek on the sand, leaving an imprint of its face. Clearly marked was a sickle-pointed devil ear on which the ghost had spent the night. Plakida had already largely mastered his imitation of the fish, the bear, and the bird, but now he had to blend into someone who would combine all of this in between two devil ears. And slowly he began to scratch his paws with his claws, to navigate with his fish tail as he raced across the glittering sand as though across the sky, and to chase away the bees from the flowers with his pointed ears while he reposed in the meadow. But it was all no use. The animal did not appear, nor did he turn into the ghost he was imitating and pursuing. But, thanks to his imitation, he did manage to identify with the role sufficiently to feel when the beast had discovered in itself something like steps and had begun to descend them one by one.

Suddenly, one evening, he heard a sobbing and, following the voice, arrived at something that could be described as a den or a lair. Squatting by the water was a big iron stove, and it was sobbing. Its front feet were shaped like bird claws, and its rear like bear paws. Its devil ears had two slits between them, and since a fire was blazing in the stove, these small bloodshot monkey or demon eyes stared straight at Plakida. It was very sick, but one could not tell what ailed it. As Plakida started to walk toward it, he accidentally stepped on a twig and, tense as he was, screamed out in fright, tripped, and fell. And the stove screamed, flapped the fish tail of its ashtrays, and tipped over on its back. Then it suddenly began to settle down and cool off. Plakida observed it through the darkness, it observed him, he wanted to get up, but so did the stove, and he decided it was better not to tempt fate. He sat there and waited. When something whitish slowly began to rise out of the fire, Plakida dozed off, and he did not awaken until morning.

Sitting before him in the sand was a young man, laughing at him, revealing three dimples on his cornbread-colored face. He had very fine warm eyes and a touch of snow on his eyelashes. He still had metal bird claws in place of hands. Before Plakida's very eyes, the wrinkles on the stranger's brow slowly curled into the letter gamma. The spectral beast was turning into Plakida. And then it softly uttered the prayer that makes beasts submit to the hunter.

4 DOWN

My soul is a virgin who gave birth to my body. And to my voice within it. That voice I wash every morning, the way one washes bread and one's face. That voice, like bread, has its body in heaven, and I, like any face, have my celestial archetype face. My word has already been uttered by someone somewhere up above before me; my word merely follows its unattainable model. And I long to get nearer to that Unknown with song. Because every known thing in this world is only half the thing and teaches us about its other, invisible, divine half, the one that is to us unattainable and unknowable. Therefore, my word and my voice are only half the Word and half the Song, and they teach me about their other half whenever I have their favor. For the Spirit breathes when it wants and on whom it wants. Otherwise, why would my song and my mind have days of utter obtuseness and days of great insight and inspiration? Why is man on Wednesday also stupid for Tuesday, and on Friday for Wednesday?

But my link with this celestial side of my nature has been ruptured. After my fall into sin with Razin and my departure from my home-land, after the death of my children—for which I, above all, am to blame, because I left them at a time when a mother does not leave her children—the celestial half of my voice, the other side of the book of my fate, and Razin's place in it are no longer legible to me. That book is for me now closed and gone forever. And all that remains of the only love of my life is the mustache, on which you can brush your teeth.

That is why I seek the One who will read and interpret for me the book of my fate. Who will once more pave the way for me to the other half of my voice, to the celestial model of my song. He must exist, just as over every centennial shade there must stand a centennial lime tree.

But if in heaven I have a celestial brother after whom my soul is shaped, then inevitably there also exists the other side of the coin, the bottom side of the echo; if each and every thing on earth has its model in the ideas of heaven, then the dark side of their nature (because here there are only beings that have also their dark side; even I, Vitacha, have a dark side to my nature and to my voice), then this dark side of my song does not and cannot have a prototype in heaven, but in the underworld; there, in hell, is my other, my dark lover, there, in the even mirror, my right hand again turns into my left, just as two eyes look together but each is blind for itself. So if I, Vitacha, and my song (like everything else that exists here and can be known in this world) teach about invisible celestial matters with one part of my nature, then with the other part of my nature I, this same Vitacha, also represent a symbol and teach about the invisible matters of hell, about the underground echo of my soul. My celestial lover measures what ill others have done to us, I, here on earth, measure what ill we have done to ourselves, and the dark lover of my song measures what ill we have done to others. If I am drawn to heaven by my celestial lover, whom I divine, above me, while I sing, and upon whom my life depends, then there must also be that other, dark lover of my soul, the prince of the nocturnal region, the murderer of my voice, who will inevitably appear to drag me to the underworld, into silence and death. That is why I longed to find the former before I was found by the latter.

This is my confession of how I found him. How I found the One who is health and eternal youth.

. . .

I always spend a long time rearranging things in the rooms to obtain the best possible acoustics. The building looks out onto two streets, so that one can see a car turning the corner twice through the windows and a third time in the mirror in the room. The bedroom has double glass doors, and in these doors, as if on a shelf, are books. When Razin and I took that house here in Milan, I did not get dogs; I do not go out on Saturdays after the performance, and I listen to the keys rattle by themselves in the keyholes of the apartment, which makes my maid, Nicoletta, have a fit. Every morning, Nicoletta washes the leaves of the rhododendron in the dining room with beer and brings me breakfast in bed. We lived simply; it was rumored that Tuesdays and Fridays did not enter our home, but we dismissed that with a wave of the hand; and in the evening, after a performance of *La Traviata* or *Aïda,* I would look calmly at my nose, the same one that had torn all my nights above me.

One evening (Nicoletta reckons it was on Chicken Christmas), it happened.

Lying there in the dark, I heard something chime, like the clinking of glasses. I put on the light and looked around the room, but there was nobody. I went back to bed and in the dark again heard the clinking of glasses and another strange noise, like bone rubbing against bone. I'm not superstitious, but the hair on my head stuck to my ears, and the hairs on my back rippled like grass in the wind. I was silent behind my teeth and suddenly, clearly, made out a conversation. This time I did not turn on the light. I remembered how my father used to do target practice at night, closed my eyes, put out my right hand, and followed the sound, pointing my index and middle fingers at the dark. It was autumn, the moment of truth was approaching, and truth knows not grammar or spelling. And then my hand struck against something cold and smooth; I stopped, opened my eyes, and saw everything.

Standing before me were those double glass doors, and behind those doors, instead of books, sat the two of you, playing dominoes. I immediately noticed that you were buxom and that you must knead dough often, because your dresses were frayed at the chest; you had patches sewn on each breast. Your hair crackled and glowed around your head. And over there, in the half-shadow, I saw you as well.

You were reading something and would move the dominoes when your turn came. Every so often you two would clink glasses, and the sound, along with your words, rang out in my room. You smoked, and on the table had a knife and a candle to absorb the smoke. I looked around to see whether you were not just a reflection in the glass of the door, but here in my room there was nobody. Admittedly, facing the door were the same table, the same chairs, and everything else you had, but you yourselves, the players, and the wine and the dominoes were not there. On the chest in my room were an unlit candle, a knife, and a closed box of dominoes.

"It's as though your soul sits crosswise," I thought, and yanked open the door. There, in the shallow darkness, was only the shelf holding dusty books that had not been touched since who knows when. There was nobody.

"Ghosts!" I cried. "You know everything about us, but we know nothing about you!"

And you two over there in the glass picked up the candle I had knocked over when yanking open the door, and you lit it again in your mysterious world, accusing one another of negligence. You didn't notice me at all. I stood in my nightgown in the middle of the room like that, and for a long time, long enough for a small pinewood forest to grow under my bed, I watched you play. You, the female, had your back turned to me, and I could see all your dominoes.

"The eye judges the price of the horse," I thought, staring at those dominoes. And you, the male, were seated in the shadow as if in your name and only a wisp of smoke rose from that shadow.

"So burly his tear could shatter a glass," I whispered, and began to signal to you her next moves. You gave no sign that my information was reaching you, but you began to win. When you had won seven thousand in this way, the two of you left, and the double doors were now empty and silent. Only the candle still burned in the glass of the doors, and it kept me awake. You had forgotten to put it out before leaving. I wanted to blow it out, but then I remembered that was not the way, and so I lit the candle in my room. That same instant, its double in the glass went out. Up above the city I saw two skies, which seemed to embrace the space equally. But one was low, full of clouds, and the other high and clear, overhanging that grim sky and pressing the earth with it. . . .

I didn't see you again in the glass doors until a few days later. I observed you quite clearly; you were sitting on the floor, alone, your head propped on your knees, and between your legs you were reading a book placed on the rug behind your own heels. The calves of your legs touched the pages of the book, stopping the read pages from turning back. Every book in the world has this secret passion of stopping you from going on. You looked younger to me than the first time, and I thought you might perhaps continue to get younger and younger, and that attracted me irresistibly to you, and I knew that one day it would lure me completely to your side, because I have always been fond of little boys. And then I leaned over to see what you were reading. Over your shoulder I read for myself what was written in your book:

"A young man brought to a girl a flower. The next one who came calling brought nothing, and threw even that flower away. She asked him why he had done that.

" 'One cannot decorate the moon,' he said, and received a kiss from the girl.

" 'How sweet that kiss was to me,' says the first young man. 'I shall remember it all my life. Instead of the girl, my flower decorated the moon, and henceforward will accompany the name of the moon.'

"But she said:

" 'Since you haven't eaten, wash the spoon.' "

The hour of midnight began to strike. That surprised me, because on my clock here in the room it had already been five past twelve only a moment ago. But now the hands overlapped on both clocks, and the one in the glass door began to strike the hour, while my clock in the room remained silent. I shuddered; I could hear my eyelashes scratch the inside of my glasses, but I was not about to give up. Softly I opened the door. Darkness. Just that book lying on the floor, and the candle burning in the corner. I took the candlestick to illuminate the book, to see what the title was, but although the candle moved with my hand, the light stayed where it was, it did not move an inch, as though it were detached from the candle. I got accustomed to the darkness like a mouth to silence, and in the darkest corner of the room noticed a bed. The same one that was in my bedroom out there, in front of the glass doors. And in that bed I saw you, you who win at gambling and read that book. You were asleep now, with your boots on, gritting your mustache between your teeth. Sleep weighed heavy and hard on you like a bell. But in your sleep you mumbled a word. A name. My name. So I was both in your dream and here at the same time. This gave me the strength to try. To touch you. I don't see why the present time should always have to carry into all succeeding times the same amount and the same kind of time. All of us have in our dreams a half-time or between-time where we stand still even though it flows, but sometimes it stops, and we plunge headlong through it. It is only partly the present time, or it is only partly here, because it is at the same time a part of past and future time, because there is more of the future in our past than in our present. Indeed, there is none of it in our present. And, like little girls, we see ourselves in this time as already old and blind. Well, like this half-time, there is also in our dreams something one might call a half-person or between-person. That, I imagine, is how you experience and see me in your dream, or whatever it is. I am here to you, but invisible, or half-visible; in other words, I am only partly present in your dream, I am prevented from being completely present, but also from being completely absent. Or else I am that partial person, merged with some other person, and this is a whole, not a half-person. Thus in your dream you have half-relatives or half-mistresses, the half-living who meet the half-dead. And I am among them. And I know that you alone belong not to a dream but to reality; I distinctly see the salt glittering in the corners of your eyes. I steal up to you very softly and trace my signature on your back with my breast, I nudge one of my purple nipples into your ear, you mutter something but do not wake up. I lie down by your side, and you embrace me, half-asleep. I am surprised and burned by the heat of your teeth when we kiss, but then desire overpowers my fear, and I press myself against you, I join my two breasts in your mouth, you suck from my breasts into your dream a beverage that neither of us knows. And as you lie by my side and suck, I know you are dreaming that you are in bed making love to somebody. "Sprinkle me with your mercy the way one sprinkles salt on the dead," I whisper into your ear. But somebody is lying across the bottom of the bed at our feet while we make love. And when the blanket slips off, you see that it is me. Who is it, then, making our love, who is making love to you? And while you wonder about it, suckling at my breast, your boot suddenly starts to fill with something warm. The more lustfully you suck from me, the more fluid there is in your boot, and I feel, while we are joined like that, I distinctly feel something warm flow out of me and into you, filling your boot. . . .

Somebody then knocks at the door and comes into the room. The person who appears has a hairy forehead; peering out from under the white cloak are its feet; the hairy nails are sunk so deep in the toes that they cannot be seen, but they can be heard scratching the floor. Eyelids without lashes, as big as lips, blink, and the person looks as though it is chewing its own eyes. But the eyes themselves are nowhere to be seen. Instead of eyes, the person has three pairs of mouths on its face, a tongue poking out of each. . . . In short, standing there is my maid, Nicoletta.

I angrily motion her to get out, but Nicoletta merely points to something under her arm. She is holding a rooster there and, as usual, the papers, with a review of my latest performance. And this rooster stretches out its neck and begins to yawn. It yawns once, a second and a third time. And every time it yawns, a bit of light spills out of its beak. I realize that this is the rooster crowing, announcing the break of day, only I don't hear it. I give your hot teeth a quick kiss and jump out of bed. I look at your boot, it has brimmed over. . . . I dash through the double doors into my room and flop onto my bed, thinking:

"There must be some reasonable explanation for all this. A simple solution to this mystery, acceptable and clear to everyone."

And then it dawned on me.

"Vampires. Not you, but us, on this side of the glass—we are the vampires. Why should others always be werewolves, everybody but us? Both Nicoletta and I behave like real vampires, that's clear. So we are from the other side of the line. But what about you? Where are you and who are you? And what about that woman with the patches darned on her breasts?"

And then I remembered that there are even mirrors and uneven mirrors. And I decided to use them to try to penetrate the secret. The question is simple: What is the time seen by the person looking out of the mirror at the clock on your wall? In other words, what is the time your image in the mirror sees when looking out of the glass at your real room and a real clock, not at the clock's mirrored reflection? How do you in your mirror see me, and do I see you accurately? No, most assuredly not. But there is a way to cure us of this myopia. There are, as I said, even mirrors and uneven, there are echoes that can be counted off in pairs, like soldiers. This is what I mean.

Compared with the original, with the face, the image in the mirror is marred, distorted. The right side becomes the left, one minute before twelve on Wednesday becomes one minute past midnight on Thursday. In its first echo the voice loses its *forward* and its *upward,* and in their place acquires a *backward* and a *downward.* But that is why there are even mirrors and even echoes, to correct the defect in the uneven mirrors. If in an even mirror you catch an image or a clock from an uneven mirror, the impairment is cured: the right hand, transformed into the left in the uneven mirror, will again become the right hand in the even mirror, and it will again be the same time it really is in the room. Catch a devil crossing himself with his left hand in a mirror and he will cross himself with his right and cease being a devil. If, after the first time a voice echoes (when its forward has become backward, and above turned into below), it echoes yet a second time, then the damage is repaired, the echo in the echo returns the original *downward* back to its place down below, and restores the *forward* back to a forward.

It is the same with a person's face: it is impaired in relation to its celestial model. One must look for even echoes and even mirrors, one must catch uneven mirrors in even ones in order to perceive the true archetype face. Only thus can accuracy and eternity be restored to the face. The same way that coffee casts a dark shadow on the tablecloth through its fine porcelain cup, and wine a red shadow through its glass. It is for this even echo of your face that I must search. But one cannot take this search into infinity. For as the image and the echo move farther away, as the uneven and even repetitions multiply, the image and the voice become darker, until they are finally lost. Both the impaired and the unimpaired parts pass together from the domain of light and clear divine illumination to the deaf domain of darkness, the domain of Satan. But one can try once. . . .

So next to your doors I placed a mirror, an even mirror (assuming that the mirror in the doors themselves was uneven). Now, if you did appear, I thought, I would see you as you really are, because even mirrors see better than uneven ones and restore the soul to order. But you were not to be caught in this trap of mirrors. So I forswore tricks and sorcery. Instead, I remembered the seven thousand you had won at dominoes. I went down to the chest where I kept my money. I unlocked it and counted. Exactly seven thousand was missing.

"Just as I thought," I whispered, "my beloved cannot be caught in a trap of mirrors and echoes." But you who win what I lose, you can be only one person: the enemy of him who loses what I win. You can only be the One who turns my world inside out in order to understand it. And so the veil slowly started to lift from my eyes.

When I woke up in the morning, I found my room strewn with unfamiliar dresses in the most beautiful colors and cuts. After taking a good look, I recognized my old dresses, which in my haste the night before I had thrown off, turned inside out. . . . The same thing happens whenever I strip my memories of you in haste, my love. At first I can't recognize you. But now I know, I know who you are. You are the one who holds the book of my fate in your hands, the book entitled *Landscape Painted with Tea,* and right now you are reading the following lines:

"And so Vitacha Milut, the heroine of this novel, fell in love with the reader of her book."

"The heroine of a novel in love with the reader! When has that ever happened?" you will say, and you will not be wrong. Those who have their own love story are in no need of another's—on paper, yet! But those who haven't . . . Anyway, isn't it unfair that for so many thousands of years all those heroines, from Homer's time to the present day, from Boccaccio's stories to yesterday, remained blind and deaf to the charms of the young handsome fellows who from them learn their first dreams of love, who with these women's tears nurse their wounds, who eye their breasts far more devotedly than any lover from the same book, standing guard over the text into which these heroines are walled? Think about it, isn't it all the same whether you first fall in love in a book or in life? Isn't it all the same whether you die first in a novel and then in reality, or first in reality and then in a novel? Admittedly, all of us—Iphigenia, Desdemona, Tatyana Dmitriyevna Larina, and I along with my Nicoletta—all of us are vampires! But do not take my soul away from me with sorrow! There is a difference. Such female vampires do not suck your blood. They may sometimes appear in your dreams and steal a little of your male seed, sweetly spilled to fertilize the imagination. And they nurse you generously with their milk, with their song which you do not hear, and with their love which longs for you as for the living earth that can give birth to man, but you turn it all into a boot full of blood. Real blood. So who is the vampire now?

Perhaps you belong to that most humble order of ordinary provincial folk, as a Russian once put it, perhaps you come from a circle of the petite bourgeoisie, and who knows, perhaps only I, Vitacha Milut, have turned you into this imaginary person who stops my life whenever he blinks. Perhaps only the brave deserve the fair. Perhaps. But to me you are braver and fairer than all the heroes of the book in which your Vitacha lives imprisoned, and perhaps you really do deserve a meal made out of those seven little devils expelled from woman.

It is now autumn and night again in my dreams, and you have left there a few unswept shadows and the scent of fruit. Waiting for you once more, I swept the room and decorated it with flowers, I combed my hair with a comb made of goat horn, but my dreams are unswept, and in them my hair is disheveled, and there are no flowers that smell in reality and blossom in dreams, and there is no comb that can comb both you and me . . .

But what great love, my love, has not faced such insurmountable difficulties? Juliet's for Romeo? Héloïse's for Abelard? Is it that you are castrated and troubled by what did not trouble Abelard's love? Since when is an ordinary page in a book more of an obstacle than death? Have you never been enraptured by the heroines in *Crime and Punishment* even if they are wiser and better than you, my only one? Why shouldn't it be the other way around? Why do you think that only you have a right to the book, but the book has no right to you? Why are you so convinced that you are not a figment of somebody's imagination? Are you sure your life isn't a mere invention? Concocted, if not like *Hamlet,* then at least like Chernyshevsky's *What Is to Be Done?* Don't you know that all readers in the world are inscribed in all books, as in the registries of death, birth, and marriage? Will you never marry in a book?

Look at your Vitacha! Look at my sinful self, at me, who counts on your fair judgment to settle my claim. Look, your Vitacha first lowers her gaze, so that one can see the lovely shadow her lashes cast on her cheeks, and then opens wide her sparkling eyes, speckled like glass marbles. To her it is more important to look than to see; she knows better than you that the eyes are more beautiful if they are a feast to others but fast themselves. And what does she ask? What do I ask of you, my love? I know that wisdom does not save us from anything and that all wisdom is like a man's day: the further it is from one night, the closer it is to another. So I neither ask nor offer you wisdom. Just as the writer is an emigrant from his world to the world of the reader, so I, Vitacha Milut, have tried to emigrate from my world locked inside this terrible book, where they kill and sell my children in the name of some higher cause, to another world, your world, which I divined only vaguely, but through a great power, the power of love. I have had my fill of sleep in bedroom mirrors, I have had my fill of baths in bathroom mirrors. Now I want to go out, out into life. You could become my homeland, and I your abroad. Is this desire of mine not to be forgiven?

Envelop me with your mercy: in each corner of my mouth, a putrid tear learns about the clear celestial tear that heals. You are eternal, ever younger; I am not. And you will soon forget these words I address to you, but they are my only words and there will be no more. You are a young and inexperienced God, and I am still articulating my first prayers of faith to you. We are only just learning what we can do for one another. Hear me and counsel me, because I am alone, even He who created me is already washing His hands of me and my life with brandy, like Pilate, and you are now my only hope. Redeem me with your love! I know, whoever saves the hero of the story kills the story itself, but try to save my life without killing your story. Fighting ruthlessly before your eyes are my two souls, black and white, locked in this book, which is mine, just as you own your one and only life. If by your gaze you prevent one of my souls from killing the other, then you need not give me anything, for I shall have everything. . . . If you close your eyes forever, I disappear forever. Imagine that this may be our only meeting before that terrible end. And permit me to worry about you as we worry about those who are our life. Because it *is* so.

"So spoke Vitacha Milut, Razin by marriage," you will say, but you will be wrong. God forbid, she never spoke like that: she sang like that, and this is merely an attempt to recount what she sang. A difficult attempt, to be sure, because Vitacha Milut can whistle our life or her dream more beautifully than we can recount her song.

But that attempt is not so important for this novel, this Testimonial, or these crossed voices. It is not essential to know whom Vitacha Milut loved while she sang: the Saviour, the celestial soul of her song, her almighty lover, who listens to her life through her song and interprets it for her, or for you, the reader of this book. What is important is that she loved the One she loved, and that this was clear from her song, and that it was also clear to her husband, architect Razin, the hero of this book. And that he finally decided to do something about it.

And this is what drives the story on. Just as the cartwheel sometimes propels the horse.

5 DOWN

June 28th of this year
Milan

To Don Donino Azeredo,
into his almighty hands

Dear Don Azeredo,

There is an anecdote about Signor Razin being told here. It describes him well. A recent acquaintance of his said, after several months of business contacts with him:

"I'm surprised he no longer keeps up on developments in the profession, he no longer knows what's happening in the world of business, he's well steeped, like Christmas yeast, but he isn't rising, it's pointless to discuss either money or chemistry with him. He's cultured, but it's as though it all comes from mere listening, as though he's never read a line in his life. . . ."

I held my tongue, because I know that Signor Razin is always as wise as necessary with the wise, stupid with the stupid, cultured with those who are cultured themselves, and uninformed and uncouth with the uncultured and uninformed.

It is not easy to deal with a man like that, as you well know. He thinks quickly and works as slowly as he can, as if he were under the influence of a heavy wine. One must always consider possibilities that are the inverse of what everything points to. One must, therefore, consider the possibility that he saw through our game, that he realized Signora Vitacha had been unfaithful to him not in a woman's way, with another man, but in your way, because of you and us, whose language she had begun to speak and sing, though she understood not a word. In that case, his jealousy of Knopf is merely a mask concealing another, greater, and more terrible rivalry.

Either way, our recent reports all show that architect Razin has stopped all payments to his wife, who, as you know, is completely impractical in terms of everyday life and has never had any money of her own. Razin returned to California alone, while here in Milan Signora Vitacha has acquired a permanent companion. Hired specifically for the job. Whether he was picked by Signor Razin or by somebody else is known to whoever needs to know, and I don't ask. Because that is not a question one asks. But he was well chosen. He appeared out of the dark, musical and mute, the music boiling inside him but unable to get out. This is how it happened.

One evening, just before the Puccini premiere at La Scala, Signora Vitacha came down with a strange twofold indisposition. She was in the street in front of her hotel, on her way to the opera house, which is quite near. There, in the middle of the street, she was stricken by a dizzy spell with a touch of blindness. Her right leg started to hurt as she walked; she could clearly feel the pain in the next street. Her pain was walking about two hundred meters away; it circled something— a newsstand, maybe—and turned at the corner. Then the pain stopped, perhaps in front of a shopwindow or a billboard. She clearly felt that the pain was drawing closer and that now it was walking along the same street, when suddenly the dizziness and touch of blindness left Signora Vitacha, and the pain merged with her, entering her right foot. It was then that Signora Vitacha heard that voice. She thought she heard, in the crowd of people, somebody talking in a very familiar voice, and she followed him as if in a trance. The voice was saying something, stuttering in a deep alto, and at first she did not know whether it belonged to a man or a woman. Rapidly moving away, the voice spoke in her onetime language, in Serbian, which she no longer spoke, which her soprano did not sing, but which she still remembered well. It was the same hoarse, cracked alto with which she had once caressed her children and rocked them to sleep, when she was not yet Mrs. Razin, she who lapsed into sin, when she did not yet carry the death of her children on her soul. She called out to that voice:

"Petka, Badlyika, Amalia, Vitacha!"

But no answer came from the crowd. And so she ran after that voice, leaving behind La Scala, which was itself dying in its plush velvet and gilding, leaving behind forever the audiences that applaud like rain pounding the streets of Vienna, leaving behind forever her magnificent voice, the first soprano of Italy, for this soured and torn alto which, like a cracked pitcher, held nothing that was not frozen.

Birds, when they want to take wing, catch the warm air currents and soar easily and swiftly into the skies under the clouds. So had Vitacha soared easily and swiftly on the warm currents of her misfortune and burning sorrow into the skies of opera. Birds, when they want to land, catch the cold air current and descend quickly to the ground. Such a current now carried Vitacha. She only followed the steps and the odd word, but it was hard, in that crowd, to follow the voice. In the street ahead of her, one could hear somebody in the dark, planting steps in the night. And then the trail was lost.

Vitacha's legs gave out on her, and she caught a ride back to the hotel. Outside it was October; clouds sailed through the somber sky, and you could see they remembered nothing. Dry leaves scraped the sidewalk as if they were metal. Waiting at the doors of time was the huge state of the Future.

We judge this element differently, depending on our powers. I and those like me believe that time is curved. He who has his eye aimed in the right direction does not need to predict the future, he simply sees and reads it behind the curves of our days. Because the future (and in it death) is already visible from the present, as are the past and our birth. For man does not see much of the past either. A day from three years ago looks just as unclear to us as tomorrow's day, allowing us to conclude that the curving of time applies to the past as well. As much of the future as that curve reveals to us, so much of the past does it conceal. That is what we think.

But you, Don Azeredo, teach us devotees something entirely different. You say: The future and the past have been invented by people themselves. They certainly have not always existed. Then again, you teach, every man has not one but three futures. Just as there are Sulfur, Mercury, and Salt. For the moment, we mortals are at a phase of development where we have discovered and use only one of our three futures. But with time we may learn to distinguish and use that other future of ours, which for the moment remains unused and hidden from us. However, we will never learn to use our third future, which you invented, Don Azeredo, not we.

In this connection you write to me, Don Azeredo, that Vitacha Razin may not succumb to this common fate, that she may be on the way to discovering that second future, still unknown and unrevealed to the rest of us, and I am doing my utmost to determine which of her two futures (there being no question, of course, of the third) Vitacha Milut will enter. And I will let you know if Signora Razin wrests herself free from the confines of her one and only future. But I think that you will judge all this better than I. Here is what I have learned.

It was almost midnight; the icy stars glittered outside. Vitacha was lying down in her hotel room, tired after her unsuccessful search for the stuttering voice. And then, from the room next door, a song reached her ears. There are such powerful songs in a man's life and in this world, songs that are first heard in dreams and forgotten for a long, long time, almost forever, and only later, after everything, are they in that life heard again in reality, like the pronouncement of a punishment or a pardon. This was such a song. The very same song that Vitacha Milut had sung so many decades before, as a little girl, and had forgotten, tossing her combs into the tub of bathwater. The song she had tried to recall for decades and now recalled, to her misfortune. It was "The Last Blue Wednesday," and it was being sung by the same stuttering, cracked voice she had been chasing that evening.

There was a Florentine mirror in Signora Vitacha's hotel room. It had hinges, and on the other side a picture. Vitacha ran over to the mirror, with an effort turned it around to the other side; there appeared a picture of a beautiful young woman astride a horse that was wearing socks. Where the mirror had been on the wall, there now appeared a connecting door to the next room. Without thinking, Vitacha rushed into that room. There, by the balcony door, stood a man with a head of curly hair, as though he had dipped it in resin full of feathers. He had a small mouth that seemed to have been cut out with a dinar, and he wore a ring on his thumb. He was biting his nails and humming. When she came in, he turned around, and his eyebrows and mustache somehow flew apart when he caught sight of her.

"Do you know who you are? Do you know who you are?" Vitacha whispered, not understanding what she was asking, but he did not understand her Italian. He inquired very politely whether he had disturbed her and said that he had become her neighbor on the same floor two days ago. He spoke Serbian, which showed that he knew who she was, and asked why she had missed the performance at the opera that night.

"The sky is high and the ground hard," Vitacha said thoughtfully. "Imagine that you are a river and that you flow only at night. And at night the thirsty come to drink your water. Now, if just two or three oxen give voice at the watering place by roaring, won't you think that all the others at the watering place are the same, that you're watering only oxen? . . . Anyway, I've had enough of left-mouthed tenors who can bite their own ears off."

Vitacha and the stranger burst out laughing. It was Vitacha's first laugh offstage. The first in ten years. Then they began to see more and more of each other. They were observed on their hotel balcony (which joined their rooms) playing cards with the autumn leaves, as lovers have done since the beginning of time. But it did not last for long.

The story ends somewhere in Tuscany, by a well in an orchard. That same autumn. After that evening when she missed the premiere at La Scala, Vitacha sang no more. Following your instructions, Don Azeredo, we saw to it that her contracts with the opera houses were canceled and Signora Vitacha rapidly declined into poverty. Thus she came to the end of her road, like the venerable Amalia Riznich, née Nako, who once spoke out from Madame Yolanta's egg, and whose rich husband left her in the lurch of despair and poverty in Trieste and death in the street, after having caught her with a young curly-haired man who had a ring on his thumb and the name Alexander Pushkin.

Madame Razin's curly-haired beloved accomplished his mission with the precision of a well-wound clock. He describes the further course of events himself, speaking into a mike during the interrogation we conducted prior to that of the police. We enclose the tape and the transcribed statement in the original and in Italian. Don Azeredo will understand that the young man used the language of fables or, to put it more precisely, that instead of relating the actual event, he recounted on tape something that could not be used against him in court:

"Our body carries its soul on its back like a huge stone or starry mist," he said in his feminine voice. "The boundary of that soul or that starry mist is not here, where you stand, but, rather, extends as far as your eye can see, as far as your ear can hear, or as far as your mind can stretch, up on high or down under the ground. Your body cannot be in the place of another body, but the mist of your soul, like a huge irregular ball or a milky way, can intersect with another such mist, with the milky way that is carried as a soul by some other body, on its back. There, where they cross, mutual injury or fecundation occurs, long before the bodies themselves touch. There your soul discovers or forgets and buries things. . . . But the same applies when the paths that cross are not those of two souls, but of your soul and your body. Then begins the story with two titles:

THE STORY OF THE SOUL AND THE BODY

That morning, when we no longer knew where to go but were already in the street, we hired ourselves out as caretakers for an orchard. We moved into a small cabin made of twigs and stone, where we spent several days, eating out of tins and frightening the birds off the fruit trees with clappers. When the food had run out, I thought Madame Petka would go out and pick some apples. She did not do that, however, and we went hungry the whole day. Then, in the morning, she asked:

"Can you go out into the orchard and pick some apples for us to eat? My stomach is contracting and expanding as if it were breathing."

I was a bit surprised and said that I couldn't. On instructions from above, I had to pretend to her that I was blind.

"Look at me," I said. "Don't you notice anything in my eyes? Don't you see in them that darkness is the natural nest of every eye, its origin and its peace? Don't you see that daylight is merely the disease of that other light, which cannot age, which is seen when one contemplates one's navel for a long, long time? In short," I concluded, "I am totally blind to this light and cannot go to get the apples."

"Now I know," said Madame Petka.

"Know what?"

"I know why he hired us to take care of the orchard for him."

"Why?"

"Because, with you blind and me the way I am, we can't steal but we can take care of the apples."

"Can't you go and pick them?" I asked in surprise. "You at least have good eyesight."

"Do you really think," Madame Petka then replied, "that I came here to take care of apples with you because I like it? The fact is, I can't take another step by myself. It's finished. Just as you can't see, so I can't walk."

"You know what?" I then said, my ears going numb with hunger. "You climb on top of me and look for both of us, I will walk for both of us, and you do the picking!"

And so we rode off into the orchard and picked the apples.

We lived off them until one day our employer caught us and fired us. That was really the end. As we stood at the crossroads I desired Madame Petka one last time. But I wanted that last time to last as long as possible. And an idea came to me:

"Climb on top of me one more time!"

And, carrying her, I walked while I was inside her, and she looked at the path we left behind us. And so we loved one another one more time. When it was all over, I said:

"We are not for one another anymore. Even when we are as close as can be, making love, you look in the direction that I can't go in, short of walking backward, and I go in the direction that you can't see, short of looking backward. . . . Oh, my soul, you who hold my body inside you, I am tired. Let it out of you so that it can rest in the open, and look for another body to carry you."

Thus we parted, as do all others when they come to the end of

THE STORY OF THE SOUL AND THE BODY

Except for this, the young man would say no more without his lawyer. But I made an added effort. I said to him:

"The human soul is a small house, and the room of the soul has its own furniture. This furniture is our *present*. If we nurtured, educated, and brought up our present, if we devoted the same attention to it that we devote to our past and future (which are the walls of the soul), perhaps it could develop, perhaps it could expand, burgeon, and grow at the expense of these walls that are the past and the future, and go back to its original measure and order, which we deprived it of so long ago by cultivating our past and our future at the expense of that repressed *now,* which is becoming increasingly stunted. . . . If you're not smart, I'll find a way to break off yet another little piece of your already chipped *now. . . ."*

Cornered, he revealed to me in confidence the following.

On instructions from the man who had hired him, he had come from New Orleans via Lyon. The orchard where it had all happened belongs to Signor Razin, which Mrs. Razin is unaware of. In that orchard there is a well, although it has more mud than water, but the young man had been given special instructions regarding this well.

"I had been instructed," he said, "to act in the following way. Every evening when the moon is full, they told me, Signora Vitacha sooth-says. She looks in a pan full of water or in a well to see whose face will appear in the water. She believes that her future and the fate of those she loves depend on the face that appears there. With the first full moon, you go with her and see what face she summons in the water. If it is a male face, they told me, if it is the face of a man, kill her and toss her into the well. If it is the face of a woman, let Vitacha go wherever her eyes lead her. . . .

"On the first night of the full moon, I went with Signora Razin to the well. She said she wanted to cool some fruit in the well. When she pulled out the bucket, I looked, because I am blind only in my story. Vitacha took no notice of me and leaned over the bucket, waiting for a trickle of moonlight to drop into it. She waited, and the stars fell off their light like leaves. Waiting, she said:

" 'Let Sunday wed Monday, Tuesday Wednesday, Thursday the female Friday, and the male Friday Saturday. Leave the year twelve male Fridays, and on those days don't eat fats, don't go on a trip, to war, or to bed with a woman. Let the female Fridays remain older, let the first Friday after every phase of the moon remain female. That is the Young Petka, the saint, the goddess of horses; let Paraskeva protect fertile women; leave twelve such Fridays in the year. And let Thursday remain a widower (when the week with the male Fridays is in progress), and the Sabbath a widow when Saint Petkas are in progress in the female weeks. And let not the male days fight over supremacy with the female days of the week, but let peace be with them and with him who says . . .' Just then I saw a face emerge in the well bucket. I took a good look to see whether it was male or female. And I did exactly as I had been instructed."

After you read these lines, Don Azeredo, please play the tape. Something can be heard on the tape that cannot be written down on paper. Unlike the voices of the rest of us, the recorded voice of the curly-haired young man is a deep, cracked alto that stutters and has no echo.

But maybe you already know that.

1 DOWN

When this Testimonial to architect Atanas Razin, alias Svilar, was completed and assembled, we all felt like dogs whose ears were crushed from being stroked against the head. There were six hundred deluxe editions to be printed, with those numbered one to one hundred to be placed at the disposal of ABC Engineering & Pharmaceuticals in California, the next one hundred, in keeping with Atanas Fyodorovich Razin's own wishes, to be deposited in his mother's grave at the cemetery in Belgrade, and the remainder to be released for circulation.

But first we had to obtain the approval of the honoree himself. So the manuscript, along with the family photographs included in the Testimonial, was sent to architect Razin. He received it but did not reply for a very long time. He had his reasons—business affairs and worries. I'll throw my mustache to the dogs if we didn't in some way put him in a spot with this book, and I was not surprised that there was no answer. But the work had to go on, and so I telephoned him. He was amiable; he spoke into the receiver while smoking his pipe. He said:

"Far be it from me to judge your book. I have only two things to say. First, I think that one of the stories, or whatever you call it, escaped me while I was reading. I lost it somehow. Second, I was unable to look at the photos. I kept thinking there would be a more propitious moment. It was only after I read the book (if I read it at all, considering that runaway story) that I undertook to look at the pictures, but then this conversation came along instead. The trouble is that now I already have the feeling it's not just one story that's escaped me from your book, but several. And the number keeps growing day by day. You know where that leads. More stories have already vanished from your book than it's got, and since they continue to disappear, by now more stories have fallen into some 'black hole' or 'quasar' than you ever wrote. We must therefore end this conversation. It doesn't have anything to do with you and me anymore, but with a third person, because who knows whose stories are disappearing from your book now?"

And he hung up.

When we met later, the Testimonial was already going to print, because he had never opposed its publication, but I asked him all the same what he thought about it. At the time, he had dropped his old habit of touching his mustache with the money when paying the bill in a café (to make the money breed); he was quiet; every morning he shaved his beard, eyebrows, and hair with a single stroke of his razor; Vitacha was no longer in his life; and it was rumored that he was slowly pulling out of business, under some kind of overpowering pressure, and that he was turning his fabulous wealth, possessions and factories, stocks and houses, into cash.

"My favorite story is the one about the fourteenth apostle," he told me.

"The fourteenth apostle? Why, there's no such story in our Testimonial."

"There isn't, you say? Ah, you see, there we disagree."

"I'll burn my beard if it's there!"

"You know," he said, as though he hadn't heard, "there isn't a sentence in a book that sooner or later doesn't become the truth. I often find that I can recognize words from our Serbian language in some foreign tongue or stage play. In the Japanese No theater, one can clearly hear the resonance of Serbian folk poetry, or chanting, which at moments sounds like the chanting in a Russian church. I am convinced that one could find in the works of Shakespeare the most magnificent story in our language (which Shakespeare didn't know at all, although some of his heroes spoke it) if only one listened carefully, if one caught the right resonances and the right places. One could put together a story that boggles the mind, with sentences pulled out of various chapters of a book. . . . In other words, not only do stories keep disappearing out of a book, but ever-new tales keep appearing in it. This is a matter of the reading, not the writing—a matter of the eye, not the pen. And that brings us back to those intruder-stories, which you mention yourself in this very same book. Why are you now surprised? Don't you believe they exist?"

I looked at him, shaven as he was, with two of yesterday's tears loath to spill from his eyes, and said firmly:

"No, I don't."

"You don't?" he asked. "What is this, then?"

And he handed me a piece of paper on which was written:

THE FOURTEENTH APOSTLE

When Christ was lifted up together with the cross on which they had nailed him, a stranger appeared out of the desert, collapsed in the dust under the cross, and started to lick the blood that ran down the crucified one's leg.

"Who are you?" asked Christ's disciples, assembled around the crucifixion.

"I am the fourteenth disciple," replied the stranger.

"We have never seen you until now. Where were you before?" they asked.

"Before?" the stranger asked in surprise. "Before I didn't need Him. He was not my teacher. I have come to learn not how to live, but how to die. And that is what I am doing now. . . ."

"What's this?" I asked Razin.

"What do you mean, what is it? Why, it's the story I read in your book and liked the best. I collected it by going from sentence to sentence like those women gleaning in one of Courbet's famous paintings, collecting, grain by grain, the wheat left in the reaped fields. You know, that story is the only thing I need right now from that Testimonial. Anyone who reads finds in books what cannot be found elsewhere, not what the writer shoved into the novel."

I was disconcerted and took his piece of paper. If the reader likes, let him do as I did. Let him check and he will see that our Testimonial to architect Razin does indeed contain all the words and sentences that Razin assembled into a story, and the reader can do the same himself, unless he decides to look in this book for a third tale, his very own, which is dearer to him than the one that we recounted or the one Razin found. Because dragons recoil from the cock's crow even when the cock doesn't know where they are.

A friend of ours, a police expert in codes, searched the length and the breadth of our text with his instruments in hand, the way mine fields are searched, and by going from word to word in this crossword, or this Testimonial, he composed another little story, besides Razin's. This, then, was not an isolated case. There are other such cases in the book. But one should not go overboard with such searches, like the man who wanted to shake the future out of his watch.

We have done enough observing of others' dreams in our own, the book has now moved from the right hand to the left, like a mistress, and the reader (the one who holds the night in his mouth and grazes the clouds with his eyes) will wonder what kind of a book we've been reading. Does it have an ending or not?

It is clear, of course, that the reader has not been given an answer to the basic question: What happened to the heroine of this book, to Vitacha Milut, Razin by marriage, on the night of the full moon, when she, following the custom of her great-great-grandmother Mrs. Yolanta Ibich, soothsaid by gazing at the water in the well, in the pan, or in some other receptacle? What was done by her paid companion with the echoless voice, who had been instructed to observe whether a woman's face or a man's appeared in Vitacha's vessel?

He who has been taught to steal his own cap will steal another's as well. But this young man with a ring on his thumb and a small mouth as though cut out with a gold coin—did he, watching behind Vitacha's lovely back, see a woman's face in the water and spare Vitacha's life, as instructed by his wayward employer, or did he see a man's face and kill Vitacha Razin, as he had been ordered to do in such an event?

The reader who does not believe that there are novels with double endings, novels that end happily and unhappily at the same time, that have a happy ending and a tragic ending, the reader who wants to know whether the heroine of this novel, Vitacha Milut, was or was not killed, need not wait for the solution in the next number, like other solvers of crossword puzzles; he need only look in the index at the back of this book. Because the denouement of this novel is to be found in the index.

This index, like any other in the world, is presented in alphabetical order, but of course it can also be organized differently. If the reader writes out the words of this index in their order of appearance in these crosswords or in this Testimonial (following the page numbers given next to them, rather than the alphabetical order), he will get a short, clear answer to his question, and the denouement of the novel will be there.

"But isn't it too much," you will say, "to ask the reader to turn into the writer at the end of the book?"

"And isn't it too much," I shall reply, "to ask every solver of crosswords to use a pencil?"

In return, the compiler of this Testimonial or these crossed voices promises every reader that he will get, based on merit, his own separate, personal ending to the story, like a nobleman receiving his inheritance.

In the meantime, the author will amuse himself one last time with the hero of this book, architect Atanas Razin. Because Razin's notebooks beckon both to us and to him. Landscapes painted with tea are waiting for us.

4 ACROSS

2 DOWN

They say one should never turn the lights out in the house at exactly midnight, but always either a little before or a little after. And it is the same with a story. One should not finish it when the reader expects the end, but, rather, a little before or a little after. Premonition is an ore out of which the money has yet to be minted.

These past few years, news of architect Atanas Razin reached us from overseas less and less often, but it was more and more incredible. He was said to be as quick as in the old days, when he had two left legs, but it was also rumored that he had sold his famous ABC Engineering & Pharmaceuticals for a fabulous sum. One morning, in North Carolina, where he now resided, architect Razin for the first time ordered a report on his cash-flow situation. Until then he had lived by the rule that anyone who knows how much he has is not rich. And then, when the information came in, and when it turned out that he had more than he thought, he did something quite unforeseen.

He was without Vitacha, he was retiring from business in a big way, his long accustomedness to his own body and the vanity of victory had worn him out, his eyes were weary, as though he had spent his whole life peering through the wind, but it was evident that he was contemplating something new. No one knows when he made his decision.

On one of those days which will remain unrecorded, he opened his notebook with its paintings in tea and searched for something. He looked for and found the note on what Yugoslav President Josip Broz Tito liked to drink and smoke. Then he collected his pipes, washed in cognac so that they played like trumpets, put them in the pouch made of goat balls, and threw them away forever. He unsealed a fresh, newly acquired box of Havanas and a bottle of Chivas Regal, poured himself a drink, and lit up. Then he signed the first document submitted to him, as he used to once upon a time in Belgrade: Atanas Svilar, Architect. He chewed the tip of his whiskey-dipped cigar, and one could tell from his ears that he was going to employ all his speed once more. . . .

The horses of a Russian troika do not look pretty while the team is idling: they bite and kick, graze, and bother one another. But once the troika gallops off, there isn't a prettier sight: they pull hard, their heads mingling, and turn the grass into speed. In very much the same way, all of Atanas Svilar's virtues got in each other's way when he was idle, they jostled and tore him apart, but once he embarked on business, like now, all his virtues fell into step. He reverted to his youth, his onetime habits returned to him one by one. He changed skins once more and gave up day for night. He felt again that his hair was like straw, his sleep so swift and heavy it could shatter a glass, and his left eye aged faster than his right, because his right eye did not age at all. And he unsealed the trunk containing his architectural instruments and rulers, which he had not opened for decades. He licked his glasses with their one nonprescription lens and from the notebook painted with tea extracted and enlarged a plan which said:

PLAVINATS, J. B. TITO'S SUMMER HOUSE
ON THE DANUBE
OUTSIDE BELGRADE

He smiled through the smoke of his Havana; he was completely relaxed; these were all, one might say, preparatory, preliminary works.

From his homeland he obtained additional, detailed drawings of the inside of this villa where Josip Broz Tito spent some of his vacations within reach of the capital and the big river. Then, outside of Washington, on a small hill overlooking the Potomac River, he bought land that in size and appearance corresponded to the area by the Danube where Plavinats stood, and in an unparalleled burst of construction, as though he had come down with building fever, procuring everything necessary with the greatest speed and energy, he began to build. There were always dozens of people around him so agile they could fell a bird in full flight with a snowball; orders smelling of Chivas Regal flew in all directions from the smoke of his Havana.

The work was as fleet in its passage as late summer.

Very soon, there by the Potomac River in the United States stood a huge house, with winter and summer reception halls, the walls all in glass and French windows, with black-and-white marble floors, and the ceilings vaulted with beams. Besides the said halls, the ground floor had another three rooms with their annexes, and on the floor above there were five rooms with views of the Potomac, the fountain in the garden, or the capital. It was an exact replica of Plavinats, the summer house that belonged to the general secretary of the Yugoslav Communist Party, Josip Broz Tito. Parallel with the architectural work, he had vineyards planted on the four and a half hectares of property surrounding the house. Exactly as they were over there, by the Danube.

When everything was completed, architect Svilar sat in his empty new summer house, wiped his glasses, and brought in the people commissioned to furnish the house. He said to them gently, "Sit down, that my hens may lay eggs," and issued new orders.

Using the itemized lists of furnishings and decorative articles he had obtained from Yugoslavia, architect Svilar wanted to create exactly the same effect as the Plavinats villa, which, for the needs of President J. B. Tito and the First Nonaligned Conference in Belgrade, had been decorated with objets d'art, purchased abroad and from old Belgrade families between 1958 and 1961 by the artists Pedja Milosavlyevich and Miodrag B. Protich, based, of course, on what had been found in the old Obrenovich summer residence. In American, European, and Yugoslav antique stores, architect Svilar's agents purchased, at prices that remain secret, items from the list they had been given, and within record time architect Svilar's villa on the Potomac River was furnished with, if not the same objects and pieces of furniture as Plavinats on the Danube, then at least similar articles and objects from the same artists or studios. Because Svilar's aim was obvious. To do everything, absolutely everything possible, the same way it had been done over there. He wanted to have everything just like Josip Broz. Even the scorching squeak of the gate, which he deliberately left unoiled.

And so Svilar's summer home had: a sitting room furnished in Biedermeier, with two-tone wood incrustations; two sets of Louis XVI furniture, Italian-baroque furniture, a small authentic Venetian green glass mirror that created the effect of an aquarium, a four-tiered chandelier glazed in blue and white (a product of Sèvres in France), a white porcelain figurine, "capo di notte," depicting a suitor kissing a woman's hand, like the unique original made for the Serbian Queen Draga Mashin, which is to be found at Plavinats. Svilar's dining room had a Louis XV table, small eighteenth-century Dutch-baroque glass cupboards, metal vessels collected in the regions of Kosovo, Metohija, and Skoplje, Meissen porcelain dishware, silver and porcelain cutlery, and fine cut-crystal glasses bearing the Obrenovich coat of arms. Finally, architect Svilar had brought in a nineteenth-century "sheruh," a musical instrument that operates with the help of cylinders, identical to the one at Plavinats, which the Viennese court had, in its day, presented to the Serbian patriarch Rayachich. He covered the floors with Persian carpets, embellished the corners of the rooms with Chinese vases, placed an Empire clock on the mantelpiece, and above it hung a portrait of a woman painted by Vlaho Bukovats. He placed fresh flowers in front of the portrait, just as Marshal Tito had ordered fresh flowers to be placed in front of the portrait of Queen Natalia, painted by this same Vlaho Bukovats, which hung over the mantelpiece at the Plavinats villa.

When everything was finished both outside and in, architect Svilar invited a friend over to show him the villa, and served him dinner out of ceramic plates bearing on the inside a portrait of Obrenovich, and on the outside the Serbian crown, like those at Plavinats. After admiring the collection of old metal dishware done in rustic Dutch baroque, and numerous wooden statues dating from the same period, architect Svilar offered his guest and associate coffee from an earthenware cup bearing the Serbian coat of arms. He watched his visitor sit in front of him like a foaming horse, waiting for orders. Architect Svilar then ordered a ship to be readied for him without delay, and saw off his visitor.

Three days later, he was already sailing the seas of the Caribbean, with a pair of binoculars in his hand. "How wise we were, and how little that is!" he thought, watching the fish flee from the birds' shadows in the water. Strewn on the deck of the ship, a huge training vessel that bore a striking resemblance to the *Galeb,* the ship on which Yugoslavia's Marshal Josip Broz Tito made his voyages, was a Bukhara carpet, and on it were a table and two armchairs. On the table was one of architect Svilar's notebooks. The landscape painted with tea on its cover depicted the fourteen Brioni islands, the summer residence of the general secretary of the Yugoslav Communist Party and president of the republic, J. B. Tito.

Atanas Svilar now cruised the seas of Mexico and the Caribbean in the hope of finding similar islands. His real-estate agency had already received two offers, and architect Svilar was now going on inspection. He was prepared to buy fourteen isles, similar to those of Brioni, somewhere in the Bahaman archipelago or the Lesser Antilles, whichever proved more propitious. . . .

And he decided on the Lesser Antilles, where he had an offer to buy fourteen islets, their earth coral-red, west of Barbados. He bought them, started surveying, and gave each a new name. The islands, in keeping with architect Svilar's orders, were now called: St. Marko, Okrugliak, Gaz, Supin, Little Brion, Supinich, Big Brion, Galia, Grunj, Madona, Vrsar, Yerolim, Kozada, and Vanga.

He felt like the old Svilar again, the Svilar whose belt turned moldy on his back from the strain and the sweat; he wore Vitacha's earring as a ring, licked his glasses, watched the armies of masons arrive, and worked day and night.

First he devoted his attention to the green belt and vegetation. Meticulously following the plans obtained from his homeland and the data on the Brioni isles' plant and animal life, he replanted, there in the Antilles, all the vegetation that grew in the archipelago of the Istrian littoral, creating an identical copy of J. B. Tito's park in Brioni. His people are said to have planted a thousand specimens of field and forest plants like those that graced the Yugoslav president's summer residence; as though praying, they quickly planted mangos, kiwis, bananas, and eucalyptus trees, mandarin and palm trees, cedars, bamboo, yew, and juniper trees. They toiled to make this soil yield malvasia, hamburg, afusali, and plemenka grapes, and to press out of them the "Brioni Rosé."

And while all this sprouted and flourished, architect Svilar began building again. Like the time before, he proceeded chronologically. First he built a copy of the Roman aqueduct—that is to say, of the ruins found on Big Brion; then several replicas of the churches on the Brioni isles—the Byzantine church in the Bay of Dobrika, the three-nave basilica in the Bay of Gospa and the Benedictine monastery, where he placed copies of the sixth- and seventh-century Brioni mosaics. He built a donjon, a small castle, the little churches of St. Germanus, St. Roch, and St. Anthony. He built hotels, indoor swimming pools with heated seawater, a racetrack, and a golf course. He set up port facilities, a small museum in the tower and fortress, built three residences and 275 kilometers of road, exactly as many as in Brioni, and let the large pool of cars with no license plates cruise all over the roads. . . .

Indifferent to food and shy by day, at night he became so ravenous, eloquent, and hardworking that his collar buttons popped. He whispered, "What won't the years and mouthfuls, the mouthfuls and years bury?," washed down cigar after cigar with whiskey, and continued to build. He called the residences Brionka, Yadranka, and the White Villa; he built the latter with a twelve-columned porch and paved the walk with yellow, blue, and white marble slabs, like those where Josip

Broz Tito had signed the 1956 Brioni Declaration with Nasser and Nehru.

On Vanga, an island so small one could throw a stone across it, he built his second home. He built the pier, placed a statue of Neptune by the hedge-lined path, opened the fountains, reproduced the Indonesian Salon, the Slovenian Salon, the House for Work and Recreation, the kitchen, the Mandarin garden, the vineyard, the terrace with the pergola and bower, the old cellar and the new, which one entered through a huge wine vat with doors. The Macedonian Salon he furnished with pieces crafted by the Ohrid school of wood carving; on the beach he lowered a rubber carpet into the sea, set up a table, sunshade, and chair; in the garden he placed white garden armchairs with purple cushions, and on the windows of the stone house he added red wooden frames. In the study he installed a wood-carved writing desk, and underneath it he spread a huge tiger skin. The walls were lined with shelves holding liquor bottles; he embellished the White Salon with a stuffed leopard, built the kitchen out of flagstones, overlapping them to obtain a gradual arch; in the wall he built a hearth with a grill, and a hood for the smoke, with a window in the fireplace and a skylight in the ceiling. In the wine cellar he cased the niches with baked clay so that only the necks of the bottles showed. Over each opening he wrote out the vintage year, and stocked wine starting with 1930 (the year of his birth), so that, like J. B. Tito, he could offer every visitor younger than he a wine that was the same vintage as the guest. He equipped the workshop with a lathe and tools, set up a photo lab, and in the Blue Salon, identical to the one in Brioni where Josip Broz Tito received heads of state, he received his caretakers, drivers, and builders, because he had no business friends left. Next to one of the residences he had a coach house built for the old barouches bought in Europe and made in Austria in the nineteenth century, which bore little metal plates inscribed with the names of high-ranking Yugoslav officials from the seventies, and engraved over the Austrian coat of arms were the initials J.B.T. . . .

He sat by the fishnets hanging from the rough wall, looked at the stone gusles he had been given, modeled after those in J. B. Tito's collection, and for days on end issued orders to the game wardens. He noticed that they were broader under the arm than in the shoulder, saw his eyes in the spoons of fish chowder, and did not stop working even when eating. Because he also had to see to the animal world.

He built three zoos and an open-air safari garden on six thousand hectares of land, pumped up water from a depth of 260 meters, and built an obelisk with an inscription where the water gives thanks for its newfound freedom. Then, ever faithful to the data regarding Marshal J. B. Tito's summer residence, into the holm oak forests and wide-open meadows he released prize stags and mouflons (four males and eight females), Somali sheep, dromedaries and llamas, white camels, chamois, does, axis deer, bucks, and, at the risk of letting this enumeration drag on, he let loose on his islands Tibetan bears, pumas, zebras, cheetahs, lions, panthers, three yaks, a Canadian lynx, desert dogs, two Indian elephants, and three giraffes. In the marshlands he bred rare birds, the gold-winged wild duck, Japanese quails, and parrots. And he bought a gun.

At just the right spot in this safari park, he erected a watch post and covered the arm and gun rest with bear fur.

And then he sat in his plane and returned to Washington. Actually, to his Plavinats summer house on the Potomac River near Washington.

Reposing in his German language as though it were a hammock, because he reverted to German whenever he thought about architecture, he read one out of every five letters from the pile of mail he had received in the meantime. His forehead, wrinkled like a stocking, bore a pair of silver unshaven eyebrows and was cold, although summer was raging outside. A huge chestnut tree stood in front of the open window, and its every leaf rustled like a tiny wave, while the entire tree roared like a lake. When he had finished with his correspondence, architect Svilar rubbed his hands impatiently and, under a seventeenth-century wooden statue, opened the next notebook, the one whose cover had the tea painting of the White Palace in Dedinye, the official residence of Yugoslav President J. B. Tito.

He had calculated long before that less than two kilometers separated the White Palace from Josip Broz's private residence at number 15 Uzhichka Street in Dedinye. And so in Washington, the capital of the United States, he paid a fortune for a plot of land that would allow the two points to be within easy communication. The moment had now come for him to carry out his most solemn intentions on this property. It was finally time to build the White Palace here, not far from the White House.

He examined the previously prepared plans on the basis of which, in the coming weeks and months, this property was to give rise to a one-story house that on the ground floor would have the reception rooms, a dining room, a study with a conference table, and a library. Next to the study he planned to build a small photo lab and kitchenette for making coffee, decorated with Ceylonese masks. On the floor above he planned to put the bedrooms and bathrooms and, at the very top of the small wooden staircase, a room with a barber's chair and mirrors in the shape of a three-leaf clover. The façade, as he envisaged it, was to be the same as at number 15 Uzhichka Street in Belgrade. The triple-winged doors would rise under and above the balcony, ending in arches. Over them he would put a tympanum; the façade was to be the color of cocoa, streaked with yellow borders, yellow consoles, and white stone doorposts. . . .

Hunched over his drawings, architect Svilar worked as if his ears did not grow on holes; nothing existed for him outside of this work; he was deaf, and the only thing he felt was that, as in the old days, his saliva was changing taste. He flopped into the armchair for a moment of respite and imagined the building already completed, standing in the middle of a park planted with the 165 specimens of plants— sequoia, Spanish firs, cedars, and magnolias—that Josip Broz had brought back from his travels to India, Burma, Korea, Africa, Egypt, America, and other corners of the world to plant in his Dedinye park, and which Svilar had already prepared in balls of straw and sacks for his own residence in Washington. He imagined himself moving into the palace, arranging, according to the Dedinye catalogue, the selected works of the painters and sculptors Hegedushich, Pedja Milosavlye-vich, Stiyovich, Meshtrovich, and Kun; hanging up on the walls his gun collection and hunting trophies, his lion skin, the stuffed heads of the great African buffalo and elk from Podmoskovlye; he saw himself buying button-up boots, a coat with buttons made out of stag horns, black swimming trunks, a Russian fur hat with ear flaps and a visor, a two-horse four-seat hunting carriage with outsized rear wheels. . . .

He imagined himself in the future palace, arranging the hunting trophies that had already been obtained and temporarily hung up in the study, carrying the same number of points as those of Yugoslavia's Marshal J. B. Tito. . . .

He thought how he still had six white Lippizaner horses to order, a German shepherd whom he would name Tiger, and two white poodles. Sitting in the summer heat, he imagined how with the first snowfall the dogs would bring into the palace and through the length of its rooms the fresh breath of winter and the smell of icy smoke.

He imagined bringing into his future palace in Washington a gold-rimmed white piano from the French Empire period, tossing a Persian rug over it, like a caparison over a Thoroughbred horse, and sitting down at the piano like J. B. Tito to play a waltz, perhaps "The Last Blue Wednesday," which Svilar actually did know how to play. . . .

And just then, when his imagination was in full flight, architect Atanas Svilar felt something strange. A cold current of air was coming in from the hall.

"What have they done?" he wondered, thinking of the servants to whom he had given the day off that morning. He strode briskly toward the study. He felt full of vigor, his knees sinking deep into his thigh muscles.

"I'll bleed them dry, I'll charge each of them a Tuesday in April and another hour as change," he thought jokingly, but when he reached his study he saw that this was no joke. A coldness that stops clocks stung his ears. The door of the darkened room was ajar but would not open. Something was resisting. Svilar slipped his hand in and turned on the light. He was dazzled by the crystal of the eighteenth-century Venetian chandelier, and his hand remained suspended in the air above the door handle. Inside the study, a heavy snow fell from the invisible ceiling. Snowflakes whirled in the air, the Persian carpet was already deep in snow, the silver ink bottle with its dishes for blue and red ink looked like two snow-swept church domes seen from afar, and the snow-covered stove looked like an ink bottle seen from up close.

Not understanding a thing, Svilar ran to turn off the air conditioning, grabbed the coal shovel propped up by the fireplace, and, forcing open the door, stormed in to clear the snow. The snow was already about forty centimeters high and still falling. Svilar applied all his strength to clear a path to the balcony door, but it kept snowing. The baroque statues donned white hats, the mustaches and hair on the African masks turned gray, snow covered the bottle of twenty-five-year-old Chivas Regal and the newly opened box of Havanas, a coffee cup bearing the Obrenovich coat of arms disappeared under the snow, the double-barreled gun disappeared in the snow along with a pair of hunter's binoculars next to it, and Svilar dug away. He shoveled with all his might, and on the wall an elk shot in 1962 in Zavidovo, near Moscow, watched him with its glass eyes, two wild boar from Poland stared at him with an air of surprise, a mouflon killed in 1977 gazed at him fixedly from between its horns, which were as wide as the wingspan of the heaviest eagle and counted for 242.15 points; peering at him through the snow was a bear, a former world champion caught in Bugoino, forgetting its 493 points, which were no longer enough.... And high above, as though in its native Mongolia, eyeing him from its Gobi Desert, was a huge agral whose antlers already bore pipes of ice.

One could no longer distinguish the books on the table; a Hasselblad camera disappeared under the drifts of snow; Svilar felt two hearts beat, one in each ear; he cleared the snow in a frenzy, nearing the balcony door. When he finally opened it, light and summer flooded the room....

And while, inside, on a little shelved table with wheels, the snow covering his collection of teas slowly started to melt, leaving streams and puddles smelling of lime and drugs, Svilar sat on the stone ledge of the balcony to rest and get warm. Then he heard a sound like a sparrow twittering or someone sucking a finger. And that same moment he noticed a cradle. It was a real cradle dumped in a corner of the balcony. Unclear as to how it got there, at first Svilar thought it was empty. But when he stepped nearer he saw a tiny, neatly swaddled infant lying there, sucking its thumb in its sleep.

At the sound of the steps, the infant was startled awake, smiled, and opened its eyes. Svilar noticed that the child had a white film in its eye. As if a drop of wax had spilled into it. It raised its head slightly and looked at him through the wax, and Svilar felt something pierce him below his chest, and then the child took its thumb out of its mouth and said quite distinctly:

"What are you looking at, you mother-fucker? Rock the damn cradle!"

Svilar had not been so stunned since his days of poverty, when he washed with his cap on, and he obediently reached out to rock the cradle. On the stone in front of the cradle his hand cast not one but three shadows.

The reader cannot be so stupid as not to remember what happened next to Atanas Svilar, who, for a time, was called Razin.

Index

(For practical reasons, all the words in this index are given in the form in which they are used in the book.)

Space left for the reader to write in the denouement of the novel
or the solution to this crossword

_____

_____

_____

_____

_____

_____

_____

_____

_____

_____

_____

_____

_____

_____

_____

_____

_____

_____

_____

_____

_____

_____

Solution

(Then Vitacha Razin caught the full moon in the bucket and leaned over to see what face would appear in the water. And in the water she and her companion saw you, who are reading these lines and thinking as you sit at your desk or in your armchair that you are completely safe and out of the game; you, who are holding this book upside down and gripping your pencil as a mother does a spoon or a murderer a knife.)

A NOTE ON THE TYPE

This book was set in a digitized version of Granjon, a type named in compliment to Robert Granjon, a type cutter and printer active, in Antwerp, Lyons, Rome, and Paris, from 1523 to 1590. Granjon, the boldest and the most original designer of his time, was one of the first to practice the trade of type founder apart from that of printer.

Linotype Granjon was designed by George W. Jones, who based his drawings on a face used by Claude Garamond (c. 1480–1561) in his beautiful French books. Granjon more closely resembles Garamond's own type than does any of the various modern faces that bear his name.

Composed by Dix Type Inc., Syracuse, New York
Printed and bound by Courier Companies, Inc., Westford, Massachusetts
Typography and binding design by Iris Weinstein